"Take a crew: human, folk – Yonakunish included. Scout to where the titan's call was answered. Find the epicentre of the earthquake: the partner sand god. Stop it from destroying our home."

Nami's mouth dropped open. She looked at Trish, then back at Mira, waiting for the punchline of the joke. Panic rolled off her in waves. She had been afraid since she had been handed Kai's dragon pearl. But Mira needed her to stop hiding behind the damned kelpie and step into the light.

"Wh-why? You are sending me away?"

"Jiang-Li will use you, Nami. You are her bridge to the Tiankawian people. A pearl, for titan's sake." Mira left the words unsaid between them: that she did not know who Nami would choose if it came down to it.

"So what you are saying is that I'm dead wood."

"No," Mira said emphatically. She wanted to shake the impetuous water dragon, as quick to dismay as she was to rage. "I'm trusting you with our lives, our city. What you find out there could change everything."

Praise for
Fathomfolk

"A thrilling, incisive fantasy of diaspora and dragons, *Fathomfolk* is an unmissable debut. If you're hungry for a beautiful Southeast Asian–influenced fantasy with razor-sharp edges, this book is for you."　　　　　　　　—Tasha Suri, author of *The Jasmine Throne*

"Prepare to be engulfed. Chan has superbly created a world as real and complex as our own, where oppression has no easy solutions and there is no success without sacrifice. Fast-paced action combined with true social depth make this an unforgettable, must-read fantasy."
　　　—Shelley Parker-Chan, author of *She Who Became the Sun*

"A vivid, textured tale of migration, prejudice, and change. Wonderful and breathtaking."
　　　—Aliette de Bodard, author of *The Tea Master and the Detective*

"Life is better down with the fathomfolk. I was dazzled by this novel, which has as many turns as the tide, and hope to see much more of this world and this author."
　　　—Sarah Rees Brennan, author of *Long Live Evil*

"Gloriously imagined and full of heart."
　　　—Claire North, author of *Ithaca*

"A richly envisioned world and finely crafted tale, *Fathomfolk* is a luxurious and thrilling story full of political intrigue, heart-wrenching characters, and edge-of-your seat tension. A glittering and magical novel from a glorious new voice in fantasy."
　　　—Bea Fitzgerald, author of *Girl, Goddess, Queen*

"Readers will enjoy exploring the intricate details of Tiankawi and its history through the perspectives of three wonderfully complex female protagonists. Fans of mythic fantasy will find plenty to savor." —*Publishers Weekly*

"Chan floats beautifully between multiple point-of-view characters, and also between different facets of Tiankawi life, from the poor to the privileged. From Nami's well-meaning immaturity to Mira's complicated feelings about her dual identity, all the characters have fully realized perspectives and goals that clash with each other in both clever political plots and exciting action scenes. The first installment in what will hopefully be a long series of undersea adventures." —*Kirkus*

"A promising debut." —*Locus*

TIDEBORN

By Eliza Chan

THE DROWNED WORLD

Fathomfolk
Tideborn

TIDEBORN

Drowned World: Book Two

ELIZA CHAN

orbitbooks.net

Copyright © 2025 by Eliza Chan
Excerpt from *The Gods Below* copyright © 2024 by Andrea Stewart, Inc.
Excerpt from *A Letter to the Luminous Deep* copyright © 2024 by Sylvie Cathrall

Cover design by Ella Garrett
Cover illustration by Kelly Chong
Author photograph by Sandi Hodkinson

Orbit
Hachette Book Group
1290 Avenue of the Americas
New York, NY 10104
orbitbooks.net

First Edition: March 2025
Simultaneously published in Great Britain by Orbit

Orbit is an imprint of Hachette Book Group.
The Orbit name and logo are registered trademarks of
Little, Brown Book Group Limited.

The publisher is not responsible for websites (or their content)
that are not owned by the publisher.

The Hachette Speakers Bureau provides a wide range of authors for speaking events. To find out more, go to hachettespeakersbureau.com or email HachetteSpeakers@hbgusa.com.

Orbit books may be purchased in bulk for business, educational, or promotional use. For information, please contact your local bookseller or the Hachette Book Group Special Markets Department at special.markets@hbgusa.com.

Library of Congress Control Number: 2024948909

ISBNs: 9780316564946 (trade paperback), 9780316564953 (ebook)

Printed in the United States of America

LSC-C

Printing 1, 2025

For all the diaspora folk
who never felt this enough or that enough.

You are enough.

The Story So Far

Fathomfolk – selkies, kelpies, sirens, water dragons and the like – have been migrating to the semi-submerged human city state of Tiankawi for decades. Mira, a second-generation half-siren, has been newly appointed captain of the border guard. She is supported by her boyfriend Kai, a water dragon ambassador and Minister of Fathomfolk. Dragons are practically royalty, each having the ability to return to pearl form, sacrificing themselves to grant one wish.

Nami, Kai's strong-willed sister, who is exiled to the city due to a protest stunt gone wrong, thinks she has all the answers, disagreeing with the current slow and legal approach. Meanwhile Serena, the human wife of the Minister of Defence, is hiding secrets of her own. She is actually the sea-witch Cordelia, a master shapeshifter, people-smuggler, healer and maker of bargains. She has no qualms about dealing with both sides of the political divide, but every bargain broken results in her body being slowly poisoned. She has little interest in her fellow fathomfolk but cares about bettering the lot of her own family even though she has hidden her true identity from her human husband, Samnang.

When someone sabotages the annual Boat Races, several humans drown and a full-scale riot breaks out across the city, heightening discrimination and prejudice between humans and the folk. Nami is drawn to the most radical fathomfolk protest group, the Drawbacks, especially Firth, a charismatic kelpie. The Drawbacks break into the Onseon Engine, where Nami finally discovers that the city is powered by fathomfolk selling their waterweaving abilities. Disgusted, she agrees to help destroy the building, realising too late that this act will also kill the fathomfolk workers within. Distraught at her complicity, she nevertheless ends up with Firth, drawn to his rhetoric and confidence when she has lost her way.

Facing insurmountable problems in the wake of the power outage, Mira, fired from her position as captain and spiralling with everything she is unable to fix, breaks up with Kai. A decade ago she struck a deal with Cordelia, giving up her siren charms for ten years to stop her mother's gill rot from spreading. Feeling that she has lost everything, she is about to renew the uneven bargain for another ten years. Kai and Nami arrive unexpectedly to fight her corner. Mira finds hope again and Kai manages to modify the terms of the bargain to exchange his full voice for the new ten-year term. Outmanoeuvred, Cordelia vows she will get her revenge.

Mira and Kai privately marry to make use of a loophole in the law that gives her his seat on the Council during the crisis. Kai was preparing to ask her to marry him anyway.

Nami is abducted by the Drawbacks, finding out that her oldest friend, the kappa Dan, has been blackmailed by them the whole time. She learns that the city is built on the back of a titan whale shark, a behemoth that many worship as a god. The Drawbacks want to kill the titan and level the city, using Nami's dragon blood as an ingredient in the poison. Nami refuses, finally realising that she values all life, not just that of her fellow fathomfolk. Against her will, however, the poison is made and the titan starts dying, causing city-wide earthquakes.

Meanwhile, using Kai's voice and her own shapeshifting, Cordelia pretends to be Kai at a press conference, ruining his reputation. As she makes her getaway, she is stunned to learn that her husband has known the truth about her identity all along. She attempts to take her daughter from the family home but is caught. Samnang gives her an ultimatum of either continuing the pretence as his human wife and staying as a prisoner in her own home, or never seeing her children again. Even though she has done everything for her family, Cordelia chooses her freedom, leaving them behind.

The titan beneath the city dies and something responds from across the seas, causing a tsunami warning. Nami, Mira and Kai lead the evacuation to the taller towers at the centre of the city, Cordelia is reluctantly persuaded to support them after Mira offers her an open-ended bargain. They use waterweaving to power a cable car to get people to safety. Halfway there, they are attacked by Firth and the Drawback leader Lynnette. Kai and Nami fight with them. Firth offers Nami a sign of his faithfulness by secretly killing Lynnette in the shadows, before disappearing.

On the roof of the tallest building in the city, they see an approaching tsunami wave that is likely to drown most of the human residents. Nami realises she can become a pearl to save them but is unable to take that final step. Kai sacrifices himself instead, as evidence of his love for Mira and everything she believes in. Nami uses his pearl to save the humans of the city. In the aftermath of the tsunami, it is clear that Kai's pearl has given humans gills. Nami, broken and guilty, runs back into Firth's arms. The city is still standing, but has forever been changed.

TIDEBORN

Prologue (Then)

"Again," said Sobekki, Protector of the Realm. He was indifferent to the choice curse words; to the scales that had come loose by the handful, drifting in the water like tiny fish. Nami kept the habitual scowl across her features as she swam into position. She pushed her long hair from her eyes, wondering if it wouldn't be easier just to hack it short and be done with it. It would certainly upset her mother, and that in itself would be worth it.

The young Academy student crouched low and waited for the signal. Sobekki dropped a lazy hand, his claws raking the Yonakunish waters as she propelled herself forward. She dived through the rings with ease, her human shape quick and lithe as she kicked her legs to undulate up and down, setting the obstacles spinning in her wake. With a boost of waterweaving behind her, she propelled herself to the surface to retrieve the flag. The change in temperature, the sharp breeze on the surface and the cackling of the gulls disorientated her a little, and as she paused to adjust, Sobekki found his opportunity. The crocodile-headed fathomfolk barrel-rolled towards her, body corkscrewing with unstoppable force.

Nami dodged to one side, then the other, but he was gaining ground. His jaws snapped at her ankles, barely missing as she kicked him in the snout. She panicked; the frothing water, the bubbles obscuring her sight, made her feel like he was everywhere at once. She was fragile and vulnerable in this form. Dragon-scale coated her lower limbs, and she felt herself doing it again. Reflexively reaching for her true form: for antlers and claws to balance the odds.

"Every time!" Sobekki roared as his grip tore into her foreclaw, sending a dozen more scales loose. It hurt like he had prised the nails from her fingers. Pulsing and taking up all her attention. "Stop trying to make yourself bigger."

"But I'm a dragon!" she gasped as she swam back, further from him and his constant lectures. "You told me—"

"I taunted you, princess. Every time you let me get under your skin. Do you think others will be more honourable? That they won't use dirty tricks?" Sobekki pursed his lips, his curved teeth nonetheless gleaming like daggers.

Nami had transformed fully, her ribbon-like dragon form longer than his, even with his tail. What he said made no sense. Constantly goading her to stay in human form, to fight in this ridiculously weak, impossibly slow body. He didn't do it to the other students. Didn't bully them and make them wake early for extra practice. She wished she had never managed to cut him that first week at the Academy when he had challenged the new intake to single combat. He had a vendetta against her now. Stubbornly Nami refused to give him the satisfaction of complaining to her mother, dragon matriarch Jiang-Li. If he thought she was a spoilt princess, then she would prove him wrong.

"You are not your brother," Sobekki rumbled.

"As everyone keeps telling me."

He hissed through his teeth. "It wasn't an insult."

"Sounded like one."

"For once in your damned life, listen! Kai could walk around all day with antlers atop his head, effortlessly making snow fall in perfect flakes. There was nothing I could teach him. The lessons he has to learn are out there."

The martial instructor was talking nonsense. The same cryptic drivel that her mother and the Senate liked to spout. She knew what they were implying: Kai was perfect. Didn't need teaching. She, on the other hand, had been signed up for additional lessons. She roared with the injustice of it, charging straight for Sobekki's belly. She could almost see the tiny nick she had made in his hide all those months ago. The same trick would not work twice. The old crocodile turned, his strong tail whipping out and slamming across her head. Disorientated, she felt herself sinking. Strong teeth grabbed onto her shoulder, and she could not counter it, could do nothing as he spun, dragging her down with him. She hit the sand bed with enough force to knock the air from her. Shoulder pulsing although he had not bitten deep. Her limbs tingled as they were pinned by his heavy legs. His pointed snout scraped over her cheek.

"Stop letting your pride get in the way."

Nami scowled but had no response.

"Again."

Chapter One

Mira and Nami stood with the welcome party, banners unfurled and long rows of chinthe, kumiho and Council members in their finest attire. The high-collared green cloak scratched at Mira's neck and she resisted the urge to itch. At least it gave her armour to hide behind. Inside she was screaming. The dragon matriarch, Nami and Kai's mother, was coming for Kai's memorial. Yonakuni was the oldest of the havens, not to mention the largest and most influential. Mira had read books on haven customs, quizzed Nami and the freshwater folk with Yonakunish heritage. She'd memorised traditional Yonakunish phrases, practising them with her mother every evening. She'd spent a month's wages dining out at a Jingsha establishment to persuade the pair of Yonakunish chefs to cater the welcome meal. Had a traditional pipa and bamboo flute ensemble at the ready. Every preparation she could make had been made.

And yet she was not prepared.

Birds rose from their position bobbing on the water. Terns and gulls that had been swooping for fish; cormorants that had been resting on small fishing vessels, their heavy wings like dark clouds passing overhead. In their wake, the waters broiled, foaming as the surface churned. A dozen objects shot up from the sea, bottlenose dolphins leaping in perfect synchronicity. Their tails trailed thick ropes, pulling from the depths a massive vessel. Front and centre, claw loosely on the reins, was Jiang-Li, dragon matriarch of Yonakuni. Her scales were an oil slick of colour: blue and green and purple, dark hues shimmering on a base of iron grey. Her spines were more prominent than Kai's had been, plates more than ridges. Mira could see the resemblance all the same. She closed her eyes a moment. She had not realised how much seeing another dragon would affect her. Could not help but compare, finding them all lacking.

The Yonakunish vessel was an impossible structure made of shell and coral. As Jiang-Li stepped onto the port, the fragments began to tremble. By the time the last of the party disembarked, their vessel had crumbled to debris floating on the water's surface. The dolphins were loosened from their reins to dive back beneath. This was the way of the haven: to live in harmony with the world around them; leave no trace of their passing. The sheer power of the waterweaving needed to transport them was tremendous.

A show of might.

Despite the marvel, despite the excitement emanating from those around her, Mira felt only a sense of utter dread. A thrum ran from her stomach and travelled along her bones like someone hammering on an internal axle. Again and again until she would surely break. She plastered a smile on her face, ignoring the sweat that ran down her forehead.

Behind her the musicians began to play. She could see now that all her efforts were for naught. Where she had thought it respectful, the pitchy music sounded like a shrill mockery of true skill.

The Fenghuang's voice was garbled under his phoenix bird mask. Only his eyes could be seen through it. "Jiang-Li, Great Dragon of Yonakuni Haven, you grace us with your presence. I wish this visit was under better circumstances, but we are glad it has brought you to the shores of our city. Long may the friendship between our two nations continue."

Jiang-Li had not transformed to human form. Her long serpentine body took up three or four times the space of a human, forcing the servers waiting with drinks and food to shuffle back awkwardly so they were not pressing on her. She moved about on all fours, sniffing at one plate, raising an eyebrow at another. All the weeks of work, undone in that one disdainful expression. None of it was good enough.

A yell drew Mira's attention. Jiang-Li had stepped right up to a server, forcing him backwards. With nowhere left to go, he'd slipped off the dock and splashed unceremoniously into the water. The dragon looked up, finally catching her eye. She smiled, whiskers flickering forward as if to taste the air Mira occupied.

"You are the one. The one my son made his wife." A statement of fact rather than a question.

Mira made a fist-palm salute and recited the Yonakunish welcome phrase she had been practising. Only fumbled over the last syllable. For a fraction of a second she was proud of herself. Of the effort she had put into this and the disparate peoples that were being brought together.

Jiang-Li burst into guffawing laughter. Tilted her head up to the sky and howled with it. The Tiankawians did not know how to react. They all looked at Mira, the Fenghuang included, for an explanation. Their resident fathomfolk expert, she could surely understand what strange new custom this represented. Mira blinked rapidly, just as confused as the rest, but ploughed ahead with her prepared speech.

"It's an honour to meet you. My name is Mira, captain of the chinthe and Minister of Fathomfolk. Kai and I married a few weeks before his death. He . . . he saved us all." A hitch in her voice stopped her, and she held back the tears that filled her eyes every time she spoke his name aloud. She hoped Jiang-Li would feel her sense of loss, share the burden of sorrow.

Jiang-Li's eyes slid from Mira's face, raking down her body. The oversized chinthe coat hid most of her shape, but she was not expecting the dragon to ask, bluntly, "Are you pregnant?"

One of the other ministers gasped, but the rest remained silent. The uniform that had provided so much protection earlier now felt like a shell grown too tight. Mira shook her head, too shocked to speak. She unbuttoned the cloak, her hand on an unremarkable belly. She'd wondered that too, almost hoped for it in the weeks after Kai's death. A distraction to take away from the loss. But it was not to be. Her monthly cycles came with a regularity that seemed to mock her.

"Then why he married *you*, and in such haste, is beyond me. My son lost his way in this city. And it looks like my daughter has too." Jiang-Li finally turned her full attention to Nami. "Come. I am tired from the journey. This can wait." She waved her claw dismissively at the pomp and ceremony Mira had spent weeks planning, her mouth pulled into a sneer on one side.

Mira did not know whether to laugh or cry. The Yonakuni entourage swept down the walkway with Nami meekly at her mother's side. In their wake, voices competed for Mira's attention. Crowded her with questions she could not answer. She would take the blame for this disaster too, but what else was new?

Nami reeled with her mother's arrival. She had expected many things of Jiang-Li, but the ruthlessness with which she had torn into Mira was not on her list. Half in a daze, she led the way to the opulent accommodation the visiting party had been given atop one of the undamaged towers in Jingsha district. It had been a rotating restaurant before the tsunami, a perennial favourite of the elite. With so many residences destroyed, it had been repurposed by the Council and hastily turned into luxury quarters. They could not afford to offend the Yonakunish representatives.

Nami's old teacher Sobekki was among the entourage. He

insisted on a sweep of the quarters, inspecting the doors and locks, muttering to himself about vantage points and exit routes before the dragon matriarch firmly bade him leave.

Jiang-Li lay down on the vast bed that dominated the room, her dragon body forming a gentle curve. She beckoned Nami to draw the shutters. Breathed in noisily against the backdrop of the rasping slide of wood and the ticking of an unseen clock. Nami's hand trembled, glad of the opportunity to turn away and compose herself. She'd not left her mother on the best of terms, nor expected to see her so soon. Kai was the link between them, the soft spot in both their hearts. Without him, what were they?

A noise behind her made her turn. Jiang-Li had fallen to the floor. "Lock the door," her voice commanded before Nami had taken more than a step forward. Even in a swoon, her mother would not be disobeyed.

Nami had been awestruck by the shell and coral vessel that had burst from the waters. The sheer waterweaving strength and precision had thrilled her to the core. Perhaps, just perhaps, Yonakuni had found a solution to their waning powers. Something beyond the barbarism of the Onseon Engine using folk like livestock.

Exactly the impression Jiang-Li wanted to give.

Here in the privacy of her room, the real toil was clear. Scales drained of all colour and whiskers pressed against her head, Jiang-Li drank greedily from the cup of water Nami pressed to her mouth. Nami had to assist her back to the bed. Her mother's body had gone stiff, like a muscle spasm drawn out along her full length. Scales flaked off in Nami's hands, scattering like petals onto the quilt. The dragon matriarch's waterweaving entirely spent.

"You didn't need to do that." Nami sat on the edge of the bed.

"They will treat us with respect now they believe we are powerful." Jiang-Li's eyes remained closed, the veins on her lids strained red tributaries.

"Mira was already treating you with respect. She tried so hard."

"That siltborn half-breed?"

"Estuary!" Nami was horrified at her mother's casual use of the slur. Siltborn. That was what they called biracial folk back in Yonakuni. She herself had used it just as indifferently back in the haven. Never thinking of the person behind the name. Hearing it from her mother's lips was like looking back into history.

Jiang-Li turned her snout in Nami's direction. "What happened to the daughter who wanted to burn it all down?"

Nami bit down on her own words, an ache in her jaw pulsing from the repetitive movement. She had started grinding her teeth, wearing down the jagged surfaces of her body. She refused to meet her mother's eye, knowing exactly the expression that would be on her face. "I lived, I learned. Wasn't that what you wanted? Kai died for them."

Her mother's claw stopped her. The curling talons were like a cage over Nami's human-shaped hands. "Kai did no such thing. *You* were the one who chose what his wish would be. You could've destroyed it all."

A breath dug against the sides of Nami's throat. She withdrew her hand, cutting herself against her mother's dew claw in her haste. A small trickle of blood welled up before she pressed it against her mouth. She knew the implied answer but persisted anyway. "Estuary and folk included?"

"The tsunami would've done that. All you had to do was stay your hand." The sentiment was merely a few times removed from the Drawbacks' rhetoric. This was not the dragon matriarch who preached about separating emotions from politics. This was a grieving mother lashing out.

"This way lies madness," Nami cautioned.

"No, this way lies opportunity." Tiankawi and Yonakuni were diametrically opposed. The abacus beads clicked audibly in her mother's head. Mira was considered Tiankawian, of course, an adversary rather than a daughter-in-law.

Nami despaired. She did not have the words, the influence to steer her mother back on course. Jiang-Li's grief lit her as brightly as the Peace Tower itself. Only someone with the patience and compassion of a sand god could unpick this tangle. Someone universally loved and trusted by both sides.

Someone like Kai.

Her brother was gone. Even though Nami had sat all night waiting for him to open the door and say it had been a terrible mistake. Even after she and Mira had boxed up his things into crates and burlap bags; until the traces of him were not quite erased but eroded, softened around the edges. Even when she'd started to forget the exact features of his face and the sound of his laugh. Even when she had tried on his shoes and found them simultaneously too big and too narrow at the same time. He was still gone.

She made busywork for her hands to push the tide of emotions back. Someone had started to unpack her mother's many chests of belongings, and Nami dipped her hand into one of them, feeling the fine embroidery on seasilk, the gossamer chiffon robes and the trinket boxes filled with hairpins. She pulled out a decorative belt rattling with small fan-shaped scallop shells. She had an indistinct memory of it from childhood. Jiang-Li shattering one of the shells in the face of a disgruntled servant, the matronly kappa cook to the household. Accusations over some missing pieces of jewellery. The roar of hantu ayer spirits released from the cracked shell, incorporeal water sprites that could merge for brief moments to make tangible shapes. The ghostly fist and haunting visions incapacitating the servant almost instantaneously. Nami snot-nosed and crying because no one would explain. She didn't understand, not for years, why their old cook had pressed a knife against her throat and called her a colourful array of names. Knowing only that strife brewed outside their insulated coral walls.

Clutching the shell belt, Nami turned. Jiang-Li seemed to have fallen asleep. Even with her eyes shut, she scowled, displeased with something or other. Nami had never expected the reunion to be straightforward. Not with the melancholy that surrounded them like boggy waters. Still she had hoped, wistfully, foolishly, to rebuild their relationship in memory of her brother.

"When is the memorial service?" Jiang-Li's eyes remained closed, but apparently she was still awake.

"At the next full moon. In a week."

"A week? Then the rites should already have started. Without me." Her voice rose with the indignation of it. To be omitted from the week-long ritual of mourning, as his closest family, was more than a slight.

"If you had remained at the port, spoken to Mira for more than a few seconds, she would've told you." Nami spoke slowly, trying to take the accusatory edge out of her voice. They'd known it would be a stumbling block with the dragon matriarch, but they would handle it. Together. That had been the plan. She took one more deep breath before continuing. "The memorial ceremony will follow local Tiankawian customs, not Yonakunish."

Her mother cursed, pulling herself fully upright. It was going to be a long day.

Chapter Two

Humans feared siren control. The manipulation of choice: of love and hate and all that was in between. Never knowing if they were being fed thoughts, emotions that were not their own. Yet when it came to loss, it was a different story entirely. A siren could earn a reasonable living by working with loss, as stigmatising as it was. Quietening the pain of heartbreak, fading the memory as if through layers of tulle. Numbing the displeasure after an argument, a disagreement at work. Camouflaging it beneath sweet tunings until it became bearable.

Mourning, though, was a special case.

No matter how many melodies a siren knew, they couldn't fill the gaping wound in a heart. A lifetime of memories woven with intricate detail could not be unpicked. A song was a life buoy but useless if no one reached out. A siren could only watch as they chose to sink or swim.

Mira sang. Her words rose into the air, catching like sails in the breeze. In the darkness she could pretend it was just her. Her and Kai.

The darkness did not scare her perhaps as it should. When she had been young, there were no lights. Not in the folk-dominated slums of Seong district. Lights were something seen in the distance: the clusters of stars in a clear sky; the bright windows of the Jingsha towers to the north; the blinking orange of a tram on its winding tracks. For those in Seong, lights were a privilege. Instead Mira had learned to count the planks along the walkways. To know which were loose and which missing altogether. To feel around the stacked crates and shuffle to avoid loose ropes. Night was not always safe, but it hid scars that could not be concealed in the harsh light of day.

Even though it was planned, even though they'd practised and coordinated, her voice faltered as the river of lights flickered into life behind her. Blue-red witchlights, buttery yellow floating lanterns, cerulean bioluminescence in the waters around them; they cascaded on and around the mile-long procession of vessels as Jiang-Li and Nami lit the brazier at the prow of their ship.

The flare of illumination made everyone's faces look jaundiced. Drawn from the long days of negotiating, hair-splitting every damned detail of the memorial ceremony with the Yonakunish party until both sides were, if not satisfied, certainly exhausted.

The procession sailed in a meandering trail through Tiankawian waters, snaking like a dragon along the circumference of the city state's outermost districts. Other voices joined Mira's in the mourning song, a drumbeat rumbling low beneath the harmonies. She allowed herself a moment of quiet, to simply marvel at what they'd organised in Kai's memory. He would've accepted the pomp and ceremony with a sheepish look on his face. Slipped a hand in hers. Not quite hating it, but enduring it with that good-natured smile on his face.

Mira's eyes were dry. She had cried all her tears. Left them unwiped until furrows ran down her cheeks. She had cried until her insides were raw. Until hunger and loss and tiredness were one and the same. Until rational thought had burned away and all that was left was the knowledge, etched with a blunt knife into her brittle bones.

He had died for her.

For his belief in her.

In Tiankawi.

This would be her burden to shoulder. To ensure his sacrifice was worth it. Every minute she did not spend improving the city was an insult to his memory.

They neared the new cenotaph. It had barely been completed on time, the bamboo scaffolding to the rear still in place. From the front, the two-storey building was raised up by six stone pillars that plunged under the waterline. For now the procession would stop here. They could not fit all the mourners under the cenotaph's roof. Here at the surface level, everyone who wanted to attend could. That was all that mattered.

The song finished, the last notes drifting like ripples. Mira could hear Jiang-Li behind her, the dragon matriarch's racking sobs like accusations. Nami had warned her that outward expressions of bereavement were the done thing in Yonakunish tradition. A mark of respect in a culture often criticised for keeping its emotions under close guard. Jiang-Li had acquiesced to human form for the boat journey. She had scratched her own face, pulled at her hair and torn her white mourning clothes. The other Yonakunish were also on their knees, battering heads and fists on the decking as they cried out Kai's name. Mira flinched at every utterance. She knew eyes were on her, loose tongues hissing at the calmness of her expression.

She reached out with one hand and cupped a handful of seawater from the bowl before her. Imagined it slipping between her fingers, falling as rain. She could not force tears, but there was water. There was always water.

Beside her, Nami matched her motion. The water dragon waterweaved from the surface of the waves with ease, a sheet of raindrops rising up before her. Each drip glistened, the globules wiggling under her hold as she raised them overhead, as high as the sails of the vessel, higher still, before letting them fall. The droplets created a barrier in front of the ship, the spray drizzling against Mira's face, providing the moisture she herself could not. Her clothes were heavy with it. Then the other folk joined in. The sheet became a curtain, extended round either side of the cenotaph until it made a complete ring. A veil of tears.

Droplets clung to her lashes, impeding her vision, and yet Mira did not have to see to feel the strength of it. The shared power and pain burning back some of the darkness. Nami brought her hands together. The muscles on her neck strained, gills heaving open as she slowly pulled her hands apart, drawing back the rain curtain with the motion, the gap big enough to allow the lead vessel to pass. They would lay offerings on the cenotaph while the others watched on.

Mira allowed her eyes to flicker closed. She only had to keep up the act for a little longer. Then she could return to Kai's apartment. *Her* apartment, she corrected herself. Wade through the piles of laundry and documents and cold cups of seaweed tea to sprawl across the bed that still smelled of him. Jiang-Li be damned, she needed this. Nami could handle her mother for a few days. Bat away her insidious questions. Each critique chipped away at Mira's shell until the whole thing threatened to crack open.

The prow of the ship passed through the droplets of water. Something landed at Mira's feet. She looked at it uncomprehending. The filmy eye of the fish stared up at her. Her initial thought was that it had leaped onboard, but then her wits belatedly caught up: it was not a whole fish. Just a head, hacked off around the gills. The smell rose up to her, a sour, pungent rot.

A thud.

And another.

Pieces of rotten fish landed with dull tones across the ship, raining down, rebounding from the people and equipment on board. Sliding and spinning across the deck. One piece slapped her across the cheek, slime leaving a trail down her jaw as the jagged fins caught in her collar. The overwhelming stench made her heave. What turmoil threw dead fish from the depths?

Those around her ducked and yelled, covering their heads and shielding each other as best they could. Nami pulled at Mira's arm, mouthing words, dragging her away from the side. It was Jiang-Li who kept her wits about her. The dragon matriarch, face red raw from crying, pressed her shoulders back and roared. The veil of raindrops around the cenotaph came to her call, solidifying into a dome above their heads.

With the noise of the onslaught dampened, Mira could finally think. The fish were not in fact leaping up from the ocean floor. They were being lobbed from nearby vessels. From barrels and buckets that had been prised open. Tiankawian hands pelted their ship, faces barbed with hate.

"Salties." Mouths gaped like empty cavities. "Bottom-feeders. Fish fuckers." Even from within the protective dome, the taunts reached their ears.

Mira's tongue was glued to the roof of her mouth. Nami cursed under her breath. The folk to either side responded in their defence. Angry voices yelling back insults just as caustic.

"Mudskippers!"

"Feathernecks!"

The insults were quickly drowned out by incoherent noise, like screeching seagulls vying for entrails. The fathomfolk, while smaller in number, were incensed. Water rose shakily from the seas, splashing against the protesters, the waves treacherous around their boats as if hands shook the hulls.

The city was simmering, and Mira had no way of dampening down the flames.

"You have things under control?" Jiang-Li's voice was a sliver of ice running down Mira's back. Neither her intonation nor her volume had changed, but the threat dangled between them like a snare. She removed the fine tiered coral necklace from around her neck. Fish guts draped across it, sticking to her neck and hair also. Someone had hung loose robes around her shoulders, covering her wrecked outfit, but the smell rising from all of them could not be masked. Jiang-Li wanted answers. Arrests. Now.

"I knew there was some disgruntlement. Dissatisfaction about the changes Kai's pearl had wrought. But that was to be expected. The Gill Adjustment Programme—"

"Your little charity project will do nothing. Trying to clear out a trash vortex with your bare hands." Jiang-Li's lip curled at one side. She continued to stare. Demanding an alternative plan Mira did not have. The dragon matriarch was diminutive in her human form and yet somehow managed to loom large over Mira. Her centuries-old bloodline justified that confidence, unlike the siltborn guttersnipe before her.

"We'll find the source of the unrest."

"And then what?" Jiang-Li asked, her eyebrow arching. "Fine them, jail them, make them work mandatory hours at the Onseon Engine? Do you see it now, the real issue?"

Mira sat down with a heavy thud, ignoring the damp of her trousers against her legs. Jiang-Li was many things – cold and critical in how she delivered information; upholding a hierarchy that was rightly fading away in Tiankawi – but she was no fool.

Tiankawi's humans were behind this. Angry, scared and adrift. Punishing them would simply cement the divide. "And I suppose you have a suggestion?"

"I do." Jiang-Li's look was smug. It would be easy, Mira supposed, to let the dragon matriarch lead. People respected her. It was clear in how folk whispered her name, touched the hem of her robes. Humans too, considering the pearls she had brought into the world. No one would haggle with Jiang-Li at a market stall – anything she wanted was hers for the taking.

"I'm sure when Kai was here, you managed. He propped you up. I can see that now. Put a pretty face out in front. A smart policy, I'm sure. But my son is gone. This is over your head, *Minister*. Yonakuni will handle the situation."

Tears finally blurred Mira's eyes, so that the room swam like paint in water. She barely heard the door click as the other woman left.

Long shadows stretched across the room as she sat motionless, tears unshed. Soft moonlight spilled from the shutters, striped across her body like she had been sliced with a carving knife. Her back ached from the hunched position she had curled up in. She blinked, unsure what she was doing there. Once she had been a stoppered bottle of energy and ideas. Concentrated, sparingly poured. Now she was empty.

The shutters were noisily yanked shut, and for a moment the room was plunged into complete darkness. Mira glanced up, blinking as Nami lit the oil lamp beside her. Trish shuffled in behind her, a precarious tray of tea held in both hands. The cups rattled, and despite herself, Mira stood to help carry it over to the small table. The smell of seaweed tea was comfortingly familiar despite the events of the day.

"You stink," Nami said with a wrinkle of her nose. She dragged Mira up by the elbow and cajoled her behind the screen. Only as Mira peeled the sodden clothes from her body did she realise how much she was shivering. A basin of warm water and fresh clothes was exactly what she needed.

The chinthe green coat still felt stiff around the collar, but it was more comfortable than the stinking mourning robes she dumped on a heap on the floor. She loathed the sight of them.

"Take it my mother gave you a telling-off." Nami crossed her legs under her, her face apologetic.

"You could say that," Mira forced herself to respond. Her hands wrapped around the cup of seaweed tea. Nami had changed out of her mourning white into her usual loose-fitting attire. She did not look as angry as Mira had expected. Not at the farce that had been Kai's memorial, nor at the fish guts poured on her head. She simply looked as she always did. A sea urchin's spikes shielding the surprising softness within. Someone Mira now considered a friend. "She implied I am not fit to lead."

"And she is!" Trish's words surprised her, echoing the self-doubt buried deep in Mira's chest. It was only her ama's harrumph, as she rubbed her sore ankles indifferently, that made Mira realise belatedly that she was being sarcastic.

The relationship between the three of them now was strong enough that words were not needed. Nami and Trish were here for her. The belief was enough to make Mira shake the growing fog from her head. Jiang-Li had intimidated her with all the power of a dragon matriarch. Condescending and cruel. But that also conveyed something more important.

Jiang-Li was afraid.

Afraid that an estuary upstart had the ear of the Fenghuang. The backing of the Tiankawian folk.

She was so afraid, she had come in strong. Pushing Mira onto the back foot, so that when a mistake happened, she could pounce on it fast and hard. Which meant Mira had to step up when Jiang-Li wanted her indecisive. She curled her fingers into fists. "Ama, Nami, I need your support on this."

They nodded.

"Nami, you've made it clear the Gill Adjustment Centre is not for you."

"Awful name, really need to rethink that one," Trish muttered under her breath. Mira ignored her. Nami mostly looked relieved. Mira had been pushing the young dragon for weeks to take over the day-to-day running of the place, but Nami always found some excuse or other, reasoning more slippery than an eel.

She could not refuse a second request, though, after so earnestly professing her willingness to help. Not when there was still the matter of her community service to resolve. "Take a crew: human, folk – Yonakunish included. Scout to where the titan's call was answered. Find the epicentre of the earthquake: the partner sand god. Stop it from destroying our home."

Nami's mouth dropped open. She looked at Trish, then back at Mira, waiting for the punchline of the joke. Panic rolled off her in waves. She had been afraid since she had been handed Kai's dragon pearl. But Mira needed her to stop hiding behind the damned kelpie and step into the light.

"Wh-why? You are sending me away?"

"Jiang-Li will use you, Nami. You are her bridge to the Tiankawian people. A pearl, for titan's sake." Mira left the words unsaid between them: that she did not know who Nami would choose if it came down to it.

"So what you are saying is that I'm dead wood."

"No," Mira said emphatically. She wanted to shake the impetuous water dragon, as quick to dismay as she was to rage. "I'm trusting you with our lives, our city. What you find out there could change everything."

The sand god beneath Tiankawi's feet was dead, murdered by the Drawbacks. No one knew exactly what its life-bonded partner would do in response, but the odds were against them. A city divided, in ruins and without military might or defences, was easy pickings. The rest of the Council buried their heads in the sand, saying it was Mira's jurisdiction as captain of the border guard.

Mira had hoped that after the memorial ceremony she could head the expedition herself. A foolish notion now the Yonakuni contingent had arrived. If he was still here, Kai would have done it. The truth of it hurt more than all of Jiang-Li's caustic words.

She needed Nami's chaos and innovation where others would tread carefully. The younger dragon might not do things conventionally, but her moral compass was true.

"That," she added to Nami's stony-faced silence, "is an order."

Chapter Three

Qiuyue's dress was brand-new. Sky-blue silk with gold knot buttons fastened tightly to the neck. Her long black hair had been braided in elaborate loops around her ears. Together the ensemble drew attention away from the gills that had been partially concealed by her collar. Cordelia only knew because she was looking: had been every time she donned another face and spied on her daughter about her daily business. Qiuyue should not have the feather gills of her human peers. She had gill lines, concealed since birth by the charmed pendant Cordelia had secured around her neck. Samnang must have had it modified, afraid others would find out about her mixed heritage if she did not look the part. It was the only piece of Cordelia her daughter had retained. All the other clothes and jewellery Cordelia had bought for her had been disposed of; her governess and the family servants also.

It made the seawitch laugh. All of Samnang's precautions made it easier for her to get closer to Qiuyue. The girl was surrounded by strangers, both at home and outside. Cordelia did not have the time to masquerade as a permanent member of staff in Samnang's household, but it had been easy enough to put an alias down for event hires, such as this private party for the Minister of Finance's birthday.

Qiuyue was oblivious. Deposited by the guest book, she had

signed her name with practised calligraphy, but in the space for a message she hesitated. There was a skill in the eloquent couplets other guests had left. A skill that a parent should be guiding her with. The girl's calligraphy brush drooped heavily, black ink dripping onto the fragile lotus paper. Her hand reached as she mouthed wordlessly to her father across the room. Samnang barely noticed. The trail of ink dotted and dashed across the page towards her skirts. Cordelia bit down on the exasperation she could not voice.

Gede leaned over and put his hand over his sister's, tapping the dripping brush against the inkwell. Whispering in her ear. Qiuyue looked up at him sheepishly as he mussed her hair. Her mouth in a more confident line now, she nodded. They were too far away to hear, but the fondness was apparent.

A junior councillor snapped his fingers at Cordelia, waving at her impatiently. She crossed the room and bowed low as he berated her. Poured the expensive soju into his glass, resenting the distance it put between her and her daughter. She had taken Qiuyue's embraces for granted. The way her small body curled into Cordelia's lap, her head at perfect height to kiss her hair. She missed the hand grabbing hers, forcing her to put down books and missives mid-sentence so that she could be more tightly hugged. A safety belt around her midriff holding them together. She would give anything to listen to another rambling story about Qiuyue's friend Finnol, or her governess, anything really.

Instead, she stood with her tray of drinks and an unfamiliar face masking her own. Qiuyue clung to Gede, the hem of his fine tailored jacket scrunched into her hand as he led the way towards the buffet table. Cordelia stared at the lotus crisps and water chestnut parcels, willing him to pile them high on his sister's plate. She wasn't eating enough.

A familiar laugh behind her prickled at her ears. Samnang slapped another man good-naturedly on the shoulder. He caught

Cordelia looking, raising his glass. Even though he had been fooled half a dozen times before, she felt her pulse racing as she walked towards him. She stooped to refill his glass, but needn't have worried. She was merely another gangly, slightly awkward server, overawed at the company. Samnang immediately turned back to resume his conversation.

"Of course the tragic loss of my wife weighs heavy on me. But my children need a mother."

It took all Cordelia's willpower to keep the gasp from spilling forth. She had heard the story Samnang told about her death in the tsunami. An easy lie when so many lives had been lost. At first when he'd withdrawn from the Council, she had wondered if he regretted the ultimatum he had issued her: be his dutiful human wife, confined within their family home; drop all her other pursuits and she would have access to their children. Sometimes she wondered if she didn't regret her answer.

The Dhinduk ambassador nodded sympathetically. He downed the expensive drink before gesturing for another. His body exuded an alcoholic fugue, like he had bathed in it. Up close, his feather gills were spotted with thin scratched lines that had healed and reformed like veins on a leaf. His eyes followed the movements of one of the female councillors, seemingly a habit more than anything. This much hadn't changed.

"I must warn you, the first families of Dhinduk city are not exactly keen on marrying into a family with gills. To them we are all salties now." The ambassador picked at his teeth, extracting a stray morsel of food. He might be bluffing. Dhinduk was hardly a city. More of a township, a semi-submerged settlement to the far west. They relied on Tiankawi for trade.

Cordelia had considered poisoning the drink. It was too obvious, though, too easy to trace back. Now she was glad she'd not gone to the effort. Samnang's attempt to rebuild his power was facing its own stumbling blocks. He was nothing without her, just as she had always known. He could not simply replace her with a simpering Dhindukian wife like refreshing a vase of fresh cut flowers.

His gills bulged against his high collared jacket, lumps at either side of his neck. He did not touch them, did not tighten a scarf around them as others did. The only acknowledgement was the deep laboured breaths he took in through his nose. It looked an uncomfortable way to live one's life.

Cordelia wandered off in a pleasant haze of self-indulgence, meandering towards the kitchen so she could dump her tray of drinks and drop her current mask. In a stroke of good luck, Qiuyue was near the doorway, deep in conspiratorial whispers with her friend Finnol. The seawitch could not risk her cover to squeeze her daughter close to her chest, but she could collect the empty glasses by the pair and listen to their playful chat. A plan to steal all the steamed canapés perhaps. Comparing notes on monotonous tutors.

"Ama always told me to keep away from the water. Not to swim in it," Qiuyue said dubiously.

"But have you tried? It really does work. I could breathe down there! I touched the very bottom of the seabed." Finnol's excitement vibrated through his body.

Qiuyue frowned in disbelief. She bit her thumb for a moment before noticing, stopping herself by putting both hands behind her back. "I don't think we should be doing that. It's dirty."

"Not all of it, and only if you stay in the water for a long time. Eun told me. It's important that we know what's down there. To see how the folk live. To remember." Finnol spoke in a superior voice. He barely seemed to know what he was talking about even as he parroted the words with an air of understanding. His half-sister, Eun, had become the city's de facto historian and archivist, seeing it as her duty to ensure everyone's story was heard. Her zeal was admirable perhaps, but what did words really change?

"It's dirty," Qiuyue insisted. "The folk are dirty. Disgusting. All of them. That's what Aba said."

A glass slipped from Cordelia's hands, smashing with a loud ring on the polished floor. The two children turned, but she ducked her head, not wanting to see the hatred on Qiuyue's face. The manager's berating words were a good excuse to keep her eyes averted. Picking up the broken shards and stumbling into the kitchen, she scarcely noticed the blood running down her hand. She took it all back.

Samnang would pay.

Chapter Four

Nami nodded as the captain of the *Wayfarer* introduced his crew. Rannoch was long-legged, each stride covering so much distance that she had to jog to keep up. He barely noticed, stroking his neat greying beard while proudly pointing out details of his vessel with explanations that Nami could only pretend to understand. The last ship she had been on was the immigration vessel from Yonakuni, and that had been a slow-moving behemoth that could transport hundreds of people at one time. In comparison, the junk ship was designed for speed and resilience. It was small, with three sails made of woven kelp fibres. Bamboo battens gave them structure like the curved dorsal fin of a fish.

"It survived the tsunami," Captain Rannoch reminded her pointedly as Nami peered doubtfully at the patchwork mending on the sails and hull. "Cut through the waves when bigger and more resplendent vessels became scrap on the ocean floor."

The first mate, Shizuku, glanced up from their charts and winked at Nami, saying nothing as the monologue continued. Their relative silence was in stark contrast to the array of tattoos up both arms and the nape of their shaved head, a vibrant tapestry across their skin. Nami filed it away to come to the first mate in future with her questions.

The crew of the *Wayfarer* were a fishing crew, out at sea for months at a time to chase the elusive deep-water shoals to the north. More than that, even though the captain was human, he had brought together a group of humans, estuary and folk. He had looked at Nami askance when she had asked him what the secret was. "An empty stomach doesn't give a shit if you have scales or skin."

The naga navigator and human shipmate were chatting as they moved barrels of supplies below deck. There was an ease between them that could not be faked. Nami understood now why Mira had chosen this crew. This ship.

"This is what we have to work with?" a rumbling voice said. The Yonakunish accent was thick, confusing the crew but not Nami as she turned. Sobekki's claws ran down the railing as he strolled on board as if he had been expected. Four other Yonakunish representatives stood behind him, awaiting further instructions. Sobekki's reptilian skin had a grain to it like the knots of a tree. He wore nothing more than loincloth and weapons: in a belt around his waist and another across one shoulder. The former weaponsmaster, Protector of Yonakuni, had a dozen throwing knives, knuckledusters, a curved khopesh and a leaf-shaped spear, but Nami knew that even without all of these, his hand-to-hand combat skills were nigh unsurpassable. Her jaw ached recalling their encounter over a year ago at the Peace Tower.

Before she could respond, Sobekki introduced himself to the crew. They were drawn to him, circling like curious birds before a predator. Nami pushed her way to the front. Forced a breezy lightness into her voice that she did not feel. "Sobekki, I wasn't aware you'd be joining us!"

"Yonakuni could not be without representation." Sobekki showed his teeth, but his expression remained neutral. His long crocodile jaw moved as he cast a glance over the vessel, not even bothering to give her his full attention. Nami heard the slight. *She* could not be that representative. Not the way her mother might once have trusted Kai.

It wasn't any different to the doubts in her own head, and yet when faced with them, she bridled. "We of course have a place for *you*, but all the other civilian spots are filled up." She threw back the volley, her chin raised defiantly in the face of her old teacher. The haven would try to fill the vessel with their people, strong enough in numbers and voices to push her to one side. Nothing was more attractive to Nami than a challenge deemed beyond her abilities. Knowing her mother had written her off, she was adamant she would beat them at their own game.

"Captain Rannoch was saying there's still space for—"

"We are full, Captain Rannoch." Nami glared at the captain, and he had the courtesy to incline his head in acknowledgement. His eyes practically bulged from his head, but otherwise he kept his thoughts to himself.

"As the young dragon says, we are full."

Nami had to stop herself from punching the air. The captain had sided with her. This time. Once they were in the open waters, things would be a lot more difficult. The ship would leave in three days, and she needed to find allies, fast.

Mira listened to Nami's request with pursed lips, giving her so little that Nami stumbled over her last words. The stallholder put a sizzling-hot plate of fried prawns on the table between them, clasping his hands over his apron. "On the house."

"I insist on paying this time!"

"Oh no, Minister, I won't allow it. Show me face by accepting it, no argument."

The ritual of the back-and-forth was comfortingly familiar. Qilin district was in ruins, but the community survived, scattered like seeds across the city. Mira had found her latest hidden gem along the rebuilt middle walkways. A bold poster behind the stall stating that it was the Minister's favourite. She endured it without the laughter and roll of her eyes that Nami had to suppress.

Mira bit down on a crispy prawn, shell and all, as hot steam rose from it. She beamed up at the stallholder, still loitering expectantly by their table. "As good as I remember," she acknowledged. When he finally returned to his spot behind the huge woks, Nami repeated her request.

"Take Mikayil," Mira said at last.

"The quiet one?" Nami was dismayed, hands nonetheless unable to keep still, reaching to deshell a prawn.

"You want Tam to lighten the mood. Make the others laugh. I know. That's why I need him. You will also need someone to represent the upper families. The Council."

"You appointed me on behalf of the Council!" Nami argued.

Mira put down her food with more emphasis than necessary. "Yes, I, the estuary whelp, appointed you, the Yonakunish water dragon with a criminal record. Can you see any issue here?"

"Point taken." Nami paused, deciding this time to hear Mira out. The sizzle of the wok behind her filled the silence. Her eyes traced a fruit seller mooring her canoe nearby.

"None of the councillors will go. It's too close to election." Mira licked her fingers before continuing. "This is a good thing, though. You won't have Pyanis or someone worse breathing down your collar. There's a junior official under the Minister of Healing, from an influential family in Jingsha but sympathetic. Interested in reforms to support gill care. She's going to be someone one day, but not quite yet."

Nami nodded. Mira had thought things out, which was good because at least it made one of them. She swallowed back the voice inside. The one that said Mira would not be on the *Wayfarer*, though. Nor Kai. She was the one who had to make the decisions.

"I'll take Mikayil then. And this junior official. But the other places are mine to decide." The false confidence worked. Mira smiled, the weary lines around her eyes softening for a moment before forming crevices once more.

Nami saw Eun's work long before she reached the library. In the built-up areas between the Palang old city and Jingsha central district, where the towering buildings had resisted the battering of waves, people still hung their washing on horizontal poles from windows and balconies, dancing in the breeze like merry festival flags. But around the library, the laundry lines had been commandeered. The lotus leaf pages of books flapped from the poles like seabirds resting together. Nami could imagine the talkative archivist knocking on every one of the doors with a handful of ruined books and bamboo scrolls, wearing down the residents until they let her in. A few tattered pages had dropped to the ground. The water damage was significant, most of the writing faded beyond obscurity. Still, Nami collected the sheets as she walked towards the library doors, loath to waste the effort that had been made.

By the time she reached the top step, she was clutching an armful of pages. At first it looked like the double doors and windows had been thrown open, but on closer inspection they had simply not been replaced after the tsunami waves. Resources were limited and the archive had clearly not been high up the priority list. Inside, more makeshift bamboo poles had been wedged between waterlogged bookcases. A murmuring sound echoed down the wide reading room alongside the rustle of papers.

Eun was talking as she attended to the lines. Taking each book in turn and flipping a few pages before reverently replacing it so it flapped open on the criss-crossing lines like drooping autumnal leaves. The archivist's light brown hair was tied back out of her face, but stray strands stuck out at right angles. She was a contradiction, stained and dishevelled while she tidied and dried the archives with the devotion of a new parent.

Nami found a smile spreading across her face. Eun was somehow untouched by the doubts and indecision that plagued her own life. She found her truth in these records, the information giving her a kaleidoscopic view of events. She was chattering away now – to the books, it turned out. Her voice didn't stumble in these private conversations. Nami was content to just watch for a moment. If someone had managed to find peace in all this, she was not one to ruin it.

"I haven't written your chapter yet," Eun said in lieu of a greeting. Her hands paused in her work and her blue-grey eyes flicked up to catch Nami's. Nami blushed, embarrassed to be caught staring. "I have the rough notes if you care to look over them, but what with everything, there just hasn't been the time."

"That's not why I'm— Wait, you're writing about me?"

Eun nodded. Her hand patted at her bedraggled hair, finding a stray pencil entangled within. "The section on Mira's reforms is nearly done. But I want to be certain that I haven't missed anything out."

Nami's mouth was suddenly dry. She'd known that Eun's life's work was to ensure Tiankawi's history was memorialised. They had crossed paths in the days and weeks after the tsunami. Eun with her ubiquitous notebook always seemed to be there, sketching, interviewing, listening. At the ropeway, the tram repairs, the partially operating sailmills. It foolishly hadn't occurred to Nami that she was a part of that ongoing story.

Her hands felt cold. She clenched them, crumpling some of the pages piled into her arms. Angry – although she was unsure at whom – that her reckless choices would be exposed for all to see. The archivist took the bundle of papers from her arms with a nod of thanks. Without the shield before her, Nami turned to leave, almost forgetting the purpose of her visit in the first place.

"I want you," she blurted out. "On the ship, I mean."

Eun cocked her head to one side, rubbing a sleeve across her glasses and smudging them even more. Nami resisted the urge to clean them for her, caught in the disconnect between the persuasive speech she'd planned and the nonsense that actually came out. "I thought it would be useful. You would be. On the *Wayfarer.*"

Despite the garbled words, Eun somehow joined the dots. Her head snapped to the centre and a dimple formed beside her mouth. She put down her precarious load atop a teetering stack of water-damaged books. "It would be an honour . . . No, that would not be the correct terminology, as obviously remaining impartial would be key to my role. Let's say it would be a necessity. Yes, necessity. Fundamental to how Tiankawi moves forward. Of course I would disclose any internal biases, including our friendship, but notwithstanding that, I do believe I'd be the ideal candidate for the position. Would there be funds for a replacement to continue my manuscript restoration work here in the city? I could write up an advertisement before we go." As she talked, her hands had somehow found a cloth bag and her arm swiped a whole load of pens and papers into it.

"Eun," Nami attempted to interrupt. Called her name while holding back a laugh. The archivist was opening drawers, dropping items as if at random into the bag and tying it at the top. Ready to go this very minute. "Eun, we don't leave for three days."

"Oh. That makes sense," Eun said, unable nonetheless to hide her disappointment.

"I'm sure Mira can persuade the Council to continue your work here, or at least preserve what you have accomplished so far." Nami was certain that the neighbourhood would continue to dry the waterlogged books, if simply to prevent the resolute librarian from knocking on their doors when she returned.

With Sobekki aboard, armed to the hilt, it was hard not to see the *Wayfarer* as a military vessel. A scout before the inevitable war. Mira had been very clear when she had refused to send a chinthe vessel north. Violence could only be the very last resort.

Nami agreed wholeheartedly. She had not the heart for more bloodshed. It had all been well and good spouting rhetoric in the Anemone Club back in the havens, but she still could not sleep at night without seeing the face of the selkie who'd died at the Onseon Engine.

It'd been a long week for Jinsei. Hard enough that he had to squeeze two classes into one, teaching forty students in a derelict warehouse at the edges of Kenabi district. His had always been a mixed bag. Merchant-class kids cramming to pass exams and get secure jobs as Council officials, hoping to work their way up into the ministries. Then the kids that drifted through from the growing shanty towns. Wandering in with scowls on their faces but staying because his lessons were as different as he promised they would be. After the tsunami, there was no curriculum. It was freeing not to be fighting with the school board any more. They had frowned on his methods, saying he never set enough homework, that his students were ... challenging. Now that their attention was elsewhere, he could teach as he'd always thought was right. Kids from other districts had started coming to his lessons, hovering at the back of the room until he gestured for them to sit.

He tipped a box of defective pakalots onto the table at the front of the room. Pakalots had started to break, mysteriously, after the tsunami. It should have been unrelated to the death of the sand god. But after the sabotage of the Onseon Engine, and then the tsunami, who was going to insist on their use? Especially when it was becoming more and more difficult to differentiate folk from human. Ambassador Kai's bill had never been passed, and yet by precedent, its legacy lived on. This was what Jinsei recounted to the students, watching as hands moved subconsciously to the gills at their own necks.

After class, the newcomer leaning on the back wall strode towards his desk. "I suspect you aren't here for remedial lessons, Nami, Second Dragon Daughter of Yonakuni."

The water dragon nodded in acknowledgement. The sleeves of her loose jacket were rolled above the elbow, and she shrugged, one hand on her hip. "The Academy at Yonakuni was a lot more traditional in its teaching methods, but you are correct."

"Tiankawi is also traditional." Jinsei tapped his ear. "I just have very selective hearing at those meetings."

Nami did not blink, looking at him as if she could figure him out. He could've told her about the bedsit in Palang district. The disgruntled ex-husband with an unhealthy relationship with fugu. The teen student at his first teaching job who'd stuck a knife between his ribs, and how Jinsei had decided to rip up the turgid textbooks rather than his career.

"The response call from the titan whale shark's death. We're going to investigate it. I thought you might come along." The words were reasonable but the delivery was sullen, as if protecting herself from the rejection that had not yet come. Jinsei recognised it from his students. The ones who kept threatening to drop out but nevertheless loitered. Despite his fatigue, his teaching brain took over.

"Why?"

"Why you? Because Trish, Mira's ama, suggested you. Said you were a good teacher and all that . . ."

"No. That wasn't my question, though I thank you for the second-hand praise. Why are *you* going? What will you do when you get there?"

"Talk to it." Nami's eyebrows were knitted in confusion. The answer was obvious, wasn't it? But Jinsei was sick of surface level. The whole curriculum was like snow on a mountain peak, never delving any deeper.

"Talk to me then, as if I'm the titan. You just killed my partner.

A partner I'd not seen in centuries. What words will you use to appease me?"

"It wasn't me. I mean, not directly." She was flustered, looking around like he was about to actually attack her. The idea was laughable. A human who barely knew how his new gills functioned against the martial and waterweaving skills of a water dragon. He sat down on the corner of the desk.

"Don't care, you were in Tiankawi. You're all the same."

"I'm sorry!" She had shrunk into herself, half the size, with the practised speed of someone who was accustomed to criticism.

Jinsei pushed on. Carefully prodded at the cracks. That was what he did. "Tough shit, I'm still angry. What now?"

"I ..." Nami gaped like a gasping fish. Out of answers. Her mouth snapped shut.

"Now ... you listen."

She looked up, waiting for him to continue. She was expecting an answer. A solution to her problems. Jinsei had seen it before, when students had been spoon-fed to pass tests.

"Now," he repeated. Emphatically. "You listen."

Nami finally heard the message. Uncoiled her white-knuckled fists and rubbed them. Let a long exhale escape her. "*This*. This is why I want you with us."

"I'll come," Jinsei said. Nami looked relieved but exhausted from the brief interaction. She'd struggle in a full week of his classes, he thought with an inward cackle.

Chapter Five

Music from the Barreleye Club blared in rolling thuds, shaking the loose sand on the ocean floor. The roving lights blinked through windows made opaque with moss-like seaweed. The full rush hit Nami like a wave as her kelpie boyfriend Firth pulled open the double doors. Bodies filled the space. Fins and tentacles, arms and legs blurring together in a writhing underwater mass. She shrank back involuntarily.

Firth sensed her apprehension. Turned a boyish pout on her. "You promised, remember? The ship leaves tomorrow. Tonight we party!" Nami smiled through gritted teeth. It was fine.

The catfish brothers Bien and Trieu, also former Drawbacks, joked around. Darting and playful still, like they didn't have blood on their hands.

They *didn't* have blood on their hands.

They hardly knew what had happened that day on the Peak mountain and during the tsunami that followed. Nodded solemnly when Firth and Nami told them Lynnette had gone too far. They had not questioned it like some of the others.

Lynnette, the leader of the Drawbacks, had murdered a titan, causing widespread destruction across Tiankawi. In the face of that, the Drawbacks couldn't exist any more. But that didn't stop some fathomfolk seeking them out. Quietly. In the submerged clubs and bars it was Firth's name that they whispered now.

"Doubles for everyone!" Trieu said triumphantly, holding up small glasses of thick brown liquid. Bien followed, gingerly carrying the rest of the drinks, the fins running along his forearms splayed for balance.

At their usual booth were a group of four young women. Fern-like gills protruded from behind their ear lobes, fanning open and closed in the water. Gone were the skinsuits and tanks that humans needed underwater. Kai's sacrifice had changed everything. The women giggled nervously, eyeing Firth. They whispered, tugging at each other's sleeves. Long flowing skirts shone with pearlescent ribbons. Bangles decorated with sea glass and pearls. Lakelanders – humans who adored fathomfolk culture.

Nami had thought their interest wouldn't last after the incident. That gaining gills would make the novelty wear off. She was clearly mistaken.

"Ladies, I hope you're enjoying your evening." Firth somehow made a fist-palm salute flirtatious. The women mumbled back, glitter drifting from them as they rearranged themselves. He had their full attention. He sat himself at the end of the booth, leaning across to help himself to the pickled seagrapes on their table. Flashed a smile as he popped them in his mouth. The women were too enamoured to protest. Finally one seemed to regain her senses, chastising him for stealing their food. The kelpie patted her on the hand, commenting on the pendant that sat nestled in the hollow of her throat.

Nami swallowed hard and turned away. "Bien, Trieu, let's dance!" The catfish twins did not notice the false levity in her voice.

In the centre of the dance space, it was easier to clear her mind. To stretch out her branched antlers and loosen the argent scales down her arms and hands. She could close her eyes and forget where she was in the pulsing beat of the drums. A naga's serpentine tail caressed her leg as her dark eyes looked for a response. Nami pretended not to notice, her head tilted up as bioluminescence burst around her like fireworks. Spinning in the water. A beautiful display that kept others at a safe distance. Despite the warm bodies, despite the press of flippers and fins, there was a cold spot of water that surrounded her no matter how energetically she danced.

Back at the booth, only one of the Lakelander women remained, sitting almost on top of Firth with her hand resting on his leg. The liquid courage in Nami's stomach was enough this time. "He's with me."

The kelpie gave an open-handed shrug, draining the rest of his drink as Bien brought over another round. It was an inconsequential thing. The Lakelander had the grace to look embarrassed as she slipped away.

"What?" Firth said. Nami said nothing, but her face, he had told her many times, told a different story. "Fastest way to get the booth back."

She pondered her response for too long. It never came out right. Discombobulated and accusatory, she'd learned it was easier to bite down.

"Hey, it's our last night together. Let's not fight. Enjoy it! Unless you want me to come with you?" Firth rubbed her scaled arm absent-mindedly.

Nami laughed, ignoring the goosebumps that trailed down her skin. He was right. The voyage would be long and Firth would not be there. The notion gave her a feeling she did not know how to interpret.

A woman's voiced shouted and Nami saw a flash of fists by the closest bar. Instinctively she darted over, swimming through the growing crowd. The Lakelander who had just been flirting with Firth was out front, her friends huddled behind her.

"Piss off topside, you feather-gilled freaks!" The bunyip was a swampy thing, mud oozing from their shaggy coat. The hantu ayer water sprites with them were spots of white light, flickering around the woman's face.

The Lakelander's lower lip trembled despite her defiant words. "We aren't hurting anyone."

"Hurting anyone? I'm barred from Jingsha restaurants and shops! After my time at Onseon. After everything at the Nurseries." The bunyip swam around the women restlessly.

"We're all folk now!" said the woman. It was a miscalculation.

Jeers bounced back from every side. Topside, folk would've probably left her be. Simmered with annoyance then taken it home. But the club was folk territory.

"You're nothing like us."

"Rich kids slumming it."

"Go home to Daddy."

"Folk is more than gills."

"Folk first."

Remarks that Nami had pondered on since Kai's sacrifice. Since Tiankawi and its people had been forced to adapt to a change no one had expected. No one had wanted. The comments grew teeth, more vicious as they continued.

"Teach them a lesson."

"Cut them and see how folk they really are."

"Take 'em out and show them."

Nami could watch no longer. "Enough!" The crowd rippled with the interruption. Turned its attention to the scrawny water dragon. She was known in these parts: as Kai's sister; as Firth's partner; as Mira's friend. "How does this help?"

They consumed her question, swirling it around before spitting it back out. The bunyip responded with a sneer in their words. "Makes a shit day more bearable."

Nami scanned the crowd, the freshwater folk who had lived in the city for longer than her time here. The words of reconciliation scattered unspoken in her head. Afraid to make the wrong choice again. Firth slung his arm over her shoulder as the silence dilated.

"I think you know what is needed." He directed his words to the human woman.

Her external gills flapped open and closed as she swallowed. Blinked rapidly. "I do?"

"Thank us! For giving you gills. For saving your fucking life during the tsunami!" He had captured the mood entirely. Laughter and agreement chorused back. Firth always knew what to say.

The edge of the animosity had been blunted, rendered into smug superiority. It did not feel happier, though. Didn't feel any more peaceable. Firth put the flat of his hand on Nami's back, shepherding her to their booth. The four Lakelanders were cajoled to the bar, heckled to hand over their coin purses to buy the next round.

Firth rubbed the nape of Nami's neck, but all it did was add to the tension. "You're still so soft." His tone was sympathetic, but the words brushed her the wrong way.

"They were going to get hurt." She pressed at her own fingers, fidgeting so she wouldn't have to look into his pitying amber eyes.

"Not our problem," he said, matter-of-fact. He tilted her face up, locking her gaze on his. "I mean it. They owe us. A dragon died for them. We hold all the cards now. Never forget that."

Chapter Six

The crew of the *Wayfarer* looked ill at ease. The drum group had gone for solemn tones, more like chopping wood than celebrating the voyage. Mira pitied the fisherfolk, chosen for their experience on long journeys rather than their political acumen. A never-ending line of officials had turned up, ostensibly to support the mission but wearing the faces of customers turning over bruised fruit at a market stall.

At least the wider crowd was enjoying itself. Tiankawians had taken the occasion to celebrate; there were, after all, so few opportunities at the moment. Kids in bright festival clothes and entrepreneurial stallholders in small boats were flogging flags and curried fishballs.

Mira fist-palm-saluted Captain Rannoch. The formal wine-red jacket the sailor had been given was ill-fitting, his broad shoulders and chest bursting the seams. The buttons were about to take someone's eye out. Everything that needed to be said had been said in private. Rannoch was Tiankawian through and through, and had accepted her proposal with a matter-of-fact approach she appreciated.

Next to him, the rest of the crew also seemed to itch in the formal garb. Human, folk and estuary alike shuffled from foot to foot, impatient to get under way. Mira understood that they had hoped to leave at dawn, not dawdle as the sun glared down with the midday heat overhead. The boatswain, Wensum, was the only one who got away with not wearing the coat. At only three foot tall, none of the hastily prepared outfits fitted her. Wensum was already garnering attention from both fathomfolk and humans because of her unusual appearance as half-grindylow, half-selkie. One of the few who could not shapeshift into human form, she had unusually large black eyes and downy fur, with scales running down her back and arms. Mira clocked the subtle freeze-branded tattoos on her spindly arm. A cresting wave was partially obscured by her loose sleeve, a pattern that looked similar to the old Drawback logos. Below it was a newer one, on the back of her wrist where a pakalot would have once been cuffed. A series of perpendicular lines like unfinished basketweave. The same pattern had been graffitied on the walkways and walls around the city recently.

As the launch party showed no sign of abating, Mira made her rounds. A drink kept her hands busy, but equally, an empty glass was a good excuse to exit a difficult conversation. A banal but personal remark reminding them of previous encounters: how did the renovations turn out; your son must be sitting his exams soon; remind me to get the recipe for your clam stew. It would never be something she was good at, but having a formula made it more tolerable.

Sometimes, as her mind drifted, she imagined the warm comments Kai would have made. The genuine interest he had paid others. Sometimes she even pushed herself to say them aloud, delighting whomever she was talking to. It didn't last long. The rush of joy washed out by the emptiness that followed.

Trish tucked her arm into Mira's, smiling at her. She had handed over a veritable chest-load of candied goods to Nami and the rest of the crew, smacking her lips together as if the mission's success depended entirely on the consumption of home-made sweets. Now she leaned against her daughter, whispering conspiratorially. "I'm calling it. The navigator and the roguish schoolteacher."

Mira couldn't help but look to where Jalad, the naga navigator of the *Wayfarer*, had reached out a hand to steady Jinsei across the gangplank. The human teacher had gone quite green, feather gills flapping in early signs of hyperventilation. "He's just being considerate. We don't all have your sea legs."

Trish said nothing, wrinkling her nose in clear confidence at her own pronouncement. Mira put her empty glass down. "They don't really have time for that."

"This is exactly the time for *that*. If we aren't building connections, what are we building?" Trish said triumphantly. She waved Nami over to share her newest matchmaking decree. The water dragon had just given her a hug when a pair of ministers interrupted, strutting cranes in their fine robes. Their families and junior officials drifted around them like fish waiting for crumbs to fall into their open mouths.

Pyanis, the Minister of Ceremonies, spoke first. Her white robes were tightly cinched around her waist with a wide gold and purple belt trimmed with feathers. She had the sense, unlike many of the others, to at least have her hems raised by a few inches so her fine skirts did not soak up the standing water from the walkway. Her high cheekbones were cutting as she looked down at Mira. "Minister Mira, I commend your quick action. The *Wayfarer* looks watertight at least."

Mira made a wordless noise, not trusting her tongue to respond. She waited, knowing the ministers had not sought her out merely to goad her. Pyanis played with her long gold necklace, lacing it between her fingers. "I don't see Chi-Mae of the Ministry of Healing. Busy, I suppose, with her new duties."

Chi-Mae was the junior official Mira had recommended Nami take on the journey. One of the few who seemed keen on

integration and innovation within the Council. The hairs prickled on Mira's neck. "Oh? I hadn't heard."

"Promoted to senior official," the Minister of Finance butted
in. His wizened face was like a prune. "Only two years since she
finished academic training. An impressive feat for one so young."

Impressive indeed that they had outmanoeuvred Mira. She
kept her expression neutral, wishing now that she still had a drink
to hold up as a shield. Nami gasped audibly. No game face, that
one. Trish increased the pressure a little on Mira's arm. That was
right, she was not alone in this. "Congratulations indeed. I look
forward to seeing the reforms she makes."

They might have scuppered her plans in the short term, but
they only looked to the here and now. Though Mira had failed
to plant one of her own in the scouting vessel, her potential ally
had been promoted in their ranks. In the long game, it was still
a win for integration.

"The former Minister of Defence has expressed an interest . . ."
Pyanis began, her face barely hiding her smug delight. Samnang.
Cooped up for months with Sobekki and Nami . . . They might as
well send a shipload of explosives and be done with it.

"My thanks for your suggestion, but we have a backup in
mind," Mira said smoothly. She resisted the urge to push Nami's
lower jaw back up from the floor. Instead she turned Nami and
Trish towards the drinks table, walking with slow but decisive
steps. Her brain went through the faces of junior officials, dis-
carding them just as quickly. Too compliant. Too conservative.
There was only one choice. Nami was not going to like it. Quietly,
so only the other two could hear, she said, "Trust me."

Trish's squeeze came immediately, reassuring and warm on her
left arm. After a hesitation, Nami followed.

At the long trestle tables filled with bamboo steamers and silver
platters of fried foods, the disgraced former Minister of Justice
stood eating a soup dumpling. There was a clear zone of exclusion

around him, a berth the other elite families gave him lest they be infected by his recent scandal and demotion. Mira plunged them straight into it, ignoring Nami's quiet *oh no*.

"Zidane," she said, with a wide wave. The former minister looked left and right as if she had mistaken him for someone else.

Zidane had risen to be Minister of Justice through the usual nepotism and corruption. His family had money, of course, and influence in heaps. Still, there was a limit to how many scandals the name could cover up. It was neither the multiple affairs nor the workplace bullying that'd been the final nail, however. It was because the money he lost belonged to the city, funnelled through fake businesses and poured into bad investments. Anyone else would've received a jail sentence, but Zidane was merely forced to resign his Council position. He still came to the events. Quaffed the drinks and ate handsomely of the free food. But even Mira noticed the injured look as yet another group sneered and turned their backs on him.

He was without allies, without connections but technically part of the elite. Enough to tick the box. "He's awful," Nami whispered insistently.

"He's also declawed. By them. He's our best option. Him or Samnang." Mira felt Nami shrivel beside her, but the water dragon made no further protestations.

Mira bit down on her own distaste. Kai would've seen the goodness in the former minister, so she could too. Somehow.

Chapter Seven

By the time the *Wayfarer* made its way out of port, the sun was low in the sky. Shizuku commented on the prudence of sailing this late, but Rannoch responded with a pragmatism that made Nami thankful he was captain. "Leave now or they'll throw another damned party tomorrow." It took her a moment to process the words, the captain's strong Tiankawian accent unlike those she had grown accustomed to. She was not the only one glad to be out of range of the blasted drumming and false interest. They'd been delayed by a good few hours more while waiting for Zidane to pack. Then a stand-off as Captain Rannoch refused to let his three heavy mahogany chests on board. The schoolteacher, Jinsei, had finally intervened, lobbing item after item out of the chests towards the delighted crowd, who yelled and grabbed for silk pants and slippers like they were gold coins raining from the sky. Nami was not there to witness the former minister's response to sharing a cabin with the teacher, but she could imagine it.

They slipped past the floating fisheries to the north of Tiankawi. The children were in the water, making use of their gills. They looked happy, splashing and waving their arms. Things had changed since Nami's arrival a year before. Her feet pulsed from all the standing, but she wasn't ready to sit down yet. She looked back to see that the centre of Jingsha remained intact, and two of the tram lines were almost up and running. There was not quite the dazzle of lights she had seen on arrival, but the city state was still a marvel to behold. Battered but not quite broken.

"A shining city in the sea," Eun quoted, coming to stand beside her. Her glasses were dashed with spray and her hands gripped the railing, but she had not resorted to spewing over the side like some of the others. Her hair swept across her face, obscuring her expression.

"Where's the lustre?" Nami's eyes did not move from the distant silhouette.

"It's there." The wind whipped Eun's voice from her mouth, making Nami lean in to hear it. Strands of her long hair jumped the gap between them, tickling Nami's face like a sea-breeze caress.

"I'm surprised you still think so. The secrets you've uncovered. The ones they tried so hard to hide."

"You can hate something and love it at the same time. People are complicated like that."

Nami blinked, the words twisting inside her, tighter and tighter. Then the wind changed. Sweeping through her clothes, under her arms and through her hair as it filled the sails. She was a bird finally released from a cage. The claustrophobia of the port perhaps, of Firth's bruised ego when he had refused to see her off, of her mother and Mira and Kai's legacy weighing on her every move. This was something uncharted. Something new.

The release made her giddy. She climbed onto the railing of the *Wayfarer*, leaning out over the starboard side as she whooped into the breeze. Bottlenose dolphins that had been following the ship leaped up, clicking as they touched noses to her raised hand. Her exuberance rang all around them. Eun tugged the back of her top, a caution and a smile in the same glance.

Nami tasted hope again. A flavour she had almost forgotten in the day-to-day trundle of putting one foot in front of another. It was not the same as the settlement vessel to Tiankawi. She had grown since then. Yanked up by the roots whether she wanted it or not. But change was coming, that much she knew for certain.

Chapter Eight

The bar at Glashtyn Square had been renovated by the couple who rented it. They'd removed the long counter, freeing up more seating space. A menu was written on long kelp strips behind the bubbling pot of soup broth. A simple selection of dumplings, in soup or fried, was being enjoyed by families on stools or workers who floated in the water as they scoffed down the quick meal. It was a good turnover, brisk and busy with all the rebuilding work happening nearby. Pleasant chatter and the clanging of the open kitchen filled the waters. The older baiji saw Cordelia enter, waving a ladle at her burly water bull disguise. They were dreadful cheery, this couple. Having operated a popular hawker stall before the tsunami, they had moved into the premises after Cordelia had decided it was too risky to continue her bar.

"Arkaig, right on time." the baiji said, addressing her by the new alias. She deposited a plate of crispy shrimp dumplings under Cordelia's nose. Her voice clicked despite the Tiankawian words, her dolphin whistles high above even the seawitch's hearing. "We were worried something had happened."

Cordelia grunted, eating as an excuse not to answer. At least that was what she told herself. The dumplings were exceptional. Just a touch of chilli oil and a burst of juicy fillings filled her mouth. She closed her eyes to enjoy it, but the chatty aunties were not quite done with her.

"It's all there," the younger wife, an imugi sea serpent, said, putting the rent money directly into the water bull's large hand. She had to duck as Cordelia turned, to avoid being impaled upon the huge curved horns that protruded from either side of her head.

Cordelia was rather fond of the tarbh uisge guise. At seven foot tall and broad-shouldered, no one bothered her. The opposite, in fact; they made more than ample space on even the narrowest walkways, her hooves a stomping warning when she approached. The fear she was already accustomed to, but the bulk was something she had not known she would enjoy until she tried it. There was nothing more satisfying than emerging from the shadows, nostrils flared, red eyes glaring, and watching someone shit their pants.

"A favour we'd ask of you." The baiji put a reassuring hand on her wife's shoulder. It provided the necessary courage for the imugi. "There's a fellow who comes by. Just ordering pickled cucumber and soup dumplings. He has the coin, on most occasions, but we'd rather he didn't sit in. You know. It's not that sort of place. We thought . . . you could talk to him. Scare him off."

The business owner was as tall and thin as her true serpentine form, a green tinge on her pale skin and a look about her that said even the lightest of breezes would knock her flat. The couple were happy to rent from Cordelia: knew that Arkaig's empire was built on more than landlording a few thriving dumpling shops. They pretended not to know any better.

Until it was useful. She was called in, as always, the thug to take out the trash. Respectable folk didn't want to get their hands dirty. Mira got to sit around the Council table and Nami was an envoy for the city. What a joke! Cordelia had done more for Tiankawi than either of them. More in trade and goods, more in getting fathomfolk jobs and housing, but no one pinned a medal to her lapel. Instead they patted themselves on the backs for having so-called morals and scruples.

She had thought it was the face of a seawitch that did it. Folk and human alike looking at her like she would devour their children, crunch her sharp teeth on their delicate bones. As a water bull, the assumptions had not changed. A different face and a different name, but the work was the same.

She picked at her teeth, not giving the couple an answer. Slowly they backed away, less certain, sliding her another plate of dumplings as she lingered. Cordelia had only come to collect the rent money. Her mind schemed with a petty vindictiveness. She would talk to this fellow all right. Tell him to invite all his miscreant friends for a meal on the house. Encourage him to set up here permanently. She could be a philanthropist too. The notion satiated her, or that might have been the double portion of dumplings she had inhaled.

The sliding door of the shop opened and a small cloaked figure swam in behind a boisterous group of shipbuilders. The baiji wife shot Cordelia a look as she plated up a steaming bowl of soup dumplings with a generous heap of pickled cucumbers on the side. All the tables and chairs were occupied, but unperturbed, the stranger plonked himself straight onto the floor, anchored against the wall. With great care he set the soup spoon and chopsticks adrift in the water and then dug into the meal with his webbed hands. Ravenously hungry, he was indifferent to the looks of disgust from the other patrons.

Even from this distance, Cordelia could see track marks on his emaciated skin. His arms shook as they lifted the heavy clay bowl to his lips. She recognised the tremors of withdrawal. A fugu addict who every so often tried to wean himself off: spent his precious coins on hearty food rather than the other substance he so craved. No sympathy; the shop wanted rid.

The diminutive figure lifted his head as Cordelia's hulking form cast a shadow over him. Scoffed down the last of the pickled cucumber greedily, as if sensing a confrontation was coming.

Better not to waste the meal he'd already paid for. Something told her this was not the first place he had been barred from.

It made her angrier than she had reason to be. Made her want to tip the tables to the ground and break the waterweaving enchantment around the kitchen so that the scalding soup blasted across the room. There was no logic in her rage. The couple were good tenants, always paid their rent on time. She had no quarrel with them.

And yet.

The stranger removed the hood, blinking up at her with red-rimmed eyes. He looked more haggard than on their last meeting, his dark hair matted and almost concealing the bald patch atop his crown. She recognised him all the same. "Dan."

The kappa's fatigue fled from his face on hearing his own name. He swam upwards, lessening the height difference in a pitiful attempt to wrangle some sort of control over the situation. He could not know who she was, not in tarbh uisge form.

"Arkaig, I'm surprised you know my name."

"It's my job to know." Cordelia kept her words clipped. The former Drawback had heard her speak often enough; he was a liability. She remembered now how deft he had appeared to her then. Not this filthy, scrawny addict, the same as half a dozen slouched in the walkways and in derelict submerged buildings around them.

Without a further word, she picked him up by the back of his neck, hefting him like a mother with a kit. Dan yelped in surprise but didn't even bother to protest. Nor did the shop owner or customers. Heads ducked as always, busy with their soup. She could gut him right here and they would barely comment.

The kappa weighed less than a shipment of fugu vials. When she reached her lab, Cordelia tossed him down, the water cushioning his fall. Pieces of fugu overspilled the bins and floated at ankle level by his face. Dan took it all in. The benches of workers, their sharp knives working fast around the deflated pufferfish bodies. The precious livers collected in a metal basin to be refined upstairs. It was quiet down here. There was no rule against chatter, but the workers chose not to indulge. Mistakes were made that way. Some, but not all, wore the thick elbow-high gloves she'd provided. A modicum of protection but one that made fumbling mistakes more likely. They knew the consequence either way.

Up one flight of stairs, above the waterline, where the rotten floorboards had been hastily patched up, rows of tables distilled and combined the toxin into the street drug. Concentrated, mixed with the hallucinogenic dreamfish, it had become the most addictive drug in Tiankawi.

On the top floor, the merchandise was packaged up, sent off to dealers across the city. Before the tidal wave, the chinthe and kumiho would've come down hard on her; closed down production in weeks if not sooner. Putting most of her resources into one drug lab would have been foolish back then.

During the chaos of the tsunami, she had struck an open-ended bargain with Mira. One she had reaped rewards from: the chinthe did not touch Arkaig's premises. A black spot in their patrols. No arrests, no enquiries. The look on that self-righteous estuaryborn's face was worth it alone. Of course the guards still arrested dealers from time to time: they had to do something to appear competent. Mostly they unwittingly took out her competition.

Arkaig, the water bull disguise she had chosen to head the operation, was only supposed to distribute the drugs, taking a cut from every dealer on the walkways, skybridges and submerged bars of the city's southern districts. Soon however, she found the demand for fugu outstripped the supply. The move into manufacturing was the obvious step, especially with the workforce begging for a livelihood. They came to her for jobs, desperate folk who could no longer rely on shifts at the Onseon Engine to make ends meet. Who was she to turn them away? She was simply filling a gap in the market.

Dan prodded at the gutted pufferfish remains scattered on the floor around him. His thick skin afforded him a decent level of protection. Only if he had an open wound would the poison seep deep enough into his system. Jaw set, he appraised the process. "There's a lot of waste."

"You could do better?"

His chest puffed out, and despite the fact that Cordelia could count the ribs under his threadbare robes, a glimmer of pride seemed to fill him. Moving to an empty bench, he hefted one of the curved knives, testing its weight and sharpness on a discarded hunk of fugu. Finding it wanting, he tried another, nodding this time. Slicing into the pufferfish on the slab, his hands moved with none of the previous tremors. The soft white belly of the fish spilled open. With impossible speed, he peeled back the skin and scraped away the black bead of the gall bladder without bursting it open. He cut around the liver next, separating the thin membranes easily and hefting the weight in his webbed hand. Cordelia could not fault his knife skills. He'd worked faster than most of her staff, without a single miscut. She moved closer, thinking to examine the precious organ Dan offered in his palm, but as her shadow eclipsed his small figure, he shovelled it into his mouth and swallowed it down with a loud gulp.

A gasp bounced around the room. The kappa's eyes clouded, and he blinked with a look of satisfaction. Unrefined fugu toxin, in a concentration high enough to kill a shark. Only a hardened user could survive that sort of dose. Only a kappa.

Dan continued to grin, inanely but with full control of his limbs. Gone was the cowed new arrival under the heel of Lynnette and the others. Life had not been kind. But he'd survived.

"That's coming out of your wages."

"Naturally." He offered his hand for her to shake. A thin transparent mucus, spotted with clots of fish blood, lay sticky on his fingers. Cordelia declined to touch him, offering a curt nod instead. The kappa's beak twitched in amusement.

Chapter Nine

Jalad opened a well-worn game box, the rectangular bone pieces yellow with age and the painted images on them faded. The weather had remained calm since their vessel left port barely a week ago, and he sat with his snake tail coiled under him on deck as he set the game up, the clatter of the tiles a welcome harmony to the low-level chat between the crew. It drew in the others, loitering in splintered groups above deck if not in their cabins. The *Wayfarer* crew got on with the job of running the ship, but the others, the interlopers, did not know what to do with themselves.

"Do you play?" asked the schoolteacher, Jinsei, half a bottle of wakame gin sloshing in his hands as he joined Nami by the ship's railings. The last time Nami had played was with Firth on the Peak mountain in Tiankawi. Back when she was convinced she had all the answers. She gave Jinsei a half-smile in lieu of an answer.

He cocked his head at her, coming to his own conclusion. "You played, but you never won."

Despite her intentions to leave it be, Nami could not help but correct him. "I won. I simply didn't realise that others were indulging me."

"Ah. And now you don't play because you're afraid of losing?"

"No," Nami said, indignant. "It's more that I don't know if it's real. Earned."

"You worry that you have nothing to offer?" His words were soft, kind; nevertheless, they cut Nami to the bone. How dare he see all her fears in one short interaction. He had been brought aboard to reach the others. Nami had foolishly not expected him to work on her first.

He pushed the bottle into her hands. "The only way to know for certain is to try." With hands deep in his pockets, he strolled across the decking towards Jalad, squatting down beside the naga as the others made room for him.

There was still space in the game. Nami pushed her shoulders back and took a swig from the gin bottle. The liquid hit her throat, not with the burn of alcohol but with the quench of fresh water. Nami spluttered with the surprise of it. Chuckled internally at the teacher's pretence. She pushed her feet forward, one step at a time. "Room for one more?"

Later, after Jinsei had won the first game and Nami had narrowly won the second, the atmosphere on the ship felt less tightly cinched. Cups of seaweed tea were passed around, and long strips of salted squid. Shizuku whittled at a piece of driftwood as Wensum played a slim tin whistle. Nami stretched her legs, strangely contented. Nothing had ostensibly changed and yet everything suddenly felt within reach.

Buoyed, she searched for Eun. The librarian had wandered from the merrymaking, craning up at the night sky. Stars sparkled overhead. Brighter than they could be under Tiankawi's city lights.

"When I sorted through the wreckage of the City Library," Eun said, eyes still fixed upwards, "I realised something. I've interviewed many people. Recorded their stories so Tiankawi does not forget. But here under this star-filled sky, I'm ... living it. The things that I've read about. Look, there's the manta ray constellation, the whale shark south of it, the turtle to the east. I memorised the star charts when I was a kid, but seeing it with my own eyes, that's different."

"Yes," Nami said, but she was not looking at the stars at all. She turned away before Eun caught her. Blustered to cover her embarrassment. "I forget which ones are paired together. Is the whale shark with the manta ray, or with the turtle?"

"Neither. A bunch of children's tales," Sobekki said, joining them. The temperature seemed to drop around his imposing crocodile hide.

"Even you must've been a child once," Nami said. The Protector of Yonakuni had stood like a sentry since his arrival on the ship, barely making any attempt at small talk. His presence made the crew and passengers alike skittish. Nami wanted desperately to tell him to lighten up, but suspected it would earn her nothing other than a cuff across the head. Getting Sobekki on side would be important, whatever they found at the end of the voyage.

"I emerged from my egg with a khopesh gripped between my teeth," he said drily, flashing teeth as sharp as that formidable blade.

Eun had a quizzical expression on her face. As if she wanted to interrogate the comment further. Sketch a diagram for her records. The notion tickled Nami.

"The only khopesh you were born with is the one stuck between your ..." Nami could not complete the sentence. Her old teacher had turned, daring her, arms folded across his impressive, ever-present armoury of weapons, and she burst into snorting guffaws instead. The noise surprised her; her own laughter was something she had not heard in a long time. She couldn't stop once she started, a stitch in her side doubling her over. Eun had clasped her hands over her mouth, giggling along. Sobekki shook his head and went to seek more sophisticated conversation elsewhere.

Nami's laughter slowly dissipated, but the warmth remained.

"I am uncertain of what just happened," Eun admitted at last. As though looking for a seminar on the proceeding conversation.

"Come on, I need a drink," Nami said.

Lighter than before, she found that Lieutenant Mikayil and Tephan, the ship's mate, had joined a new game with the others. The tea had been finished, but after some good-natured cajoling, the carpenter, Garrett, admitted he knew of a stash of semi-decent plum wine.

Jalad picked up the next tile, the end of his snake tail swishing with delight at his choice. He lined it up with his other tiles, turning them face-up for the others to see. He had won. The other players declared how close they were to their own victories, Tephan bemoaning how messy Jalad's winning sets were: not matching groups but an eclectic array.

Jinsei was the only one to shrug. "A win is a win," he conceded, offering the naga his hand. They both leaned forward to clasp each other's forearms. Trish's prediction tickled in Nami's ear and she saw it, how their hands lingered on each other. The beginning of something that could be what they all needed.

A loud yell from below deck had her scaled and armoured without even thinking. The others stared with eyes widened at the silver in the water dragon's skin. She bounded over to the stairs before the others, leaping past Sobekki even. If there was trouble, she needed to deal with it herself.

Deep in the hold, the barrels and crates of supplies were still neatly stacked. Garrett stood with a bottle of plum wine at his feet. The water dragon held her hand behind her back, waterweaving a curved dagger of water as she approached with caution. There in the shadows was neither a serpent nor a dozen kumiho with drawn swords. Emerging from under burlap sacks with hands raised and a sheepish look on his rugged face was Firth.

The kelpie didn't even have the courtesy to act embarrassed. He grinned like it was a boyish prank. Before Nami had time to think, he had smothered her against him in an embrace. His heart beat steady and calm, unlike her own racing pulse.

"What are you doing here?" she asked finally, looking up at him.

"You wanted me here. So I came." His amber eyes were bright, like sweet mead. The flecks of green like the facets of a gem. It was hard to think straight when he looked at her like this. Nami swallowed hard. She didn't remember much of the conversation when they had said goodbye, her head too full of worries.

Her face was clearly a turmoil of emotions. "Nami, you as good as asked me to come!" Firth was hurt, his arms turning stiff against her. She stumbled an apology, hastily soothing him with mumbled words.

Behind them, Garrett cleared his throat.

They'd have to turn back. Drop him off at one of the outlying fishing villages. Captain Rannoch would be annoyed at the delay, of course, but there was not a lot that could be done. "Just a misunderstanding is all," Nami said. "I'll talk to the captain." Garrett nodded in obvious relief, leading the way back above deck.

As they emerged, the silhouettes of the crew members seemed to loom larger over Nami than they had but a quarter of an hour before. Not even a week out from Tiankawi and so much had already gone wrong. Her feet dragged heavily across the decking, dread roaring in her ears as she searched for the right words.

"Found a stowaway." She tried and failed to keep her tone light.

"By the waves! Firth!" Wensum gasped. The boatswain covered her mouth with both hands, face a picture of sheer rapture. Nami recognised the look. She had seen it many nights at the Barreleye Club.

The responses of the other folk and estuary members of the crew ranged from quizzical to impressed, but the humans' expressions all fell. This was Firth's power. His personality eclipsing all others. Nami raised her hands placatingly, hoping to defuse the situation, but the kelpie spoke first. His arm rested heavily on her, making her shoulders droop with the weight of it.

"Good evening, everyone! I apologise for my sudden and abrupt appearance. Nami and I thought it better this was done quietly. Now we are away from the Council, from all the paper-pushing bureaucrats who would disapprove, I can be revealed."

Garrett's face scrunched in disagreement. There'd been no plan. The carpenter looked pointedly at Nami for the clarification she'd promised.

Nami's face reddened, but she stumbled out the words. Her voice was tinny in comparison to Firth's easy manner. "I didn't realise he was aboard. We can drop him off somewhere."

"Nami wasn't involved. It was my decision and mine alone." Firth spoke with exaggerated pauses, winking as he did. Everything she said was recast in his genial tones, rendering her own words insignificant. Both Wensum and Jalad nodded in understanding, magnetised to the kelpie's indisputable energy.

Sobekki folded his arms. "Yonakuni will not accept a stowaway. Drop him over the side; he can swim." A wave of conflicting emotions surged in Nami's ribcage. Sobekki could be the villain here and leave her hands clean.

Captain Rannoch came down from his place behind the ship's wheel and looked at Nami. Looked and failed to find what he sought there. Nami did her utmost to avoid his eye, glance sliding about the decking like floodwater. Stall for long enough and it would not be her responsibility. Finally Jinsei broke the silence pragmatically. "We should vote. Drop him off or keep him."

"Lynnette went too far, I've always regretted that. I followed her because I believed in a world where folk are no longer the bottom of the barrel." Firth's arm moved from Nami's shoulder, leaving her cold and exposed. He paced, his words directed at the crew members. His auburn hair caught in the wind, moving as if in a warm current. Strands of kelp seaweed and shells intertwined in the tousled strands. When he spoke, it was like the ocean roared. "You *need* me. I don't have an ancient bloodline or a post on the

Council. My salary hasn't been paid. I will speak the hard truths they don't want to hear. Even if you disagree, you are obligated to hear them. That is the purpose of the mission, isn't it?"

His proposal was seductive. Nami could see it working around the crew like water underfoot, soaking into their clothes until they waded through it without realising. Subconsciously they drifted apart from each other. Humans on one side, folk on the other. When asked for a show of hands, only Zidane and Sobekki dared to vote him out. Eun's face was inscrutable. Wensum looked like she was about to kiss the kelpie's feet. Nami's own hand tingled by her side, goading her to stretch up towards the sky.

Chapter Ten

Mira had never been in the Fenghuang's quarters before. She should really be taking notes; Trish would ask later. Paint a picture for me, her ama would say. But Mira could barely keep her eyes open, never mind anything else.

It had once been a palace. A courtyard with walled gardens, pleasure pavilions and servants' quarters. The history books had shown peach blossom trees and ponds filled with koi and lotus flowers. But that was before the water had risen. They'd moved the Hall of Harmonious Eminence, brick by brick, marble pillar by marble pillar, to sit atop one of the towers in Jingsha. The rest of the palace complex had drowned, tiles and stones pilfered for other builds.

While Tiankawi had risen, on bamboo scaffolds and iron girders, the Hall of Harmonious Eminence remained as a token of the past. Its double-eaved roof was the only one tiled in a golden hue, while other traditional buildings had green tiles. Once a month the phoenix-masked leader would have an open session with his people and to ratify new laws. When Mira had been younger, she'd joined the snaking queue. Stood on throbbing feet through the night and watched the sun rise the next morning. Determined to be heard. The injustice she saw every day, in every district. The solutions that no one would listen to. If only he would see her, she knew that it would make a difference.

They'd shuffled forward only a few metres by the time the sun set and the doors slammed closed. The Fenghuang had finished for the day. He had seen half a dozen petitioners. Stubbornly Mira tried again, then again. Altering her plan of attack, camping for two nights on one occasion. She'd been the second person at the double doors. They hadn't opened at all. All she had taken home was sunburn and disenchantment.

Now, as she mounted the eighty-eight stone steps, stopping halfway to catch her breath, she wondered if she should feel a sense of awe. Satisfaction. Joy that she had finally got to the other side. Mostly she wondered if the tower really had the structural support for the sprawling stone behemoth on its roof. If the inhabitants in the floors below looked at the cracks in their ceiling beams as they slept. She smiled wryly. Here for a private meeting with the Fenghuang and she was thinking about city planning by-laws.

The double-height wooden doors were painted green. Gold studs bedecked the surface, each as big as her fist, etched with the symbols of kumiho and chinthe. Red pillars stretched out on either side, with blue-uniformed city guards standing between them.

The eyes of the closest two guards moved to follow Mira's progress towards the door, the only indication that they were anything but statues. As she neared, they suddenly snapped into action, pulling the doors open for her. Deep inside, a gong rumbled like thunder and an echoing voice announced her name with a litany of ridiculous titles. Minister of Fathomfolk, Captain of the Chinthe, Daughter of the City. The air from the hall wafted towards her, salty and sharp like opening a jar of dried squid.

The wide corridor before her was decorated with intricately painted blue flowers on white tiles, while wooden birdcages swayed on the overhead beams, filled with the busy chatter of songbirds. At the far end was another set of double doors, but these were ornately decorated with coloured glass flowers and geometric shapes. The detail was so fine, she could see beetles and cicadas painted onto the stems of the stylised greenery. There were no kumiho guards at these doors, just her and her hesitation to knock. Everything was designed to intimidate, leave people craning their necks and staring for so long that they forgot the purpose of their visit. To show how far above the waterline the Fenghuang was. Mira knew these tricks and yet it was hard not to let it affect her all the same.

She yanked open the doors, the force making the stained glass rattle. The room was vast and empty apart from marble pillars like sentries lining the way to the dais at the far end. One hundred fawning dignitaries could fill it with pomp and ceremony. Or a dozen struggling families could easily sleep on the floor. A rolling relief filled the walls on either side, carved with the history of Tiankawi. Mira could only see the section close to her: the city before the Great Bathyal War, surrounded by a dense jungle forest and a ragged mountain range.

Jiang-Li and the Fenghuang sat on the dais drinking tea like old friends. By the looks of the half-eaten plate of snacks on the circular table between them, they had been there a while. Mira felt the heat rising through her body, quickening her pulse. The apology for tardiness pushed at her gritted teeth, despite her knowing she was not late: not according to the messenger who had relayed the invitation. She held back against every fibre of her instinct; every desire to grovel before the two resplendent leaders who put her on the back foot. The masked Fenghuang in his golden headdress and robes. The dragon matriarch in human form in a voluptuous dress like the rapids of a raging river. Jiang-Li had likely not been fazed by the Hall of Harmonious Eminence. Had not felt the fabric of her worn trousers as she pushed her chipped and bitten nails deep into her pockets.

Everything had been designed to make ordinary people ill at

ease. A reminder of the things they didn't know. The life they had not lived. It was an inspired move, but it had the opposite effect on the freshwater estuary.

It boiled her blood.

"Ah, Minister Mira, we were wondering if you were joining us," the Fenghuang said. His words were polite enough, but a bitter taste coated them. Having only received the invitation yesterday evening, Mira had rescheduled everything to accommodate.

She took her time crossing the echoing room to reach them. The chair they'd put out for her was smaller than the others, without ornate armrests or a tall back, like she had been given a seat at the children's table. Titans below, the ones they sat on looked uncomfortable, the kind of chair she would rant to Kai had no purpose other than removing coin from the purses of people with too much money. Despite that, she spied another leaning against a far wall and dragged it, feet scraping on the tiles, to the table. An almost imperceptible smile perched on Jiang-Li's lips but she said nothing. The Fenghuang continued as if it were perfectly normal for visitors to rearrange the furniture.

"Do you want to fill her in, or should I?" the leader asked, with an indulgent wave of his hand. Jiang-Li unfolded her legs and put her teacup down on the table, her movements all grace and poise.

"We were discussing the pakalots. The barbaric practice must end. Permanently." Jiang-Li's eyes were steel. Selling waterweaving was still happening, despite the Onseon Engine being destroyed. Now it was unregulated on the walkways for a quick coin.

"They are still a regrettable necessity. Eddy farms and sailmills are not able to cover the whole city. Not yet. We need power." The Fenghuang was blunt. Mira was surprised he even had a grasp of the situation in the first place. He rarely attended Council meetings, and when he did, he was liable to fall asleep or leave halfway through. She would be as happy as Jiang-Li to do away with pakalots if it meant a better life, better living conditions for fathomfolk. At least, after Kai's wish, the manacles no longer prevented folk from using their powers against humans. However, siphoning waterweaving to pay the bills would not disappear overnight. Yonakuni could claim to have achieved a major victory if the Fenghuang agreed, but Mira had seen enough exploitation in the city to know that it wasn't that easy.

"Phase it out. Folk are more than batteries to be drained. We have a shortage of labour to rebuild the city. Apprenticeships – for folk and humans alike – will give Tiankawi what it needs. Shipbuilders, architects, farmers, engineers." Mira dared to imagine a future with opportunities, a walkway leading from the water's edge all the way up to the highest Jingsha towers.

The Fenghuang shook his head. "An admirable notion but one that will take years to come to fruition. We need results faster."

"You are rebuilding a city. Now is the time to change. Not after the foundations have been set." Her words bounced off him like raindrops slipping into the gutter.

The Fenghuang turned to face Jiang-Li, and although he was masked, there was something in the slope of his shoulders that straightened like a guide rope pulled taut. He issued a statement, an opening volley. "You wish to negotiate the Peace Tower Accords."

"I do," the dragon matriarch acquiesced.

"A proposal then. Given the sacrifice your son made for Tiankawi, I will release the last dragon pearl into your care."

The air in the room grew still, even the muffled birdsong from the corridor dimming to silence. The moment before a match is lit. Jiang-Li pressed her finger and thumb together, face unreadable. "And in return, you want to rebuild the Onseon Engine?"

"Time-limited," the Fenghuang promised. "Thirty years and then we close it permanently. Enough time to re-establish Tiankawi." Thirty years and the current Fenghuang would definitely have retired. A problem for his successor.

"Fifteen," Jiang-Li fired back.

"Twenty-five."

"Twenty, and you increase the number of folk visas issued. The havens cannot take any more from Atlitya." Jiang-Li readjusted one of the many pearl hairpins that covered her elaborate looping braids.

"We are in agreement."

The whole thing had happened in less than a minute. A quick rally of words that flew over Mira's head and they were pouring each other tea, the stiffness gone from their manner. They had planned this, come in with their hard lines and compromises. Mira had never been a part of it: just an eyewitness as they carved up the future of freshwater folk in the city.

"No." She stood up, her chair scraping in protest.

"No?" Jiang-Li raised an eyebrow. "You have much to learn, child. Sit down."

This time Mira unstoppered her rage, let it stream in a controlled burst. Jiang-Li was used to leading, used to being at the top of the seamount; but this was not the havens. Mira gripped tightly to the front of her chinthe green coat. "No. Any changes must be agreed through the Minister of Fathomfolk first and then ratified by the Council. It is written in Tiankawi law. I can fetch you the exact wording if you do not believe me."

"I believe you, but the Minister of Fathomfolk was my son. Upon death his title reverted to me." Jiang-Li was not afraid to weaponise her own son's memory. Challenged Mira to do the same. It felt wrong to sling his name around for points, but the weight of her betrothal bangles reassured her.

"Kai was incapacitated before death. I took on the role and it was accepted by the Council. With all due respect, you do not speak for the folk of this city. You haven't lived here. Haven't swum in our waters or eaten at our tables. You have no right."

The Fenghuang had leaned back in his chair to watch the

heated discussion with mild amusement. "The mermaid has claws. You do realise we can simply appoint another Minister of Fathomfolk?"

He goaded her with the mermaid comment, but Mira would not be distracted by insults any more than by finery. It merely showed she was getting under their skin. "You can. But it's an election year. You will have to wait until the official ballots. And you'll have to find a candidate the public support more than me." It was a basic bluff, but there was truth behind it also. It was one of her few saving graces that the general Tiankawi population trusted her more than the rest of the Council. Her chest swelled with hope. She could beat them at their game.

"My dear, your little tantrum has bought you a few months, but your re-election is not guaranteed," said the Fenghuang.

"No," Mira tossed back. This time she was the one smiling. "And nor is yours."

Chapter Eleven

It was awkward going down the eighty-eight steps of the Hall of Harmonious Eminence in complete silence with the dragon matriarch. Mira could've dashed off ahead, and yet she could not go any faster than a few steps in front without tripping over her own feet. Despite her triumph in the privacy of the Fenghuang's quarters, she did not want to show her open enmity before the watching city guards. Besides, Trish's face filled her head, finger wagging with displeasure. *If it was me, you'd offer me an arm.* Mira could only imagine the look of disgust if she offered Jiang-Li anything other than fawning admiration.

"Have you had time to do many outings?" The words fell from her mouth before she realised how crass they were. Jiang-Li had not come on a pleasure jaunt but for her son's memorial and to renegotiate the terms of a peace treaty. Not exactly the time to be buying squid on a stick by the harbour.

"Now is convenient." Jiang-Li was graceful on the stairs despite her long skirts, barely having to lift the hem from the ground. Mira was so busy watching that she didn't at first comprehend the words. At the roof level, Jiang-Li paused before the lift, her neutral expression unaltered. *"Haven't swum in our waters or eaten at our tables.* You were the one who proposed it, Minister."

Mira paled in realisation that the dragon matriarch had misunderstood her words. Strongarmed her into being tour guide once more. It wasn't a bad move. She wanted Jiang-Li on board. Wanted to know the cold-as-stone mother-in-law she'd heard so much about. It wouldn't be as pleasant as showing Kai the city, nor even Nami, but it had somehow become an integral part of her job.

Jiang-Li waved away the awaiting Yonakunish contingency at sea level. The six fathomfolk barely batted an eyelid at her dismissal, simply offering a fist-palm salute, in perfect synchronicity, before diving into the water. For want of a plan, Mira hailed a water tuk-tuk. The dugong driver's muzzle turned towards them indifferently, and then with a sharp flaring of nostrils as he did a double-take, shocked at his esteemed customers.

"Glashtyn Square in Seong district, please."

"Minister, with all due respect, wouldn't it be better to stay in Jingsha? Or Palang even?"

"Seong," Mira repeated with a nod of acknowledgement. Jiang-Li was no inexperienced ambassador on her first job. She doubted the worst of the slums would even ruffle the Yonakunish leader's feathers.

Seong district had had the biggest folk population before the tsunami. It'd been washed clean away, held together with nothing more than mud and lashed bamboo scaffolding. It'd also been the easiest to rebuild. While others waited for bricks and mortar, settling in derelict buildings and crammed into boats, the residents of Seong had simply shrugged like it was any other week, then piled the corrugated iron back up.

With the chinthe and kumiho both busy with rebuild projects, the slum sprawled like a sleeping monster, humpbacked and spilling much further than its previous borders. It welcomed all. Folk, human and anyone in between – alike in destitution – were accepted here.

Jiang-Li said nothing as the tuk-tuk driver dropped them by the edge of the Seong. The walkways had not been rebuilt, and even Mira's gills burned as they dropped into the water. Effluent from the Onseon Engine had drained into it, sending a river of silt right through the area. It had only got worse after Onseon was destroyed, the filtration system that offered some protection no longer functioning. A thick miasma lingered like sulphur in the air. Gill rot was rife, and no longer restricted to fathomfolk. Black veins throbbing against raw skin as if ink had been injected into their systems. Marks that looked like soot stains concentrated around gill lines, marks that were familiar to Mira as she watched for them in Trish every time she visited.

Mira took them through the dense areas of the shanty town, waving in response to those who called her by name. She said nothing. Didn't need to. The threadbare clothing that even sashiko embroidery could not save, hanging from bodies that were alike in how rake thin they were, no matter the scales, fins or fur on the surface, did the talking for her. The rheumy eyes of fugu users too deep in their pain-numbing trips to even move. They had to take careful steps to avoid standing on the sprawling arms or fins of the more prolific users, who barely twitched as they passed by. Jiang-Li's porcelain features remained unchanging, but she blinked erratically, a moth against a light.

A small crowd started following them. Street kids at first, hands outstretched for the few coins Mira dropped into them. Then whispers trailed like the tail of a kite. *The dragon matriarch. The dragon! She came.* Hands stretched out to touch Jiang-Li's clothing, to ask for her blessing, the more courageous reaching up to touch her hair. Voices, tremulous at first in Tiankawian and Yonakunish phrases. It bothered Mira. For all she had done for them, she had never received this adulation.

Jiang-Li was unfazed. With skilled ease she offered a wave, an incline of her head that sent a murmuring wave of joy through the small crowd. Then, without any seeming action, she removed the hands pressing at her clothes and hair. Only a few droplets of water that glistened in the air gave evidence of what she had done. She paused only once, to accept a gift one of the folk dropped into her hands. Like a piece of unfinished basket weaving, a small amulet with perpendicular straight lines, looped onto a piece of cord to be hung on the waist. Mira had seen good-luck charms for health, wealth or studies knotted to the waistband of many a folk. This one she did not recognise.

At the Gill Adjustment Centre, she offered Jiang-Li a hand up the ramp. The dragon matriarch ignored her, regal despite her skirts now being waterlogged, stained in grime and oil. She flicked a hand over the bedraggled material, as if shaking off a crumb, and in that fine movement the water sprang from her clothing, lifting off in a fluid gossamer curtain. She deposited it over the side.

The hull had been scrubbed clean of barnacles and the decks were freshly painted, but the place still looked as bleak as it sounded. The old junk ship had somehow survived the tsunami without major leaks, but both masts had snapped clean off, leaving it disfigured and unusable on the seas. Mira had a soft spot for it, had done since the chinthe guard had salvaged this vessel alongside dozens of others. She wanted symbolic sails, bright and colourful, to be commissioned. A second ship as a school and a third as a canteen nearby.

She wanted a lot of things.

Jiang-Li walked round the exhibit Eun had hastily set up before joining the *Wayfarer*. Her expression gave nothing away as she read the text, looking at the curated diaries and items the archivist had set out. She could destroy them in an instant, cut through the evidence with a blade of water, and no one would be the wiser. Mira was foolish for bringing the dragon matriarch here before the display had been viewed by the newssheets and the general public, but it was too late to backtrack.

"If Yonakuni was free of the debt, of the Peace Treaty that was forced upon us, we could've helped," Jiang-Li said finally. Her voice was low and quiet for once. She stood before the framed copy of the agreement. The one her own husband, the water dragon Alon, had signed as the first ambassador to Yonakuni. He'd made a unilateral decision to close the Nurseries. The cost: indentured labour at the Onseon Engine. Her hand reached up to touch the red seal next to Alon's signature, sharp claws curving out. She stopped herself, nails embedding in her own palm.

"He was angry at me for not letting the Iyonessians cross our borders. Even though we'd heard the rumours of the pens they were kept in. Onseon was his compromise."

"A prison by any other name."

"Yonakuni comes first," Jiang-Li insisted. Scales fanned from the neckline of her robes, up around her forehead. Argent scales more like Nami's than Kai's. "You are siren. Folk. You must know this. Your mother must've spoken of your home."

Mira laughed. A pointed sound. Jiang-Li was not the first, nor would she be the last, to appeal to their shared heritage, her obligations to an underwater realm she'd never known. They saw her face, her gills, and could not help but assume. Defiantly, despite her voice wavering more than she wanted, Mira let the feelings fill every corner of her being. "This is my home. The freshwaters and estuaries and humans who raised me. Tiankawi, broken and rotten as it is, will always be my priority. Not a haven I have never known."

The dragon matriarch turned to face her full on. The intensity of her scrutiny was like staring into the sun. Petite as she was, there was more force behind that look than half the Council could ever muster. Her expression did not change, but her scales slid back under her skin. Mira didn't know what she saw, but it was enough. Enough for Jiang-Li to nod, a movement so subtle Mira wondered if she had imagined it. An instant and it was gone, the dragon matriarch searching for something within an embroidered bag she kept at her side.

A pearl.

Jiang-Li had pulled a dragon pearl out of her bag.

Mira stumbled backwards, gripping fiercely to a handrail to keep herself steady. Her vision blurred, doubled, refocused through the sheer rush of waves crashing in her ears. Her heart pounding with fists against her ribs. It came back to her in an instant. The pulsing of Kai's pearl in her hands, the swirling colours, the way she could not hold onto it any more than she could let go. Her legs crumpled beneath her.

The first look of sympathy crossed Jiang-Li's features, a softening of her hard mouth. She cradled the pearl in her arms. It was larger than Kai's had been. Shell shiny and hard where Kai's had been supple, newly formed.

The last dragon pearl.

The Peace Tower beacon.

Jiang-Li's final egg.

"Wh-what . . . why is it here?"

"Would you have left it behind?" Jiang-Li countered the question with one of her own. Of course the pearl would always be part of the negotiations. Better to have it here, centre of the table, as a reminder of Kai's sacrifice and the bargaining chip Yonakuni still had left. That was it then, Mira mused as she considered her response. She pulled herself to her feet, wiping her clammy hands on her trousers. That, or another more maternal reason: Jiang-Li had just lost a son and wanted to keep the last hope of one close.

Which was it? The dragon gave nothing away, rolling the pearl into one hand and holding it out. The fear that it would drop, crack on the decking like any other egg, lurched in Mira's stomach. She hastened to refuse, not wanting to touch it. Not wanting to remember.

"Why are you showing me?" Mira was not Yonakunish. Had made it quite clear that she would fight in a different corner if it benefited the city she sought to protect. Why in titan's name would Jiang-Li offer her this piece of information?

"For whatever the reasons, Kai married you. My daughter vouches for you. I am no fool. To the Fenghuang and the rest of the Council, this is leverage." Jiang-Li ran her hand across the shell. Mira saw imperfections for the first time. A smattering of light grey spots on one side of the curved surface.

"And to me?"

Jiang-Li's eyes flicked away from Mira's face to rest on the betrothal bangle on her left wrist. The stylised dragon lay as if dozing against her skin. "To you, this could be family."

Mira knew. She knew Jiang-Li was tugging on her heart strings with practised ease. Leaning on her relationships with Kai and Nami. The dragon matriarch spoke in only half-truths. It was true that the Fenghuang did not give a shit about Yonakuni. That they needed someone more sympathetic to their cause. And wasn't Mira an easy mark? Already in a position of influence, already aligned through marriage, already feeling guilty beyond belief for Kai's sacrifice.

Jiang-Li was no fool. She brought the pearl back to her centre, cupping it between laced fingers. Her head ducked as she looked down, and she wasn't the intimidating dragon matriarch any longer but a protective mother, curled around her last child.

Mira knew the play, but sand gods be damned, it still worked.

Chapter Twelve

A blast shook the room, sending Cordelia reflexively under her desk. The glass-fronted cabinet in her top-floor office rattled, as did the scales on the table. When a second blast did not follow, she recalled there were no quakes now. The sand god was dead.

Which meant the explosion, the tremors, was more likely coming from downstairs.

Dan.

The seawitch groaned aloud, her back teeth already grinding as she headed downstairs towards the cacophony and chaos of the second floor. Her regular drug brewers had been taught simple tasks. Distillation and refinement. Weighing up the black powder and mixing it into tinctures. They did not ask questions. They did not offer suggestions for improvements. Cordelia liked that.

The foul-mouthed little kappa was a piranha among the guppies.

"Utter abalone," Dan said in place of an explanation. He had trimmed his hair since he had joined her operation, his hollow cheeks filling out a little with regular meals. The whites of his eyes remained rheumy, pupils turning milky as those of the deep-sea dwellers who never saw the light. Without preamble, he counted the faults on his fingers. "Excess wastage. Like they've never used a knife in their lives. Overboiled! Time and time again, like someone determined to burn the whole batch. What's the point? Where's the artistry!"

"We are selling street drugs, not fine dining at a rotating restaurant."

"Well you damned well should be! You have the set-up, the resources. They are throwing the residue in the midden. Might as well just pour your money directly down the drain!" Dan's beak snapped vehemently in the direction of the other drug brewers, who huddled together far from his wrath. The fragments of the broken distillation set in the central bench dripped with the tar-like residue he spoke of. Cordelia had found no use for it.

"You should be picking your own sea urchin needles rather than buying them in. The fisherfolk crush half the spines when they harvest them. A child could do a better job."

"Employing children?" Cordelia said. Dan stumbled in his tirade. A conflicted look flickered across his face, one that said she had read him right. He had moral lines he wouldn't cross. Shame.

"Folk with nimble fingers. Anitos, water sprites, grindylows would do."

The wave of his rage had settled a little, allowing Cordelia a moment to examine the bench more closely. She walked round it, her water bull hooves splashing in puddles of seawater that lapped up from the submerged floor below. Before her, she saw the mortar and pestle, the corked bottles he had pilfered from her shelves. She brought the one unbroken vial to her nose, smelling brown algae alongside the familiar metallic tones of the fugu toxins. "You were trying to replicate dull weed. Why?"

"Have you not noticed? The tsunami killed the spirulina harvest."

"You're wasting my expensive equipment to make a balm for grazed knees and burns?" The words rang out before the image crowded into Cordelia's mind. Qiuyue in her lap with torn skirts, showing her every last little cut and bruise from her collision at the park. Rubbing the sticky balm with small circles into her skin and kissing away the huge tears that rolled down her cheeks. She scratched at the inside of her elbow as she pushed the memory away.

"How many fugu users are there in Tiankawi?" Dan said. "A few thousand? It's a good market. You control the supply, the prices. But how many people *live* in the city? Would buy a jar of dull weed for their children, for their aches and pains at the end of the day? How many more customers if you could sell to everyone rather than just the desperate few?"

Cordelia was stunned into silence. A synthesised dull weed with the waste product of fugu. Profit for sure. Legitimacy. The one thing that had eluded seawitches since her grandmother's generation. She turned her back, her hooves thudding as if to leave imprints on the stone stairs to her office. As she touched the doorknob, she shot back, "Come."

The contract had already been drawn up; she'd written it a couple of days after she'd dragged him back by the scruff of his neck. After her whisper network in Yonakuni had updated her on the situation and she had figured out the best way to leash this particular find. Now she slid the document across, turning the rattling bamboo scroll so that it faced him. Dan's eyes skimmed it, webbed hands gripping the edge of the table.

The bargain offered him exactly what he wanted. A monthly stipend to be sent directly to his family in Yonakuni. Protection for them from anyone who would use them as leverage.

"Firth is dangerous," he said, looking up.

"So am I," Cordelia promised. Her tarbh uisge disguise no longer felt uncomfortable. It acted as proof of her claims. See me. Fear me. Fight me, if you dare. "I can get wards in place. Send messages to them if you want them to know you are alive." Neither of them said the obvious. Dan was not exactly surprised a water bull was offering him a seawitch's bargain. Had probably recognised her voice from their run-in at Glashtyn Square. For all of the kappa's insults in the laboratory, he was subdued now.

"No. Better they think I'm dead."

"This will bind you to my service. Ten years. You cannot compete, you cannot go back."

His sisters would be fully grown by the time they were done. Dan either dead or dependent on the drugs that filled his system. His eyes were clear as he signed his name with the vial of seawitch ink, put his thumb against the mark. Family was everything. A sentiment she had once shared.

Chapter Thirteen

"It's like you don't trust me." Nami volleyed the raw fear across the bed, aware of how her voice whined. With sleeping shifts in the cramped cabins, it was the first time she had been truly alone with Firth on the voyage. All her anxieties tumbled out, a dam burst with the weight of it.

"You would've run to Mira, tugged at her coat to ask permission," Firth said, removing his shirt.

"What's wrong with that? Consulting the Minister of Fathomfolk, my friend, on who should be on board."

"You think Zidane deserves a place more than me?"

Nami shook her head, her words and ideas jumbling up before she could articulate them. "Of course not, but Mira's hands were tied."

"And yours would've been too, had I told you. Come on, Nami, you know it's better this way. I did the thinking for both of us. You should be thanking me." Firth slid closer to her, a pout on his lips. She couldn't stay angry at him. Her hand sprung unbidden to touch his arm. Firth caressed down from her shoulder, across her collarbone and dipping down between her breasts. She shivered, lacing her fingers in his. She had lost her train of thought entirely, arguments dissolving as the growing heat overwhelmed all other thought.

"I missed you." His eyes were as dark as the growl in his throat.

The one that made her tremble with both desire and trepidation. The small witchlight hanging by the door swayed like a drunk in the darkness.

"Tell me," he demanded, kissing from her gills down the nape of her neck. A shiver of scales rose to the surface like goosebumps.

"I missed you too." Nami's words were hollow. She couldn't explain it. Not to him, not even to herself. The misgivings that only stilled when his mouth pressed into hers. Here in this windowless space, where it was unclear when day met night, where there were no havens or cities or sand gods or gills, she was intoxicated by him. Her hands could not help but wander across his skin, lean into the heat she felt rising between them. She threw herself without thought or repercussion into the sensation. Exhilarated. The delicious sweetness wrapped around her spine and warmed deep between her thighs. She could subsist on this.

"How much? You need to mean it," Firth insisted. His hands had continued to work on her body, making her gasp and arch across the brief space between them. Holding her gaze like he would suck the very air from her.

Nami gave him the answers he wanted. "More than anything. More than anyone."

He looked at her approvingly. Kissed her forehead. "Good."

The condescension grated on her. The way he so clearly managed her. She shoved him back onto the bed, craving the heat that warmed her belly. It was passion, it was fury. It was everything. All she could do was ride it. She undid the ties of his loose trousers. Dipped her fingers into her mouth and wetted them with her tongue. Firth's eyes widened as she slipped her hand under his waistband. Holding him, feeling him stir in her grasp. This, at least, she knew what to do with. She leaned into him, into the familiar swell of need that consumed her, slick and ravenous. For a time, she could forget everything.

Nami woke before Firth, reacting to the noise of feet on the decking overhead. From the rumble of conversation, it felt like morning. She turned in the narrow cot, disentangling her limbs from his. Firth had sprawled out in the middle of the bed, leaving Nami only a cramped sliver of space against the wall. Her body protested as she sat up, running her hands through her short hair. He looked boyish with his eyes closed. Sharp-lined, with a furrow still between his brows, but more mellow than in his waking hours. As vulnerable as everyone else. She yearned for him like this. The version in her memory blurred around the edges. The recollection of last night and the careless promises she had made. Diving head-first into a rocky shoreline as the breakers crashed over her head. She knew and yet she could not break free.

Truth be told, she wasn't certain she wanted to.

She slipped out of the bed and dressed herself, needing a moment in the air to clear her head. As she pushed the door closed behind her, she realised there was someone else in the narrow corridor. Eun stood blinking behind her glasses like a cat in the dim light. She held an armful of bamboo scrolls in her arms.

"Did I keep you waiting?" Nami said quietly, tucking her hair behind her ear. She would have to get it cut. Long hair reminded her of being a little girl: the ridiculous hair ornaments and flowing robes her mother had forced her to wear. She was self-conscious suddenly. She had not had time to wash Firth from her skin, from between her legs.

"Yes, but I mean not a significantly long period of time. Just since dawn. I was worried you'd made other plans."

"Eun, we're on a ship. It's not like I'm going anywhere."

Eun considered her response, wrinkling her nose in acknowledgement. She climbed the steep stairs to the deck, scrolls spilling from her arms. Nami caught them, had to catch Eun at one point, steadying her by the elbow as she stumbled. She couldn't help but chuckle. "You need a bag."

"I have one. But the seams burst for some reason."

"Hmm, some reason." Nami kept the rest of the sentence to herself. The sails of the *Wayfarer* billowed like a dorsal fin, the pennant of Tiankawi flapping above. The morning shift were breakfasting on steamed fish and chewy rice cakes, the low hum of chatter familiar and soothing. They were still on the hunt for the second titan, but navigator Jalad had screwed up his face when Nami took to accosting him daily, getting in everyone's way as she tried to play lookout across the endless waves. In exasperation, he finally retorted that it would be weeks, if not months, before they reached the epicentre of the earthquake that had caused the tsunami. Jinsei had to tactfully take her to one side, advising her to let the crew do their job.

Eun rubbed her smeared glasses on her sleeve and picked over the scrolls to find the one she wanted. The bamboo panels clattered open as her finger followed the carved words. "I found a precedent. In this pre-Bathyal text regarding Muyeres Haven, it says there was a visitor from above the waterline. Human surely. Certainly before air canisters were in common usage."

Nami tried to get her attention, find a reasonable gap in the endless stream of words. "Eun."

"Of course there's a possibility it's a mistranslation," the archivist continued. She opened another scroll, laying it across the first. "In Muyerian the word for human is very similar to another word describing a species of deep-sea squid—"

"Eun." Nami cut through this time, loud enough to stop the ramble. "It's okay to be nervous. But we agreed the only way to test it is to test it."

They'd been at sea for a few weeks now. Open water as far as the eye could see. The horizon a shimmering flat line meeting the cloudless cerulean sky like lovers. Nami never thought she'd miss the jagged silhouettes of Tiankawi, the cascading greenery and winding tram rails that had seemed so out of place when she arrived. A scar on the water's surface. But now it felt strange: everything flattened, drifting at the edge of the world.

The folk on the ship slipped daily into the cool waters beneath them to swim. To marvel at a kelp forest miles long and nearly as deep. A pod of humpback whales greeted them one morning with white fins waving as they gracefully corkscrewed in the water. Silver-arrowed sardines in numbers Nami had never seen, vying and dancing like the waves had come to life. The saltwater a shade of turquoise and teal, beautifully clear and soothing against her gills. She'd forgotten how foul the waters of Tiankawi were until she left them.

The folk were revived. Jalad's snake scales shone like they'd been polished. The algae patches on Wensum's back bloomed lush and green. The waters quenched a thirst they had not realised they had.

Yet for all that, the humans among them reaped no such benefits. A few ventured down the rungs of the ladder and swam at the surface. The crew members were the bravest, accustomed to being at sea. Still it was edged with a fear that kept them within touching distance of the hull. Only a perfunctory dip of the head beneath the water. Mouth and nostrils gasping rather than using the feather gills that flailed behind their ears.

They were afraid.

Every single one of them.

Despite Kai's sacrifice and the gills saving their lives, they didn't want to use them. Didn't trust them. Nami saw where this fear might lead. It was too late for her to take up Mira's offer, join the Gill Adjustment Centre when she had so adamantly refused, but she could do something here.

Several failed attempts later, she was still struggling to explain what she meant. She gestured uselessly, having not the words or the grace to explain what she could see clearly in her mind. Eun at least did not sigh in exasperation or throw something at her. "Just open your gills. Not that much. A little. Just like breathing. Relax. Let go."

"Are you teaching her to use her gills or the latrine?" Sobekki shot, folding his arms as he watched on. Nami had hoped to wake early, save Eun the embarrassment of being watched by the whole crew.

"She's human, what's the difference?" Firth said. The Yonakunish Protector of the Realm was not as tall as the kelpie, more of a coiled spring of sinew and hide. Firth towered over him, broad-shouldered but tapering lean around the waist.

"Our experiment does not seem to be working," Eun said. She had not protested when Nami made her dunk her head in a barrel of water. Repeatedly. It was no replacement for being fully immersed, surrounded by water on all sides. Captain Rannoch only raised an eyebrow but did not object as Nami moved to her backup plan, tying a rope around Eun's waist instead.

"Why do I feel like you're about to go fishing and I'm the bait?" Eun tugged at the line. Her slim hands were callused around the fingers where she held a pen, palm shiny and smooth on one side from gliding across paper.

"It's to stop you from drifting away from the ship. They won't exactly stop for swimming lessons."

Eun jerked her head towards where Sobekki and Firth were chatting conspiratorially, Sobekki's curved teeth showing even as he closed his mouth. "What if one of those two unties the rope?"

"I will never let you go."

Eun searched Nami's face, blinking slowly as she did so. Nami resisted pushing back the wet strands of the woman's long hair from where they were plastered against her forehead. Eun gave the knotted rope one last tug. A fist-palm salute of acknowledgement before she climbed awkwardly over the side of the vessel.

As they slipped under the water, shoals of fish darted away from them. It was a different world under here. A world that oscillated in blue and green, where straight lines and hard surfaces had been worn away and instead the undulating rise and fall reigned supreme. Even the ship itself was rendered more organic: barnacles and mussels like a miniature mountain range across the curved surface.

Nami turned back from admiring it to realise Eun was not at her side. The archivist was treading water, chin above the waves as she thrashed her arms. The rope around her waist was pulled taut, folding her around the middle like a clam shell. Nami shot up beside her.

"Breathe," she said, demonstrating with long, slow breaths through her gills and back out through her mouth. Their gills were not the same, though. The slits behind Nami's ears were mostly hidden in her hair, their movements all but concealed, while the feathery external gills on Eun's neck flapped like the panicked wings of a fledgling. It was difficult to explain something that came naturally. Nami had never experienced life without gills. Mira would be better at this, she thought bitterly.

Eun reached out, gripping Nami's forearm tightly. For all her book reading, it did not occur to her that without circling her hands, she could no longer keep her head above water. She slipped under, air bubbling from her mouth. Nami moved one arm under her back and the other beneath the crook of her knee as she propelled them both to the surface once more.

Eun clung to her, hands chokingly tight around Nami's neck. Sobekki's words were carried off by the wind, but they could both guess at the content. For the first time, Eun looked crushed. Her skin was ashen, without even the usual pinch of pink about the cheeks. Her glasses askew, speckled with seawater. It was her silence that was most eerie, though. She should be telling Nami about the biology of barnacles or the history of Tiankawi's tricoloured pennant. She should be smiling, face animated, hands gesturing at the wild magnificence of it all.

Nami called her name, softly, her lips against the lobe of Eun's ear.

"Eun, look down."

Around the hull of the *Wayfarer*, banded fish had started to congregate. They kept pace with the vessel, a ring of guards, as if leading the way. Nami pretended ignorance. "What are they? I don't recognise them."

"P-pilot fish. They feed off debris and parasites, often following sharks around. They've built such a close relationship, they'll take food from the sharks' mouths and remain unharmed," Eun mumbled despite herself. She twisted in Nami's arms to get a better look. Nami obligingly dipped lower.

The fish reminded her of the cleaner wrasses in the freshwater caves of the Peak. The ones that had known, and thrived, and supported the titan whale shark when it had remained hidden.

"Different to those?" she asked innocently, pointing at one of the large shoals further in the depths. Eun peered down, rubbing a thumb over her glasses. She gestured for Nami to take them lower.

"Oh, I see the confusion. Those are mackerel. Their stripes are much tighter together. You really must read Tak-Yue's *Comprehensive Guide to Deep-Sea Fish*. Her classification system makes this all much more transparent than I can explain. Mackerel shoals are dense. Defence in numbers as opposed to the pilot fish method of befriending the predators. Both reasonable but very divergent strategies."

Nami had removed the hand from under Eun's knees, waiting for her to notice. The archivist's rambling excitement about the nearby mackerel shoal continued and she started patting her robes, looking absent-mindedly for a pen to take notes. It was then she noticed the knot around her waist, touching it with some confusion.

Her face flared as she realised she was fully submerged, her gills doing all the work she was afraid to let them do. Bubbles escaped her mouth in mild panic, but this time she quickly recovered herself. Brought her hands to touch the feather-like structures and craned her neck uselessly, as if she could catch a glimpse when they were at the sides of her neck.

Nami beamed, savouring the delight in Eun's expression. She tugged the other woman's hand to bring them closer to the mackerel. The huge shoal dispersed into two halves but then merged once more, magnetised to each other. Nami swam through them, the fish jostling her as they veered away. The water thrummed with the motion of their fins. A blur of silver. Individually the fish were small. Insignificant. Together their shadow left a bigger impression than the ship overhead.

When they finally climbed back aboard the ship, Eun started scribbling furious notes, dripping over the lotus leaf paper as Nami threw a disregarded towel around her shoulders. The sun would warm them fast enough and Eun's elation was infectious. Nami could do this. She could teach the humans on board to embrace their gills. Her body felt lighter than it had in months.

Then she turned and saw them. Firth and Sobekki, drinking a fine Yonakunish wine together. The undercurrent of their expressions was cold. Stagnant water beneath their feet.

The sun slipped behind a cloud, leaving Nami shivering. Her scales dipping down despite her attempts to counteract them. Firth looked up, raising his glass to her.

Chapter Fourteen

The sound of children's laughter was a pleasant backdrop to a rare day off. Skewers sizzling on the barbecue, other equally delicious smells wafted from that direction. Mira nursed her drink as she watched the circle of kids kicking a featherball to each other. Colleagues from the border guard and their families. Lieutenant Mikayil's son was unfazed at the absence of his father, on board the *Wayfarer* with Nami and the others. The boy bounced the featherball with ease off the heel of his foot to Lieutenant Tam's daughter.

Tam's wife, Dewi, came to stand beside her. The round of her belly was only starting to show now, part of the reason Mira had refused to send her more jovial lieutenant aboard the *Wayfarer*. He was her oldest, most stalwart colleague, and had already spent the best part of a year in the waters dealing with the fallout of people-smuggling. It was only fair he spend some time with his growing family. The large man was in his element, giving piggyback rides to any of the children who asked. Swinging them round as they held onto his ample biceps.

"He is going to do himself an injury," Mira commented.

"It's his way of prepping. For the babies." Dewi said it so nonchalantly that Mira thought she'd misheard. She turned, the coy smile on the woman's face confirmation. Twins. Mira threw her arms around Dewi. Their daughter was already seven. Tam had thought they wouldn't be able to have another. Then along came two miracles at once. It was no reason for Mira to be bitter. No reason to resent that she would never have this with Kai. Yet the ugly thought surged in her brain, clamouring for attention.

"Quick, rescue me." Tam pretended to hide behind his wife, taking a long gulp from her glass. His face was red from the exertion as a gaggle of children ran towards him demanding a turn. Dewi sidestepped gracefully and the children attacked his legs, gripping onto them like gleeful little lizards. Tam declared dramatically, "What a betrayal!" as he was dragged back.

"He wants six, can you believe," Dewi said. Mira could. Had heard Tam boast of it often enough in the chinthe headquarters. *A whole crew for the Boat Races.* Kai would've got them matching tunics to wear. Mira was pleased to have thought of it. Could almost hear his voice whispering in her ear.

They chatted a bit about Dewi's work: she painted elaborate murals on the walls of Jingsha restaurants and hotels, designed the signs that swung outside shops, and had even been commissioned to create a panorama of the cityscape for the archives. People were desperate for something bright and bold to take attention away from the daily drudge.

The women were distracted by Tam being swarmed by the children. He raised an arm, pretending to drown as he fell to the ground under their weight. The kids piled in. Dewi shuffled over, prodding an exposed foot before shrugging and throwing herself atop the heap. Tam's yell of protest was muffled by the peals of laughter.

As the sun dipped red against the clouds, they huddled around the barbecue grilling razor clams and scallops in their shells. Mira sat among her border guards and their families. They had done this many times before. Weddings and birthdays, festival days and weekends. When they'd been cadets in training and now with partners and children in tow. It should have been easy.

Somewhere she could stretch out and be herself, not buttoning herself behind her chinthe coat. Yet she felt like a fly buzzing around a warm lantern, banging uselessly on the glass. Watching the banter between Dewi and Tam. Watching Mikayil's husband fill his absence with his own calming presence. Every mundane interaction stung her, singeing her skin against the flame.

She turned her head, more than once, to her right. To where Kai would've customarily sat by her side, inserting a witty comment; tipsily suggesting they go to a teahouse; squeezing her knee. She looked down at her leg, imagining his warm hand there. She'd taken it for granted. The loss was a hundred paper cuts across her bleeding heart.

The smoke of the barbecue was a good excuse for the red in her eyes. She rubbed at them, saying her goodbyes before the ice she had packed around her chest melted entirely. Tam looked like he'd persuade her to stay, until his wife gently touched him on the shoulder. A tiny look passed between them, communication that needed no words. This broke Mira even more. She had lost that; she had lost Kai.

She walked down the ten flights of stairs to sea level. The lift was operational, but she was loath to use more power than was necessary in these rationed days. Besides, her face was concealed in the unlit stairwell.

Everyone said it would get easier. Day by day. Week by week. On the surface she was coping. Leading. Arguing with the Fenghuang, strongarming the Yonakunish party. Her strength never wavered.

On the outside.

"Was it worth it?"

She almost tripped on the step, hands gripping the rail. The voice. *His* voice. Clear. Loud. She moistened her dry lips as her heart pounded. Felt foolish as she ventured, "Kai?"

"I loved you. But it wasn't enough. *I* wasn't enough."

Something moved further down the stairs. The echo of feet as Kai's off-key singing warbled up to her. A Yonakunish ballad about giant water lilies blocking out the moon. Something so specific that Mira knew it had to be him. She cried out his name, tripping down the stairs as fast as she could. Yelling for him to stop.

Wait.

Wait for me.

I'm coming.

Her hands smacked into the exit door, leaving her stumbling onto the puddled walkway. The night was quiet apart from her own cacophony. Noise rushing in her ears, screaming at her without purpose.

There was no one there.

Mira heard the sound of tea brewing and felt a blanket being placed across her shoulders. Somehow, after wandering the night, she had found herself here, again, at the Gill Adjustment Centre. Poring over the ledgers to avoid closing her eyes. Exhaustion had eventually set in.

Tam put a cup of seaweed tea by her elbow as she stretched. He said nothing as he sipped from his own cup, sliding open the doors to the classrooms. Despite the bustle of the day before, he was bright-eyed as ever.

"Teaching this morning?" he asked, as if it were on the schedule. Handing her the excuse she needed as her brain caught up.

"Yes . . . How many?" Mira's tongue was furred with sleep.

Even though his eyes moved to her smoky clothing from the night before, to the shadows permanently beneath her eyes, he didn't push. "Our most successful class to date," he said with a wiggle of his eyebrows. "A whole twelve people!"

Twelve people. That was it. In a city state of people struggling with their newly acquired gills, only twelve had bothered to reach out for support. Mira's face must've shown her despair. Tam handed her a fried doughstick in consolation.

"Can we at least change the name? We need something that sounds less like a seagull choking on a herring bone."

"What?" Mira said in confusion.

"Gill Adjustment Centre? GAC? Gack!" Tam clutched at his throat in a dramatic pose, squawking like a gull for emphasis, until his act coaxed a snigger from Mira.

"If it gets people in the door, call it whatever you want!"

Despite waiting an extra quarter of an hour, only five showed up in the end. An elderly couple who kept comparing it to the sashiko classes they had attended, and three young men who had apparently hatched some sort of plan to make their fortune as underwater tuk-tuk drivers. Mira was happy they had such energy but alarmed at their belief that folk had it any easier. That being able to breathe underwater would automatically mean high-earning jobs. Gill rot was, after all, no longer a folk-specific issue.

Trish came in to teach about the Nurseries, a mandatory history lesson in each class. The elderly couple and one of the young men listened, but the other two talked in loud whispers throughout, passing each other a newssheet without any sort of subtlety.

Finally, unable to bear it any longer, Mira walked right up to them. They tried and failed to hide the sheet between them, kicking it to each other to remove all responsibility. Instead it slid into the aisle by her feet. The headline was clear, even upside down.

Dragon directed the Drawbacks!

The *Manshu Chronicle* had been a flaming garbage fire of a newssheet for a while now. Sensationalised headlines sold, and that was all they cared about. The story was riddled with inaccuracies and pure speculation, attempting to place Kai as leader of the Drawbacks movement. The statement he had given at the press conference before the tsunami was damning. Mira desperately wanted to clear his name, but her bargain with Cordelia had sealed her lips. It was a price she'd been willing to pay at the time, a small cost to save people from the tidal wave. The same people who were the first to cast aspersions. The article continued: Kai's sacrifice was a conspiracy to make folk the dominant power in the city. The Gill Adjustment Centre nothing more than brainwashing and indoctrination.

The lotus leaf crumpled as Mira's hands shredded it in frustrated twists. Her voice cut like ice. "Tiankawi has always evolved. Our people were born in the changing tide. If you believe this trash, then stop wasting all of our time."

She turned so she would not see them go. The mutterings of annoyance trailed behind. *Thinks she's special because she's the Council pet.* If she closed her eyes, she could pretend the words did not penetrate. But she couldn't prevent the voices in her own head from sowing the seeds of doubt. The loudest of all rang in Kai's baritone. *Was my sacrifice for nothing?*

Chapter Fifteen

They sighted the seafarers in the early afternoon, the rigger hollering as she pointed north-west of their position. The dozen or so double-hulled canoes with white triangular sails looked like terns floating on the surface, but her sharp eyes were not mistaken.

Nami vibrated with excitement. She had heard of the sea nomads who spent all their lives on boats, shunning the idea of permanent settlements. Even in the havens, there was a grudging respect for these humans who lived in harmony with the waters. A heated discussion distracted her from watching the canoes cut through the waves.

Zidane, still wearing silks far too impractical for their voyage, demanded the crew members cover up. Jinsei said nothing, simply loosened his collar provocatively. Zidane snarled, disgust lining his face. Sailing did not agree with him. The motion had made him sick for days at a time. Even when he finally gained his sea legs, he still refused to share in communal meals of seafood, dried fruit and pickled vegetables, ignoring all Rannoch's advice about diet. He nibbled instead at dried biscuits, filling his stomach with sawdust.

The former minister approached the captain. "Tell them! They need to cover up. Our gills are unsightly." Rannoch's thick beard hid much of his expression, and he stared over the top of

Zidane's head. Zidane tried Sobekki next, then Firth. "Tell them! Tiankawi's reputation is on the line." Only when they too gave a nonplussed response did he turn to Nami.

"What harm is there?" she said in honest confusion.

"Fear. Loathing. Dhinduk are already afraid."

"Dhinduk is a narrow-minded flooded town that has survived mostly on rabid fearmongering. They have the same entrenched prejudices as Tiankawi, if not worse," Jinsei cut in. "Seafarers are different. They already trade with both folk and humans. Gills won't change that."

"And who asked you?" Zidane snapped.

Jinsei raised an eyebrow, answering the question obliquely. "They say you're never too old to learn." He folded his arms patiently, familiar with this type of behaviour.

They turned to Nami for a response. Her swimming lessons with Eun had been going well, and a few of the other humans had started to come into the water too. The rigger and Jinsei in particular had taken to it, confident with their gills already. To ask them to hide who they were now was to be ashamed of it. "I will not force you to the front. Not if you aren't ready. But your gills are part of you. You should not have to hide."

Captain Rannoch grunted as if satisfied as he turned the steering wheel. Jinsei on the other hand nodded thoughtfully, filing away her response as if part of an ongoing test she had not signed up for. The rest of the crew and passengers took a moment to choose. Most left their necks exposed. Only Zidane and Garrett, the gruff carpenter, seemed inclined to pull scarves about themselves.

The seafarers were as excited to see the *Wayfarer* as the crew were to see them. Relying mostly on ships for their textiles and construction materials, they were ferocious at bargaining, would've stripped the vessel to its bare bones if they could. Zidane was adamant that everything he owned was essential, but even he was browbeaten into bartering silk robes for fish sauce and a sack of water chestnuts.

After the trade, the seafarers invited those on board the *Wayfarer* to share a meal, tethering a few of the canoes together. Their leader was an old man with brown skin as tough as leather. His caterpillar eyebrows drooped down the sides of his face, giving him a quizzical appearance. The sandstone pendant around his neck had left a mark where it nestled against his chest. They spoke their own language, one that had more tones than Nami could comprehend. Conversation was in broken smatterings of Tiankawian and Iyonessian; signs and gestures filling in the gaps.

They feasted on raw tuna in lime juice and coconut milk; crab legs longer than her arms were steamed in leaves and cracked open for all to share; and they finished with small glasses of heady liquor made of fermented hijiki seaweed. The tastes were a welcome change from the monotony of meals onboard.

The alcohol loosened tongues after the meal. The seafarers were fascinated by the new human gills, wanting to stroke them, asking questions the Tiankawian humans barely knew the answer to. Did everyone have three sets on each side or did it vary? Were they able to regenerate? Would all newborns born to gilled humans also inherit? The questions were well-meaning, naïve and full of wonder, but Nami could see the discomfort mounting. Even Jinsei was struggling under the weight of the interrogation, fumbling for the right words.

It amused her to find the tables flipped. Tiankawian humans were now the peculiarity, the aquarium fish to be gawked at; but eventually even she felt sorry about the endless quizzing. As if identity was such a tangible and knowable thing, unchanging through time and the same for each one of them. She flipped it around to ask the seafarers questions of her own. Did they ever come on land? How did they repair their vessels? What had they seen out there in the open waters?

This group moved in the seas north of Tiankawi, free-diving around the tiny craggy islands scattered across the area, collecting shellfish, setting lobster pots and using spears for catches. Yes, they had heard rumours of something new out there. Land.

Moving land.

They hadn't seen it themselves, not yet, but other seafaring groups had spread the word. A sand god, they whispered in reverential tones. Bigger than the largest ship. They touched the soapstone amulets around their necks, making the same signs across their body that the Drawbacks leader Lynnette had once made. Believers in the old gods, the old ways.

The entire party of the *Wayfarer* erupted with questions, the canoes rocking as they leaned in for the answers, but the seafarers had no further information. Instead, they answered with intoxicated whoops into the night sky. One of the more exuberant backflipped into the cold waters around them, starting a trend as they continued the merrymaking by swimming around the canoes. Floating on her back, head up towards the sky, one sea nomad warbled in song. Another held onto her outstretched hand, their voice adding a harmony. One by one they linked together, like a raft of otters idling in calm waters. The music soared into the night, reverberating around the boats like a blanket of whale song.

Despite all the water, Nami's mouth ran entirely dry, tongue a leaden weight in her mouth. Part of her had hoped the mission was for naught, the other sand god too frail and old to respond to the death laments. She had clung to that possibility fervently, glad of the excuse to be out of Tiankawi and away from the disputes between haven and city, folk and humans and those who were both and neither.

Deep down, she had always known it was a lie she told herself. She had heard the titan sand god's response that day, same as everyone else.

The seafarer leader could only report second- and third-hand knowledge of the sightings. He kissed his pendant, vowing to lead the others to their god. Jinsei tried to caution them about the risks, about what had happened in Tiankawi, but the seafarers turned each warning into something joyful instead.

"Big earthquakes! Big waves!" they repeated with awe. Nami could not blame them. She also had a tendency to disbelieve unless she had seen it with her own eyes. The seafarers had no point of reference for the destruction of half a city. They lived out on the open waters, where capsized boats and storms were an everyday occurrence.

When they returned to the *Wayfarer*, Zidane immediately took Nami to task for a litany of things she had not apparently handled correctly. She had not remembered to use the traditional wording of diplomacy, had not offered her left hand in greeting as was the seafarer way, had not sat with crossed legs at the meal. A million slights delivered through her ignorance and lack of care. He puffed out with his own importance, the gills around his neck pushing at the scarf he had knotted over them. He readjusted the material under his chin. The way he saw it, the seafarers would see it all as a grievous insult. A declaration of war. "Double the watch tonight," he insisted.

Nami had no words to respond to his outburst, choosing to walk away before she slugged him in the jaw.

Firth patted the bench where he sat drinking, as was now habitual, with Sobekki. "What does the featherneck want now?"

"Featherneck?"

Firth and Sobekki shared a conspiratorial glance. "The mudskippers put feathers in their hair and clothes as it is – featherneck is apt, don't you think?"

"My original suggestion was feather-fucker." Sobekki picked at his saw-like curved teeth as if they were talking about the weather. Nami felt jealous of their ease with each other, the bonding that had happened without her. She was being made irrelevant. She piped up, wanting to be heard, wanting to be part of the group. "How about fern-face?"

Firth and Sobekki mulled it over, deciding whether her offering was good enough. At last Sobekki nodded, passing her the bottle. Triumphantly Nami took a deep swig.

"So what do you think of the seafarers' report?" She tested the waters, wanting other opinions before she formulated her own.

"Those craven pieces of driftwood? Can't trust a word they say." Sobekki folded his arms as if the matter was decided.

Firth nodded. "They'll say anything to distract. Steal the pillow from under your head. Scavengers really."

The comments were similar to Zidane's just moments before. Not to trust the seafarers, even though they had shared an amiable meal with them. Even though they had provided information vital to their search for the second sand god. A dissenting voice stirred inside her, uncomfortable with the malicious reek that surrounded this burgeoning camaraderie. Conversation built on exclusion rather than building bridges. But the louder voice drowned out her guilt, wistfully wanting into that inner circle.

She took another swig of the kelp liqueur. "Ocean deadbeats."

Firth slapped her arm encouragingly. "Gill-less vagrants."

"Yellow-bellied mudskippers," Sobekki yelled to the stars overhead, raising both hands. They all laughed, cracking up at their own humour, ignoring the glares from the rest of the ship. The words were merely spoken in jest. They were neither knives nor pakalots. Gone as soon as they'd left her lips. They could not hurt anyone; at least that was what Nami told herself.

Chapter Sixteen

Even if they'd heeded Zidane's advice, it would not have been useful. When the attack came, it came not from the seafarers, but from another, unexpected quarter. In the middle of the day, with everyone awake and watching; and yet not one of them saw it coming.

Nearly a week after they bade goodbye to the sea nomads, they spotted a trio of small vessels in distress. One had clearly capsized, debris littering the calm waters around them. As they neared, they could see a body or two clinging to the floating wreckage. Nami freed her long whiskers, letting them flicker in the air for a scent of survivors as Captain Rannoch readied their own smaller rowboat for a rescue mission. The subtle aroma of the air was confusing. She could smell people. Dozens of them. Not the *Wayfarer*'s crew, whom she had more than grown accustomed to; new scents. Humans. Strangers. All around them. She turned this way and that, growing more and more perplexed. The surface of the ocean was still, not another vessel or landmark in sight. How could she possibly—

The water around them burst into life, something flying towards the hull of the vessel. A sturdy iron hook slammed into the deck near Nami's feet, sliding back towards the water before it lodged against the railing.

"Pirates!" Rannoch shouted in warning, drawing his short sword.

Marauders clambered up either side of the boat, blades already drawn before Nami could react. One stood directly before her, eyes concealed by a simple diving mask. He jabbed with his right hand, grinning as Nami avoided the blow easily. His left hand, the one without the blade, punched out, making contact with her hip. It stung more than it should, razor-sharp pain that flared and stayed. She looked down, seeing the black urchin spines embedded in her skin. Tearing them out, she tossed them to the side. The pirate wore knuckledusters covered in the sharp bristles.

She sensed something behind her, raising the hair on her nape. She threw on her silver scales: releasing them across the breadth of her back first, then on her soft abdomen and down all four limbs. The sharp edge of a blade caught against the natural armour, glancing off. Reaching for the seawater, she turned, grabbing at the spear shaft aimed at her chest. Water streamed up from the side of the vessel, coating her hand and solidifying around the wood. The heavy weight of the ice made the pirate drop the weapon, eyes widening in a panic as they recognised the strength of her waterweaving. Nami stamped down on the spear shaft, breaking it just above the ice. She grabbed the broken pole and used it to strike the pirate on the head, knocking them unconscious.

The first pirate was not done with her, though, aiming more urchin spines at her vulnerable face. Nami flicked her head out of the way so they only glanced against her cheek. Then she held out both hands, weaving a thin layer of water before her like a shield. It spun, swirling towards the centre. The urchin spines glanced off it, the tiny projectiles easily spat to one side. She stepped forward, pressing the pirate back towards the side of the boat, pushing the water against his body until it filled his mouth, making him gag. She directed it lower, tightening into coils that pinned his hands about his midriff. Tapping the water, she turned it to ice.

Immediate danger averted, she scanned the battlefield. Sobekki had easily subdued four pirates by himself, and was currently stalking another panicked intruder around the perimeter of the vessel. The crew of the *Wayfarer* were holding their own. Shizuku had several large cuts on their long arms, but the marauder they had been fighting lay slumped at their feet. Eun and Jinsei were huddled behind Lieutenant Mikayil and Captain Rannoch. Eun had shrunk right back but her eyes were as round as saucers. Nami felt a lump in her throat calcifying. The archivist was perfectly safe, she knew that in her rational brain, and yet the blood pumping through her said she wasn't safe enough. A thread existed between them, one that reverberated down its length with Eun's rapid panicked breaths. All Nami could do was cross the ship to be near her.

"Pearl!" Zidane's voice. "She's a pearl!" Time dragged as Nami turned, realising the former minister had been cornered behind some crates. He gesticulated frantically in her direction. The marauders left in the skirmish turned to look, to size up their chances. She heard the hiss of steel as extra blades were drawn. Heard Sobekki's clipped Yonakunish curse as he halted his pursuit to come towards her. Heard Eun call her name softly, no more than an exhale. And then everything happened at once.

Nami reached towards the puddles of water on deck, lifting it all at once so that droplets were suspended in the air. The water zipped together, cutting those who did not move out of the way. In her hands she weaved it into a long, taut water rope and whipped it underfoot. Half of the marauders were quick enough to jump out of the way, the others tripping on the sudden hazard. Sobekki tackled one, lifting the lad clean off the floor and tossing him over the side of the ship. Nami kept turning, adding a water dart to the end of her rope as she pulled it back, swinging it off her foot and knee to send it lashing out once more. It struck at the shoulder of a pirate who got too close, throwing her to the floor with the impact.

They were resolute, though. More determined than when there was simply loot at stake. Zidane might as well have served her up on a platter. They kept coming, despite the cuts and bruises she was inflicting, an unflinching grimness in their expressions. She bit down on her lower lip and swung the water rope around her back. She aimed for the kneecap of one assailant, hearing it shatter as she struck true. The woman screamed and fell sprawling.

"Put down your weapons!" Nami said. Her voice belied her fatigue and rather than responding, the marauders inched closer.

"Never," one of them said. An older man, chest tattooed with intricate black designs. Ugly scar marks riddled his face. Nami had already struck him once, the water dart jabbing into his thigh. It bled in thick dark trails, but he acted like it was nothing. Their leader. A fatalistic gleam shone in his eyes.

Nami yanked the rope back into her hands, turning to face him squarely. "What is it you so desperately want? What is worth your life and those of your crew?"

She said it so that he would be forced to acknowledge the truth. So that the other pirates knew they were expendable in his eyes.

"You are a pearl?"

"My name is Nami, water dragon of Yonakuni. Envoy to Tiankawi. Two nations will be on your head for this. What could possibly be worth that wrath?"

"You think we care about havens or cities? Your threats of repercussions? Your petty wars and feuds?"

"Then what?"

"Land. An island of our own. Somewhere to lay down roots, to build our homes, bury our dead."

Nami looked at him, incredulous. She wondered if he was mocking her, but he did not seem the type. There was no land for anyone, never mind a group of bloodthirsty marauders. She noticed then the resemblance between him and several of the others. The matching tattoos across their collarbones.

"You are not seafarers?"

"Nomads? Pah, they want this life. We were forced to it when our homes flooded. We do not want to live in your city towers. We want what we once had." Longing was threaded through his words. Pride, too. The waterline had risen long before this man was born. He had never lived on the island he yearned for; it was nothing more than a tale from the past.

Something else he said rang in Nami's head. "You have lost people?"

"My grandfather, the last of us who once put his feet on the sand, passed away." His lower lip trembled, but his words revealed none of his turmoil. "We promised him, vowed his body would—"

His words were cut off. He looked down at the blade piercing his chest. Blood gushed red, a river of it pouring from the huge wound. The dagger twisted and the man's eyes rolled up in his head. He slumped to his knees, then face-down on the decking. Behind him, Firth, held the bloodied water blade in both hands.

The pirates erupted, rushing towards the kelpie with a fury beyond control. Screaming the fallen leader's name. Screaming *aba* and *brother* and *son*. All Nami could do was defend, holding them back, not thinking beyond parrying blades and dodging blows.

Then, before she even realised how, it was over.

Bodies lay strewn across the deck. Blood stained the wood grain like a fresh lick of paint. Someone was wailing: rambling, incoherent sobs. It was the pirate Nami had tied up in ice. His bonds had melted but he made no effort to escape, crawling instead on his hands and knees to the leader's body.

Nami wanted to wail alongside him. The dialogue had been working, she was certain of it. Her head buzzed, refusing to believe what her eyes saw, refusing to believe it was anything other than a terrible nightmare. A mistake.

"Well done identifying the leader. The distraction worked well," Firth congratulated her. Depositing the blame firmly at her feet.

Nami couldn't answer, her hands shaking. Had she accidentally given him a signal? Winked when there was dirt in her eye? She did not recall, did not even remember where he was standing before she saw the bloody weapon in his hand. How had it gone wrong so quickly?

Only three of the marauders were left alive. The ones who had been knocked out or restrained before Firth had murdered their leader. Their kin. Sobekki yanked the weeping lad to his feet. "How many more of you?" When the pirate didn't answer, he backhanded him across the cheek. His reptilian skin drew blood from the young man's lip. It stopped the crying at least. "How many? Waiting for news of your raid?"

"I don't... I'm not sure. Ama and Massey, the kids. Volin has an injury and..." The lad blurted it all out, unthinking in the shock of what had happened.

It was hard to infer if Sobekki agreed or disagreed with Firth's actions. What was done was done. Nami followed his question back to its true intent. How many people to avenge these deaths? How many ships chasing the *Wayfarer* through the night? Weighing up their options, the value of finishing the job.

"Let them go," she said. She had to step over bodies to get to Firth and Sobekki. She was tall, but the other two were taller, forcing her to look up at them.

"We will be watching our backs every night from here on in," Sobekki warned.

"Better than a massacre."

"Nobody needs to know," Firth said insistently, hand on her arm. His voice was lowered as if the rest of the *Wayfarer* were not listening, riveted by the tableau.

"Eun," Nami called. She was thankful when the archivist responded, feet shuffling as she stepped forward. "I want this reported. All of it. Honestly. Do not omit a single detail."

"Understood."

"I will provide an eyewitness account," Jinsei added. There was no covering this up now. Firth gave Nami a half-smile, unsure what all the fuss was about.

"Captain Rannoch, let them go." Nami finally let herself look at the corpses sprawled around her. People. A family. A way of life that was not her own but was no less valid.

"And the bodies?" The question rang into the silence. A reminder: they had only wanted to bury their dead.

Nami nodded towards the decoy boats. The capsized hulls more like omens now. "Send them home."

Chapter Seventeen

Mira couldn't sleep. Her head hit the pillow, desperate for the restorative power of slumber. But when she closed her eyes, her mind would not switch off. It clamoured instead, the loudest of the petitioners: all the things she hadn't done; all the time ticking away. An hour or two at most, fitful, tossing and turning. Then she would sit up, convincing herself that if her mind could not rest then she would put it to use. Sometimes that even worked, getting through the never-ending paperwork that surrounded her position.

Mostly she just listened for Kai's voice.

She told Trish after the first time, confessing to her mother about the voice she had chased down the stairs. Her ama said nothing, holding her, stroking her hair. Grief moved at a different pace to time. She would never forget, Trish promised, but one day the pain would be bearable.

For a few days that logic bought her a reprieve.

Then she heard his voice again. The Ministry of Healing had opened a new gill rot clinic in Kenabi district and Mira attended the ribbon-cutting. Before she had even taken a sip of her lotus liquor, she heard Kai whisper, as he used to at such events, his breath tickling her ear, "What would you give for my arm to lean on?"

Mira turned. The corridor stretched out behind her, empty

apart from servers at the far end. She blinked, doing her best to ignore it. It didn't mean anything. It was natural.

"Perhaps it was only ever my pearl you were after."

This time she let out a noise. A strangled yelp that she somehow managed to turn into a sputtering cough. Thank the titans the band started playing not long after that. She made an excuse, slipping out into the night. Most people would run from a voice that haunted them.

Mira chased it.

Through the wet shine of Tiankawi's walkways and skybridges, at an hour when most people were in bed, she wandered. Walked until her feet ached, until she was light-headed and dizzy from it all, the street lights blurring like spots in the corner of her eyes. Sometimes Kai spoke. Her name carried like a lament over the rattling lobster pots and the slow, steady knocking of taraibune boats in the marina. His ghost taunting her from just beyond the next corner. Mira pursued it, even though she worried she was descending into a pit from which there was no way out. When she had felt those worries overwhelm her before, she could stop herself. But she did not want to; not if it meant Kai's voice would stop speaking to her. Not if it meant she might forget the details she so desperately clung to. The way her name elongated in his accent. The little noises he made when deep in thought, hardly aware. His enthusiastic and off-key singing, warbling like a kite in a gale.

"They are all thinking it. The people, my mother," Kai's voice said.

Mira followed it up the spiral stairs, onto the roof of a squat building. The garden there was empty: winter greens growing in neat rows on raised flower beds. The leaves fluttered in a sudden breeze that made her wrap her arms around herself. She couldn't help herself, feeling foolish nonetheless for asking. "What are they thinking?"

A moment passed. She wondered if he would answer after all. "That you never loved me. That you were using me."

Looking out across the roof, Mira could see the taller buildings around her like silent sentries. Among a hotchpotch of graffiti art, tags and pasted posters was a giant mural of Kai in dragon form. His branched golden antlers reached right up into the top corners of the building and his serpentine body curled around the sides. *THANK YOU* had been written down one wall. Mira's heart had been fit to burst when she had first seen it, the unsanctioned art giving her strength on the longest of days.

It looked different now. The moon emerged from behind the clouds, illuminating the mural more fully. Someone had added external gills at Kai's neck, black and thorned as barbed wire. Red dripped from his antlers, eyes and ears, seeping between the scales like oozing blood. The message of gratitude had been scored out, and above it was the words: *NOT OUR CHOICE. NOT OUR WISH.*

Mira had seen the slogan in the last few weeks: graffitied on the hull of the Gill Adjustment Centre, in banners flapping from skybridges and occasional residential windows. A direct response to the spurious newssheet article about Kai. She gave statement after statement about fathomfolk and humans working together, cooperation and solidarity, the words ringing hollow even to her. And then something else happened, taking up all of her attention.

The first robbery was relegated to a line in the newssheets. A motorboat stolen from the home of the Finance Minister. Such episodes, while rare, were not exactly sensational enough to hit the headlines. The minister was acutely critical of the kumiho's response, but otherwise licked her wounds and business moved on. Then the Triton of Iyoness was stolen from the tempered-glass and security-locked display case at the Jingsha Cultural Museum.

In its place, the thieves had left a single pakalot.

Unlocked.

❦

Days later, as Mira's boots crunched on broken glass underfoot, she tried to ignore the flash of camera bulbs and huddles of city guards. The kumiho were bristling tonight, throwing their weight around in wild swings, desperate to hit a target. As captain of the guard, Gede was directly in the firing line. Everything from his hairstyle to the way he pronounced words was suddenly up for ridicule in teahouses and hawker stalls across the city.

The Ammonite Atelier was an exclusive members-only club and rooftop garden. It was not simply about affluence; as well as a generous monthly fee, joining also required nomination by current members, something that kept it firmly in the upper echelons of Tiankawi society.

In other words, filthy rich, well-connected humans.

Mira had only ever been there once, forcing her way in with her chinthe badge when she had tried to get Serena, Samnang's wife, to free Nami from a jail cell. That had gone as well as could be expected. She had been in too much of a rage to do more than glance at the rooftop garden then, but her second viewing didn't exactly leave a better impression.

The club was spread over three floors of a Jingsha tower. It had been left unscathed by the tsunami, pristine as if freshly painted. A private lobby led onto a lush restaurant and bar. A huge aquarium filled the longest wall, the sheet of glass defying belief. Neon tetra fish and pink jellyfish were dotted about, but the tank was mostly empty. Mira knew the kind of entertainment they hired in the evenings. Mermaids mostly. Covered in glittering body paint as if to differentiate them from those in the Palang teahouses.

There wouldn't be any shows for a while. Across the glass, etched into it in unmissable jagged letters, were the angry words: *FATHOMFOLK FIRST.*

Inside the tank, the water had turned a peculiar shade. A tinge of rust red about it. Mira moved closer, not understanding the shapes that lay between the stones.

Birds. Songbirds, the kind that filled the cages in the Fenghuang's hall or in rooftop gardens. Pretty little things with speckled brown feathers and yellow throats. Hundreds of them. They lay at the bottom of the huge tank, drowned by the pakalots that had been clamped about their small bodies, sinking them to the tank floor.

Mira had heard what folk called their newly gilled human compatriots. Likening their external gills to feathers. The message loud and clear.

"The real issue is upstairs," a familiar voice said behind her. A grim-faced Gede ushered her up to the next floor. Mira did not comment on his misbuttoned kumiho coat and the pen stains that marked his jaw. He looked too harried for such details.

"We've been seeing more and more petty crimes lately. All with this same slogan, or the thatched logo they've come to adopt," he said as they took the stairs. Mira knew the symbol he was talking of, had seen it more and more in Qilin and Seong districts, an innocuous pendant or lucky charm dangling from a folk market stall. She had not understood its significance. "My intelligence suggests they've replaced the Drawbacks as the most radical voices in the folk community. The one difference is, they are getting access. It's not just throwing rocks at rich houses. Someone is letting them in. This place had security locks, seawitch wards, night guards."

It made sense. Hit the humans where they thought they were safest: in their plush private club where all manner of corruption and debauchery took place. Mira almost marvelled at the audacity of it. The next floor housed a tailor, a jeweller, a bank and repository. The damage the explosion had caused was clear: the whole front window of the tailor's had been blown out. When that had failed to break the security wards of the bank and the jeweller's, more drastic methods had been used.

"They cleaned out the repository. The jeweller's as well. Sand gods know what was in there; they're certainly not telling me the true worth of it. I suspect millions. Enough to make anyone rich."

Mira crouched to touch the jagged edges of the waterjet-cut door. Precision. Skill. "Enough to fund a war," she said finally. This was no ordinary heist. They had been well funded, well planned. They had taken out the reserves of the wealthiest, the ones with the ear of the Council, if not Council members themselves. The Drawbacks had gone, Mira was certain of that. Their numbers scattered and mostly drifting in the power void. Try as she might to recruit them, few were enticed. A new power had filled the vacuum, offering the folk something far more tempting.

Yonakuni was behind this. It had all the signs of organisation and skilled waterweaving. The haven using the rhetoric of Fathomfolk First to further divide the city. Mira knew it in her bones; she just didn't have the proof.

Chapter Eighteen

Mira was getting very drunk. At least she was trying to. She pressed the bottle against her lips, but her throat refused to swallow, gagging and closing up. For a while she had tried to hunt down her ghost again to ask for advice. *Hi, Kai. Ordered your sister to find a titan, but now I think your mother is trying to destroy the city. Families, huh?* Tonight, however, his voice remained silent. The clear liquid burned her palate and tongue until she half coughed, half choked it down. The siren with her rubbed her back, not unkindly.

It had seemed like a good idea at the time. Another night when she couldn't sleep. Another hour of her life chasing a memory. Other voices crowded her head, judging her in Kai's absence. So she had gone into Palang district, where the noise from bars, theatres and teahouses still thrummed at this time of night. The proprietress's eyes widened only a fraction as she listened to Mira's request, nodding with businesslike acumen. She had been ushered into resplendent private chambers with a tea set for two laid out on a round lacquer table and a bed discreetly hidden behind rice-paper screens.

Here she was. Opposite a siren with a handsome face. Long dark hair had fallen past his shoulders as he had poured the tea, but he was too severe-looking to be Kai. Nobody could be Kai; who was she kidding. That was when she had ransacked the drinks cabinet in the corner, balancing the squat bottle of spirits on her trembling knees.

She took another swig, this one going down a bit faster. It was still peculiar, like she had forgotten how to do something as simple as drink.

"You have to remove your barriers," the siren said patiently. He could weave an illusion for her – one convincing enough to satisfy. Perhaps then the voice would stop hounding her. Perhaps then she could finally sleep.

She removed the internal barriers against charm compulsion and illusions. Fully clothed, she nonetheless felt naked without them. The siren took her hand in his and sang. His voice was beautiful, like the warming crackle of a fire on a cold night. Mira closed her eyes, letting herself be carried along in it. The knots and tightness in her shoulders stretched themselves loose. When she opened her eyes, her husband was there.

Kai.

He smiled at her, a sadness about his lips. His touch light, as if afraid to hurt her. It felt like a glass had distorted her vision, rendering everything just that little bit off. A copy of a copy until the original had got lost somewhere. She concentrated, trying not to let her panic overwhelm her. *Stop. It's him. Just believe it's him.*

She stood, leading him behind the screens. The massive canopied bed was draped with silk curtains and sheets. It was supposed to look sensual. Instead it felt too expansive, too exposed.

Kai ran a finger down the side of her face, to the hollow of her neck. He stepped in closer, leaning down to kiss her. Mira tilted her head up, waiting for the hand on the small of her back. He put his hands on her waist instead. He smelled wrong, all wrong. She shook her head, taking a pace back and turning so she did not have to look at him.

Staring resolutely at the wall, she undressed. Dropped her clothes on the floor around her, tearing them from her body as if the mere contact hurt her skin. Her fingers fumbled, numb and cold. Somewhere, distantly, she wondered that her heart was not beating a thousand times a minute. If not excited, she should feel nervous. Instead she felt indifferent. Something she just wanted to get over and done with.

Behind her, Kai placed a hand on her bare shoulder. Waited as if for permission. When she did not brush him off, he moved to caress the line of her collarbone, then reached down the curve of her breast and brushed a thumb over her nipple. He kissed the back of her neck as his hands worked and Mira screwed her eyes shut. Her brain was telling her that he was too tall, his kisses different to how she remembered.

"Let's get into bed," she decided, slipping under the cold sheet. Kai moved to turn down the lights, leaving only the small witch-light by the bedside to illuminate them. It was a wise move; helped a little when there were only shadows to see by. Mira heard him rustle between the sheets, his head on the pillow next to hers. Her eyes sprang back open despite herself. It was Kai. Her husband lay next to her, scanning the angles and planes of her face. Sweeping a thumb over her wet cheek.

"I miss you so much," she said, voice cracking with the weight of her words. She tucked in tight in the crook of his warm arm as he held her against his chest. His hands ran over her, stroking back and forth along her arm until she was no longer a shivering sliver of ice. He moved them down over her thighs, taking his time, assured and practised. Knowing just what to do so that her breath quickened, her legs loosening as his confident strokes delved deeper. She felt the warmth spreading across her body, her heartbeat finally quickening.

She cupped his face, the rough stubble on her husband's chin. She leaned over and kissed his full lips, felt his tongue in her mouth and—

"No," she said abruptly. Breaking off all contact. Revulsion crawled up her arms. The touch of his lips was entirely wrong. The taste of him unfamiliar. All feelings of comfort, of home fled her body. The illusion shattered around her and she sprang apart from this siren, this stranger she had paid, pulling her knees and the sheet up around her. It had been a stupid, foolish idea now she thought of it. She had scarcely lusted after anyone before Kai came along. Going through the motions because everyone else did. Desire had not meant anything until they had started their tentative relationship; friendship had come first.

The glamour faded along with the hum of music, and the siren's face was no longer Kai's. Instead it was a sombre stranger, seeing the hurt he could not heal. His voice broke any last illusion, the curls of his Tiankawian accent apparent. "We don't have to."

Mira pressed her lips together hard, trying to stop the tears from coming. She was just so tired of crying. She shouldn't be here. Should have gone home. Every night she still hesitated before turning the key in the door, hoping against all logic for him to be there. For the sounds of cooking, the smells of the dinner he had made, the warmth of his smile as he welcomed her home. She could not face that for another night.

"Could you ... Just one more thing. Face away ... and pretend to sleep. As him," she said, flustered at the peculiarity of her own request.

The siren took no offence. He lay down, turning on his side so that his back was to her, and sang the illusion around him. Mira stared at the distant and familiar slope of his shoulder. At the antlers pressed against the pillow. The rise and fall of his upper body as he breathed. How many nights had she turned in bed and caught a glimpse of that back? Taken it for granted. She longed to wrap her arms around him, press her body to mould into his curve. She reached out a tentative hand, wanting just to touch: the hair sprawled on his pillow, the lean shoulder blade, the bare arm above the sheet. Her hand wavered, a finger's breadth from his skin. A moment from shattering the delusion.

She pulled her hand back to her side.

Sleep did not come that night either.

Chapter Nineteen

Gede was taking his sweet time. Long enough that Cordelia convinced herself the whole thing was a trap. That the blue-coated city guard would fire harpoons at her again, dragging her through the saltwater like a prize catch. Her shoulder twinged in memory of the wound. It still ached when it rained, swelled and warped like water-damaged timbers.

At last she saw the familiar slouch of her son, hand in hand with his sister as they made their way through the fair. It had sprung up almost organically. A few performers, the theatres and music halls low down in the priority of rebuild projects, had realised they could take their shows to the open air. The walkways didn't have the space needed, but lashing barges to make stages on the open water was a cheap and easy solution. A dozen acrobats at first, spinning plates on sticks balanced on their hands and feet. Folk using their waterweaving to make water shows and ice sculptures. The musicians came next with their barrel drums, bamboo pipes and zithers. The street vendors were magnetised, offering candied kelp, dulse cakes and skewers of grilled prawns. The people of Tiankawi, desperate for distraction and reprieve from the endless clean-up and rebuilding; from the tensions and sporadic violence across the districts – humans and folk alike, on boats and in the water – were drawn to the fair like moths fluttering around a light.

Gede and Qiuyue had disembarked from the family vessel and were walking through the fair across the floating platforms. Qiuyue held her brother's arm in a vice with both hands, clearly afraid that she would slip at any moment into the deepest, darkest of waters. A selkie family approached them, the three boisterous children making the platforms bounce as they ran up and down, trying to keep their paper balloons aloft. The folk were oblivious, but Cordelia saw her daughter tense and shrivel as the young folk girls bounded past. One brushed her arm and Qiuyue let out a small noise like an animal caught in a trap. Gede leaned down to whisper something as his sister furiously shook her head, chin tucked against her chest.

Cordelia let herself fade. Her skin took on the colours of the warped planks and painted boats that bobbed to the sides. She camouflaged herself entirely, slipping noiselessly after the pair. At a nearby stall, a wizened old man proudly showed his array of tiny blown-sugar animals on sticks: elegant birds, fish and dragons. Qiuyue shook her head at all the examples, asking for something else. The man rolled a ball of molten brown sugar in his hands, stretching and pulling it with deft precision, blowing it as he pinched tiny arms and legs into being. A thick long tail, a second, then a third. The nine-tailed kumiho fox of the city guards emerged from his careful hands and he presented it on a stick. Qiuyue was captivated. The joyful expression kept Cordelia's three hearts beating.

"I want to give it to Aba," the girl said, loud and proud enough to pierce Cordelia's ears.

"Of course," Gede said, as he steered her to the next stall, searching for Cordelia in the faces of others around them. After weeks of her prodding, he had agreed to arrange this meeting. Wearily reiterating that she should not get her hopes up. Whale piss, he was making excuses, and she told him as much. Too afraid to cross Samnang, to risk his new position as captain of the city guard. Qiuyue would be fine. Cordelia just needed an opportunity to explain to her daughter what had really happened. Get her away from the influence of Samnang's rhetoric and show her who she was.

They stopped to watch the performers. The dancers threw their long blue silk sleeves in the air and twisted them into loops until they looked like waves rolling across the surface of the water. Puppeteers hidden by the movement held rod puppets aloft, telling the crowd-favourite tale of the Great Flood after the Bathyal War. The leader's wife, left behind in Tiankawi as her husband struggled to get home in time, hundreds of miles away after negotiating peace with Muyeres haven. The unnamed wife sure despite everyone else's advice that the floods were not like those that had come before. That the ceaseless rain would be their downfall if they did not prepare. The Council who supported her vision and built a fleet of ships, stilthouses and fortified foundations, even while critics called her a fool, even when she lay dying on her sickbed. And the tragedy, of course, that she died having saved the city but before being reunited with her loyal husband. He wore the robes of the fenghuang, the mythical phoenix sunbird. A reminder that her leadership had brought peace and prosperity to Tiankawi and that the fenghuang would always watch over them.

Qiuyue was engrossed in the performance, barely touching the bag of lotus candy Gede had bought for her. The softness of her face had gone, elongating as she hit adolescence. Her hair, habitually in double buns or looping braids, had been brushed into a fancy chignon jangling with pretty flowers, pearls and jade beads. Cordelia could almost see the adult she would become. She was both elated at the image, at Qiuyue's poise and confidence; and terrified. Coming into her own in a time that was so tempestuous and unpredictable. The fear made her want to pick Qiuyue up and hold her tight. Never let go.

The next performers were folk, painting pictures with water,

sculpting ice into the likeness of water dragon and tiamat, levia-
than and kraken. Cordelia had taken her daughter to shows like
this before, having to drag her bodily away from the waterweaving art. Qiuyue had been entranced by it, throwing her hands in
the air to copy the movements of the artists until Cordelia had
to make her stop, worried that her enthusiasm would somehow
break the charm keeping her powers dormant. This time, however, the girl turned away, tugging her brother's sleeve to move on.

The platforms and walkways were getting busier, making
it more difficult to slip unseen through the crowd. A couple
of people called out in surprise as they tripped over Cordelia's
unseen lower limbs, or bumped into her body when there was
nothing there. She cared not, mind consumed entirely with the
notion that Qiuyue was evolving without her ama's guiding
hand. Her children stopped at a paper-cutting stall, browsing the
fragile cuttings, holding them up to the stall's lights. It was okay,
Cordelia assured herself, the little girl who had fallen asleep in
her arms, crusted drool on her face, was still there.

Soon Gede would be turning homewards. If she was to do it,
it had to be now, regardless of the flip-flopping of her stomach.
She had grown accustomed to her water bull disguise. On the rare
occasion when she was completely alone, she would stretch out
her octopus limbs, unfurl the suckers and pulse through all the
colours of her true form. But it had been months since she had
been Serena. Small. Delicate. Like the first bud of spring, without
the armour and size of her other masks. Dressed in the lightest
skirts, silk and chiffon. She didn't like the vulnerability. She never
had, but she had endured it, to keep her family above the waves.

It was the only face her daughter knew.

"Qiuyue," she said hesitantly, approaching from the shadows.
"It's me, it's Ama."

Her daughter's face blanched, mouth open as if she would
scream. Gede put his hand over hers, talking low and urgent.

"Listen to me, she's been hiding, that's all, like I said. She missed you. I told you, right? That she really missed you. That we would find a time to meet her."

"Ama's dead. The seawitch . . . Aba said the seawitch killed her," the girl stammered.

"Samnang lied." Cordelia couldn't help but cut in. Ignored the look Gede shot in her direction. He had explained, of course, that Samnang had been feeding his daughter stories and they would have to move carefully. Her promises to her son dissolved when faced with Qiuyue's disbelief. Nobody knew her little girl like her ama. Her voice cracked despite herself. "Your father and I . . . had a disagreement. I had to go away for a while, but I'm back now. I've missed you."

Qiuyue's eyes widened. Lashes that had no right to be that long fluttered against her light brown skin. She wanted to believe it. Her trembling fists said that she just needed a little more coaxing, that she could be won back. Cordelia came forward, one small step at a time, as she kept talking. "I missed taking you to the shops, having our cake and tea, listening to your stories about Finnol and the others. Come back to me Qiuyue, come with me."

"Ama," Gede said, the single word filled with warning. He had only promised to orchestrate a meeting, not an abduction. But would there be a better chance before Samnang realised something was wrong? Before Qiuyue blurted out by accident that she was meeting with her mother. *Now* was the time. Cordelia had places, above water and below, where Qiuyue could be safe, could be trained to use her shapeshifting and waterweaving. It was an adjustment, that was true, from her life of privilege, but perhaps it was what she needed. What they all needed. Her hopes raced on ahead, conjuring up a future with her daughter by her side to take over the empire she was building.

She took the girl's hand, the one still clutching the sugar-spun kumiho. Qiuyue snatched it back like the contact had scalded.

The nine-tailed fox slipped between her fingers to land on the ground. Sticky and coated in gritty sand. She took a step back, then another. "No, you're not my ama. She's dead. You're trying to hurt me. Hurt Aba. You're wicked – a seawitch. A murderer!"

"I am both your mother *and* a seawitch. You are half-seawitch too. Estuary. I can teach you. Remember the funny faces I made that you used to love. You can do them too. You can shapeshift. And so much more." Cordelia struggled to keep the plaintive edge hidden. Desperation clung to her and she longed to shake off its clammy grip.

"No, I'm not estuary. I'm not folk. Folk are filthy!" Qiuyue said. Cordelia's hearts bled out.

"Qiuyue—"

"I won't listen to your lies. I won't!" Qiuyue said. The fear was real. The absolute belief that Cordelia meant her harm. It hurt more than being shot with a harpoon or having a limb ripped off. It hurt in a way she could not ignore, like she had been pinned to a board and dissected alive. The girl had turned entirely, her face buried in her brother's chest, hands over her eyes as an extra precaution. Despite Gede's reassurances, she refused to engage any further. All he could do was bring her into a hug, mouthing an apology to Cordelia as he complied with his sister's wishes and led her away.

Cordelia stood unmoving. Uncaring that people were looking at her. What they saw convinced them to give her a wide berth. In that moment, she did not care which face she wore. Finally she took a few steps forward, stomping deliberately on the candied kumiho sweet that lay discarded on the floating walkway. It stuck stubbornly, flattened to her shoe, like stepping on a pile of steaming shit.

The seawitch whistled, a sound so high that it was only

perceptible to certain folk. Within a few minutes, hantu ayer spirits drifted over to her. The incorporeal water spirits mostly resembled firefly light in good moods, miniature storm clouds when they were less inclined. Overlooked by most as a nuisance akin to mosquitoes, they floated through all strata of Tiankawian society, making them excellent spies. Neither were they as innocuous as most believed, able to come together in a humanoid swarm for brief periods of time.

"Where is she?" Cordelia asked. The spirits moved like pinpricks in front of her face, floating into position until they created an outline that hovered before her. The Gill Adjustment Centre. She pursed her lips. The bead containing Kai's voice had come back to her by pure chance. Rifling through the stalls at the Glashtyn Square underwater market. The jangjamari rag-picker knew the value of the pearls and obsidian he had collected in the seaweed strands that covered his body, but not that of the bead with an off-key voice. Cordelia had bought it for a mere copper piece.

It had started as a one-off. Messing with Mira by whispering that voice into her ear. Watching her stalwart face twist awry. A satisfying treat that Cordelia savoured. It niggled her still that Mira had risen through the ranks, courted by the Jingsha officials for what she and the dragon had done. Remembering how Kai had outwitted her by offering a like-for-like equivalent in his addendum to her bargain: a lovelorn water dragon's pitchy singing voice in lieu of a siren's charm. It bothered her more than she would admit that the folk loved Mira. For better or worse, it was the half-siren they talked about at every floating market: her successes, even her failures. Every stallholder with a tail had a Mira anecdote, a Mira opinion, a Mira critique to offer. She was the favourite daughter of the freshwater folk while Cordelia was and ever would be reviled.

It was easy to put on his voice. A diversion. Hounding the

Minister of Fathomfolk with Kai's words was a great stress-reliever at the end of the day. Stalking her while camouflaged and watching those pitiful tears spill down her face. Cordelia would bottle them all up if she could. Mix them into her seaweed tea in lieu of honey.

She gestured to dismiss the spirits and then turned south towards the Gill Adjustment Centre. Today had been one of those days. A little light torment was just what was needed to clear her mind.

Chapter Twenty

"No." Jinsei did not elaborate. He twisted with the borrowed knife, scraping another curl of wood from the surface of the mainmast. The first mate, Shizuku, had taught him the basics of whittling and he had been etching all over the ship ever since. The captain had not been best pleased at first, until Jinsei had surreptitiously carved Rannoch's name with elaborate flourishes at the helm.

"But you're a teacher. Teach!" Nami persisted. Jinsei blew away the wood dust, running a thumb over his carving. The scales of the naga navigator's broad snake tail were rendered by small but effective cuts of the knife edge.

"There are two things I cannot do," he said pointedly. He raised a finger for each. "Firstly, I can't teach a subject I don't know anything about. And secondly, I cannot teach a lesson when no one is listening."

He meant it. Nami had hoped he would bridge the growing divide between the humans and folk on board. Trish said he had managed it in the classrooms of Tiankawi after all, so why the titans did he spend his days whittling and drinking tea? It was beyond her.

"Well, *I* can't do it," she muttered.

"Why not?" He threw it back, hands finally stilling. "Nearly everyone on board can now swim. I am hardly an elegant baiji in the water, but it does the trick. That was you. What's holding you back?"

"Because waterweaving is different. I was the lousiest student in the whole Academy. I can't do it by the book."

Jinsei's indifference had forced her to blurt out the real worry. His eyes lit up as he slid the knife back into its sheath. "Teaching doesn't have to be by the book. It doesn't even have to feel like a lesson at all."

"I thought you said you can't teach when people don't want to be taught," said Nami, utterly confused now.

"I said when no one is listening. People are listening whether they mean to be or not. The best lessons are often the ones learned despite themselves." Jinsei ran his hands over the carvings of the *Wayfarer* crew he had made so far. They were crude, but nevertheless Nami liked to watch him progress daily with them. They all did: contributing unasked-for critical feedback, laughing when he had given Shizuku one arm significantly longer than another. It was the place they all seemed to converge.

She shook her head with a laugh. "Perhaps I would've learned something if you had taught at the Yonakuni Academy."

Jinsei shrugged, but his eyes danced merrily at her comment. "Or perhaps you've already learned more than you realise."

"Hmm," Nami said drily. "I've learned what doesn't work."

"Isn't that a valuable lesson?"

She refused to give him a response, even though he was right.

"Try again," Nami encouraged. She stretched out on the rowing boat they had borrowed, tethered to the *Wayfarer* like a kite. The mid-morning sun was pleasant on her shoulders and face, not as hot as it had been in Tiankawi, where it sent everyone scurrying like bugs to hide in the shade. Eun wrinkled her nose habitually, a tell that Nami had come to recognise when she was searching the archives of her memory for further information. Unlike Nami, she was sitting with both legs folded under her, the traditional first position.

"The Yonakunish texts suggest meditation in the first to eighth positions for weeks before the initial sensation is even apparent. That tuning out the world allows folk to hear the rhythms of their own bodies."

"Oh, the elders like to make everything into a ceremony. Take the fun out of it." Nami remembered how she had hated those meditation sessions. Her feet numb under her and her legs burning with white-hot pinpricks when she tried to move. This was not how she had found her waterweaving skills, by a long shot. "It's like that feeling you get deep in your stomach when you're anticipating something good. The bubbles frothing to the top."

Eun hesitated, a hundred questions of clarification on her lips. She would want to know the length and breadth of the feeling, how to measure it, describe it, write it down for future generations. Nami could not teach her like this. Not with words and scrolls the way Kai might have. She only knew how to lead by example. Sobekki and Firth were leaning over the railing, watching the lesson with knowing smiles on their faces. Betting against her like when she had offered the humans swimming lessons. Nami did not know what to do other than ignore them, staunchly pretending the comments didn't dig under her skin in serrated barbs. But this, *this* was a step too far, even for her: trying to teach humans to waterweave.

"Let's get a bit more space," she said, cutting the umbilical cord that attached the rowboat to the larger vessel. The salt spray tickled her bare arms as she used waterweaving to propel the boat forward over the waves. It was freeing to be away from the burden of their expectations.

"If you come here, I can show you what I mean." She took Eun's hands, ignoring the peculiar sensation in the back of her throat as she did so, resisting the urge to rub at the other woman's writer's calluses. "Listen."

"You will need to be more precise than that. There are a number of sounds currently within hearing distance: your voice, naturally, the waves, the gulls, the—"

"Eun, listen," Nami repeated. The archivist looked like she would say more, but bit down on her lip with a nod. Closed her eyes with a little frown. Nami counted to ten in Yonakunish, slowly so that her voice carried in the breeze.

"There is water around you, waves carrying us on the tide. There is water beneath you, cradling this boat. Above you, in the clouds overhead. Within you, running through your body like tributaries towards a lake. Here is the source of it, deep inside your belly. Here it lies waiting, a tranquil pool. Can you see it?"

A pause, where Nami wondered if Eun had fallen asleep. Finally, "Yes."

"Focus on it. Call to it. Imagine it in motion, swirling and bubbling. Catch those bubbles in your hands, as fragile as eggshells; don't let them pop."

Eun's hair had flicked into her face, strands of it spreading across her cheeks and lips. Her grip tightened as she tried to do as Nami had instructed. Her nose pink as she concentrated.

Eventually she sighed, her hands pulling away. "It's no good. Perhaps the others were right. Gills do not automatically mean the waterweaving to go with them. It isn't even well established among all folk communities. We should stop."

"If folk can work in Onseon, have their powers drained from their bodies, then they can waterweave," Nami insisted. "They have not been taught to use it, control it, but they have it. I can feel it in my scales. You too." Left unsaid was what separated Nami from the freshwater folk in Tiankawi: less the antlers and whiskers and more the tutors, the teachers, the resources her mother had expended on her. Of course her waterweaving was better; she had had every advantage within claw distance but hadn't truly appreciated it until she saw how else life could be.

She had sensed something, after all, when they had powered the cable car during the tsunami. It had rung clearly in her mind. Only the fugue of time and distance made her doubt herself.

"Turn around," she suggested. "Focus on the ripples rather than me." She looked out over Eun's shoulder, gazed with her at the shimmering waters. The mist formed hazy layers just above the waterline.

"Bubbles, right?" Eun murmured, exasperation laced through her voice.

Nami leaned closer and placed one hand on the other woman's belly. Felt her stiffen. "Is this okay?"

Eun was quick to confirm it was. The fabric of her loose-fitting robes tickled Nami. She tapped her fingers gently, like strumming a zither. "Bubbles," she confirmed, her voice husky. By the abyss, she wanted to touch Eun. Unwilling to say it out loud, but the lessons were a convenient excuse.

The feeling inside her own body was entirely cloud. Rising like it would lift her off her feet. She hoped Eun could sense it too. At the same time, she was afraid – afraid Eun could see through the layers of propriety that were holding her together.

A warm hand reached down and covered her own. Nami forgot to breathe. Her mouth and ears and eyes ceased to work, shutting down entirely. Everything blurred. Every part of her body focused only on the skin that touched her own, the fingers resting atop her knuckles.

Eun called to her. Through the wonder and growing realisation, Nami heard her voice. "Is that . . . an island?"

The hand on her own was simply directing her attention. It had not meant anything at all. Nami blinked rapidly and she could see it: the obscure shadows she had presumed were simply the fog were indeed a group of tiny islands. Strange angular shapes on the horizon.

"Captain Rannoch said there was nothing out this way. Not for hundreds of miles," Eun said.

"Nothing . . . except a titan."

They watched for a few minutes more in silence. The islands seem to rise out of the water as more shapes were revealed. Another island to the far left joined the cluster before they all slipped back under the waves. Up and down. Like a beast coming to the surface for air.

They had found the sand god.

Nami and Eun's hands separated, neither of them even aware of it as they pulled apart, too busy looking at the sight before them. Nor did either notice the seawater by Eun's feet. Droplets danced for a moment, straining towards the archivist before settling back into puddles.

Chapter Twenty-One

The Wayfarer thrummed with activity as they climbed over the side. Eun rushed straight down to her cabin, to get her scrolls no doubt.

"Walk with me." Sobekki's tone left no room for refusal. He and Nami moved towards the back of the vessel, the wind almost tearing the words from his mouth. "Your mother has a plan."

"Why am I not surprised." Nami slouched, elbows on the railing, chin in her hands. Ready to be told what political manoeuvring Yonakuni had in store.

"If there is no peaceable agreement with the sand god, I will give a signal. Jiang-Li will in turn use her last bargaining chip."

"What bargaining...?" Nami did not need to finish her own sentence. The last dragon pearl. Her mother had brought it then, to Tiankawi. Had not deigned it important to share this information with her own daughter.

Had not trusted her.

The notion incensed Nami at first, made her want to snap and storm away from Sobekki. A year ago, she would have done so. Screw them all. Instead she turned her gaze to the ocean waves, the bubbles she had so recently taught Eun about dissolving in her stomach as bitter acid. Where did her allegiances lie? Would she take Yonakuni's side against the Council? Yes. But against the freshwater folk? Against Mira? She was less certain. The currents pushed and pulled, but Nami continued to drift.

"You have done nothing to inspire confidence so far."

She ignored his stinging remark. Circled back to his previous comment. "Use it how?"

"You think we came all this way to renew a lopsided treaty? When Tiankawi lies so low in the water?"

"You want the city for your own?"

Sobekki nodded, satisfied that she had finally figured it out. "They owe us. And they will never be as weak as they are now."

Thoughts exploded like firecrackers in Nami's head. Yonakuni was acting, rather than being a passive observer of the troubles across the sea. Finally. Seizing the moment. This was what she had wanted, wasn't it? All they could do for the fathomfolk of the city.

A smaller part of her, a portion she tried to quell, had doubts. The Senate would be a Council by any other name. And then what? There would still be an underclass, it would simply be humans instead. Always one or the other, as if there were not space enough in the wide ocean for both. For everyone. No room for the messy but hopeful future that Mira and Kai had strived for.

"There must be another way ..." she said, more to herself than him.

"Against my better judgement, I promised your mother I would give you a chance. Only one. I will remain neutral for now," Sobekki said, gritting his curved teeth so the lower ones protruded. "But what have you actually achieved here? On this ship or in the city?"

"Don't do it. Don't raise this signal, whatever it is. Give me more time. I can show you, show all of them. It isn't all or nothing. We can figure this out together."

The crocodile-headed fathomfolk turned his back to the railings, eyes scanning the ship. While the view of the waters behind them was one open expanse, in front was a scene of chaos. Captain Rannoch barked orders across the hull, and there was a discordant panic of activity. Zidane was throwing up again, noisily, over the side. Eun had dragged a sackload of scrolls on deck but now they were rolling around underfoot as she furiously made notes on lotus leaf paper as if her life depended on it. The crew tripped over their own feet as they tried to run the ship, all while their necks twisted over their shoulders towards those looming shapes in the distance. Firth had climbed halfway up the rigging, confident in his precarious position. His hair streamed like a pennant in the wind and he let out a vicious laugh. Nami could barely hear it at this distance, but it carried all the same.

"*He* will always stand in your way." Sobekki spoke a truth that Nami had refused to acknowledge. One she had hoped would disappear if she left him behind in Tiankawi. None of the word-mincing of Eun or Mira.

"Then why are you suddenly best of friends?" Nami said, her words sounding defensive even to her own ears. She was jealous, not of Firth's attention but Sobekki's. Once upon a time she would've done anything to earn a word of praise from her martial instructor, but nothing she did was ever good enough for him. Watching Sobekki and Firth drink and laugh together was a slight she had not expected to hurt so much. Firth, who had none of the discipline Sobekki had always lectured about.

"Because he is the strongest person on this ship." Sobekki called her out, challenging her with his words as he once had with his claws.

Prove me wrong.

Chapter Twenty-Two

Trish had put on her second-best outfit. A bright yellow skirt with matching fitted top. A teal scarf trimmed with gold was folded and draped over the top to bring the ensemble together. Her eyes were wide when the Fenghuang's boat pulled up by her sampan. The narrow vessel was longer than Trish's whole house, carved with the silhouettes of graceful birds down the prow. The four oarsmen waited silently without the slightest sign of impatience. Trish yelled at her daughter to hurry up. Mira pulled open her old clothing chest, dragging her feet like a heavy anchor on the seabed. She hated that she had been strongarmed into this. More than that, she hated that Trish was so excited. The punishment the Fenghuang had dispensed for every concession she had squeezed from him during the prolonged negotiations was a loan of his boat and booking her a table for dinner with her mother and mother-in-law.

It was done. Mira could hardly believe it. They had pushed and pulled, arguing over every little detail, talking until the sun rose at dawn over the Hall of Harmonious Eminence and her voice was no more than a rasp. She refused to be cowed by the two bigger personalities of the Fenghuang and Jiang-Li, standing firm until finally, against all the odds, they came to an agreement. It was not perfect, but neither were they.

She didn't know what to do with herself. Without the focus that had been driving her every day, she was adrift. And so, as the Fenghuang had graciously commanded, she was trying to enjoy herself.

Trish had heard about the Behemoth. Her neighbours had been twice already, venturing below the water even though they had only recently acquired their gills. The waiting list for reservations was weeks long! How had Mira managed to get a table? With Kai's mother! She had been hoping – but didn't want to put any pressure on Mira, of course – to have a good natter with the dragon matriarch. A hard egg to crack. She had an armful of gifts for her already, mind. Nami said they had the best dulse cakes in Yonakuni, but Jiang-Li had not yet tried Trish's recipe.

Mira raised her heavy head from the camphor chest and pulled on the first thing to hand. She owed it to her ama to endure this dinner. Realising now how neglected Trish had been while she herself had been in endless meetings. The brightness in her mother's ruddy cheeks was reward enough. The bottle-green tailored jumpsuit was looser since she had worn it last. She looked at her reflection in the smeared mirror as she fastened the collar. She had worn it at the charity gala with Kai last year. It no longer hugged her curves but instead hung off them. It would suffice – none of her clothing fitted any more.

Trish's nattering silenced for a short while as Mira joined her on the Fenghuang's boat. Her ama took her arm and there was an immense feeling of comfort. Her familiar wrinkled hands extended a blanket around them both, sheltering Mira from the worries that followed her like a cloud of mosquitoes. The rowers moved in eerie synchronicity, their oars slipping in and out of the water with ease.

"Ama, you don't have to," Mira said, trying to pull her arm away.

Her mother's grip tightened like a clam shell around her. "It's my prerogative."

Mira gave a tight smile, acknowledging and accepting the lapping siren song that emanated from Trish's chatter.

They neared the sailmills, the slim white structures like giant cranes wading through the water. More would be commissioned shortly, the much-needed apprenticeships part of her deal with the Fenghuang and the dragon matriarch. Employment for people from the local districts, as well as providing work visas for those from the havens. Money was also to be allocated for gill rot research, looking into remedies that would work for folk and humans.

Perhaps the Fenghuang was right. She did deserve a night off.

Diving underwater still gave Mira a few seconds of disquiet. A decade of avoiding the water had made her somewhat hesitant to dip under. She had to forcibly stop herself from holding her breath.

At a distance, the Behemoth's exterior looked like pre-Flood architecture, with jewel-green roof tiles and red pillars. On closer inspection, even the most casual observer could see the eclectic mismatch of statuettes, broken and chipped, that had been fixed to the railings and roof. For many years it had been an institution in Tiankawi, a rite of passage for people to talk about. The food something of a lottery and the service notoriously irate. Everyone had an anecdote about the Behemoth. Then it sank.

After the tsunami, it had been reclaimed by folk in the district. Spread over three floors, it still had all the fixtures and fittings to continue as a submerged restaurant. Another evolution – folk and gilled humans working together to create fusion cuisine the whole city was abuzz about.

In the main dining hall, many were wearing extravagant seasilks and layered robes. A special occasion event rather than an everyday bite after work. Mira looked, as was habitual, for the fathomfolk. They were servers and customers both, packed onto round tables of families and friends; sharing their meal in some cases with gilled humans. The hardened shell around her cracked a little. These were the humans who embraced their gills. Here, in this microcosm, was the future she fervently hoped for.

Jiang-Li was already seated. They had been allocated an alcove, panelled on three sides, with a curtain of shells dividing them from the main dining area, allowing them the illusion of privacy. The dragon matriarch stood on their arrival, her loose sleeves billowing in the warm current of the restaurant. Mira gave a fist-palm salute, taken aback at the level of courtesy. She waved to introduce her ama, but Trish swam straight over the top of the table and embraced Jiang-Li. The water dragon stiffened, arms straight at her sides, although she did not push the elder siren away.

"Now we are family," Trish said triumphantly, as if her small act papered over the cracks of Kai's funeral, the terse negotiations, Mira's suspicions that Yonakuni was funding extremist sentiments.

Jiang-Li was as if folded from a sheet of stiff paper. Angles and lines from her sharp chin down to her elbows and hips. Trish, on the other hand, was like soapstone: solid and yet somehow soft, a comforting ease about her person. She thrust the parcel of dulse cakes into the dragon's hands, shaking her head and refusing to take no for an answer as Mira sat down. Foot panels were discreetly located under her chair, helping her to remain seated without floating off mid meal. These tiny adjustments were springing up throughout the city. Unremarkable and yet important all the same.

The shell curtain rattled open and a rusalka server came to waterweave drinks from a swan-necked jug. A school of striped clown loach darted through the opening in her wake, swimming around the table for stray morsels. Mira thanked her, noticing that Jiang-Li barely glanced in the server's direction. It irked her. She wanted to slap her hands on the side of the water dragon's head and force her gaze. Look. These are the people of Tiankawi! Not the Council, nor the Fenghuang. The everyday folk and humans scraping a living.

"Tell me, how did you come to live in this vibrant place?"

Jiang-Li said. The question was innocent enough, but Mira heard barbs in the words.

Her ama was oblivious, sitting on Jiang-Li's other side. "I've lived here longer than the haven I was born in, or the outer islands I worked in. I always meant to go back for a visit, of course, but time moves faster than the waves. Not sure if my old bones could make it all that way. I came as many of us do, lovesick and certain it would last. The relationship ended up being fleeting, but I found a different sort of love in its place." Mira resisted the urge to sink under the table as her mother turned the full glow of fondness upon her. Not a single ounce of siren charm there, and yet she felt the effects all the same.

"You have done well to raise your daughter under the circumstances."

There it was again. The insult somehow masquerading as a compliment. Mira tried to catch her ama's eye, but Trish was nodding along, telling an anecdote about when she had first moved to the city. Was Mira simply imagining it, overworked and seeing things again? She had not heard Kai's voice in days, and while she should be thankful for that, she felt empty without it. He had moved on when she could not.

"Your appetiser this evening is pickled water chestnut with steamed water spinach and a taro crisp." The rusalka swam next to Mira's right side, her arm stretching out to place the dish down on the table. The bubble of waterweaving keeping the food fresh wobbled as she did so. Mira turned to give her a closer look. The rusalka was tall, her skin the colour of dappled leaves at dusk, her hair long and loose to her waist, heavy, thick strands like spongeweed. Not someone Mira would forget easily. And yet the voice . . . set her teeth on edge. She scanned the room, waiting for the ambush that every muscle screamed was coming.

"Cordelia?" Trish exclaimed from across the table.

Of course. Her ama had attended enough of those damned

healing sessions at the seawitch's apothecary. Mira launched herself forward, hand on her dagger. The rusalka gave a gasp of horror before dropping the act, laughing to herself. "I was just messing with you, saltlick."

Cordelia's eyes changed to her own yellow irises, the horizontal black pupils narrowing. The seawitch had a perverse sense of humour, popping up now and again when Mira least expected it. It made her wonder if . . .

"My, my, what a peculiar sight. The Dragon of Yonakuni dining with a siren and her estuary pup. Here I was thinking the mudskippers were the ones dirtying the water."

"Minister Mira, I do not know who this is, but give the word if you would like me to intervene." Jiang-Li's words were cut ice. Mira itched to let the water dragon loose on Cordelia, but the seawitch was, regretfully, her problem.

"What are you doing here?" she said.

"Can't a seawitch make a living these days? Must you assume the worst at all times? You of all people should know better." Cordelia put a hand on her forehead in a mockery of real tragedy. She was enjoying this. Perhaps being caught had been part of the plan.

"Cordelia, sit down," said Trish. "There's plenty of food to go around. I've missed our chats. I have to say, the new healer simply doesn't have your touch. His herbal soups are too bitter. Look at this, surely you could do better?" She moved her thick braid from where it hung over her left shoulder. Mira could not help but wince at the gill rot veins spreading up her neck. Her ear lobe was starting to discolour.

"Oh, Ama, why didn't you say?" The pang of guilt struck her like a blow to the stomach. Trish shrugged. In the silence, Mira filled in all the words her mother did not say: because you've sacrificed too much for me already; because I'm old; because you've been busy; because I knew you'd worry.

"It matters not. Sit, sit, Cordelia!" Trish acted like it was the simplest thing in the world. An old friend rather than someone Mira could not, despite all her efforts, disentangle herself from. She had been forced to allow Cordelia a free pass with her drug business. Swallowing the bitter pill and telling herself she would deal with it later. She was not a fool, though. Chinthe guards sent her weekly reports on the thriving black-market business, and Mira pretended she did not know the drug baron Arkaig and Cordelia were one and the same.

The seawitch, still rusalka-shaped despite the giveaway eyes, considered Trish's invitation. Then, to Mira's surprise, she sat on the empty chair. "Are you eating that?" she asked innocently, before pulling Mira's plate over and making short work of it.

Mira finally sat back down, patting her dagger to ensure it was still there. Things could not get worse than this, surely.

"I do not think we've been introduced," Jiang-Li said, inclining her head towards Cordelia. "I am Jiang-Li, Dragon of Yonakuni Haven."

Cordelia wiped her mouth with the back of her hand, taking her sweet time finishing her food and washing it down before responding. "Cordelia, seawitch, healer and entrepreneur, at your service."

Jiang-Li's eyebrow twitched but she was too well bred to react otherwise. "How do you know Minister Mira and her esteemed mother?"

"Oh, you know, the usual way. Mira made a bargain to sell a decade of her siren abilities in exchange for healing sessions to prevent her ama's gill rot from killing her. Then, when the bargain was due for renewal, your paragon of a son offered himself as a replacement and traded his voice rather than his powers. That sort of thing." The seawitch did not quite lick the plate clean, but every last morsel had been eaten. She stretched her arms overhead. "Anyway, it has been delightful, but I really must ..."

Before the sentence was finished, her whole body blurred. Mira blinked, but it wasn't her eyes; it was Cordelia's camouflaging skills. The seawitch's outline could be tracked briefly, but then the shell curtain jingled and she was gone.

"She is clearly a very lonely woman," Trish commented.

"What? How did you decide *that*?" Mira practically yelled.

Trish gave a sad sort of smile. "I've met people like her before. Some use levity, others anger and spite. She's lost something. Someone."

"Was it true, the story she spun?" the dragon matriarch interjected.

Mira nodded, not knowing what else to say. What excuses would make it sound less embarrassing, less ridiculous. She kept her eyes averted from Jiang-Li's for as long as she could. But the appraisal she was steeling herself against did not come.

"Your self-sacrifice, although foolish, is laudable. All for your mother. You are a person of surprising depths, Minister Mira." Jiang-Li's tone softened, and for a moment there was a crack in the facade.

Trish's words rang in Mira's head. She wondered if her ama had been talking about the seawitch or the water dragon all along.

The meal ended up being more of a success than expected. Despite Mira's apprehension and Cordelia's unexpected appearance, Trish and Jiang-Li were, if not firm friends, at least further along the waterway.

A sense of relief spread like wings as they said their goodbyes. Mira squeezed her ama's hand. "Can I stay at yours tonight?"

"Of course," Trish said. "I deep-fried a batch of coconut puffs yesterday. They'll still be crunchy."

"How can you think about food? I'm so full." Mira's protest was only half-hearted. She was already looking forward to changing out of the stuffy clothes and sleeping on the floor of her ama's sampan like she was a kid again. The warmth of her overfilled stomach made her drowsy and calm. Perhaps for once she would be able to sleep through the night.

"That stuff? It was okay. Better than the places in Jingsha, I'll give you that, but it barely touched the sides." Trish would've added more, but the oarsmen suddenly stopped.

"Minister," one of them interrupted. In front of them, four small boats were blocking their way.

"What are they selling?" Trish asked, squinting. The banners held aloft filled Mira with dread, as did the familiar slurs they shouted across the short distance.

We are the Cleaven.

We will not rot.

No more gills.

Not our choice.

Human protesters. They were more and more vocal these days, finding traction with those struggling to accept the changes. Mira had tried to engage them at the Gill Adjustment Centre, but it was difficult to combat a sentiment that grew like black mould in unseen corners. She had hoped the rest of the Council would step up, but no one could decide if they were in favour or against the cause. It was an election year, after all.

"Can we go round them?" she asked.

"We can try," the front oarsman said, but his expression was doubtful.

The vessel pivoted with ease, giving the protesters a wide berth. It kept ahead of the small boats, but not far enough to escape the heckles. The ruckus started to draw a small crowd of nearby boats and people watching from the walkways, pointing and pondering at what was going on. Exactly what the protesters wanted.

Just as the coordinated strokes of the Fenghuang's oarsmen were making progress, two more rowing boats pulled out in front of them, set on a collision course. They would force an encounter one way or another.

"We could ram a path through them?" the front oarsmen suggested, breath laboured now.

"We can't risk hurting anyone. If they want us to listen, I'll listen," Mira said.

Up close, the Cleaven protesters gave triumphant cheers. A disparate group of humans, they had bandages wound tightly around their necks. Mira blinked, trying not to show her horror that some of the bindings were stained with blood.

"You! You did this to us. You didn't give us a choice!" the lead woman said, a finger pointed like a knife.

"The tsunami would've drowned the whole city," Mira said. Her voice remained steady despite the hairline fractures running through her. She had lost Kai for this. For these entitled fools to throw the gift back in her face. They knew, and did not care he had given his life for them.

"We would rather have drowned!" another shouted.

"Be my guest!" Mira lashed out before she could stop herself, gesturing at the dark waters around them, aware of how her words carried to the watching crowd. She reined in her rage. "But you can't speak for every human in Tiankawi." The human oarsmen on their vessel remained silent, thoughts imperceptible behind their professional demeanour.

"Nor can you! Just another bottom-feeder with a pretty face. Fucked your way to the top." The Cleaven vessel rocked as the woman and her companions pulled the coverings off something. The side of their boat jostled into the Fenghuang's vessel like a warning shot. It was hedged in by the smaller craft, by people whose rage burned like a forge. The heat of it scalded Mira's face even though she had not put her hand into the fire. She could only protect those around her: her ama and the oarsmen were her main concern.

She turned her head, speaking in a low tone to the crew. "Can you swim?"

Three of the oarsmen nodded, but one shook his head. Mira feigned confidence. "We've got you."

The protesters hefted their burden across. It thudded heavily onto the Fenghuang's boat, rocking it precariously. Mira gripped the sides, barely registering the alacrity on the lead woman's face. "A gift. Comparable to the gill rot you forced upon us."

It was a crude effigy, made of driftwood and torn rags, stuffed with newssheets, the print bleeding grey on the thin paper. Humanoid in appearance, it had a faceless head but the curves of a woman's breasts on its upper half. From waist down, it had the body of a fish. A crude rendering of a mermaid, mami wata, lamia or melusine. An effigy of *her*. Siren, as depicted by the fools who did not know or care where story ended and person began. It was folk as the Cleaven saw them.

A heady smell rose from it.

Fumes.

The woman flicked a lit match across the prow. The tiny flame sat atop the effigy like a flickering candle at the end of the day. And then it caught. Ravenous tongues of orange and yellow curled possessively down the stiff body.

The oarsmen did not wait for Mira's command, diving away from the burning figure. Trish already had her arm under the man who could not swim. Mira stood for a moment watching the flames ripple down the length of the boat. She knew what would happen next, knew with a foreboding that tasted like bile. The fire reached across to the nearby protesters' vessel. The woman stood triumphant and unyielding as flames flickered at her feet. She would not jump into the water, would not push her boat away.

She would rather burn.

Chapter Twenty-Three

Mira stood beside the other Council members outside the Hall of Harmonious Eminence. Her habitual chinthe green coat was replaced by a heavy ceremonial cape, a carp brooch and chain, denoting her position as Minister of Fathomfolk, fastened neatly at the collar. It was just as well; her chinthe coat still smelled of singed flesh. The screams of the Cleaven woman echoed in her ears, her skin blistering before she had finally been pulled into the water.

It was going to be a long day.

Inside the hall, a drumming troupe had started the solemn rhythm of the procession. It instinctively instructed her steps, moving as if one with the other Council members. They walked between the rows of chinthe, then kumiho, to reach the ceremonial room. Mira could not help but beam at the border guard. Once they would have stood on the steps outside the door; now they had a prouder place within.

The drumming stopped and the Fenghuang entered, accompanied by the warbling tones of plucked zither and bamboo flute. Mira had grown accustomed to the smaller phoenix mask that covered only half his face, allowing him to eat and speak freely. Now he wore his full ceremonial mask. Gold-plated, with a sharp, bird-like nose, it swooped over his forehead and hair like a crest. Rubies lined almond eye holes and the cheekbones were delicate fretwork butterflies. Atop his head it had been worked into beautiful golden feathers, beaded with pearls and jade stones.

His floor-length robes were warm yellow, with purple details embroidered onto the upward curve of the shoulders and on the wide belt at his waist. He looked like a statue atop the grandest building. A symbol of what Tiankawi could be. For all Mira wearied of the pageantry, in this moment she saw the appeal. A ritual that made sense when all else was crumbling about them. She hated how the traditional was used as an excuse to exclude, but with the shiver of the musical instruments and the panelled circular ceiling above them, she felt the power of it.

A gong shimmered as the musicians finished. The Minister of Ceremonies, Pyanis, was almost unrecognisable in her formal robes and made-up face. Her voice reverberated down the hall as the list of previous Fenghuangs stretched like ghosts between the pillars.

Finally she reached the present day. The Council had unanimously re-enthroned the current Fenghuang. He embodied their will and the will of all peoples of the city. Pyanis took the ceremonial sceptre from its stand. Made from a whale bone, the handle was long, with a gentle curve ending in a head fashioned like a stylised mountain in the clouds. The bone was carved filigree, hollowed out with detailed depictions of birds – from songbirds to birds of prey, cranes to swooping gulls – set between the leaves and vines of mangroves and banyans.

The drums began once more, their beat growing faster and more insistent. Mira felt her heart beating in time, pounding with the anticipation she had been afraid to feel until now. The Fenghuang would stand. He would make his speech and finally introduce the new agreement between humans and the folk – Tiankawi and Yonakuni. Everything Mira had worked for came down to this. From the moment she had chosen not to accept the injustices piled upon their backs but to question them. Pushed back against every loophole, giving her life, her love, all of herself.

Everything thrummed in perfect harmony. The gong sounded again, shimmering in a quiet hiss.

The Fenghuang stood, the sceptre cradled in his arms like a babe. "I have the great honour of continuing to serve as your leader, as your Fenghuang, in the years ahead. Tiankawi has changed more in my lifetime than ever before. It is time to move with that change. To build before everything is eroded before our eyes." He inclined his mask towards Mira. This is your moment too, he seemed to say. He readjusted his grip on the sceptre, holding it vertically in one hand.

The hissing noise had not subsided. Too long now to be the fading gong ringing in her ears. If anything, it was getting louder. The Fenghuang hesitated, looking at the sceptre more closely.

It moved.

The bone twisted in his hands. Writhed. Before he could react, before Mira or anyone else could make sense of what was happening, it leaped towards his face with a forceful snap. He struggled, tripping over his hem, and fell to the ground.

Mira stared, not comprehending what she saw. A scarf wrapped around his neck, tightening. No, not a scarf. A noose-like rope. The Fenghuang looked up at her, rasping as his hands grabbed at it ineffectually. Stripes moved, and finally Mira saw. Scaled skin. A viper. The sceptre, merely a receptacle, was broken in two where it had fallen from his hands.

Jiang-Li moved fast, pressing her hand against the serpent. Ice crystals formed along its length with a crackle as her waterweaving froze it solid. She prised its fangs loose from the Fenghuang's skin, tearing its body away and flinging it behind her. People shrieked and skittered away. Gede yelled, and the kumiho drew their swords, brandishing them wildly at the crowd. It was pure chaos.

Mira ignored them all, crouching beside the Fenghuang. The neat puncture wounds just below his jaw were already swelling up, blood trickling between his fingers as he tried to staunch the flow. Against all protocol, she gingerly removed his mask. It was clear even before she had prised it loose from his lower face that the venom had already worked its way into his system. His face and neck were paralysed and swollen. A purple hue spread across his skin. His limbs quivered involuntarily. His breath came in short, shallow gasps. His bloodshot eyes widened, trying to communicate something. It was hard to look away. Mira grabbed at his free hand, giving him comfort when she could not think of anything else. Aware dimly of the shouts and panic around her.

The healers finally scrambled forward, pouring a vial of liquid over the bite. The brown fluid sizzled, cauterising the wound, but everyone could see it was too late. Without the mask, the Fenghuang was just an old man. Unremarkable, like any she might pass in the market or sit next to on the tram. He wheezed from the floor, vomit filling his mouth as the healers turned him onto one side. They examined the snake, shaking their heads, whispering frantically. The other vials, the jars and powders spilling from their bags, were untouched. Useless to heal such a wound.

Mira, almost invisible despite continuing to hold the Fenghuang's hand, spoke finally. "Will fugu help?"

The lead healer said nothing.

"Will it make things worse?" she insisted.

"No," the healer said finally. "It won't make things worse."

"Give it to him. Give him his dignity."

The Fenghuang's hand squeezed hers for a moment. They had their differences, but he had genuinely come round to this change. Perhaps simply to bask in the praise, but he would have offered more to the fathomfolk than all the Fenghuangs before him. He did not deserve this.

The Minister of Healing, Kelwin, was the first to come out of his shock, standing by Mira to give his assent. The other Council members stepped up too, united for once. A first. They formed a wall around the Fenghuang, sheltering him from the gawking eyes of the others in the hall.

The healer injected a large dose of fugu into the Fenghuang's arm. The leader's contorted features relaxed a fraction. His shallow breaths slowed, and then finally stopped. It was not peaceful, but he was gone. All that remained was a waxy husk. Mira slipped the mask back over his face. He would not want to be remembered as a frightened old man. She looked up at the Council members around her. Their expressions were fearful. Confused. Angry. A fragmented mirror of everything she herself felt. She spoke the formal words, desperately throwing them into the stunned silence. "The Fenghuang is dead. May his words and deeds rise upon the breaking waves, his name carried by the highest tides."

The crowd murmured the response, lacklustre in their shock. The temperature of the hall had dropped noticeably. People wrapped their arms around themselves, looking at those standing to their sides. Only a select few had had access to the hall before the ceremony. Whoever had murdered the Fenghuang was probably in this room.

Gede's formal kumiho uniform was a size too big for him. This was city guard jurisdiction and Mira did not envy the position the young Minister of Defence was in. He licked his cracked dry lips, confirming, "This is now a murder investigation."

It was an election year; any one of the Council members could have plotted this, coveting the phoenix mask. Perhaps a servant was simply sick of mistreatment. A dignitary planning to further their nation's cause. The gill-hating Cleaven or Fathomfolk First dissidents. Gede could arrest every person in Tiankawi and they would likely all have a motive.

"No one is to leave the building. No exceptions."

The questioning went on for hours. There were hardly enough chairs in the room for all the people present; it was supposed to be only a half-hour ceremony after all. Some paced the room, frustration shuttling between pillars. Most sat on the marble floor, cross-legged or squatting like dock workers. Intricate hairdos wilted like cut flowers.

Colourful shadows moved across the room from the stained-glass doors at the far end. Mira looked at her own brown arms under the rainbow hues, imagining they were body paint on a festival day. Enjoying the holiday she never got round to taking, rather than standing next to the shrouded body of the city's leader.

Jiang-Li stood beside her, staring down at the Fenghuang. Her antlers formed a sort of crown above her head, elaborately draped with golden threads. "The young Minister of Defence is a bamboo shoot pretending he is a forest. He will arrest someone regardless of their guilt. They will not accept anything less."

"He knows who did it?" Mira said.

"I did not say that. But there will be repercussions, for both you and me." Jiang-Li touched her hair, fiddling with her hairpins. It was an anxious tic that Mira was now familiar with. Gold gleamed as pins were pulled out, checked, carefully replaced. One of them looked familiar.

"Consider this a warning, Minister. This city is a powder keg and that young man is about to light the fuse."

"He didn't murder the Fenghuang! He's just trying to do his job," Mira hissed, surprising herself by coming to Gede's defence. Jiang-Li clearly saw something she didn't, reading between unspoken lines.

"When the silt settles, you should remember you will always be folk. Freshwater, estuary, your fanciful words might make you feel like you have a place. But ultimately they will always treat you as an outsider."

"And you don't?" Mira's nerves were worn down by Jiang-Li's cryptic comments. She would've added more, but Gede had entered the room, and all conversation stopped. He wavered for a moment with his back to the closed door, eyes sliding to Mira's. She could not decipher his expression, however: the pained look like his arm was twisted up against his back.

"My esteemed friends," he began, "apologies for keeping you. I hope you can appreciate the necessity of the minor inconvenience. You are free to return to your homes for now."

A ripple of relief ran through the room.

"With one exception," he added, hand raised. "Jiang-Li, Dragon of Yonakuni, you are under arrest for the assassination of the Fenghuang."

Chapter Twenty-Four

"It's Iyoness," Firth said, collapsing the telescope with an abrupt snap between his hands. He handed it back to the navigator, Jalad, with more force than was warranted.

"How do you know for sure?" Nami asked.

The kelpie turned his gaze upon her. The hard line of his mouth pulled her up short. He pointed at the peculiar oblong shape on the centre-most island. "That was the highest point on the seamount, Manannán Keep, where the Elders would meet. The last thing I saw when we left. The shape of it is for ever seared into my memory."

There was a little lost boy hidden beneath the confident exterior. Nami reached for his hand, but Firth didn't seem to notice.

"My youngest brother was only eight when we left. We swam – what else could we do? Swam towards the chinthe patrol ships. Begged for sanctuary, for aid. We thought we'd be safe in Tiankawi, but they locked us in a cage."

The others gave sympathetic nods of their heads, Wensum welling up as she pressed her hands to her heart. Even Zidane said nothing, keeping his barn door of a mouth shut for once. The only scrutiny was the one in Nami's head. Wondering why this was a different story to the one he had told her. Different again from the story he'd recounted at Drawback rallies. The reality did not matter as much as the picture it drew.

The inhabitants of Iyoness had had a reputation. Tough, sullen folk who could endure hardship. Tarbh uisge and kelpies were highly sought after in physical labour jobs. Seen to be stronger, more resilient, less likely to complain because they were too busy working impossible hours on building sites, drilling for oil or whaling in the deepest oceans. Their stoicism so legendary that no one believed the rumours brought back by traders at first: that their haven was fracturing. Hairline cracks became crevices that consumed whole neighbourhoods. The filmy waters, thick with oil from spillages, coated gills and fur, making folk more vulnerable to gill rot, to freezing in the sub-zero conditions as their natural coats lost their waterproofing. But it was disease that secured its demise. Children falling sick, gills unable to work as they should. By the time healers arrived from the other havens, it was already too late. Acute gill ulcers. The illness took a quarter of all young. Caused by the oil spillages, by the mining they had been persuaded to continue by their own elders, by the contracts with human trading partners, despite all the warnings.

People had thought the Iyonessians were quiet folk. They soon learned that when pushed to the brink they were anything but. The uprising was short but brutal. A small group slaughtered the whole of the Senate, arranging their bodies on ice floes for all to see. They pulled stones from the bases of the tallest buildings and let them fall, destroying whatever was in their path, including themselves. Most of the ordinary folk fled, swimming south, pleading to be let into Tiankawi. They brought stories of the devastation, horrifying but hypnotising first-hand accounts. With the morbid curiosity of youth, Nami had listened to her teachers, to her mother's repeated warnings. The northern fathomfolk are fools. We are not.

The sand god, the life-bonded partner of the titan whale shark beneath Tiankawi, had lain dormant under Iyoness haven. Even after the fighting, after the structures crumbled and the folk abandoned their homes, it had not awoken. It was only the death knell of its partner that roused it from its slumber. Rising in lumbering movements from the deepest waters of the north; rising still as water poured from the newly exposed structures.

Was there a sand god under every settlement, folk or human? Under Yonakuni? Something that would've been ludicrous to Nami a year ago now seemed entirely plausible. During the Great Flood, earthquakes had destroyed many of the smaller folk settlements, lava sheets spreading rapidly across the sea floor so they were unable to rebuild. Pollution spilling from human territories corralled folk into smaller and smaller areas of safety. Fathomfolk sought refuge by going topside, or heading to the havens; sanctuaries that were inexplicably more resistant to the disasters and rising water levels. Now she knew why. The titans had lain down to give them a base to build a future. What they assumed was good fortune was actually another sacrifice Nami could not imagine making.

"I wish I could've shown you Iyoness in its heyday. I've never seen anything as beautiful as the jellyfish bloom on summer solstice," Firth went on. His voice carried far beyond Nami's ears. Loud enough to reach the entire crew. At some point he had moved away from her, addressing each of the crew members in turn. "My kelpie clan, the selkies and boobrie kids next door. We stayed up all night, long past our bedtimes, telling the old stories. In spring, we dared each other to the surface, leaping between the drift ice, sending flocks of noisy gannets skywards."

Despite his earnest expression, a discomfort spread from Nami's stomach. She had seen it one too many times: the charming stories, the captivated audience. Wensum nodded along, their shared Iyonessian ancestry tugging at her. Sobekki was difficult to read as always. Even Eun was watching intently, hand paused in her ubiquitous writing. It was the archivist's expression that made Nami break.

In three strides she could've crossed the *Wayfarer*'s deck, taken

Eun by the shoulders and shaken her. No. Don't listen to him. To his honeyed words and handsome face. To the excuses he spins with the practised ease of a spider: never accountable for the destruction he has wrought. He uses and discards people when they no longer fit his purpose, nothing more than bodies falling from the scaffolding in Tiankawi.

It had taken a long time for her to see through the smoke and mirrors, longer than she cared to admit. Perhaps she had always known but hadn't wanted to face up it. The fact was, she was no better than Lynnette, than the Lakelander girls, than every lovelorn mermaid, rusalka and nymph Firth had left in his wake.

She had let him insert himself into her life, into the crew. Let him undermine her until it was too late to take back her support; too late to call him out without implicating herself. She had faltered and fallen beneath his cajoling, his coercion, from the first moment they had met.

"It's heading for a direct collision course with Tiankawi," Jalad said. He merely confirmed what was clear from the moment they had sighted the risen haven. How could they stop a sand god, a creature older than the foundations of their cities, bigger than a flotilla of ships?

Nami had to do something before Firth took the initiative. "We should open a conversation. Reason with it." It sounded weak even to her own ears.

"Reason? Talk?" Firth scoffed. Sharp like needles in her back. "What use is talk? What has the damned Council ever done for us through talk? Cages, enforced labour and manacles on our wrists is what."

"Change is happening." Nami forced her voice to be louder, to drown out his criticism. "The elections will be under way by now and Mira—"

"That brown-noser? She might as well call herself human and be done with it."

Nami drew in her breath sharply, her train of thought entirely derailed. All eyes watching. She was the leader of this mission, was she not? Now was the time to cut down his lies and sluice them off the side of the vessel.

Firth beat her to it. "None of you have the courage to say it. The question isn't how do we stop this disaster. How do we avert this sand god from levelling our beloved city. It's why should we. Why *not* level it?"

It was deliciously bold. The chaos Firth proposed always had been. Level the city and its inequalities. An obvious choice from the outside. But nothing was as simple as that. Titans below, Nami had been a naïve fool once, thinking that stealing her mother's last pearl would somehow solve everything. Destruction would always impact folk and poorer humans the most.

"Kai's pearl changed things. I believe we can reach a better understanding now. Change takes time. This crew, this mission, is proof of that: folk and human; haven and city. If we can make it work here, together, then Tiankawi is simply a matter of scaling up." Nami was desperate for a friendly face, a kinship with someone, anyone, against the look of sheer disdain on Firth's brow.

"Tiankawi will never be anything more than a city built on blood." His amber eyes looked pitifully at her, green flecks as sharp as broken glass.

"Everything is built on blood – you, me, everyone! What we need is to learn from it," Eun interjected. Her eyes were trained on the shape of the islands but her words were meant for Firth. He glared at her, making a noise out of the side of his mouth, but she hardly noticed.

"What does a Jingsha-born human who interacts more with books than people know?"

"I know that books, like people, tell their own stories. Stories of just cause and heroic deeds to mask ugly truths beneath the surface." Eun was pushing back. She would not be cowed, a tiny fish biting at the tail fin of a great white shark.

Jinsei cleared his throat, hands out placatingly. "We need to start somewhere. Why not with a conversation? There's no harm in trying." They could argue all day, but the schoolteacher was right. Someone had to take the first step.

Nami nodded in agreement. "I will take a small party to talk to it."

Everyone agreed, relieved that the tension had been alleviated. Nami could not take both Eun and Jinsei; everyone knew she had grown close to them. It would give Firth more kindling for the fire. She chose carefully. "Zidane, Mikayil and Shizuku, you are with me." Without waiting for a response, she made for her cabin.

Captain Rannoch shouted overhead, readying the rowboat. The thud of feet as the others completed their tasks. She stared at her burlap bag, somehow unable to comprehend what it was and why exactly she was holding it. Waiting, simply, for the door to creak open.

"How could you?" she said without turning.

"It was really quite invigorating, wasn't it? Reminded me of when you first came to Tiankawi." Firth was pleased with himself, his hand curving possessively around her waist. Nami pushed him away, his softest touch like bruises blooming across her skin.

"You mean it, don't you? That you'd rather the sand god destroy everything. Everyone." She turned finally, afraid to hear his answer. Knowing what it would be.

"Yes. You knew that. Sacrifices have to be made. You agreed."

"No! You kept me in the dark. Time and time again: at Onseon, at the Peak. How could I agree when you never told me?"

"Face it, you never wanted to hear the whole ugly truth. You just wanted to hit something. Head in the direction of the nearest fight rather than asking why. I took care of everything else, for both of us." His thumb rubbed on her cheek, a gesture he must've made every day of their relationship. She had found it a comfort before. But coupled with his blunt words, the touch felt like a collar. Choking her. She had helped him fasten it about her own neck.

"That's all I ever was to you. A pearl. A means to an end."

Firth raised an eyebrow, lines enclosing his half-smile. "And? Would you like to pretend I wasn't being used also? A common low-born rebel. Oh, you loved it! Slumming with us. Someone your mother would disapprove of." He stepped in closer, the warmth of his breath brushing her lips. There was enough truth in his caustic words that she couldn't answer.

"Fuck you," she whispered finally. Her fist wrapped around a weapon she had not even realised she'd waterweaved. One that came unbidden to her hand, responding to the fury within. An ice dagger, plain and lethal. She raised it to his neck, the edge sliding to the side of his jaw. The bristles of his facial hair scratched against the blade.

"Yes, you did," he smirked. "Two, sometimes three times a night."

Her body still burned for him, longed to close the minuscule distance between them and succumb to him. It would be easy. Pretending that want and need meant that they were good for each other; that making her gasp his name over and over again somehow meant that he loved her.

A drop of blood trailed down the blade and onto her wrist. Do it, he goaded silently. She tore herself away, pulling at the invisible knots that bound them together. The ice blade cracked as it slipped from her hand and melted into puddle water at her feet. She shuffled backwards until there was space to breathe; to think for herself rather than letting him do it for her.

"Goodbye, Firth."

He tossed a parting shot. "Go on then. Run to her."

Nami knew exactly who he was referring to. He could hear her heart beating faster, giving her secrets away. "If you—"

"If I what? I'm not the one throwing myself at the next lifeline. Hoping her books and words will save you. I see the way you pine. Everyone does. Lost little seal pup, falling for anyone who offers you a scrap. Be honest with yourself – you want to be on a leash."

Chapter Twenty-Five

The rowing boat rocked precariously, a strange feeling after their weeks aboard the much sturdier *Wayfarer*. Zidane grumbled the whole time but had not outright refused when Nami had called his name. The former minister realised that his inclusion was something not to be scorned; or perhaps he feared what would happen if he was left behind on the larger ship with Firth and Sobekki. Shizuku's long arms were perfectly suited to the oars of the small boat and Nami only had to use short bursts of waterweaving to move them over choppier waves.

A mist of spray made it difficult to discern the former haven at first. Clouds and foam merged as if into one, shrouding everything. Overhead, they could hear seabirds calling, but none could be seen.

Then, as if out of nowhere, they saw it.

"Titans save us," Lieutenant Mikayil said, slowly rising to his feet. Shizuku pulled the oars in securely to their waist. Zidane was resolutely staring the other way, only glancing out of the corner of his eye like it was a bad dream. Nami was transfixed. Body and mind seeing and yet failing to understand what she gazed upon.

A god.

The titan moved at a glacial pace, the water churning around it as if boiling. An archipelago of three small islands emerged from the depths. Water poured down from the broken structures, the abandoned homes that made up Iyoness. Then it partially dipped back under the waves, the weight of the haven on its back, a clumsiness from lying dormant for so long perhaps, hampering it.

Iyoness had been the smallest of the havens, a northern coldwater nation that had fallen two decades before. Fathomfolk had lived in Tiankawi city before the demise of the haven, but not nearly as many. A large portion of those Iyonessians displaced – kelpie and merrow, tarbh uisge and selkie – were the ones who had endured the Nurseries' cages. The ones who had been forced to wear pakalots and were desperate enough to work at the Onseon Engine, exchanging their waterweaving to feed their families. These were people who had come to Tiankawi not out of choice, but because they had nowhere left to turn.

The former haven was already being reclaimed, the cacophony of the bird colony growing louder as they approached. Nami could spot nests and perching spots. She knew it was not true land, and yet her eyes said otherwise. Thick emerald strands of seaweed matted many of the buildings. The stone and coral walls were coated in uneven coats of limpets and barnacles. The first glimpse of the titan was overwhelming, but as her racing heartbeat quelled, the waves of shock dissipated into urgency.

The titan was swimming for Tiankawi.

The southernmost point of the former haven was too rocky to moor on, so Shizuku gave it a wide berth, manoeuvring them to the east. Nami left Mikayil in charge of the rowboat as she and the changbi first mate dived into the water. The structures of Iyoness were huge, a decaying labyrinth of derelict buildings subject to a changing tide. They formed an armoured barrier upon the titan's back. It would be far easier for them to communicate below the surface.

The temperature here was brisker than Nami was accustomed to. She shivered as she transformed into her true water dragon form. Her body lengthened around the waist, stretching like an unfurled ribbon. Her silver scales slipped over fragile human skin, an insulating layer that pushed back against the freezing waters. She arched her neck, her antlers twisting from her head.

Firth's cheap shot earlier in the day resurfaced in her mind. It had put a barrier between her and Eun. Despite wanting to confide in the archivist, she had kept a distance. Pretended not to notice the woman loitering while they'd loaded up the rowboat. The disappointment when Nami had given her no more than a perfunctory farewell.

Nevertheless, Nami was excited. They were about to make contact with a sand god. A creature of legend. Her interaction with the titan in Tiankawi had been so brief, so tinged with Lynnette's betrayal, that she had not appreciated the magnitude of it.

This was a chance to make reparations. To use the communication Kai and Mira spoke of. To build bridges. To speak to someone who had lived through history, who might have the answers they all sought.

Nami and Shizuku swam downwards through the currents. Underwater, the remains of Iyoness were different. Near the surface, anemones and coral had started to discolour, bleached pale. The stress of the haven's collapse and the rapid change of environment of a sand god in motion. She had seen some of it in Yonakuni also. Pollution from Tiankawi's industrialisation did not recognise border markers on maps. Further down, sponge and finger corals still thrived, dotted across rocky surfaces. Sea anemones waved petal-like tentacles in vibrant yellow and orange hues, greeting her as she passed. The life that remained gave her hope. Not everything here had died.

She pushed them further, deeper, until they were beneath the behemoth. The shadow of the titan eclipsed the dim light from the surface, leaving her colder than she had ever felt. Her chest ached, unaccustomed to the water pressure since she had been living topside. She turned her head towards the light, towards the haven being dragged overhead.

White. Dazzling as staring into the sun. An expanse of it, stretched out before her. A diamond-shaped plain as wide as a glacier. The sand god's mouth alone was the length of the *Wayfarer*, and the long tail dragged behind like a steady stream.

A behemoth manta ray, placid angel of the sea. Known for being one of the gentlest beasts of the ocean waves. Something so big was rarely so graceful and calming. Relief suffused her. It would be okay. It would listen to reason. There was still a chance to talk this out.

She beckoned to Shizuku as they approached one of its massive eyes. They still had to be careful. The titan was so huge it might not even register their presence, assume they were merely another barnacle on its hide. As they swam under the rows of gill lines filtering water, Nami felt the suction pulling her upwards. She struggled to swim against it, Shizuku using their long arms to tug her out of the current.

Before they got any closer, one of the titan's great eyeballs swivelled down, pinning Nami under its gaze. The floral words, the niceties, the courteous greetings she had in mind dissolved like salt in the water. Dread rippled down her spine with a certainty that quickened her heart. She had got it wrong. All wr—

The titan manta ray bellowed. Long and low, a single note that made the water around them tremble. It spilled over Nami, batting her back with wave after wave of emotion, so much pain that it felt like someone had prised her ribcage wide open, reached inside to crush her soft innards with a fist. A tide that would not turn lapped over her with the inarticulate raw edge of anguish.

Of anger.

With a certainty sandblasted into her bones, Nami knew its intent: the overwhelming desire to conceal grief beneath another, more immediate sort of pain.

"Shizuku, go! Get everyone off the *Wayfarer*! Now!" Desperation lined her words and the first mate did not even question her. With a twist they darted under the titan's bulk, back towards the ship.

Nami sought to distract the sand god with her presence, but the swell of waves kept pushing her back. Churning foam swept her away like flotsam before she had got anywhere near it. After the fourth time of being tossed to one side, she changed tactics, snaking forward into deeper waters, placing herself in front of the behemoth.

The titan manta ray lumbered onwards, a whole haven ploughing towards her like a mountain. Ignoring the inner voice telling her to move, Nami curved her serpentine body into an undulating knot, rolling waves of waterweaving outwards. One after another, sheets of ice solidified before the titan's path. Walls of it, freezing together in vertical honeycomb slabs as wide as she could stretch, thicker than the length of her dragon form. She kept going, ignoring the ache in her limbs, the knowledge that she was nearly spent.

The sand god pressed its head against the improvised barrier, not even pausing to consider the obstacle, shattering it into slivers of ice. All of Nami's waterweaving at its limits, and it had done nothing. She could not move away quickly enough, the manta ray smacking into her. She fell, dazed, drifting down through the deep waters as brightness dazzled her once more.

White light filled her vision as far as the eye could see. Not, as she first thought, concussion, but the body of the manta ray. It chilled her to the bone, blocking out the sunlight as it lumbered overhead. Something beautiful and frightening in equal measure. At the periphery of her vision, she could see its gigantic, district-sized pectoral fins rising and falling, disorientating her like the sky was changing trajectory. Unhurried as the rising of the sun itself.

Nami had no concept of time or place, still falling through the water. She was transfixed as the belly of the sand god moved above her. The white skin took on mottled grey marks around its pelvis, narrowing to a tail as thick as a river. The size of it was terrifying, but the titan made no sudden movements. Perhaps she had raised the alarm for nothing. Misread something in that baleful song. Perhaps.

Then its tail whipped round and came down. Right on top of the *Wayfarer*.

The ship was split asunder, sliced through the middle like it was nothing. Everything lurched, spun, turning like a water-wheel. The waves foamed, greedily guzzling down the mainsail. Only the sight of the broken mast snapped Nami from her daze. She swam back up towards the surface, just as pieces of the haven crumbled from the titan's back into the waters.

Regret could come later. She swam as fast as her limbs could push her, forcing water through her gills, pushing it out of the way with broad strokes of her faltering waterweaving. Fast, but still not fast enough. The mast plunged through the saltwater, barely missing her head. Her focus was entirely on the people beyond, drowning in the turbulent waters. They must've abandoned ship, they must have, she repeated as a litany in her mind. Shizuku would've cajoled them into the other rowboat, into the water even.

She shot forward, pushing until her chest and sides screamed in protest that they could not, would not go any faster. That this was no Boat Race accident. The entire sea roiled and tossed, the waves so choppy she could barely keep upright. She moved towards a flailing body, belatedly realising it was nothing more than barrels tangled in canvas. Her eyes, even her whiskers could not see, could not help when everything around her was chaos and danger. Splintered planks falling like hail; bigger pieces that threatened to batter her as they sank.

She saw the hand first. Outstretched as if reaching for her. She flared with optimism until she followed the line of sight to the motionless body it was attached to. Face-down, spread-eagled, the only movement the dark bloom of blood spilling from Garrett's broken skull. Further away, she saw the rigger, her wounds less obvious but her open-eyed stare telling Nami enough. Back down she dived, looking for others. They had gills, she told herself. But the sand god's tail had crushed them like some inconsequential beetle running across a table. A strike that hard, that sudden . . .

Nami roared. The sound from her true dragon form deeper than her human voice, bellowing low and rumbling. Her grief ripping raw across her scales, articulated without words, molten and dripping through her. Burning her skull, tearing claws down her chest until her voice gave out and she had nothing left to give.

The sound of her call was a beacon, although she had not intended it to be so. It rippled out from her position and she finally saw a wave for help. It was Tephan, the ship's mate, struggling in the water, tangled up in the ropes of the sails as they had fallen. She cut him free, rising through the water with his arm over her shoulder, glad to break the surface and leave the turmoil beneath them.

They both gasped as water ran down their faces. Above the waterline, more debris from the *Wayfarer* floated on the surface. But the ship itself was gone. Their vessel, their supplies, their way home.

Nami looked up at the island-like crops of stone, the behemoth manta ray continuing its unhurried journey as if destroying their entire vessel had been but a minor inconvenience. There was only one way back: they would have to hitch a ride.

Something pulled at her eyeline, a movement unlike the broken pieces of the vessel. Kicking. Fatigued and uncoordinated but nonetheless kicking.

"Over here!" It was Zidane, clinging to the capsized rowboat as best he could. Nami paddled over to his position, careful not to dislodge Tephan as she did. Despite her best hopes, the boat could no longer hold water. It would at least float, though, something for the humans to cling to as she pushed them towards one of the derelict Iyonessian structures. She hauled herself out of the water, catching her breath. There would be more survivors: clinging to floats; swimming over to the other buildings. They would find each other and make a plan.

She had to believe it.

She scanned the structures above water. Manannán Keep she recognised after Firth had pointed it out. A tall, slim tower, only the top few floors emerged from the waterline at the moment. A silhouette stood on its roof, a shadow as she squinted into the sun. It was hard to tell who, but her stomach knew it had to be Firth. Who else could move so quickly, knew the lie of the land so well while the titan's wrath crashed over their heads. Someone else joined him. A stocky figure, the captain, pointing over to them. Nami waved her tail from side to side, comforted by the knowledge that the others would know what to do. In a couple of hours they would have the energy to reunite and . . .

The two distant figures appeared to be talking. Rannoch gesticulated at Nami's position. Firth's response was clipped. They turned towards each other, something else going on. The sun came out from behind the rolling clouds, glaring directly into Nami's eyes. She looked away for a moment, and when she turned back, they appeared to be hugging. Then Rannoch's silhouette crumpled, folding in half like nothing more than a shadow. Firth kicked him off the roof, and the dark mass of the captain's body fell into the water below, a heavy stone.

The weight of the splash made Nami flinch.

Firth looked directly at her. She cowered behind some fallen masonry as if she could pretend she had not seen.

As if he had not done it exactly for her to see.

Chapter Twenty-Six

Lieutenant Tam of the border guard nodded, giving the order with a downward motion of his fingers. The hand-held battering ram slammed hard against the inconspicuous door, its ornate liondog head splintering the painted wood. Two more strikes were all that was needed to break the hefty lock. A skylight opened two floors above and figures scrabbled down the roof, sending loose tiles into the water with splashes. They hastily slid a plank across to the nearby rooftop, hesitating only briefly before making the precarious crossing.

Mira and the second team were semi-obscured by the flapping laundry on the adjacent flat roof. The woman in front noticed them, yelling a warning before she was tackled to the ground. As she fell, she reached out, pulling the washing line down. Mira swerved as the taut line whipped towards them, striking some of the guards and fouling their vision with sheets and clothing. The second figure took his opportunity, leaping across the three-metre gap to another lower rooftop. The impact of his fall dented the corrugated iron with a ringing thud. He rolled off it, limping but still running.

Mira swore under her breath as she yelled orders left and right. Not waiting to hear if they had been received, she shimmied down the rickety drainpipe after him. The corroded metal groaned but thankfully did not peel away from the side of the building. The walkways here were still under repair. Massive gaps had planks or reclaimed signs placed over them. The man stepped on one, the metal sign slipping backwards and flying towards Mira. She jumped to dodge it, teetering on the walkway's edge, where railings were notably absent. Beneath, the sea was placid, but twisted metal and broken house stilts jutted upwards like teeth. Even the most confident of fathomfolk would hesitate before diving into the water these days.

He was further away now, halfway up a ladder to the upper walkways. Mira flicked a throwing knife in his direction, aimed to knock him off kilter. It whistled past his cheek, cutting into his ear lobe. Blood dripped onto the bandages wrapped around his neck. Mira swallowed. She was rusty. She had been aiming for his outstretched hand.

When she scaled the ladder, he was nowhere to be seen. A group of construction workers on the skybridge looked in her direction. Half-erected bamboo scaffolding was scattered around them and the group sat on upturned crates having a tea break. They stared, united in stony expressions. She knew the type. People who trusted neither the border guard nor the people who would run from them. Who wanted to get on with the matter of living and cared not for the churn of politics swirling around them. They would not talk.

Further down, street vendors were selling fruit, green mangoes and pineapple sliced into long fingers, dipped in salt and chilli to refresh in the heat. Seaweed tea was brewing over a portable stove. Lotus-leaf-wrapped parcels of rice and fish were heaped on mats, waiting for the midday rush. Mira slowed down as she approached. These street stalls were always bustling, filled not just with the hawkers but with their families and friends. A makeshift community with aunties aplenty to watch the children, people prepping food but also mending, gossiping, existing. The chatter had already petered out before her approach, the air thick enough to cut with a blade. Her target was still here.

Most of the street vendors and customers looked to the ground, avoiding her eye. A couple trembled as she stepped around them. One woman alone raised her chin, meeting her gaze defiantly. The boy beside her shook, his feather gills flapping in a panic. Mira's hand was on her dagger as she gave a curt nod. Mouthed a countdown to the woman.

As she reached zero, the stallholder yanked the boy down in one swift motion, slamming both their faces against a pile of sea cabbages. Mira sounded a single high note of siren song. A command. *Stop.*

The word blasted in a cone towards the people behind the stallholder. The aunties caught in her clumsy charm clutched at their throats in horror as her song sucked out their breath. The hooded man, her target, stood frozen, knife held in an outstretched hand. His eyes were the only things that could still move, straining to evade her gaze. Mira disarmed him, ending her song before the life was choked out of the bystanders. She had only done it to protect them, but she knew that no amount of explaining would stem the suspicions. It was why she kept such a tight leash on herself; as the most prominent Tiankawian with fathomfolk powers, she could afford to be nothing less than perfect.

Other border guards answered her whistle, running towards her. The man looked so bland. Insignificant. Just another of these gill-hating Cleaven, with their angry rhetoric.

Back at the illegal clinic, blood was encrusted over the headrest of the treatment chair. On the white-tiled floor, despite attempts to clean, the pink hue bloomed like cherry blossom. These gill-removal places had been springing up with alarming frequency. Mira had seen the infected bandages, smelled the sour pus that made her retch. Oozing yellow liquid between crude stitches that were pulled so tight they puckered. The kumiho and chinthe could barely close one clinic down before another appeared a few walkways over. Charlatans even working from mobile units on leaky boats.

Lieutenant Tam shook his head. "No sign. I could've sworn the tip-off was a good one."

"It was," Mira said, putting her finger to her lips. Silence had its own uses. The border guard had turned the room inside out. Yanking open drawers, shouting orders, keeping the curious crowd from the door. Too much noise.

Almost indistinguishable from the lapping waves outside, it could be easily missed. The sound like gas leaking from a pipe. Long and rasping but at times intermittent. Mira followed it to the far wall lined with cabinets and bookcases. Crouching down, she could see long scratches on the white tiles. The cupboard was filled with bottles and jars of various fugu-derived painkillers. The whole industry was getting out of control, a bigger money-spinner than anyone had expected. She rapped on the hollow back of the cabinet.

"Should I get the battering ram?" Tam asked. Mira grunted, pushing the medicine bottles to one side until she found one that would not budge. Yanked it like a lever. Something clicked and the hidden door creaked open.

Snakes. A room of poisonous caged snakes under hothouse lights. They had been searching for this since the Fenghuang's death. At first the Minister of Defence, Gede, had insisted the city guard would sort it, but after weeks without answers, the Council was angry at the lack of results. Unlike his father, Gede was willing to ask for help. He had reached out to Mira and the border guard, combining their forces in the search.

The snake that had poisoned the Fenghuang had been bought here: from an illegal hack who mutilated gills. Mira held onto the thread, but she knew the spool had much more to unwind.

"Well, fuck. I'm not eating snake soup again any time soon," Tam said.

"Didn't you hear? The Council are banning it altogether. Out of respect."

Her lieutenant guffawed, and then caught the look on her face. "You're kidding, right?"

"If only. Voted yesterday, comes into effect next week. A good use of our time, I agree."

The snakes barely moved, coiled like ropes or vines mostly. All highly poisonous specimens. The whole enterprise made her shiver. The hooded snake in the nearest cage slid towards them, its forked tongue tasting the air. Its body was as thick as her forearm. She could imagine it coiling around her, twisting tighter and tighter until she could hardly breathe. Little different from what she already felt.

"Find out who owns the building. Where the shipments come from. One of those we captured might talk."

"They won't," Tam said confidently. So many of the Cleaven had been arrested and questioned, but very few were willing to spill anything of note. People fanatical enough to self-immolate were not bothered by the threats of the border guard.

"Then question the neighbours, the water tuk-tuk drivers who work along this stretch, the kid who delivers the newssheets." Mira refused to be disheartened. The net was tightening. Pull on the tail for long enough and the head was bound to show its fangs. She flicked open her pocket watch and wished the time on it was wrong. The second hand kept ticking, a warning of everything else she still had on her plate. "Speaking of vipers . . . I have a Council meeting to attend."

"Have fun," Tam said cheerfully.

Chapter Twenty-Seven

Nami awoke to an ear-piercing scream. They had taken shelter in one of the hollowed-out husks of a building, and despite her best intentions, she had collapsed on the rough granite floor. She had meant to keep watch, wondering if Firth would swim up to their position and quietly slit their throats in the night. Her eyes desperately scanned for Eun's silhouette among the ruined buildings and bleached coral until the light had completely faded, as if she could will the archivist to be safe if she looked for long enough.

Zidane was pointing, one shaking hand gesturing. Titans knew how Tephan could sleep through the racket. The fuzziness of sleep filming her eyes lifted, and she realised that that was what Zidane was yelling about. The ship's mate had passed away in the night. At least, she thought with inane calmness, he looked peaceful. She envied him that.

She glared at Zidane, quelling his yells to a stuttering halt. A twinge of guilt prodded her. She should not be so unkind. Most people had rarely seen a dead body before, never mind woken up beside one.

"We should look for the others," she said, helping him to his feet. She considered Tephan's body. After last night, the idea of pushing him into the water around them filled her with absolute horror. No. They would take him home to Tiankawi. If the sand god was planning to be a funeral barge, then what was one more body?

The opinionated ex-minister for once had nothing to say. He was so far beyond his comfort zone that he followed meekly, his uneven gait scraping as they climbed over the rocky ruins. Glossy strands of seaweed lay like a thick carpet, slick under their feet, as they carefully navigated the terrain. The buildings were unlike anything Nami had ever seen. The occasional coral structures were similar to those in Yonakuni haven, but Iyoness mainly comprised wide-based mounds of porous rock, eroded over the years into cones and mushroom shapes, bubbling like squat loaves of bread in the oven. The Iyonessian fathomfolk had carved into them, forming windows and doors that looked at a distance like honeycomb in the sand-coloured rock. Among them, black basalt columns towered in uneven hexagonal pillars. A broken staircase descending into the sea.

Far to the north, where bitter winds and flurried snowstorms held court, Iyoness had the reputation as the most inhospitable of the havens. The drift ice on the water's surface sent beautiful mottled patterns into the depths in summer, but formed impenetrable sheets in the darkness of winter. No wonder the selkies cared so closely for the blubber of their seal pelts. It was not about returning to the sea; it was about freezing in fragile human form without it.

Nami left Zidane grumbling, clambering along and up a series of basalt columns to find a vantage point. The titan manta ray beneath them was moving fast enough that she could feel the motion, a rumbling sense of unease like staring up at the clouds for too long. At least its journey south meant they were not freezing among the ice sheets. It was colder here than she was accustomed to, but she did not need thick padded layers of fur and cloth to keep the biting wind from piercing her bones. Her breath did not frost as it escaped from her mouth. She was thankful for these small mercies at least.

She inhaled deeply, using the moment to collect herself as squat little seabirds eyed her from their perches. They seemed unruffled by her leaning over their ledge, making warning noises only when she came too close to their nests, their colourful beaks jabbering from their black-hooded, white-faced bodies.

The four sections of Iyoness above water were like an island archipelago, the water between them like a wide river. She could swim across to the next one if needed, but she was not certain that she should. Their ship had been destroyed; the titan was their only ride back to Tiankawi – and Firth was out there somewhere. She needed a plan of action before running into him. Their survival was more important than any false bravado. Her defensive armour was nothing more than glass shards pressed into her skin, embedding all along her until there was not a single part of her untouched. Unbroken. She blinked, but the myriad versions of herself were still fractured.

A motion distracted her from her reverie. More survivors, only a short distance away, waving excitedly. Nami tripped as she slid down the uneven basalt column steps, dragging a protesting Zidane to where the others waited. She threw her arms around Eun, muffling her small sound of delight. The shorter woman returned the embrace more tentatively, her hands flat against Nami's back. Moments passed before Nami thought more clearly about her actions, about Zidane and Mikayil watching awkwardly to one side. Heat rose to her cheeks, but she held on just a little longer, feeling a burst of energy filling her now they had reunited. Then Firth's stinging words resurfaced. She was just replacing him with Eun. Predictable. Pathetic. She pulled away.

"I'm glad you're alive," she said awkwardly, running her fingers through her hair with a nonchalance not replicated in her tightening chest. The freckles across Eun's nose were more prominent now, sun-kissed from weeks on the ship.

"Alive is certainly the preferable state of being, given current circumstances, or indeed most circumstances," Eun responded in her usual manner.

Nami felt obliged to offer an awkward embrace to Mikayil also, sensing the grimace in the chinthe lieutenant's shoulders as he patted her as quickly as he could get away with.

"Mira will be happy I didn't let her second-favourite lieutenant drown," she said. She might have imagined a twinge of a smile on his face, but the reserved border guard said nothing.

With four of them, things felt more achievable already. Eun and Nami searched the ruins for a building that could shelter them until they reached Tiankawi. Somewhere that was not liable to collapse about their heads. Somewhere – Nami said aloud what they were all thinking – that was defensible.

There was no point pretending any more. Mikayil knew it; even Zidane had figured it out. Firth would have little interest in humans, even less in ones who were part of the establishment. As much as the ex-minister complained, his best chance of survival was with them.

Eun's encyclopedic knowledge of history was essential as the group stumbled around the ruins. What looked like a mass of tangled brown seaweed was, she pointed out, a uniformly planted kelp forest when it was underwater. Cultivated both for sustenance and to feed the fish at the nearby salmon farm. The buildings nearby were nothing more than squat honeycombed mounds, the dilapidated housing of the folk farm workers. Nami knew that meant a grander, more secure dwelling was nearby. She held out against resting in the vulnerable broken structures, against Zidane's complaints and his limp, which grew more pronounced as the day wore on. Her stubbornness was rewarded when a two-storey building came into view. She had guessed more than anything, seeing the farming lands and piecing together what it meant. It didn't matter if it was haven or city; the wealthy lived in fear of those beneath them. Up high, in stilthouses, on the upper slopes of a seamount or in towering fortified properties, they were protected from the masses.

She looked inside. A gaping hole in the south-west corner let the light into the ground floor. Internally, however, the building was intact. Built to defend against raiders, thieves, or perhaps simply irate workers who had been abruptly dismissed. With no windows on the ground floor and only ones as wide as her hand upstairs, it was the most secure building around. There was no need for stairs when it had lain underwater, but the heavy trapdoor would've been locked from the first floor, protecting the family within. They were in luck, the trapdoor wide open and requiring only that they find some way of climbing up safely. Mikayil made quick work of fashioning a rope ladder out of braided kelp strands, something that could be pulled up as they slept.

None of them asked the question. Not even Zidane, as Nami used careful waterweaving to assist him up to the first floor. The opposite, in fact. As she slammed the trapdoor shut, the tension dissipated just a little. It was inevitable Firth would seek them out. Dispose of them one by one as they reached the end of their usefulness. As he had done with Captain Rannoch, there for all to see. She just didn't know if the hunt had already begun.

Nami took the first watch. They had forgone a fire, lacking the firewood and anyhow worried about giving their position away. The narrow windows prevented attackers from gaining another point of entry, but after weeks of seeing the entirety of the ink-black night sky, the blurred reflection of the bright moon shimmering on the water's surface, the ceaseless motion of the waves all around them, the curtailed view from the window was rather claustrophobic.

"Fireflies caught in the firmament of the night," Eun said, somehow following her gaze in the darkness. Her voice was lined with fur, sleep blanketing her. Her silhouette shuffled over until she sat beside Nami, shoulders almost touching.

"Poetic," Nami said with a wry smile. A memory rose like a soap bubble. "When we were kids, Kai told me that stars were the scales the goddess Tiamat sloughed from her body as she ascended into the sky."

"Dead skin?" She could hear Eun's amusement, almost see her raised eyebrow at the remark. "I thought your brother was a renowned public speaker?"

"He was. But he was also a boy, winding up his rather naïve brat of a sister." Recalling the memories, saying them aloud felt like a way to celebrate him.

"You know there could be something there . . . In one of the oral histories of Tiankawi, there's an obscure reference to serpents that held up the sky."

"Don't, Eun, don't give credence to his nonsense."

"We are sitting on the back of a sand god, Nami. There is a grain of truth in every lie . . ." Eun's voice faltered, both of them hearing the implication of her words. The lies Nami had bought into for so long. The silence was so long, she thought perhaps the other woman had fallen asleep. Then, without warning, Eun's small hand reached across Nami's lap and rested atop her own.

Perhaps it was the darkness hiding her face from scrutiny. Perhaps the touch of skin on skin. Nami let the words flow from her before she could overthink it and snatch them back. "I have been a fool. A monumental idiot. All this time, all those people who warned me. I believed Firth . . . because of what? Because he was folk therefore must be righteous? Because someone with that jawline could not possibly be that cruel? He told me to trust him, and so I let him tell me what to do, how to *think*. Sand gods help me, I mocked people like that. I was so proud of being different, of having my own mind." She had been carrying this burden, lashed to her back, for so long, she did not know how to stand straight any more. Saying the words aloud was cathartic.

"I met a water dragon," said Eun. "In the City Library, looking for the truth. In the Nurseries, searching for answers. Helping humans to escape the tsunami waves, teaching them to swim. Perhaps she listened to the wrong answers. But asking questions is never wrong."

Being with Firth had burned. Like running her fingers over a candle, closer and closer to the naked flame. Nami had embraced it because it felt like all she deserved. To make up for the privilege of who she was, the sacrifice she had spectacularly failed to make. She had wrapped her whole self around him, knowing that it would consume her. But Eun ... Eun was something else. A seed of an idea. Delicate, fragile. When those roots were planted, they would unfurl in networks more extensive than the eye could see. Growing, nourishing, healing below ground and above. Eun offered no easy answers, but the canopy of a shelter from the rain.

"How did you get so wise?" Nami said. Eun made a pleased sound in her throat as she adjusted her position on the uncomfortable floor. She smelled like the books that had been drying at the library, of lotus leaf paper with notes of resin.

"A lifetime with a nose in a book is good for something."

"Don't tell my mother that. She'll send me back to the Academy."

"Ah, but the Academy only tells you one side of the story. The side the Yonakunish Senate want its people to know. The side that paints it benevolently. What haven, what city would admit its faults so readily? Walls and cages and pakalots are there because of the difference. Because the easier option is always blame."

"Then how does this end?" Nami's voice rang out. Zidane moved in his sleep, snoring a little more deeply, but did not wake. She breathed out, not realising until now how desperately she wanted someone to give her a solution.

"With a conversation," Eun said finally.

"A conversation?" Nami couldn't mask her incredulity. She pulled her hand away, gesticulating as she forced herself to keep to a whisper. "You think chatting can resolve this?"

Eun didn't reply immediately. Her voice remained unraised, forcing Nami to lean forward to catch it. "You think violence will?"

"Firth won't listen, we both know that." Eun made it seem so easy. Here in the darkness, while the world around them slept, they could talk about it all they wanted. In the grey light of the morning, it would never be that simple.

"Firth relies on people listening. To him. His version of events. He doesn't get his hands dirty; he persuades others to do it. That is power, Nami. More than your spines and claws combined." Lynnette's broken body tumbled through Nami's memory. The Drawbacks leader's unexpected advancement made a lot more sense through the lens of Eun's words. She had merely been another puppet in Firth's plans.

Nami longed to retake the hand that she had shaken off in her annoyance, never noticing how much comfort she had gained from it until it was no longer there. With her dragon eyes, she could see more of Eun than the archivist could see back. The outline of her profile as she stared off across the room, chin tilted upwards as if she could feel the stars outside the building, eyes glittering in their light. Her hair spread over her shoulders like a cape, straight despite all the saltwater and harsh winds. She pulled her knees up and wrapped both arms around them.

Over the course of the journey, Eun had become important to Nami. Someone able to call her out as Dan once had. Now here she was daydreaming about reaching out and touching her face. Titans damn her, she was doing it again. Just like Firth had predicted. Throwing herself at the nearest person with a kind word, as if she would drown if she did not attach herself to someone. She would not do this to herself. To Eun. They were friends, that was all. Why was she contemplating destroying everything by giving credence to this foolishness?

"Nami?" Eun said, her voice strangely strangled.

"You should get some sleep." Nami stood up, moving lest she give herself away.

When Mikayil woke up to relieve her watch, Nami settled down to sleep beside Zidane. The man's snoring was like a boat engine, but it was more than that that kept her awake.

Chapter Twenty-Eight

Cordelia had been burning for days. A low-level hum in her ink sacs like a migraine that would not shift. It went undetected at first, but she could feel it all the same, making it difficult to think straight, to do anything other than home in on the source of the distraction. Someone was trying to change the terms of a deal. Tiny chips at the edges.

She knew exactly who it was.

She had hidden in the chest of contraband overnight, waiting for them to make their move. Envisaging the various ways she would mete out her punishment. In the morning, the jostle of being hefted onto a boat awoke her. Water lapping around the container, muffled voices, and then silence. She had reached her destination.

Her lower limb threw the hinged lid open as her suckers spread wide, her cephalopod body almost exploding from the tiny box. She propelled herself upwards in the water, ready to catch the kappa who dared betray her. She knew what she would see: another drug baron, one of the kingpins of the underworld, weapons out and ready to take her down. Well, she was prepared. The thugs she had hired were meatheads, but they would storm the building and cut everyone down at her command. She had a reputation to uphold.

She was not prepared for the sight of a stunned merrow

propped up in bed with what appeared to be a large family around him. She spied parcels of dulse cakes, familiar jars of dull weed, and the black veins of gill rot running down the merrow's neck and upper limbs, and came to the conclusion that perhaps, just on this one occasion, she might have made a mistake.

"Kraken!" one of the younger merrows shouted with a point of his finger. The two younger kids screamed in gleeful horror, using it as an excuse to bounce and tumble off the sickbed as their father tried to quieten them.

"I am not a—"

"Cordelia, what are you doing here?" Dan interrupted as he swam in through the open door. He crunched on the bowl of lotus chips in his hands, perplexed but certainly not displaying the guilt of a deal-breaker.

Cordelia tucked her lower limbs back in, floating in the water just above the chest of contraband. Trying to regain control of the situation, she glared down her nose at him. "Following up on stolen goods and reneged deals."

Dan nudged one of her tentacles aside to reach into the chest. "You mean these?"

The seawitch had not looked properly when she had concealed herself. Glass vials of liquid were stacked within the chest, vials pilfered from her lab; what else did she need to know? Except now she saw it was not fugu. It was not even the synthesised dull weed tincture they had started to manufacture.

"The lab pretty much runs itself. So I've been experimenting with your gill rot potions. You know the snow ear fungus near the Onseon Engine grows red now?" Dan nibbled on another crisp, animated as he continued to talk. "Mutated due to proximity to the effluence. It got me wondering if it had developed resistance to the pollutants causing gill rot."

Cordelia finally put the pieces together. "You've been cheating on me . . . by developing more drugs?"

"Cheating?" Dan barked in laughter. "I told you, the lab is a well-oiled machine! I was just tinkering in my free time. And, well, Roanan here was game; you can see how far the gill rot has spread. We've been doing some trials."

"And dinner," the merrow added, as if that was of the utmost importance. "Don't forget you get a free meal out of it."

Cordelia glowered, her horizontal pupils thinning to a faint line. She slid across the room, the folk children scattering at her approach. The sick merrow said nothing as one of her lower limbs turned his head to one side to better see how far the rot had spread.

"What have you given him?" The healer in her could not help but ask. There were white scars down the merrow's arms as if the rot had receded. Interesting.

"One part red snow ear fungus to four parts the usual gill rot remedy."

Cordelia's head snapped back to the kappa. "*My* gill rot remedy?"

Dan shrugged, licking crisp crumbs from his webbed fingers. "I reverse-engineered it from samples. A way to pass the time."

Cordelia's ink simmered in the glands beneath her jaw, her body just as confused as she was. She rubbed at her temples. "I think we need to add another clause to your contract."

She stayed to watch Dan administer his concoction, questioning, advising, theorising in a way she did not want to admit excited her. Roanan dozed as they argued dosages over his head, the rest of the family no longer interested in the novelty of a seawitch appearing in their house. Outside, someone was calling in Yonakunish, offering free hot food. The merrow children made eyes at their father, who shooed them out with a gesture of his hand. Cordelia stretched, glancing out at the light that refracted through the waves to their position. It was already late afternoon.

Tiankawi had erupted after Jiang-Li's arrest, fuelled by the

Yonakunish delegation. They were in Qilin and Seong districts daily, giving out charitable hot meals alongside unabashed opinions. Outrageous, wasn't it, that the humans had arrested a dragon! After the sacrifice Kai had made for them and all. Absolutely no respect. On what evidence? Because the kind-hearted Jiang-Li had rushed to the Fenghuang's side? The first one to react to the assassination attempt? Because she was here negotiating on behalf of the haven?

Or simply because she was folk?

Cordelia watched the haven's rhetoric sweep through the southern districts like water looking for the path of least resistance. The local guards were not prepared for the intensity of the response. The bone-weary tiredness after everything that had happened, finally snapping the freshwater communities into action. Full-on protest marches crippled Jingsha for days. Fathomfolk took to the streets, blockading crucial walkways and skybridges, refusing to work at the docks, vertical farms or construction projects. It was tolerated at first, sympathised with even, until it turned. A drunken altercation in one corner of the otherwise peaceful protest resulted in violence. Ugly words, fists, then bottles and blades. Two city guards in a critical state and a dozen folk arrested.

See, the newssheets sneered. In parlours and private members' gardens they whispered the rhetoric. Then they grew louder. Bolder. Pakalots were no longer functioning and this was the result. Folk were nothing more than savages. Animals.

The critics were more subdued when the retaliation happened. When groups of marauding Cleaven took to trashing fathomfolk businesses. Threatening to cut the gills from anyone who looked at them askance. Protecting their own, muttered the humans safe in their Jingsha penthouses, shaking their heads as if it was a tragedy that could not be prevented. As though it was not being fuelled by repeating the rumours, the headlines, the words that slipped so easily from loose tongues.

After a week of it, a week of burned-out boats, smashed-up shops and kumiho whistles echoing all hours of the night, Tiankawi was subdued again. Stall owners swept up the broken glass and set their stools back out. People dragged themselves back to work, back to putting food on the table. The animosity remained, but need put it on the back burner.

Cordelia and Dan swam up to the surface late that evening, deep in discussion about the modifications they could make to the gill rot formula. Talking about it made her own gills itch, as if the long day in polluted waters had already had an impact. She shook the notion off as she donned her water bull disguise, telling herself it was the ink in her body still thrumming until she settled the loophole Dan had eked out for himself. As they crossed one of the skybridges, a figure at the opposite end froze. The stranger clutched at the bandages around their neck and ran in the opposite direction with a single long whimper.

Dan was subdued after that, the whirlpool of energy suddenly stagnating. Con artists who called themselves healers had started offering extra services in back alleys and walkways. Pain-free gill removal for cash payment. No questions, no names. Which made it easier, of course, to shirk all responsibility, packing up their filthy mobile infirmaries when anyone came back to complain.

The problem was the assumption that the external gills could be trimmed off like a haircut. They had not considered, these charlatans and the fools who paid them, that Kai's pearl had granted them the ability to breathe underwater. Gills were not merely decorative but were integrated with the body's circulation. Blood ran through them, branching capillaries needed to filter the water. Cutting them was akin to cutting off a finger and expecting it to heal. Even when out of the water, the humans' gills supplemented their lungs, making use of the moisture in the air. But no, those who hated their unasked-for gift could not see that.

Cordelia had been called on several times already after a

botched gill removal. "I do not enjoy cleaning up other people's messes. The state of them. Absolute frauds. Butchers."

"Don't," Dan said. The single word more of a throat-clear than anything else.

"Don't what?"

"You're thinking about it. How you could remove gills better than what's on offer. Turn a tidy profit."

"And you think I couldn't?" Cordelia said, bristling. If she was in true form, she would be pulsing purple stripes right now.

"You could. You're an excellent healer. An astute business-woman. You would make a fortune." Dan's response punctured all Cordelia's counter-arguments. "But you would be complicit."

"Money is money. Why should I care?"

"Because you are folk. Because where does it end? Frustrated estuary kids? Babes in arms?"

"I do not need advice, from you or anyone. You are in my debt, my hire."

"If you say so," Dan barked, concealing the sound of mirth with a cough. He did not push the matter.

Cordelia closed her eyes for a long moment, resisting the urge to continue the verbal sparring. She had learned much from the kappa, even though she would never admit it. The dull weed tincture, for example, was a riotous success. They were selling it as fast as they could put it in jars, labels not even fully dry. The street vendors, selling along the skybridges and walkways with their shoulder poles, came back twice a day to refill their baskets. Dan had been right. Now this gill rot medicine. She did not want to get her hopes up, did not want him to know how important his discovery might actually be. But she knew.

He needed more to bind his beak to her service.

Back at the lab, she made him wait as she unlocked the strong-box in her office. Handed over the knotted rope messages that had made the long journey from Yonakuni. Lotus paper and bamboo scrolls were rare in the havens, rarer still in the hands of the common folk. Instead, knotted messages were like telegrams, getting the main message across. Less likely to disintegrate in the saltwater during transportation as well. She had received the replies weeks ago, but the kappa did not have to know that.

Dan turned the messages over in both hands, fingers rubbing the knots that denoted his ama and sisters' names. Cordelia had pulled strings. Full apprenticeships for his two oldest sisters. The youngest, by lucky coincidence, had reached the top of a waiting list for a school scholarship Dan had apparently applied for on her behalf years before. A distant unknown relative had died, bequeathing a small but perfectly reasonable residence on the other side of Yonakuni. Stability. Opportunity. A future.

His hands clenched around the messages. He knew what she dangled before him. No matter his personal opinion on it, he had signed the bargain.

"Now … about this new gill rot medicine." Cordelia unrolled the agreement. There was space, plenty of space, for amendments.

The crown of Dan's head, visible with their height difference, was like looking down on a pond in an ornamental rooftop garden. The clear water she never saw him topping up remained full to the brim, barely stirring as he nodded. "Let's talk business."

Chapter Twenty-Nine

"Finally. We were wondering when you were going to grace us with your presence," snapped the nasal junior official who was taking the nominations. If she rolled her eyes any further they would pop right out of her head. Mira shrugged, sliding into the empty seat next to Gede. They had come to an amicable accord. An unspoken agreement to keep certain topics off limits and focus on their mutual interest, that of narrowing the gap between Jingsha and the rest of the city.

Responsibility suited him. His face had slimmed down, cheekbones as prominent as the dark circles under his eyes. He still wore outfits far too pretty for Mira to take him seriously. Gold and silver embroidery about his cuffs and lapels, seasilk handkerchiefs and perfectly coiffured hair. But the few times he had spoken up in Council meetings, his points were pertinent. He had backed her to divert city funds to the sprawling shanty towns to the south. Amendments that the Council had rejected were reconsidered when Gede rephrased them. Mira had sought allies in the Council, but she'd never expected Samnang's son to be one.

The nominations for Minister of Healing concluded. No one stood against Kelwin, who nodded as if it were to be expected. All nominees had to have rank: either an official who had passed the citywide scholar exams, or in one of the guard divisions. Voting, however, was open to all citizens of Tiankawi. As it stood, few fathomfolk had full citizenship. They were on long-term visas or spousal permits; even their children, born and raised in Tiankawi, were only considered settled permanent residents. A narrow distinction perhaps, but a separation all the same. The process to become a citizen was laborious, prohibitively expensive and incomprehensible. Another thing the Fenghuang had actually been willing to change. But he was dead now. The status quo remained: citizens voted for the Council, the Council voted for the Fenghuang. Trickle-down equality. As if that was even possible.

Gede's leg shook as the nominations for Minister of Defence were read out. Mira could hear his teeth grinding and she impulsively patted his knee. He stilled for a moment. Standing when his name was called, he pushed his shoulders back, making a short statement about his suitability. The anxiety could not be completely concealed. His eyes kept flickering to the door, his gaze so intense that others, Mira included, twisted in their seat to see who was there. No one. There had been talk, of course, of Samnang – who had resigned due to his wife's death – returning to power, seizing the mantle back from his inexperienced son. One of the kumiho lieutenants stood in opposition, but in the end that was all.

It was Mira's turn.

"Are there any other candidates for the Ministry of Fathomfolk?" the junior official said, hardly concealing the boredom in her voice. Mira was more than happy for other folk to stand against her, but she could see none in the crowd.

"Yes, I nominate my daughter, Reimi," the Minister of Finance announced.

Mira couldn't help but laugh aloud.

"Minister, I fail to see what is funny about the matter. Aren't you all for the Gill Adjustment Centre?" The Minister of Finance had a triumphant look upon her features.

Of course. Another seat on the Council that they could put

an ally on. After all, they all had gills now. Never mind that the feather-gilled humans had never had to endure a pakalot around their wrist, or the decades of injustice that went with it.

It made sense now how willing they were to fork out the funds for the centre. Mira had naïvely believed she'd won them over; instead she'd let them build an irrefutable argument against her.

"By all means. I have no quarrel with other suitable candidates standing for the position."

The Minister of Finance's daughter was about Gede's age. She was a senior official in the Ministry of Agriculture, but the opportunity to seize office early was clearly too good to pass up. Had she shown the slightest interest in folk needs, Mira wouldn't have minded. The brazen ambition was what rankled. Two more nominees came forward, both relatives of current Council members. Nepotism on display like a preening bird-of-paradise.

The door opened.

Samnang.

The former Minister of Defence sauntered down the long aisle to the front. "I'd like to nominate myself."

The stunned junior official spluttered a response. "Minister of Defence nominations have concluded."

"Oh, I'm sorry. I didn't make myself clear. I'd like to nominate myself for Minister of Fathomfolk." His gaze slid to Mira's. There was more white in his hair, more black in his eyes. But it was the high-necked collar of his jacket that alarmed her most: his feather gills bound and gagged beneath brass buttons.

"Mira, Mira, wait," a muffled male voice called. Mira pushed her hair back, throwing open the door into the corridor.

"Kai?" The ghost she would have welcomed, but instead Gede stood in the doorway. The blue of his uniform mocked her. She had exited the nominations meeting as soon as was politely possible, head reeling from having to stand against four other candidates: all human, one of them the man who had made it his career to stand in her way. She had stumbled into the first quiet space, a small unlocked office, to gather her thoughts. She did not think herself irreplaceable; far from it. But she would not – could not – relinquish the position to them. Not when they would sully everything she and Kai had sought to achieve.

Gede grabbed her hand to stop her slamming the door shut on him. She yanked it away. Snapped at him with a coil of rage. "Was it fun to watch? Right after I found our snake dealer! *Our* lead!"

Gede flinched. "I had no idea. Titans believe me, he didn't tell me a thing!"

"He's your father. How do you expect me to believe a word you say?"

"Not all parents are like your ama." Gede's expression was so vulnerable it stopped Mira's anger in its tracks. It was the first time she had glimpsed behind the velvet curtain. Her vehement disgust for his privilege and lifestyle a barrier between them despite their burgeoning alliance. She did not want to know more than that. Easier to sneer at the gold-gilt surface than uncover the cracks that had been papered over. She was the one who steered the conversation onto other topics, ignoring those distress signals. She did not have time for someone else's problems.

A couple of officials trickled past them, slowing right down with heads swivelling to follow the tantalising interaction in the doorway. Mira smiled directly at them. "If you'd like, I'll transcribe the conversation and have it posted to your apartments." They hastily moved on.

"You know it's going to get worse than that." Gede took a step forward so his words would carry. "Public speeches, mudslinging, debates. You need a thick skin."

Mira looked up at him, surprised by the wisdom in his words. She was guilty of always building walls, hadn't Kai said that?

Perhaps she should not be so quick to dismiss Gede's overtures of friendship.

Another group of officials came down the hallway. "Minister of Defence, Minister of Fathomfolk," one said politely.

Their greetings were enough of a reminder to snap Mira back. What was she thinking? This was Samnang's son. She could see his father's sneering lips and sharp chin echoed in his features.

"My thanks for your concern, Minister. As you have reminded me, I'm going to be rather busy in the next few weeks. Perhaps it's best if we conduct our investigations into the Fenghuang's death separately for now."

Her words were like a bucket of cold water in Gede's face. He looked to respond, try once more, but in the end he nodded. A perfunctory fist-palm salute. "Good luck, Minister Mira."

Mira could not help reading his farewell as something else.

Chapter Thirty

They fell into a sort of routine. Nami wouldn't call it familiar, but it structured their days. Surviving occupied so much of her time that she almost forgot where they were, what they were travelling on, and who lurked beyond their perimeter. They scouted out the nearby buildings for anything salvageable, moving in widening circles around their base camp. Containers that could catch precious rainwater for drinking, driftwood that could be dried to start a fire. Nami dived to catch an occasional fish while the others foraged for whelks and mussels from shallow rock pools.

On one occasion as she and Eun were scavenging, they opened a door to a storeroom to find a massive spider crab. With spindly legs and claws, the crustacean was nearly two metres across, squatting in the middle of the room like it had been expecting them. Dried anemones covered a carapace as wide as a human torso. Nami moved without thinking, a water spear summoned to her hand as she leaped forward. It was only when Eun halted her, prodding the nearest leg with her toe, that they both realised it was a shed shell. The actual creature, bigger than this cast-off, was out there somewhere. In wordless agreement, they both returned to the others earlier that day. Iyoness had been reclaimed by the sea and Nami wasn't sure if they should take it back.

"It's slower than the *Wayfarer*, but not by much considering the size. We'll be back to where we met the sea nomads soon." Mikayil was a man of few words, but those he spoke were always important. He was best able to chart their journey, using his chinthe training and the position of the stars to calculate how fast they were moving, and that yes, Tiankawi was still their destination.

"We need to warn them." Knowing the damage the sand god had wrought on their own ship, Nami was worried for the nomads. Their awe and admiration of the old gods would put them in harm's way. She felt a duty to protect them after what Firth had done to the pirates. No more standing back and letting others decide for her.

"Pfft, why? We should be worrying about our own hides, not theirs," Zidane interjected.

"By the abyss, can you be any more self-serving?" Nami was sick of hearing his complaints. The fish they caught were not to his taste, the floor was hurting his back. As if she had chosen to shipwreck them and could do anything more about it. "You were the Minister of Justice once. You had a seat on the Council. Surely, between all the greased palms and back-alley deals, there were a few things you actually cared about? Once upon a time, there must've been a cause that even you thought was worth protecting."

Zidane puffed up, about to launch into a tirade about salties or women or outsiders telling him what to do. Like a record stuck in one endless loop. She knew he was in pain. The limp had grown more pronounced over the days, his gait lopsided as he gripped his hip with each winced step. It was one of the reasons she had not abandoned their base, and mostly assigned him to collect shellfish rather than scout the ruins. She had tried to protect his dignity, not draw attention to it, but at the same time, she could not simply conjure a water tuk-tuk for his convenience.

"The Welfare Act," Eun cut in. "You failed to pass it by a narrow margin, against the grain of most of the other Council members . . ."

The former minister's face flitted through a series of emotions, but he remained silent.

"I remember that," Mikayil added, appraising Zidane as if for the first time. "Mira and I were cadets at the time. She was disappointed when it failed to pass."

Nami was the only one out of the loop, her bafflement finally loosening Zidane's tongue. Subdued. "My housekeeper was folk. A mermaid, although you wouldn't know it; she had worn her legs for so long that she might as well have been human. She'd been with us for decades: raised our children, nursed my wife on her sickbed. I know she was paid help, but she was also family. One day she was at the market, after a week of heavy monsoon rain loosened the mortar. All it took was a single roof tile, falling twenty floors onto her head. They said at least it would've been instantaneous."

Many affluent humans employed folk: as housekeepers, cooks, tutors and cleaners. Mostly female, they were often at the markets, a gaggle of human children by their sides as they piled the week's shopping into their baskets, somehow juggling the multitude of tasks. She had seen them, and pretended not to see them. Living and working at the feet of humans, eating the scraps from their tables, sleeping on the floor they had to sweep and never being able to speak back. It was not the kind of life she could tolerate, and she thought little of it; never delving deeper into the complicated bonds that might form in the privacy of the luxury homes.

Zidane looked down at his hands. "She had two children, both still in school. No partner or family to take them. It was only right that they stayed in my house until they came of age."

"The proposed Welfare Act would've allowed humans to adopt folk and vice versa. Removed the barriers that insisted each should stay with their own," Eun said.

"They panicked, didn't they? The grown offspring afraid of losing their inheritance. The wives and husbands who knew of secret affairs and bastard children. The purists disgusted that it would lead to more fraternising, more estuary babies," Mikayil added.

"I didn't know! I hadn't even thought about it before. Didn't realise the whole folk issue was so damned fraught." Zidane still looked perplexed. The first time, perhaps, that things hadn't gone his way. Nami always thought humans actively hated folk, but most were like him. They did not question things because they did not see them. It was only when prejudice veered like a boat ramming into their placid existence that they looked up and listened.

"What happened to her children?" Nami asked.

"They were placed in a folk orphanage. I, um, tried to set up a fund for them, but the people who ran the place wanted the money to go towards the whole home." Zidane frowned as if it was an unreasonable request. He could certainly afford to sponsor an orphanage, but that wasn't what he'd wanted. His guilt was only towards two individuals – not all folk, nor all children.

"We each have people we want to fight for. Want to protect." Nami's eyes lingered on Eun's face but hastily turned away as the librarian looked in her direction. "That's exactly my point. The sea nomads have the right to know what's heading their way. This kindness costs us nothing."

Zidane acquiesced with the briefest of nods, Mikayil and Eun more enthusiastic in their confirmation. It was a step. A decision that had not come from her mother or Firth or the rest. Hers. The feeling was strange. For so long she had felt like invisible threads held her up. Tearing loose from the Yonakunish web, straight into Firth's. Along the journey, the strings had pulled taut in all directions. Now, as she saw the confidence the others had in her, it was as if she'd cut through the remaining strands.

Nami was the only one fast enough to scout out the sea nomads. She needed to get ahead of the sand god and make sure the sea-farers kept a wide berth. Their curiosity would otherwise get the better of them, seeing this beast of legend, the titan with a world upon its back. Eun accompanied her to the water's edge. Nami sensed her apprehension. The way she tripped on unseen obstacles, muttering to scold her own clumsiness.

The water reached Nami's ankles as she slipped into the shallows. The cold lapped over her feet, making her shiver. Fully submerged, she would not feel it: it was balancing between two worlds that was the most challenging. "I'll only be a couple of hours. Do some foraging if you can, but don't take any unnecessary risks."

"Unnecessary risks are more your forte than mine."

"I don't know about that. Paper cuts can be lethal," Nami teased. She kept wading until she was waist-deep in the water.

Eun had wrapped both of her arms around herself. Her eyes were more grey today, to match the overcast sky. A sliver of a thing, a bamboo stalk bending, but stronger by far than Nami. Despite the water and distance that separated them, it felt like Eun was by her side. "Documenting this for your records?" Nami shot, needing to say something, anything to alleviate the pressure building inside her.

"Not for the official records … Just for me." Eun's words threatened to undo her entirely, and Nami could barely nod in acknowledgement. She closed her eyes, forcing herself to concentrate on her own body rather than the gaze that dissolved her into foam.

With an audience of one, it felt more intimate than any transformation before. Like undressing, slipping out of each item of clothing, revealing all the blemishes and imperfections along the way. Her scales unfurled like lotus petals, a river of silver stretching down her torso and up and around her neck. She lengthened like a ripple through the water, her tail coming back up in a loop with the iridescent fins like a silken fan. She rested on all fours as her limbs grew thick with sinew, ending in sharp claws. Antlers burst from her head, delicate branches that reached back as thin whiskers tumbled from her jaw. The world was brighter through her dragon eyes, as if she had cleared a film. She tasted the movement of the waves, the flapping of Eun's loose skirts like they caressed down her arms. Her serpentine body could not help but curl, coil and flourish, tail swinging behind her like a sail.

"Well," she said. Eun's eyes widened at the rumbling tones, the growl that rolled under her words. "I am seen."

"The stories, the books … they say many things. But they do not speak the truth."

"What is the truth?"

"The power is not your pearl. It's you." The certainty of her statement was like a confident sword stroke, Nami almost gasping with the sharpness of it. Praise given unconditionally was something she was unaccustomed to. She looked down at her reflection in the shallow water. Seeing herself for the first time in a long time. Raising her head, she met Eun's gaze, the words unsaid and yet the silence speaking for them both.

It took a while to find the seafarers, but she could cover the open waters with ease, her sleek body fast as it moved. There was movement to the south-west near the surface, but as she neared, she realised it was not the sea nomads but a pod of humpback whales. She drew close enough for them to see, but at a safe distance. Even she was dwarfed by them, a reminder of how insignificant one individual was in the vast oceans. In days past, fathomfolk had ridden on the backs of whales, harnessed them to pull huge underwater craft across the deep oceans. They were respected and revered as the living descendants of sand gods. Until they weren't any more. Until the push-and-pull of their own problems was magnified a hundredfold, and even these magnificent creatures were forced into irrelevance.

The lead whale scrutinised Nami from beneath an ecosystem of barnacles, scattered down the matriarch's jaw and fins. In halting mangled whale song, Nami asked if they had seen ships. The matriarch did not respond, but one of the smaller whales behind did. *East of this place*, it said. The phrase repeated over and over as the other whales took up the chant. The sound rumbled around her, sonorous echoes that swept in waves. Every fish and folk would hear it.

The sand god would hear it.

She interrupted with her thanks, asking them to quieten the call. The whales corkscrewed upwards, laughing at her request, their pleated throats flashing white and their huge fins moving like the blades of a sailmill. They could not dampen their song any more than she could extract her pearl. It was part of who they were. They breached the surface of the water, Nami entirely forgotten as they played. Out here, whales were safe. Free. A pang of jealousy lodged in her throat. What if she simply swam off now? Away from the sand god, from Tiankawi and Yonakuni and the multitude of unsolvable issues.

It was too late for such dreams. Eun and the others from the boat; Mira and Trish back in the city; even her impossible-to-please mother. Too many people needed her.

Once she spotted the sea nomad flotilla, convincing them to stay away was easier than she expected. *Where is your ship?* they asked. Her answer, delivered in a mix of signs and Tiankawian, turned their expressions from pure joy to horror. They might not comprehend the waves that had destroyed Tiankawi, but they had seen the *Wayfarer* just a few weeks before. The vessel bigger than any of their double-rigger canoes. Its destruction was much more tangible.

"The gods, angry," the leader said, making a sign across his body.

"Keep your head low," Nami advised. They were more than happy to give the sand god a wide berth, kissing their soapstone talismans and even pushing a few into her hands.

It had taken a little longer than expected. Nami swam back towards stricken Iyoness, snaking her way through the waters as the sun started to dip over the horizon. She wondered idly if Eun would still be waiting for her, down by the shallows where they had parted. Imagined saying the words that stuck in her throat, that would change the timbre of their friendship.

She was so busy daydreaming, she almost swam straight into the *Wayfarer*'s first mate, only halting when she felt the push of waterweaving batting her away. "Shizuku, you're alive." She realised the triteness of her words as soon as they escaped her mouth. "Are there others?"

Shizuku's eyes narrowed. They seemed to be making their mind up. The two of them were near the sand god now, close to what Nami could only assume was another group of survivors.

"Listen, Shizuku, the captain, he—"

"He's dead. I know. My crew, *my family* are gone because you thought you could reason with a god."

Nami's tongue wouldn't cooperate, wouldn't line up neatly to tell her side of the story. The disgust on Shizuku's face pressed out all other thoughts, making her words stumble and trip. "I ... No. I mean yes, I didn't realise how angry the sand god was. I didn't expect it to destroy the ship. I miscalculated. But Rannoch wasn't dead! Not from the wreckage, I mean. I saw Firth—"

"You're both as bad as each other!" Shizuku's hands rubbed their shaven head, frustration etched in their actions. Firth's glossy lies against Nami's stuttering explanation. She needed to put it right. Before others appeared and reinforced Firth's stories, digging the barbed hooks in deeper.

"This is what he does. Charms, manipulates, makes you doubt yourself. He hates humans, but that doesn't mean he cares for the folk. For anyone. Don't make the same mistake I did."

Before Shizuku could respond, a clicking sound carried through the water. Nami spotted Wensum first, the diminutive grindylow-selkie giving a curt wave through the submerged ruins. Her hand looked misshapen at first, until Nami realised she was gripping a short blade. A hundred nightmarish possibilities ran through her mind. "What did you do?" she asked.

Shizuku had the courtesy to look ill at ease. Wensum, on the other hand, was positively gleeful. She twirled the blade a couple more times before sliding it back into her underarm scabbard. Each movement washing the blood on its keen edge. Nami could taste iron in the water. Her group had spent their time scavenging for food; Firth's group had found weapons instead.

"If you aren't with us, you're against us," Wensum said, as if it was obvious.

Chapter Thirty-One

Nami did not waste her time on a response, streaking past them, an arrowhead in the water towards the sand god islands. Barely stopping for breath as she clambered over the ruins, her claws clumsy and clattering. No time to transform, no time for anything. She raced towards the safe house, looking for signs of a fight, plumes of smoke or caved-in walls. Everything was as she had left it.

"Eun? Mikayil? Zidane?" she shouted desperately, not caring who could hear. Her own voice echoed back in fading mockery. Then only silence.

"Nami?"

She turned, practically weeping at the sight. Eun and Mikayil carrying their makeshift fishing rods, Zidane curiously poking his head over their shoulders. Nami collapsed, shrinking back down into human size like a puddle of water. Small and vulnerable as Mikayil asked her what was wrong, drawing his baston stick and circling her position as if giant squid were about to peel themselves from the walls. Zidane commenting about folk hysteria even while he put his jacket over her bare shoulders. But it was Eun who knelt by her side. Took her shaking hands and held them between her own. She said nothing, her head touching Nami's with the lightest of grazes, her hair a waterfall masking them from view.

Here in the eye of the storm, there was peace. Nami knew it would not last. Knew that if her group were safe, Wensum's blade had simply blooded another instead. The violence had not ended because it was out of sight. For now, the reprieve was enough. Eun's presence was enough.

It didn't take long to find Wensum's victim. Mikayil was an excellent tracker, and between his skills and Nami's heightened senses, they were able to pinpoint the direction. The land that had risen above sea level had expanded, and the distance to the next topside part of the haven was a narrow strait, the water only waist-high although the ground beneath their feet was unstable. A thick trail of blood was smeared over the dried coral and rocks heading towards one of the derelict honeycombed settlements.

In the dusk light, Jalad, the naga navigator, lay unconscious in human form on the ground. The blood was his, flowing from a wound in his upper thigh, despite efforts to staunch it. His rich brown skin was ashen, a sheen of sweat coating his whole body as his dried lips muttered incoherently. His head was cushioned on Jinsei's lap. The teacher barely noticed their arrival, mopping Jalad's head with an intimacy that had not been present on the *Wayfarer*. Called it, Trish's voice said in Nami's head.

"Jinsei," Nami said. She did not want to break the moment of affection, but time was not on their side.

The schoolteacher didn't look up, his voice wet as he spoke. "They tried to recruit him. Folk first, they said. But he wouldn't leave me, even when Wensum told him the price." The grimy rag he was using to wipe Jalad's face simply smeared the dirt around. Jinsei did not bother to hide the tears speckling the surface. "They were a crew. Sailed together for years. How could she . . . just like that? How does something turn to hate so quickly?"

Nami unwrapped the blood-soaked makeshift bandage from

around the naga's leg. Jalad groaned a little as air nipped at the wound, but otherwise gave no reaction. The cut was deep, the blood continuing to ooze out without signs of clotting. They had neither healer nor seawitch on this forsaken haven. "Jalad, can you hear me?"

The naga's eyes fluttered open briefly, unfocused although his head turned towards her voice. He mouthed *yes*, although his throat was too tired to work.

"You've lost a lot of blood. Possibly too much. The wound is deep to the bone." Jalad blinked in acknowledgement. She had spelled out what was obvious to everyone, her own harsh words making her wince. She had to get through to him how important this was. "There might be a solution. A risky one, though. Do you have the energy to shapeshift?"

"In this state?" Jinsei said in distress. He shook his head adamantly. "It's too dangerous – broken bones get lost in the shift."

"It's his best shot." Eun's sharp mind saw what Nami was hoping for. "Shapeshifting can move the position of a wound. On a human leg, a cut this deep will drain you of all blood, but on a naga tail? It could be more superficial."

Nami had learned about it during monotonous charity visits to healing houses back in Yonakuni. During lessons she had only partially paid notice to in the Academy. Shapeshifting when severely wounded had possible positive outcomes; negative ones as well.

"Could?" Fear tore through Jinsei's single word. His head swivelled between Eun and Nami. "You don't know for sure?"

"No," Nami said honestly. "But it's a subject I know something about. It's up to Jalad to listen or not."

Jinsei's eyes narrowed. Nami had absorbed his previous advice, returning the volley to him. He wiped the rag across Jalad's forehead once more, giving no further argument, teeth clenched tight in his jaw.

"I'm tired," Jalad said. His eyes sought Nami's. "Decide for me."

This was what she feared the most: the mantle of leadership spread across her shoulders. People expected her to know more simply because of her birth. None of the tutors in Yonakuni could prepare her for the pressure. They called her princess. Saviour. She was neither of those things.

Her one trait was stubbornness: headstrong in the face of all odds. She would not let Firth win. She would not let him cut them off, one at a time. She crushed her hand into Jalad's. This navigator whom she barely knew had put his faith in her. "Shapeshift, Jalad. I know you can do it."

She took Jinsei's hand and mashed their grips together, pulling away so the two men were clasped tight. A notion that had bothered her a year ago: human and folk together. It felt like such a straightforward thing now. More than that – it felt right.

She reached for water from the nearby strait, calling to it with her waterweaving. It trickled in streams up between fallen stones, threading dark channels across the yellow sandstone, like the veins of the haven pulsing with life. She directed it to cover Jalad's lower body, making the transformation easier.

Jalad's face strained, wincing as his eyes moved beneath closed lids. His grip tightened on Jinsei. Shapeshifting should not be that difficult, but Nami had never tried it when so heavily injured. She reached forward to second him, but before she could touch him, the naga seemed to gain strength from somewhere else. From Jinsei. His eyes flickered open, fastened on one person only. A small smile tugged at his lips. Beneath the blanket of water, his human legs merged, fusing together. The skin around his hips and below turned obsidian black, with a white diamond pattern mottling his long snake tail.

Nami let the water around him go, dripping off his reptilian scales and slipping down between the cracks around them. The wound was still there, below where his hips became a tail, but not bleeding so profusely. The width of his naga lower half had saved him: ballooning outwards like the hood of a cobra around his hips, wide enough to preserve him from what would otherwise have been fatal.

Nami closed her eyes and tilted her face up towards the sky. Spread her hands out at her sides and let the brisk breeze dry the saltwater from her skin. She had done it. Made a call that was for good. That was for . . .

Them.

Her eyes opened again. Jalad and Jinsei were still holding hands, a white-knuckled grip between them. Eun didn't know where to look, her eyes drawn towards the scene of affection as if to document it, then swivelling away again, blushing furiously. Zidane had sat himself down on a short basalt column, Mikayil standing beside him, warily guarding the group without ever being asked.

They needed to fight. This she would always believe to be true, no matter how Firth had twisted her ideals. But it was a different sort of fight. Firth's group had brought blades to the battlefield; Nami would have to go one better.

She finally had an idea how.

Chapter Thirty-Two

Another day, another opportunity to preen themselves in front of the public. Camera bulbs flashed and the audience at the debate swivelled, awaiting the parry. Reimi, one of the other candidates to be Minister of Fathomfolk, almost fell off her stool as she triumphantly threw the focus on Mira. "Kai, the previous Minister of Fathomfolk, *your husband*, declared in front of the whole city that he didn't give a damn about Tiankawi. Why should we believe you are any different?"

"As I have already responded," Mira said, trying and failing to keep the exasperation from her voice, "Kai sacrificed himself for this city. What further evidence do you require?"

"Convenient, wasn't it, for him to martyr himself. Didn't the *Manshu Chronicle* have evidence he was involved with the Drawbacks leader, Lynnette?" Reimi would not let go of the topic. Her confidence had grown after the third or fourth debate, focusing her efforts solely on destroying Mira's reputation.

"The *Manshu Chronicle* has no evidence whatsoever, as well you know." Mira pinched the bridge of her nose. "I'd prefer to return to the matters at hand. Your policies if you were elected Minister of Fathomfolk, for example. It's really not clear what they are."

"And yours?" rushed the Minister of Transport's nephew, another of the candidates. A thin, heron-faced man who had a tendency to join in a pile-on but had few ideas of his own.

"You were at the launch of the *Wayfarer*, were you not? I sent a scouting party to investigate the answering call."

"Then what? I would've sent the best of the kumiho city guard to destroy the titan out at sea before it ever reached our shores," the man said smugly.

"With what army? We have none. Ask Reimi; her mother is the Minister of Finance and knows the state of the city's coffers. We are struggling to fund the rebuild as it is; do you believe in the money tree stories from childhood?" Mira snapped. That clamped his mouth up, temporarily at least.

"We should be evacuating the city," Reimi said. "A fleet of ships to take us to a safe distance until we know the titan's intentions."

"Mm, a sound proposal. Except we do not have a fleet big enough to evacuate everyone. We did not before the tsunami and we certainly don't now. Kai gave us all gills. We can take the plunge into polluted waters if we must, but not yet. We know now that humans and folk are susceptible to gill rot – I do not believe in spreading panic just to win an election."

Mira stared until Reimi finally broke her gaze, flustered. The young woman might have some nerve, but she could not match the mettle of a cityborn estuary who had been standing up for herself her whole life. Mira felt the thrill of a win, turning her attention to another of the candidates. "Anwar, I believe you might know a thing or two about ships, though."

"Me?" Anwar said, startled into actually speaking. He had lurked in previous debates, clearly not wanting to be there. Rumour was that his husband, the Minister of Agriculture, had forced his hand in an attempt to get another vote on the Council.

"Yes, I've heard that the hull of your new family vessel is already packed full of dry supplies that would last months at sea."

Anwar did not even have the acumen to come up with a plausible excuse. "Indeed, and why not? If the titan does strike down the city, I want an escape route."

"And when you and your well-to-do friends have bought up all the usable long-haul vessels, driven up the price of food with your hoarding and abandoned Tiankawi, what exactly should the rest of us do?" Mira asked innocently. Anwar had no answer.

She leaned back, letting the other two candidates peck over his remains. It was a bitter victory. She did not enjoy playing their cruel games, but after they had cumulatively decided it was far simpler to chip away at her rather than each other, she needed to throw them another target.

The most frustrating thing about the endless debates was Samnang's marked absence. There was a chair, a podium for him at each session. Always glaringly empty, as if it did not warrant his precious time.

"Don't take it personally," Trish said, linking her arm through Mira's after the debate ended.

"They are the ones who keep making it personal. Dragging Kai's name through the mud ..." Mira drained the water flask her ama offered.

As if she didn't already have enough on her plate, the investigation into the Fenghuang's assassination had hit a dead end. Finding the head of the snake, the Cleaven mastermind behind it all, was proving more difficult than expected. Every lead had gone cold, with Gede reluctantly confiding that evidence had been tampered with by someone in the kumiho city guard. He wanted to hold onto the dragon matriarch for a while longer, so that those watching thought he was pursuing the wrong trail. The truth dangled frustratingly out of reach. Mira shook her head, trying not to dwell on it. "Let's talk about something else."

"The thing you sent me to do? I've done it," Trish said.

"The ... thing?" Mira repeated. She could feel a migraine

pulsing at the corner of her vision, hardly comprehending the words tossed at her. She did not recall setting her ama any task.

"You said you might as well try to recruit the Drawbacks." Trish opened her paper parasol, using the motion to hide her grin. The shade it provided was a welcome reprieve, although it did not lessen the stickiness on Mira's skin. Her shirt was damp all down her back, and even though she'd tied her hair up, it was slick around her neck and forehead. The pungent odour of fish from the market filled her nostrils. Her feet lingered before the fruit stall, a slight breeze running under the tattered canopy that protected the produce. The sweet mangoes and fragrant durians momentarily masked the other smells that jostled for attention as the stallholder offered her a lychee to taste. The prickly skin was rough against her palm, jolting as her ama's words sank in.

"I was . . . joking." Her voice was faint.

"Were you now? I had no idea." Trish's response too glib to be believed. "In any case, we have three."

"Three?"

"Former Drawbacks. To teach at the Tideborn Centre. That's what you wanted, isn't it?"

"Tideborn?" Mira tried again. The words were in a language she understood, and yet she could not parse sense from it.

"It's what they are calling the centre. It's certainly less of a mouthful than the Gill Adjustment Centre. Honestly, Mira, I warned you that name was awful."

"It's functional," she protested half-heartedly.

Trish wrinkled her nose. "There's function, and there's inspiration. You need both. No point doing all the hard work if no one is coming through the door, is there?"

Her logic was hard to argue with. Mira had said something offhand during one of her many visits to her mother's sampan, that was all. Might have mentioned that recruiting to the Gill Adjustment Centre was proving harder than expected. That they needed people who understood what it was to transform. Reform.

The stallholder looked between the two of them, waiting for a break in the conversation. She tapped at the bowl of lychees at her feet. Barked out a price. Without missing a beat, Trish snatched up one of the round shells and peeled it deftly. Plopped the white flesh in her mouth and spat the stone into her hand. "Sweet but overripe." The words bounced over Mira's head, the familiar haggling batting back and forth. Melody and counter-melody.

"These are all the way from Dhinduk! The lychee crop hasn't recovered since the tsunami. You know how hard they are to get hold of?" The stallholder's sales pitch was reasonable. The price of fresh fruit and vegetables had increased significantly since everything was in short supply.

"They are already rotting. I'll take half," Trish said, offering a couple of coins.

The stallholder ignored her, putting two red dragonfruit atop the pile. "I'll throw these in for free. Take the whole lot. What use is half to me?"

"We don't need that many. Look at her, she hardly eats," Trish said, dragging Mira unwillingly into the interaction. The stallholder evaluated her, nodding in agreement. Minister of Fathomfolk and captain of the chinthe meant nothing: auntie appraisal cared not for age or status.

"Dry them. Good to sweeten your tea in winter. You just need to peel them, put out a fine layer—"

"I know how to dry fruit! Not like those Jingsha types, who don't know how to wipe their own arses," Trish harrumphed. She had been cornered, her pride making her delve into her purse for a couple more coins. The stallholder smiled with a toothy grin, pouring the bowl of fruit into Trish's woven basket. She thrust the basket into Mira's hands. "Carry this for your ama. Show some respect."

Mira took it without complaint. She would have carried it anyway, but it wasn't worth pointing this out to the stallholder auntie. Glimmers of truth shone through. Mira might not have meant for Trish to recruit Drawbacks, but there was a logic to it.

"Tell me how," she said as they walked out of earshot of the stallholder.

"You know my sashiko group?"

"Since when did you do embroidery? I thought your eyesight was bothering you?"

"I can still have hobbies. Not just sitting in my sampan worrying about you all day," Trish said, as if affronted. "Anyway, I bumped into Ibhar there. You know, the Drawback dugong. She's only a few years older than me. Very good with a needle and thread."

Mira suspected her ama had only joined to connect with Ibhar, not for a love of ornate darning. It was a reasonable excuse, one she herself had neither considered nor would've feasibly managed: infiltrating a sewing group of elder folk.

"Anyway, she introduced me to a few others. A shellycoat called Coburn, and a couple of catfish, although the quiet one doesn't trust me. They are adrift. Without Lynnette, without Firth, they don't know what to do. It's been so long since they've had to think for themselves. They will listen to you. Show them the evidence you've gathered at the Tideborn Centre. Let them come to their own conclusions."

"What if those conclusions are more anger? The records aren't exactly glowing with praise about how we've been treated."

"No, but you're offering a solution they haven't considered before. That means more than you give yourself credit for." Trish gave her a look. The same one she gave when Mira complained that no one was listening to the needs of the folk; when she had torn up her second, or was it third, examination results, another apparent failure to meet the minimum requirements of

scholar-official; when she had been on the brink of refusing cap-
taincy, certain that her gills did more of the heavy lifting than her
attempts to enact real change. A look that said: it doesn't matter if
others don't believe in you, if *you* don't believe in you; I do. Trish's
love was unconditional and her belief unwavering.

Mira was still considering her ama's words as she crossed the
city in a waterbus. The cramped boats were the cheap way to get
around until the trams finally reopened. Barely seaworthy, they
spluttered between stops, heaving with passengers, in the aisle,
on the roof and dangling from the railing. It was not a pleasant
journey, but swimming all the way round would take hours and
increased exposure to gill rot. The districts passed in blurs of
broken buildings and bamboo scaffolding. The boat slid into
the next stop, graffiti sprayed on the side of a building catching
her eye. Alongside the usual tags and slurs, there was a quietly
devastating mural. Crashing waves filled the bottom of the scene,
but rising up from them were the silhouettes of humanoid figures
with wings. No, she realised, squinting, feathered gills stylised to
look like wings. Like they were birds emerging from the waterline.
She stood up, peering over an annoyed passenger's chair as the
waterbus reversed out.

Tideborn.

It had a ring to it.

Beating people over the head with a book only worked for so
long. There were other ways to change the narrative. To change
the public perception of gilled humans, from something to be
worried about to something joyful and empowering. Murals like
this, graffiti on a derelict building, were an excellent canvas for
the message. The people Kai had protected were the Tideborn. If
they could make that into a source of pride, then half her work
was done.

Chapter Thirty-Three

Mira's voice creaked as she stammered through her speech. Her notes dissolved before her eyes. Somehow her body continued, the words seared into her skull. Perhaps she even said them in the right order. None of the hundreds of audience members, the scholar-officials and guards, the newssheet journalists, the other folk and humans, seemed to notice her floundering in the shallow water. All she could hear was the click of camera shutters and the inordinately loud tapping in her own gills as she cleared her throat.

The ongoing investigation into the Fenghuang's assassination haunted her more than Kai's voice of late. The niggling feeling that while Jiang-Li wouldn't be so arrogant as to murder the leader of Tiankawi in broad daylight, her hands were not entirely clean. Quietly she tasked Lieutenant Tam to round up the rest of the Yonakunish delegation for a litany of minor offences: unpaid mooring fees, noise disturbance, lacking the correct paperwork. Her years of being entrapped in bureaucratic nightmares were suddenly of use. Some crimes they didn't have to fabricate: the border guard caught the delegates agitating bored youths with snappy slogans and a plentiful supply of spray cans; organising rallies under the pretence of soup kitchens in the submerged city. The hatched symbols of intersecting perpendicular lines graffiti-tagged across the city were not something as complex as she had initially guessed: simply three interlocked Fs.

Fathomfolk First.

She sat back down. It was over. No matter the outcome tomorrow, she had given it her all. Part of her, the part she dared not acknowledge for fear of the gnawing guilt, hoped that someone else would take the position of Minister of Fathomfolk, and the burden that weighed her down could be handed over. It had always been a heavy mantle, but lately it dragged, long and ragged, catching on every splintered plank along the walkway.

As Samnang took the podium, Mira forced herself to listen. After all the missed public debates, she was curious to hear his position. No one really knew what he stood for now. What angle he played. His daughter, Qiuyue, stood next to him. The girl Mira had rescued in the Boat Race riots no longer wore the short tiered skirts of childhood. She had stretched out, gangly legs and arms that looked disproportionate to her body as she entered those confusing teenage years. Her skirts were ankle-length now, in demure mint-green and pastel-blue hues. The standing collar of her dress swept into her braided hair, quite concealing the wraps around her neckline where her gills were. She stood with both hands together, a porcelain doll more than a person.

Next to her, Gede shifted his weight from foot to foot. He was in ceremonial kumiho blue, but his immaculate hair had fallen across his face, dishevelled by the hands he kept running through it nervously. He noticed Mira's gaze and held her eye for a long moment, trying to articulate something across the stage to her. She had neither the energy nor the interest to decipher it.

Samnang had always been tall, but today he looked like a blade honed at the whetstone. He said nothing, waiting until the murmur of conversation quietened down. Then slowly he unwound the white bandages from around his neck, hands moving round and round. He would not be hurried, despite the supposed time limit on each nominee's speech. Never doubted his right to speak, to govern, to lead.

He dropped the long strip on the floor next to him. Released, his gills stretched out like fledgling wings. They were discoloured, purple and almost scaly compared to his deep brown skin.

"Gills," he began. "We have them now. Whether we wanted them or not." He scanned the crowd, but failed to find what he sought. "Rotten. Infected. Altered. By people who claim to have our best interests at heart.

"I say no. No to fathomfolk, no to gills, no to this change that they forced on us. No!" There was a blade in his hand, a curved dagger that moved upwards without hesitation and slashed at one side of his neck. He threw the amputated gills into the audience; they seemed to fly for a second before thudding at the feet of the journalists in the front row. Blood poured out of the open wound, streaming down his neck and white tunic. Gasps and small shrieks of horror from the audience as they backed away from the scene of self-mutilation.

Mira took a few steps forward, feet moving automatically. He turned before she could get anywhere near him. Words blasting her like a wall of waterweaving. "Not our choice. Not our wish. We will not rot!"

The words of the Cleaven. Mira felt light-headed as the pieces came together. Samnang was one of them. No. He was not the type to follow a crowd: Samnang *led* them. The whole Minister of Fathomfolk nomination simply a stunt to amplify their platform. Something soared through the air towards her, and instinctively she caught it. Samnang's second set of gills lay cupped in the palm of her hand. His warm blood splattered across her face as the gills twitched with residual movement. She dropped them on the ground, her blood-smeared hands shaking in disbelief.

There were times, in the days before she had made her first bargain with Cordelia, when she had fantasised about cutting herself. Reaching down her own throat and ripping out her vocal cords and tongue. Disowning all the parts of herself that made her different, that made people look at her askance and talk to her in the patronising tones of ignorance. Slough the skin and emerge as something new. Someone ordinary. Someone who fitted in.

"Stop, no!" Gede shouted. The anguish cut through Mira's introspection. Samnang, his shoulders stained with crimson blooms, still brandished the knife, blade and handle slick with blood. He was gesturing with it, and his daughter moved towards him. The shock and horror that rippled through the audience did not seem to reach the girl. She tilted her head to one side, exposing her swan-like neck and the frilled gills beneath her ornate collar.

Mira bound towards Samnang just as Gede grabbed his father's arm, stopping it from swooping down, twisting until the blade clattered from Samnang's hand. Mira placed herself in front of Qiuyue, her voice finally rising above the chaos. "Hypocrite! It's her choice, not yours! Not a choice you should pressure her to make, here in front of this crowd, just to further your own sick agenda."

There was no word of command in her voice. No siren song. Simply the heartbreak of someone who knew what it was to be caught between two places. Qiuyue was still young. Still fluid in her understanding of the world. Taught only hate against a section of society she had barely had the chance to interact with would turn her hard and immovable. In that direction lay only misery.

"Don't lecture me on ... how to bring up ... my daughter." Samnang's words were a gasping hiss. He was forced finally to attempt to staunch the flow from the clumsy wounds at his neck, but blood continued to pour between his fingers.

Mira turned to look behind her, to offer comfort to Qiuyue whether the girl wanted it or not. The space was empty.

In all the confusion, the girl was gone.

Cordelia found it difficult to keep her colours under control. A riot was written across her skin. Vivid purple hues of bitter rancour swept up her limbs, clashing with pulsing white rings of terror. Samnang had meant to cut their daughter for some political stunt. She had seen him search for her face, for Serena, in the crowd. The message pointed: she is mine to mould in my image.

The seawitch had not moved. For once in her life, she had frozen. Unable to launch herself as Gede and Mira did to protect Qiuyue. Fear overrode everything, like all her ink had turned to poison. She used to scoff when the Council wives and husbands told stories about watching in slow motion as their precious babes tumbled off a climbing frame or stuck their hand in the fire. She had merely seen it as an excuse, a bad one at that, to alleviate the guilt. Their slow reflexes. She had felt it today, though, anchoring her eight limbs from her position at the rear of the crowd. She could not move. Could not breathe.

She could do nothing but watch.

Now she looked at the girl staring balefully at her. Somehow Cordelia had collected her wits. Slid between the legs of the other spectators, invisible as she mounted the stage and carried Qiuyue to safety. Here she was. Finally! Her little girl, reunited with her.

She did not take it personally when her daughter had kicked her in the face. They had all the time in the world to mend their bridges, to undo the harm her father had inflicted. She did not know her ama in this guise after all. The seawitch stayed back, blending the wild array of colours into a subdued burnt orange.

"I know you are frightened. I'm sorry I had to grab you like that. I was afraid you would be hurt."

"Aba would never hurt me," Qiuyue hurled across the distance between them. Her bottom lip trembled, but her chin was thrust defiantly outwards, masking the quiver in her voice. Cordelia was perversely proud of her.

"He was going to use that blade on you," she said, in what she hoped was her gentlest tones. Her loathing nevertheless seeped through. No denying his ill-intent as he'd waved the bloody knife at his daughter. People would see him as unhinged, unable to lead anything and unsafe to be raising children. Her mouth turned upwards despite herself, grateful he had handed her this easy win.

"I know," Qiuyue said, halting Cordelia's internal celebration. "He discussed it with me."

She tried to explain it in terms the girl would understand. "It would've hurt. The blood loss alone could kill you. And it's permanent. Gills don't grow back."

"I knew the risks. Aba told me. It was important for the cause that we separate ourselves from the bottom-feeding fish fuckers." She swore with casual ease, like it was something she'd been taught at school.

Cordelia held back the reflexive tirade of vitriol. She had to go slowly. She had learned that much after the aborted meeting at the fair. Gede had been right about the situation, even if he had not realised how far Samnang was embroiled with the Cleaven. Qiuyue was just a child, but she had been fed lies. Lies reflected through broken mirrors, close enough to reality to convince, distorted enough that Cordelia was the only monster in view.

"Remember the faces? You used to like them. They were always me, Qiuyue. I am still your ama, whatever face I wear. It is a gift. One you have too, if you want to learn it."

"Don't!" Qiuyue snapped. Cordelia had not even realised she had moved towards her, that her body had instinctively shifted into Serena's demure features. "Don't lie to me."

The seawitch did not know what to say, how to convince the girl. She longed to scoop her up, hold her in her arms. Bend over to kiss her ebony hair and inhale the smell of peach-scented soap and sticky coconut cakes. To push her somehow back into her womb so that they could start over again. Erase those deep cuts that were chiselled into stone.

Instead she showed her daughter her own hand, the white rings pulsing through her body, subdued but still present. She bit down on her fleshy palm below her thumb, her sharp teeth easily puncturing the skin. Blue blood dripped from the nicks, trailing down her hand and wrist. "This blood runs in my veins. In yours too."

"Lies. I've bled before. My blood is red. I am human."

"Your blood looks red because of the charm around your neck. One I made for you many moons ago, to allow you to pass as human."

Qiuyue's eyes darted, blinking rapidly as she parsed the new information. Her hands fiddling with the necklace subconsciously before she caught herself. "Aba said you would twist the truth. That you have been for years. That we would never know for certain when you started impersonating Ama." Her words cut across the distance. "Tell me, when did you murder her? I want to remember my last embrace with her."

"The day of the press conference. That was our last embrace. When I asked you to pack, to leave with me. Every embrace was mine. It's me, Qiuyue, it's always been me!" Cordelia resisted the urge to reach out with her lower limbs. To touch a strand of her daughter's hair; to rub her cheek. She had taken every moment for granted, too busy planning for the future to enjoy her daughter's adulation while she had it. Even though she was right there, Qiuyue might as well be a million miles away.

"How can I believe anything a saltie says?"

Cordelia did not cry. Her precious water was already spilt: the blue blood dripping onto the floor, the black ink lying dormant for her next bargain. She would not waste more on tears. "If I release you, you will go to your aba. You will let him cut and mutilate you and hate all that is folk. All that is you."

"Yes," Qiuyue said, as if it were no decision at all. Her trust so completely misplaced.

"Then I cannot release you." It was not the outcome she wanted. Not the one her daughter deserved, but she would rather Qiuyue hate her and be safe than the alternative.

"Let me go!" the girl protested. She must've seen something in Cordelia's features that frightened her. Dawning on her, perhaps, that no one had yet come to her rescue.

Qiuyue's voice rang in the seawitch's head, but her mind was made up. She turned her back, locking and barring the door behind with a slam. She pretended not to hear her daughter's screams.

Chapter Thirty-Four

The massive chandelier at the Jingsha tram station had been remodelled. Nestled among the crystal shards they had manage to salvage, a blue-green sphere of fused sea-glass pebbles sat like an egg in a nest. The marble floor had been repaired with golden seams, the fractures displayed proudly. This was where Tiankawi nearly fell. This was where it was rebuilt.

Mira moved towards the red-ribboned carriage where Gede and the director of the tram company were idly talking. The director's small talk stammered to a halt as she came within earshot. Gede's kumiho blue tailored coat was a trim fit, the tassels of his Minister of Defence epaulettes perfectly framing his shoulders. Despite everything that had happened, or perhaps because of it, he had been voted back into post with a landslide. No doubt about it, even though he had not officially been sworn in yet.

They were touting him as the fresh face of the Council, a voice for change, even though he was from one of the elite families in the city. In Gede's Jingsha accent, the same things Mira had been saying for years were suddenly palatable.

The Minister of Fathomfolk position, in contrast, the one that no one had even cared about until several months ago, was a shambles. After Samnang's gill-mutilating stunt, the Council had agreed to postpone the vote.

Gede made room at his side. Mira pretended not to notice the tramway director take a few steps back, as if whatever she had was catching. Samnang's performance had revived a distaste towards fathomfolk, the chasm wider than ever. At first the newssheets declared he was mentally unstable, the actions of a man grieving for his dead wife and abducted daughter, even though the abduction had happened afterwards. Then a narrative evolved. Sympathy like weeds between the flagstones. The Cleaven had friends in high places. He cared enough to hurt himself. As if folk had not suffered silently for decades. Goldfish memories. This was different. This was something people could empathise with.

Something human.

Newssheet after newssheet threw their full weight and support behind this self-mutilating widower and grieving father. Inside, Mira screamed. She had sacrificed more to a city that barely paused to notice as it swallowed all of her down. Sometimes she wished she had a haven to pledge herself to instead; but as Jiang-Li had reminded her, she had no such roots.

The only home she knew was here.

"Minister Mira. I wasn't sure you would be joining us." The director recovered politely.

"I'm glad to see this essential service up and running again." The smooth lines came more easily to her lips these days. It was easier to fake enthusiasm when she kept her comments for the most part honest.

"Indeed. Now the northern lines have reopened, the city will start moving again."

"Is there a timescale for the other lines? Folk in the southern districts would be glad to be reconnected."

She had her own reasons for asking. She had quietly set up apprenticeship projects in Qilin and Seong districts. The Drawbacks had mostly responded well to rehabilitation efforts, integrating well into the Tideborn Centre. But it was frustratingly slow. She could not reach everyone this way. People – fathomfolk and human alike – struggled with what had happened at the tsunami. Uncertain about what the future looked like and therefore clinging to a past that had never truly existed.

"All the districts are important to us. We are hoping to get to the south, of course. Just as soon as the … most essential areas are reconnected."

"Of course. You mean the industrial heartlands to the west, right? And the port at Seong, for goods and services, must be a priority."

The director gave a faint smile, waving down one of the servers with a tray of drinks. He grabbed two, thrusting one like a poisoned chalice into her hands. "You really must excuse me."

Mira watched him go, amused but unsurprised at his response.

"We need to talk," Gede said, steering her by the elbow towards the pristine tram carriage. The glass had been polished to a mirror shine and a fresh lick of yellow paint coated the exterior. They pretended to admire it.

Mira sipped the overly sweet cocktail. "Congratulations, by the way, on the votes."

A boyish grin lit up his face. "Thank you."

"You're the son of the previous minister. Easy on the eye. Human." Satisfaction mixed with guilt as Gede's expression fell. That had been unnecessarily harsh. Gede had proven himself, little by little, to be a force for change. She would do well not to destroy all of that because of things outside his control.

A small brass plate near the carriage door caught her eye. *In memory of Hue, beloved wife of Director Ramon.* They had all lost someone: Gede had lost his mother, had he not? "I'm sorry, that was uncalled-for. You must miss her too, your mother?"

"I … guess," Gede said after a long pause. "I'm not sure if I miss her so much as wonder if I ever knew her at all. Was it just another mask she showed me, or the person underneath. Does that make any sense?"

"Sometimes we keep up the masks for so long that we forget we are still wearing them."

Gede read something in her tone, in her face perhaps. He turned to her fully. "Are you okay, Mira?"

The question confounded her. What a peculiar thing to ask. She had heard it often enough from her ama, from Nami before the *Wayfarer* set sail. Brushed off their concern as a nicety. A remark about the weather. It hit differently coming from Gede. He did not know her well, and yet those words struck an unexpected blow in the centre of her chest.

"No," she confessed in a whisper. Before common sense could stop her, she continued, "I don't remember when I last ate, when I last slept. Kai haunts me, everywhere I go."

As soon as the words left her mouth, she regretted them. What sleep-deprived foolishness had convinced her to spill this to Samnang's son, at a public event? One kind word and she'd immediately fallen apart. Before Gede could respond, before he could do anything else that might dissolve her into a flood of tears, she moved the conversation on. "Has there been any news about your sister?"

"No leads. I mean, no substantial ones. As yet. Still investigating." He did not comment at the abrupt change of topic. His voice rose, just in case it was not obvious he was talking a pack of lies.

"You are worse at this than me." Back on an even keel, Mira tied down her emotions with slipknots.

His voice dropped, quiet enough that only she could hear. "She's safe. It's ... complicated. Family stuff. And if she remains missing, she won't be dragged into *this*." He sighed, desolate. "We are not so dissimilar, you and I."

It was the second time in as many months that he had said something along those lines. "In what way?" Mira asked.

Gede loosened his collar, a red flush around his neck and up around his ears. "I ... I've never felt like I belonged. Like I was hiding part of myself. For years I just chose to ignore it. Drink enough, party enough and the questions tend to take a back seat. But something happened after the tsunami. Seeing gills on everyone, everywhere. It felt like I didn't have to pretend any more."

Mira arched an eyebrow, but Gede was earnest, leaning in conspiratorially until their foreheads were almost touching. People around were watching, glancing out of the corner of their eyes and drawing their own conclusions. Whether deliberate or not, Gede was giving an impression of intimacy that would send tongues wagging and newssheets not far behind.

His gills moved under his collar. They looked different to the external gills of most other humans, but like many, he had kept them well hidden. He took her silence as assent. "I'm scared to say it out loud."

"Say it," Mira said. Something in him was vulnerable, a limited window where the doors were open.

"I feel like what I am, what I truly am ... is fathomfolk."

"What?" Her tone was more cutting than intended. "What do you mean, you feel like fathomfolk? Because you have gills? You do realise that being folk isn't window dressing? You can't just *feel* like it."

"No, you misunderstand—"

"*You* misunderstand. Being folk is about culture, community, it's ... eugh, it's more than gills! More than our music or food or whatever is in trend right now. It is something that cannot be separated from our identity, from what makes us *us*." The semantics of the election debates boiled inside her, released like scalding steam. Gede drooped, his nerve gone, doors slamming back shut. Perhaps the force of her condemnation was heavy-handed, but she was not going to say sorry. Not for any of them. Sand gods give her strength, Gede, her only ally on the Council, was some Lakelander idiot.

She swallowed down her discomfort, burying it alongside the

other distasteful compromises she had made over the years. She was not in a position to turn away his support, but she had been a fool for expecting friendship to come of it. To expect anything from someone born into the elite of the city.

"Let's just stick to Council business," she said with her brightest, most polite veneer. She even gave him a smile, albeit one that resembled a grimace more than anything.

"I hear you. Loud and clear. But I do have a proposal. A *business* proposal," Gede quickly added as the Minister of Finance walked towards them. "Someone will reach out. Promise me you'll at least listen?"

Before Mira could ask anything further, a few of the other scholar-officials came over to offer congratulations. She had monopolised enough of his time, and let herself be swept back into the crowd.

The tramway director's speech was brief, the Minister of Transport's less so. They droned on for so long that someone in the crowd nodded off, waking only as those around applauded after the ribbon-cutting. The most esteemed guests were ushered into the first tram. Mira was thankful when the doors slid closed, leaving her milling with the junior officials on the platform for the next.

The tram she finally joined was four carriages long. It was easier to move between the new cars, something she took full advantage of to raid the buffet table. Thankfully, most of the junior officials had neither the nerve nor the interest to engage her in conversation. She pretended a purpose with her plate of food, seeking a space to curl up. Too much socialising rendered her prickly to the touch, a spiny sea urchin.

The tram line ran north into Manshu district. From their elevated position, the crags of the Peak mountain loomed into view, the harsh rocky face seemingly within touching distance. The mountain had always been a familiar part of Mira's childhood.

While towers rose and the skyline was forever changing, the Peak was the one constant. Except since the tsunami, since the death of their sand god, the mountain had become unstable. Landslides had become commonplace despite the dearth of earthquakes. The houses around the Peak's base had been abandoned altogether after a dozen workers were crushed in the rubble. It was unclear if the mountain would continue its rapid erosion, discontented until it had levelled itself altogether.

In the final carriage, there were only a couple of waiting staff. They glanced up at Mira in surprise as they tidied away used cutlery and drinkware. She made a vague gesture, one that said *don't mind me*. Squeezing herself into the window seat in the far corner, she savoured the assortment of steamed and fried dumplings.

"Minister." One of the servers offered her a cup of seaweed tea. Mira took it gratefully, the aroma of the smoked kelp filling her nose. She looked up, the words of thanks on her tongue, to catch horizontal pupils in the server's eyes. It was only the two of them in the carriage now; and the only door out was behind Cordelia.

"Brewed just the way your ama likes it." In outward appearance, the seawitch was a siyokoy. A dorsal fin ran from the top of her head down the back of her neck, with smaller pectoral fins concealing her ears. Her eyes were huge and globular, her skin reptilian in hues of green, taking on the appearance of the notoriously taciturn deep-sea merfolk.

"Poisoned?"

"Only if you'd like it to be."

"Wait, are *you* the person Gede mentioned? The business proposal? Oh no. No and thank you. I'll be going now." Mira put the cup down on the seat.

"Sit down, *Minister*. I'll admit we don't always see eye to eye."

"Eye to eye?" Mira's voice rose with incredulity. Neither Trish nor Jiang-Li was here; she did not have to be civil on this occasion. "You cashed in your open bargain. I have not even touched the fugu trade. I know you are thriving, Cordelia, and I know my hands are tied. Titans below, there's no point in even feeling guilty about it."

"For that, you have my gratitude. But I'm here to discuss our common friend."

"Friend?" Mira did not understand. The seawitch rubbed at her gill lines, her double rows of shark teeth bared as she did so. What friends did they have in common? Cordelia cared only for the profit, not the politics. Here she was, disguised as a siyokoy, choosing to keep others away with the appearance of a folk that was maligned even within freshwater communities. She wanted to sense their fear.

Their hate.

It dawned on Mira. Trish was the one person who did not judge on outward appearances. Who saw the best in everyone. "What do you want with my ama?"

"What if I could reverse her gill rot? Everyone's gill rot." Cordelia brandished a small jar of pills, the purple spheres rattling against the glass. "With this."

Mira unscrewed the lid. The pungent smell of herbs was overwhelming, but beneath it was a more familiar smell. Like her ama's snow ear soup. "This isn't fugu."

"No."

"Nor is it the dull weed you've been selling," she pointed out. She had the reports on Arkaig's new side-hustle in legitimate painkillers, and despite herself, she hoped it succeeded. The seawitch was not the folk businessperson she would have chosen, but all the same, she wanted some freshwater folk to prove it *could* be done.

"Also no." Cordelia toyed with her, words clipped so Mira had to do the heavy lifting.

Mira tipped some of the pills into her hand. The size of salmon roe but hard as seeds.

"So what is it?"

"Secret formula." Cordelia winked. "But it works. It's reversed the effects of gill rot in a dozen fathomfolk so far."

Mira could barely hear her above the din of her rapidly beating heart. Reversing gill rot. It was … impossible. They had been trying for decades. But no, that was a lie. *Folk* had been trying. The Council, the humans, had not bothered to spend much on it, an obscure condition that didn't impact on them, after all. Her ama could be free of it, finally. And not just her. "It works on humans too?"

"I don't see why not. But to know for sure would need a larger-scale trial, funding, licensing … Perhaps Auntie Cordelia's Special Formula? Auntie Delia's Gill Rot Cure-all? I like the sound of that." The seawitch held up her hand as if envisaging a sales banner before her. She nodded in satisfaction. "It's not just for us, saltlick. It's for them too. Your poor unfortunate little humans who don't know what to do with themselves. The Cleaven and your Tideborn students alike. This changes everything."

Mira read between the lines, her mouth going dry. It was the one thing that could take all the wind from the Cleaven's sails. Their rhetoric was compounded by panic over gill rot: take that away and humans having gills could be something positive again.

She imagined districts prospering under the waterline, filled with humans and folk. Money finally being funnelled into submerged housing and healthcare. A bridge of understanding built on shared experience. A fate that could be far more alluring than the divisive hatred the Cleaven and Fathomfolk First offered.

For that, Mira was willing to bargain.

"If what you are implying is true … *if* these pills works – and I will be thoroughly checking it – what do you want in return?"

"I want to take down Samnang."

Mira blinked. She had been mentally preparing for all sorts, but not for the level of vitriol that oozed from the seawitch's pores. Whatever Cordelia had to do with the former Minister of Defence, it was clearly personal. If she had learned anything from the seawitch, it was that when emotions were high, people did not make the best decisions.

"On one condition. Wind down the fugu sales within the year. You sell the dull weed, this gill rot cure too if it passes all inspections. You will get on every shelf in every healing house across Tiankawi. Licensed. Regulated. But the fugu goes. Completely. Off the walkways, out of the water – it stops. That is non-negotiable." Mira made the most audacious demands, deciding it was worth a shot. Cordelia would negotiate it away anyway, nibble at the edges until everything was much smaller.

"Deal," the seawitch said without hesitation, pulling out one of her ubiquitous scrolls. Mira did her best to hide her shock. It was too easy. Whatever her history with Samnang, was Cordelia willing to give away her entire illegal empire for it?

Chapter Thirty-Five

Cordelia set the various items on the tablecloth. It made the room a little cheerier, the bright batik patterns swirling across the surface. Candied lotus seeds, whitebait in chilli and lime, rice balls with sour plums and steamed water chestnut dumplings filled the small table. The smell was enough to make her mouth water, and it would be difficult for her daughter to resist. Qiuyue looked wild, her eyes bloodshot as she huddled in the far corner, hair falling in greasy strands across her face. Cordelia had set up a pallet for her to sleep on, but she had managed to twist one of the wooden legs free and had used it to dig into the gills at her neck. They still looked infected, wood splinters embedded despite Cordelia's attempts to remove them.

"I've brought your favourites. The sweet shop in the Meridian building closed down, but I was told these are very similar." Cordelia popped one of the candied lotus seeds in her mouth. The powdered sugar was a mite too much for her taste buds, but she chewed on it anyway, simulating enjoyment. It was an act. Wasn't everything? "The dumplings are fresh from the street seller on the Arimo Bridge. The lady who can wrap them with one hand. Do you remember how I used to have to drag you away from watching? I got you a double portion."

Qiuyue had moved just an inch or two forward, eyes trained warily on Cordelia like a wild animal. Since bringing her here, the seawitch had tried – as Serena, as Samnang, as her governess, even as Finnol – to talk to her daughter. Each attempt met only with distrust and barbs. In the last few days she had dropped all the disguises, letting the girl see her true form, even though horror was illuminated in her eyes. At least the disgust had started to lessen, her daughter growing accustomed to how the seawitch's lower limbs slipped across the floor tiles. Sometimes she was tempted to creep in, camouflaged, to watch the girl sleep, as she had done when Qiuyue was little. When all she had to worry about was colds and grazed knees. The maternal guilt tangled worse than any fishing net around her.

She sipped her seaweed tea, pretending a nonchalance she did not feel as her three hearts thudded in time. No sudden movements. Nothing to scare her daughter back to the dank corner of the room. A hand slipped out of the dirty dress to grab at one of the rice balls. Swiftly as it had emerged, it sank back behind the curtain of hair. Cordelia willed her daughter to eat, to gain just a little energy, enough to listen, enough to understand. She would bring all the rice balls in Tiankawi if it would win her over.

"I've brought fresh clothes. And a basin of water. You can get out of these rags, feel more like yourself again."

Qiuyue gagged, spitting out grains of sticky white rice. She stuck two fingers in her mouth, bringing up the meagre meal with a retching vomit. "You poisoned me!"

"No, no, Qiuyue, you've got it wrong. It's not poison, I would never—"

"Something was in that, something wrong." The girl was certain.

Cordelia cursed internally. She had been confident there would be no taste, no smell to discern a difference. That she could get away with one tiny subterfuge today. "It was just a sedative, honestly. Strong dull weed. I just ... You needed to sleep. I thought ... I hoped—"

"Can you hear yourself? You're mad. A deranged bottom-feeder."

"I am your ama!" Despite telling herself to remain calm, Cordelia heard her voice hurtling across the gaping expanse.

"You are not. You think my ama drugs her daughter? For the last time, she is dead! What sort of sick relationship did you think we had?" Qiuyue's voice cracked, parched despite the water Cordelia had left her.

She had thought watching from afar, watching Samnang poison their daughter's pure hearts, was the worst that could happen. But here she was, and at this distance there was no wall between them to temper the pain. The full force of it blistered and charred across every inch of her being. She wanted to haul Qiuyue to her feet, shovel food and water down her throat. Scrub her clean and order her to bed. But forcing her to do anything would simply push her further away.

Straight back to Samnang's embrace.

She pushed away the feeling of desperation. "The food is there if you want it," she said, no longer pretending enthusiasm. As she turned, she heard Qiuyue's screams of frustration. The table upended, contents scattering on the floor. She should probably take away the tablecloth. Something else that could be used to self-harm. But she was too tired to do anything other than lock the door behind her; containing the mess in one tidy box so that it didn't spill into the rest of her life. She just needed a moment.

Gede stood outside.

Her son's reaction was written across his youthful face. Distress. Revulsion. He swallowed and said nothing, turning to leave. It would have been easier if he'd berated her. At least one of her children would be talking to her.

"What else would you have me do?" she demanded, the words more to herself than him.

"Let her go." He said it as if it was that simple. Blowing

dandelion seeds to the wind and letting them drift, never minding where they ended up.

"She'll go back to him. To his brainwashing."

"And?" Gede's tone was incredulous. He loomed taller than he had ever done before. The kumiho blue had always looked awkward on him, like playing dress-up in his father's clothes. At some point, without her noticing, he had shed the tight shell and grown into a new one. "I thought she'd be safer here, away from it all. I was a fool. You manipulate, Aba manipulates, how is it any different?"

"He is teaching her to hate a part of herself."

"You taught us to hide it," Gede countered. It was clear now, like the storm had suddenly passed, clouds parting to let rays of sunlight shine down. He hated her. Qiuyue hated her. For what she had done to keep them safe. To ensure they would never be at the bottom of the barrel. They thought she was cold. Just like the stories said. Seawitches cared for nothing but the bottom line.

"I taught you to survive. Cutting off your gills is not survival."

"You cannot keep her locked up for ever. You cannot conceal every blade in the whole city to protect her. What you need is her trust."

All she had ever wanted was for them to be stronger. Better. Successful. She had sacrificed so they would succeed in a city that did not expect people that looked like them to amount to anything. Being an indulgent fool was only an option for people whose place was secure. Cordelia didn't have that luxury. Her children hated her, but they would survive *because* of her. Look at Gede, at the fine young man he had turned out to be. He would never thank her for it. He probably thought his success was in spite of rather than due to his upbringing. Cordelia alone knew the truth.

"Trust is not a trait our family is known for," she said, inclining her head towards the bolted door behind her. Gede looked like he would protest, make one more bid to change her mind. She slid against the wall, not waiting for him to move aside. The desire to get out, to escape from the hounding, was a flight-or-fight response. Everything she had done, thrown back in her face.

He called one more time. "Ama?"

Cordelia looked, a reflex despite her whole body telling her not to. Gede wore Kai's face. Imperfectly formed: the water dragon's nose had not been so long, his topknot not so sloppy. Once upon a time, shapeshifting had been their special time together. When she had unclasped the charm from around his neck and taught him the basics, practising the different faces all through his teenage years until he was exhausted with perfecting them, until he had thrown it all aside, saying he would never be good enough for her, so why bother trying.

"You're fucking with Mira, aren't you? Impersonating Kai." Her son's voice emerged through Kai's forlorn face. The auditory illusion was discombobulating. Cordelia's skin rippled blue and black before she could hold it back. She had given him an answer without speaking. He shook his head. "You want my help against the Cleaven, against Aba – stop messing with Mira."

"What does it matter to you?" Cordelia cocked her head as the Kai mask wavered a little on her son's features. She had assumed Gede was like her, uninterested in romance or physical relations unless there was leverage there; but perhaps the silly fool had fallen for the chinthe captain after all.

"Because I want my allies alert and watching my back. Not driven to distraction by ghosts at every skybridge. Nothing else."

His head swivelled back towards the locked door. He did not demand that she let Qiuyue go. Did not even look in and check his sister was okay. Showing his face would imply he was part of it, that he had taken sides with Cordelia against Samnang. He did not want to show his hand yet. Gede had learned a little about the game, but not the risks needed to win.

"A deal. I will stop harassing Mira if you stop questioning my methods," Cordelia proposed. She gave him exactly what he wanted: something to ease his conscience and the plausible deniability he sought.

He considered her offer, or at least pretended to mull it over. She had taught him that. He offered his hand to shake, pulling back when she extended her own. "And you hand over Kai's voice."

"You don't trust me?"

"Trust is not a trait our family is known for." He threw her own words back at her.

Cordelia shrugged as if it was of no consequence. "The novelty was wearing off anyhow."

They shook on it, Gede's eyes dancing. He thought it easy, striking a bargain with his seawitch mother. Charging in to protect his new friend. Except the damage was done now, whether Cordelia bothered to continue the charade or not. Mira would always be haunted. Meanwhile, Cordelia had gained the upper hand.

Samnang would pay for turning their daughter against her with a gift in kind.

Chapter Thirty-Six

"Isn't it just an observation tower?" Nami asked, squinting up at Manannán Keep. The same tall tower Firth had thrown Rannoch from. She shuddered.

"Ostensibly," Jalad said, "but Firth and his lot seem to think there's a passageway down. A shrine room."

"A means of communicating with our slumbering host. It makes sense," Eun said. Perhaps the Peak had been that for Tiankawi also. People had forgotten, deliberately or otherwise, that they owed their survival to the titan beneath the foundations of the city.

"That's where they've holed themselves up. The one place we could actually communicate with the sand god." Nami chewed on her lower lip.

"Easy enough to avoid," said Mikayil.

"No." Nami's words formed steps along a treacherous path. "That's exactly what they're expecting of us. Hiding until the titan ploughs straight into Tiankawi and destroys everything. We take the fight to them."

"Fight?" Zidane said with incredulity. He gestured around. What army? What skills? Their small, broken group didn't exactly inspire confidence. A corrupt politician, a severely injured naga, a quiet chinthe, a schoolteacher and a librarian. Not Nami's first choice for a team, but she could sit and complain about it all day or she could do something. She would always choose the latter.

"There's more than one way to fight. We have our differences, but none of us wants Tiankawi to be destroyed. It's a mess, but it's *our* mess. Our home, our families and friends. We have that in common. Firth has nothing but doubts. Hate." She caught Eun's eye, the other woman's expression encouraging her. "He hates humans. He hates fathomfolk. All he knows is how to manipulate and lie. There is no trust there. We can use that."

A painful silence followed her impromptu speech, one that made her certain she had said the wrong thing. Screwed up yet again. Against the odds, it was Zidane who broke the lull. "Well, you all think the Council is full of self-serving liars. Let's put my experience to good use, shall we?"

Jinsei and Jalad were delighted to spend more time together, palm to palm under Nami's tutelage. Jalad waterweaved handfuls of seawater from one rock pool to another. Then it was the schoolteacher's turn. He squinted at the innocuous puddle, brows scrunched as if the vein popping on his forehead had the strength to lift the liquid. After a number of minutes, Jalad yelped, shaking out the hand Jinsei had squeezed too tightly.

"Anything?" Zidane asked hopefully as he watched. His own lessons had been just as dire, except he was significantly less enthusiastic about having to hold hands.

"I saw a drip, I'm certain of it!" Jinsei pointed emphatically at a squiggle of a damp shadow on the stone.

Jalad rubbed the back of his head with embarrassment. "That might have been me. I got too excited to hold back."

As they argued good-naturedly, Nami decided it was a good a time to break. She moved away from the others towards the water's edge. Her waterweaving pulled at the saltwater and lifted streams of it overhead. She held it between her fingers, glittering rivulets running wet around her wrists and hands. Teaching waterweaving was difficult, but practising it gave her some peace.

Eun was behind her. It wasn't a smell or a sound, simply that invisible thread tying them together. Even in the abyssal darkness of the deepest oceans, Nami would be able to sense her.

"You might need these," Eun said, putting a couple of hollowed-out gourds on the ground at her feet. The librarian had sensed her task without being told, instinctually knowing.

Nami pulled her hands further apart, stretching the streams of water like they were on a loom. In the Academy they had practised turning water into ice. Useful as weapons or barriers, waterweaving in this way came easily. The other direction – changing water to vapour – was rarely used. Scalding someone, hitting them with a water dart that burned as it pierced, was not something Nami had ever grown confident at. In the factories, they hired folk who could heat vats of water, for distilleries or manufacturing. People like Firth would be good at this, she thought with an internal bitterness. Vapour took up more area, harder to manage as it spread like wisps of clouds. Easy to lose control over and send boiling rain lashing down on those below.

"I might hurt you," she warned.

"No, you won't."

The conviction in those three words made her resolve crack. After all the hours of fruitless lessons, she could feel the doubts pressing at her skull. "How are you so certain? You've seen my track record."

"I've seen someone backed into a corner. Whenever you've made the choices for yourself – to help, teach, listen – I've never been afraid."

You should be. Nami swallowed the words down, turning away as if to block out the noise, as if she could hold her breath and deny herself air. Spreading her hands as wide as they would go, she formed the water into a sheet like misted glass between them. It vibrated against her weaving, wanting to bunch back together and find the natural channels down towards the water's edge. It took all her focus to refuse that pull, to instead send a vibration through it, faster and faster, until the liquid hissed and turned to steam. The water vapour formed a dense cloud. Heat dampened her brow and made her shirt cling against her skin.

A movement out of the corner of her eye nearly made her drop it all. Eun had taken a step closer. Another.

"What are you doing?" Nami hissed.

"Trusting."

"I've already told you, I can't promise—"

"But I can." The crinkle of fabric was Nami's only warning, and then she felt Eun's body press against her back, her arms wrap around Nami's middle. The touch sent a crystal clarity through her whole body. Every inch of her skin glowed where it touched Eun's. Tingled in response to the blanket hold she found herself in. She closed her eyes and wondered if she could bottle this moment, hold it for ever in the storehouse of her memory. She could sense Eun's waterweaving pool, untapped and deep as a well, the strength of it seconding her precarious hold on the water vapour, allowing her to loop the nebulous mass around and cool it enough to pour it into the empty gourds.

Eun's hands stayed on her as all the water was secured. Drinkable now, the salt crystals left behind on the ground. Nami's whole body shook, although she did not know if it was from the waterweaving or from the way Eun was looking at her. A confession spilled from her lips. "I am not Kai." The grip she had held so tightly loosened. Like letting a fish off the hook and watching it continue to struggle, not realising the barb had already gone. "I'm not the water dragon my brother was. My mother is. The stuff of legends. The one with all the answers. I'm ... broken."

Eun held her so that their heads bent towards each other and their brows touched. Her hair tickled at Nami's cheek and her breath warmed the air between them. She leaned into that secret space, talking to the hollow of Nami's collarbone. "We are all broken. Crumbling away in the tide. But I will be here holding on at the shoreline. For as long as you need."

"You are my mangrove forest?" Nami said, unable to help herself. Eun had slipped back into her overwrought language. Nami's defence mechanism was to be glib. The librarian wrinkled her nose, not at all put out by the remark.

"Yes. I like that." She contemplated the words as if they were much more than a flippant comment. The tangled roots of mangrove trees slowed the movement of the tide, stabilising the land beyond. Ecosystems for marine and land animals alike, providing shelter and food. "I'd like us to grow roots together, you and I." Sunlight played across her face like the sky itself was in collusion. It dappled her skin, running across her delicate cheekbones and swooping down her jawline.

She closed her eyes, face tilted up. Her plum lips aching to be kissed. To seal the promise that had formed between them. Nami was halfway there, moving before her brain caught up.

She froze. It was all too much. The way Eun looked at her as if she had discovered a new colour in the depths of her eyes. The touch that brought her so much comfort and yet scared her, knowing the mess she made of things. She could not risk Eun becoming a pawn, not when she had seen what Firth had done to Dan, what he would do to manipulate and control her. It would not be fair on Eun, on the rest of the survivors, on the task Mira had set for her.

She forced herself to step back, her hands empty when they had been so full. Eun's eyes fluttered open. Disappointed.

"I can't give you what you need. Not right now, Eun. Not while Firth is out there." If he had his way, what future would there be? One where Tiankawi was destroyed, or one where Nami had to sacrifice herself as a pearl to prevent it. Either way, she could not think past the current crisis.

Footsteps disturbed them before Eun could try to change her mind. Mikayil cleared his throat. "The message has been sent."

Nami nodded, picking up the sloshing gourds at her feet. "Right," she said, as if Eun did not long for her with eyes that hungered. Ignoring the distracting response of her own body in kind. As if she had not torn out her own aching heart and locked it within an iron safe, walls too thick and dull to acknowledge any more of its persistent beating. "He acknowledged?"

"In all truth, I couldn't tell," Mikayil said.

"We'll have to assume he got it. Tell the others the plan goes ahead."

"And if we are wrong?"

"Then we come up with a new plan." Nami cocked her head to one side, nonchalantly, as if she had all the confidence in the world. If she could convince the others, perhaps she could even convince herself.

Chapter Thirty-Seven

Gede closed the door to the visiting room quietly behind him, back turned for a long moment as he composed himself. Samnang glanced up, but then returned to examining his neck in the huge wall mirror, craning like an injured swan. The healer had reopened the wound and cleaned the infected area before sewing it back up. The skin was tighter on the left-hand side, as if someone was pulling at him to turn his head, looking for something just beyond sight. He smiled as he placed his fingers on the swollen stitches, proud of the ugly black knots that bristled like barbed wire.

"They kept me away from mirrors until now, you know. But I rather like the effect."

Samnang could not be kept in an ordinary healer house or prison cell. The Council had granted the Minister of Defence unprecedented powers to keep his whereabout from the Cleaven and the press, moving him to a new location every few days.

"Aba," Gede said, hands behind his back.

"It's been years since you've called me that. Even then it usually preceded a guilty confession. Crashed the family boat, drank the house dry of wine." Samnang stood up, cricking his neck as he moved through his warm-up exercises. Sliding his feet and arms from first to second position, his movements practised and assured. Every morning it had been his routine: through monsoon rain and sticky heat. Ten set positions that remained unaltered, uninterrupted by the rest of the household, on pain of his wrath for the rest of the day. It was uncannily familiar, even when they stood in this unfamiliar room. A goldfish bowl of a locked room in an obscure healer's facility. "So, what is it this time? I take it you've failed to recover your sister?"

"I know where she is."

"That's not exactly impressive. She's with the witch, of course. Where else would she be?"

"She is with her mother." Gede's eyes flashed in warning despite trying to keep his cool.

"Gede, that octopus is no mother to you or Qiuyue. You know that. She manipulated all of us to get her own way. Lied to you. Qiuyue understood. She saw that the Cleaven are the only way forward."

"Qiuyue is a child! A confused girl whom you have done nothing to educate. Nothing to prepare for the difficulties of this world. All Ama wanted to do was protect her!" Gede's breath was ragged, his voice bouncing off the thin walls of the room. He saw himself in the mirror, a scared boy playing at being an adult. He gritted his teeth.

"*I* protected her, not that damned seawitch! I kept Cordelia's secret long after I had figured it out. I thought she was having an affair, besotted husband that I was. Ready to ensnare a couple of lovers tangled up in bedsheets. Too unimaginative to consider the truth was much more terrifying. And then? Finding out that my dutiful wife was a fucking saltie whore, I *still* didn't abandon her! I let her keep her home, keep her little games. *She* was the one who betrayed *me*!" Samnang slammed a fist on the wall.

"You honestly believe that, don't you? That you were doing her a favour by offering to keep her caged. That you are protecting Qiuyue by convincing her to cut out every fathomfolk part of herself."

Samnang didn't have to answer. The insidious love between him and Cordelia had turned a bond that once shone with the brightness of polished metal into a dull and rusted thing. Something that should have been thrown out a long time ago. It had been built on a foundation of lies, and the sand had eroded beneath their feet.

Gede shook away the regret, the sentimentality that threatened to ruin the plan. "And in this world, where you are protecting the city by encouraging humans to cut off their own gills, where do the fathomfolk figure? The freshwater kin born of folk and human? Or the tideborn humans who choose to keep their gills? Where is their place in this Tiankawi of yours?"

"Tideborn." Samnang spat the word from his lips, disliking the rallying call it had become. "When I am Fenghuang, you will be my Minister of Ceremonies. We will rewrite these half-baked laws for the better."

Mira's plans had started to take effect. People were no longer talking about the Tideborn Centre in the sceptical tones of months before. Instead the whispers were cautiously optimistic. People learning to swim, to make sense of the broken history of their city. Cordelia's gill rot medication was undergoing trials sanctioned by the Ministry of Health, and the early reports were positive.

The mood had changed in the city. Samnang was hopelessly out of touch already, perhaps always had been. The Cleaven might have gained a foothold in the face of gill rot fears, squabbling ministers and lack of leadership, but Gede and Mira had managed to unite the Council for now.

"You poisoned the Fenghuang, didn't you?" Gede asked.

Samnang quirked his lips. "And why would I do that?"

"Because you knew the proposal he was about to announce. The one Mira had been negotiating for weeks. Complete shutdown of the Onseon Engine. Increased visas for folk from the havens. Apprenticeships, housing."

"He went soft in his old age. Agreed to anything so they would erect a statue of him in Jingsha."

"So you had him murdered," Gede carried on. "Used your Cleaven contacts to get the venomous snake into position. Put the blame on Yonakuni."

Samnang shrugged, no longer caring to conceal it. "I couldn't have planned that timing better even if I'd tried."

There. The confession Gede and Mira had long suspected would be coming. But it might not be enough for the Council. The Fenghuang's murder was something singular. They would chalk it up as a personal matter. Gede needed to prove it went further than this. He stared his father down, not turning away as he once might have done. "You would have humans in pakalots also? Working at Onseon?"

"If they act like bait, they should be treated as such." Samnang shrugged.

"Anyone who disagrees with your ideology – not just folk, but humans – is to be indentured?" Gede spelled it out like he had an audience.

"Yes!" Exasperation making Samnang gesture as if his son was the bonehead everyone had always suspected him to be. "Has saltwater blocked your ears?"

A loud clanging sound drew both their attention, and Samnang swivelled his head to the mirror covering the far wall. His own reflection faltered. A bright overhead light illuminated the room beyond, filled with people who had been observing the interaction through the one-way glass. Journalists from all the newssheets, newly elected Council members: they had heard everything.

Mira leaned down over the microphone at the front. "I think we have enough."

"You double-crossing siltborn sneak," Samnang snarled. He turned on his son, but Gede had already drawn his kumiho blade in warning, keeping a good distance from the father he had betrayed.

Mira turned towards the other observers in the adjacent room, ignoring Samnang entirely. "This verifies our suspicions. Samnang was responsible for the murder of the Fenghuang. On top of this, the Cleaven are a radical group with concrete plans to harm humans, freshwater and fathomfolk within our community. As their leader, Samnang must be placed on trial and serve jail time. I motion their members be treated with a degree of leniency, that we immediately enact a programme to support and educate. They were lost after the tsunami. We all were. We let the people of Tiankawi down. It is our duty to ensure they know this city is still their home."

Once upon a time, Mira had hated public speaking, even with the notes in her shaking hands. Now she held a captive audience with her improvised words, charming them despite the lack of siren song humming in the background.

The Council members were quick to murmur their agreement, to quell the questions of the onlooking journalists as they filtered out of the room. Samnang and Gede forgotten entirely now that the tableau of the confession had run its course. Only Mira paused, looking in their direction before asking hesitantly, "Shall I call for the kumiho?"

"Give us a moment ..." Gede glanced back at his father, leaving the words unspoken between them. Mira closed her eyes for a moment, her conscience wrestling for control. There was nothing she could do here. She had signed the deal after all and would be obliged to delay the city guard. Only one way remained to change the outcome: she needed to find Gede. The real one.

"Thank you, saltlick," Gede said softly to Mira's back as the door clicked closed. He sheathed his sword and counted slowly to ten, ensuring they had all gone. He had time. Samnang, on the other hand . . .

The wards he had embedded in the room activated, cutting them off entirely. His eyes swirled yellow, pupils turning horizontal as water started trickling in through the vents.

The water slipped underfoot like snaking eels. Samnang backed away from the walls, but there was nowhere that remained dry. He rattled at the door Gede had come in through. Noticed for the first time that the lock had been sealed shut. As had the door frame, edged in a thick layer of ice.

Cordelia let the disguise fall. Gede's face was simple enough to replicate, one with which she was abundantly familiar. He would not mind, when he woke, drugged and without his voice, that she had borrowed it for a short time. After all, the bargain had been specifically worded so that he could not question her methods.

She unrolled her lower limbs, the suckered arms twisting around the legs of the chair Samnang reached for. Her humanoid arms stretched overhead as she cricked her back, looming large. The pinprick dots of iridescence pulsed across her cephalopod skin, ready to burst into colour or camouflage her at the slightest provocation. She had adapted well to the changes in the city, to the changes in her relationships. The coral growths on her crown scraped at the ceiling as she pushed herself to full height.

"I would have forgiven you for ruining me. Ignored the insult at least. It was of little consequence. But you turned Qiuyue against me," she hissed, baring her sharp teeth.

"Ruined? Admit it, you're thriving," Samnang replied. The casual tone of his words could not conceal his bobbing throat and how he hastily clambered on top of the furniture.

The ink thrumming through Cordelia stopped her from retorting. He was right. She had diversified her business to great success following their separation. Spending more energy on the healing arts was an unexpected challenge. She'd always thought bargaining was the ultimate achievement, but watching her empire emerge from the water gave her a pride she had never expected. Nevertheless, this was due to her ability to adapt and survive. She refused to give him any credit for it.

"You turned Qiuyue against me," she repeated.

"And you turned Gede. So we are even." The water continued to pour in, spilling over the bed. Samnang moved gingerly to the adjacent tabletop.

"Gede is an adult. He made his own choices," said Cordelia.

"Did he? How could I ever reach him when you were both keeping secrets from me? Whispering in your office and concocting plans. Moving me around like a game piece. Even when you disdained his help, it was your approval he always sought. Not mine. My only son!"

It had never occurred to her that Samnang might have resented being left out. "So you did it out of jealousy? Because Gede preferred me? Taught our daughter to hate herself?"

"I taught her to have principles. She sticks to her words, unlike you ... For better or worse. We made that vow."

"Until the river of life parts us," the seawitch said, the traditional vows of their wedding day all those years ago. There was nowhere else to climb to. Nowhere higher than the desk that would keep Samnang's head above water. Still it poured in. Gallons and gallons of seawater she had procured. Calling in bargains, blackmailing powerful folk to her bidding.

He'd tried to stay her hand by making her recall their joyful days together. Kindle the spark of affection she had once felt for him. But Cordelia had brooded over this for too long. Retribution had become a hard stone that weighed her down. She knew there was no going back: any chance of reconciliation with Qiuyue would be destroyed if she did this. And yet ... she had to.

She had made a bargain with herself.

Literally.

To ward against changing her mind, she had written up a contract in her own ink. She would kill Samnang, or her ink would poison her from the inside for failing.

The water continued to rise, the salty brine cool against Cordelia's skin. She rippled in calming purple and blue stripes. Patient. Prepared to wait for as long as it took. She would not be foolish enough to take her eye from her husband's face. She wanted to remember his death, savour it to warm her on the cold nights ahead. Samnang flailed as if he could push the water away from him, with the air of entitlement that had propelled him through his whole life. He should know by now.

Water would always flow.

The door of the adjacent room was thrown open. Gede and Mira rushed in, staring through the glass at the macabre scene. Samnang an ailing goldfish in a tank, floating in helpless circles near the top.

Gede could not question her, but he had unclasped the charmed pendant around his neck. Showing his true self. For the first time in a decade, she saw him take in water, the mantle cavity just above his collarbones opening so that his internal gills could absorb the oxygen he needed. His cephalopod skin had taken on the colour of the stone walls.

He was a boy again, crying because he did not have the temperament for the endless lies and charades she piled upon him. Telling him to be a man, to grow up faster than he wanted to. He had pulled away from her, hiding his worries in drink and debauchery; in friends who were no better than parasites.

He threw something at the glass. A chair. It bounced, not even making a crack. He struck again and again, relentless. It would break eventually, of course. Everything did. But by then it would be too late.

Samnang trod water, mouth gaping like an ornamental carp for the inch of air left in the room. Behind her, Cordelia heard Mira banging on the glass, pleading to let him face justice. So much wheedling. Negotiating. Didn't they know?

A seawitch never reneged on her bargains.

Samnang's eyes locked with her own, but he did not even have the energy to snap at her. The water rose over his head. He held his breath, eyes screwed tight as his cheeks puffed out.

Saltwater streamed across Cordelia's gills, which filtered it effortlessly, clearing the grit from her eyes until her vision was clear. Paradoxical that the same water that revived her would drown him. She would not look away, but Gede should. She released a burst of black ink into the water, corkscrewing upwards towards her husband as she did so. The ink muddied the waters, making it difficult for them to be seen from the outside.

Samnang pressed his lips together against the protestations of his body. He was fit for his age, could hold his breath for longer than expected. But in the end he was flesh and blood, just like the rest of them. A crying shame he had cut away his own gills. His mouth involuntarily flew open, sucking in a lungful of water. Coughing and gulping down more, twisting as if there would be a pocket of air somewhere in the corner of the flooded room if he ordered it into being. He clutched at his throat as he jerked. Drowning in agonising increments, his body twitching, contorted.

It was done.

The seawitch wrapped her suckers around the corpse of the man who had once been her husband. She fondly caressed down his side, the lines of his body as familiar as a well-worn piece of furniture. This dent in his hand where her thumb would fit against his. This shoulder where her head would rest after yet another boring function. She had never loved him, but she had grown accustomed to him after all these years. She turned, presenting her prize to Gede and Mira as the ink obscuring them dissipated. The glass had finally started to crack. One deep line tore through the centre, smaller ones fracturing off.

Cordelia showed all her teeth in that crescent moon of a grin. Most would back away in disgust. Mira and Gede were not everyone. She did not like the way they looked at her. Pity. Sadness. She threw down the body still enfolded in her octopus limbs, slammed it hard against the glass. The cracks grew. In a thunderous rumble, the window gave, and the water exploded from the room.

By the time Mira and Gede picked themselves off the floor, drenched and confused, she had gone.

Chapter Thirty-Eight

Mira stared at the broken glass littering the floor like diamonds. At Samnang's face-down body, reminding her of so many, too many bodies she had seen before. It had been personal. Cordelia, Serena ... it all made sense now that Mira had the pieces before her. Her bargain with the seawitch had kept her silent as the masquerade had unfolded. Samnang was dead. Her stomach was queasy with her complicity, but she would do it again, every time, to obtain a gill rot cure and the hope it represented. A small part of herself, one she would never admit aloud, secretly celebrated his swift demise. Cutting off the head of the beast before the Cleaven's rhetoric spread any further.

Gede crouched, a query on his lips that she barely heard. His skin undulated in a prism of colour, rippling with anxiety. He had been right all along: they had more in common than she'd realised.

"Do you trust me?" asked the son of a self-mutilating human and a double-crossing seawitch.

"Yes," Mira said simply. It was true. They were not their parents. They could shoulder neither their burdens nor their expectations any longer. They had to find a third way.

"I need to do something. Don't ask me for the details, but I need to go now or it'll be too late. Can you ..." He gestured around at the debris, at the questions and demands that would be only moments away from their position.

She nodded, watching as he blurred, colours merging into that of the wall and floor beneath them. Hesitant as a fledgling bird taking its first steps, unlike the confident changes his mother had just exhibited. "I can still see you," she teased, following the shimmering outline to the exit.

"Yes," he replied, the rueful smile unseen but heard all the same. "Perhaps you finally can." The door clicked closed with an exhale behind him.

Mira was flustered by the remark, recalling how she had quashed his confession at the tram platform. *What I truly am . . . is fathomfolk.* Even she had made a mistake, leaped to the assumption that she knew all there was to know.

For now, the reflections would have to wait. She had only a few minutes to prepare. To sing as she had not sung in a long time. Her siren compulsion coating the devastation around her like a fine dust, until her voice was hoarse and her eyes dull from the scene she had set. The door burst open.

"Yonakuni did it," she said, reaching out a shaking hand. One of the city guards helped her to her feet. "They sought to mete out their own punishment after we accused Jiang-Li of the Fenghuang's assassination." She gestured helplessly. Keeping her words to a minimum meant she needed only a little of her song. A quiet hum hidden by the gasps and mutters and the one shriek at Samnang's body on the floor. Half a dozen kumiho guards and a few of the ministers had responded to the noise. They had the strongest sense that she was telling the truth. Evidence at the scene that made the link to Yonakuni irrefutable, even if later they could not recall exactly what that was.

The newly elected Minister of Justice paled. She had not expected to be making these sorts of decisions quite yet. Mira used that to her advantage. "This must be kept quiet. On top of everything else, we cannot risk outright war with Yonakuni haven right now."

The minister nodded, too busy ruminating on the repercussions to consider the holes in Mira's hastily constructed story. The fear tactics felt sour on Mira's palate, but she did not have time for qualms. Nami, even Cordelia had taught her that much. Sometimes rules had to be broken. "Let me talk to Jiang-Li. Privately. Smooth over this misunderstanding before it gets to the newssheets."

The Minister of Justice nodded slowly. "While left unsupervised, Samnang, former Minister of Defence and confessed leader of the radical Cleaven movement, took his own life. That is what we are telling the newssheets. That is what everyone in this room saw."

The city guards outside Jiang-Li's apartment were playing wunlan, the board perched precariously on a three-legged stool between them. They jumped to attention with guilty looks on their faces as Mira approached. The dragon matriarch had been confined to her luxury quarters in Jingsha district since the Fenghuang's assassination.

"Who's red?" she asked. The taller guard rummaging for the right key on his belt looked up. His nostrils flared. "Me. Why?"

Mira pushed out her bottom lip. Nodded to herself. "A bold move." Neither guard had much of a strategy, pieces taken haphazardly. Mira had learned something since being on the Council and massaging the pride of so many scholar-officials. Giving them credit for something was the greatest of distractors. Egos took over. The taller guard would try his hardest to figure out what he had accidentally achieved, the other suspicious and annoyed that he had been outmanoeuvred. So engrossed that they would not bother about the discussion happening within the room. After all, Mira had visited several times before. The topics never more interesting than terse exchanges about the weather.

Jiang-Li was standing by the window. Despite being detained, the dragon matriarch was elaborately dressed as always, her hair knotted in looped braids atop her head as if she were about to go to a banquet. Her hand was on the floor-to-ceiling window, the ghosts of other imprints marking the glass.

"It looks like rain," she said towards the ominous overhead clouds. The top of the highest towers disappeared into them, like pillars holding up the skies.

"Good for the crop walls," Mira said. Growing up in Tiankawi, it was an instinctive reply. The vertical farms could survive on saltwater alone if needed, the hardy vegetables and fruit having been selected for just such a reason. Precious rainwater – collected in rooftop storage tanks and huge terracotta pots at the sides of properties – was, however, always welcome.

While she would never be fully comfortable in Jiang-Li's presence, she was no longer intimidated by the dragon matriarch. The clothing, the words were simply Jiang-Li's uniform. Protective layers that allowed her to obfuscate beneath the dazzling curtain of ceremony. Imprisoned here, within these impersonal quarters, Jiang-Li looked smaller than she did upon a dais.

"There's a song my ama would sing me when I was little. It was supposed to sound like the trickle of rain chains." Mira sang softly, in time with the drumming of her fingers on the window frame. She caught Jiang-Li's eye, giving her a warning as she layered her siren song into the tune. An inobtrusive touch, hardly noticeable unless the guards had sensitive warding amulets. No cry of alarm sounded as her charmed song seeped out into the corridor. No hands on weapons or door unlocked. She had muted the sound from inside the room, siren song telling the guards that Jiang-Li and the Minister of Fathomfolk were discussing the mundane and the mundane alone.

"Where is it?" she asked directly. No use skirting around the topic. Jiang-Li had shown her the dragon pearl; it had to be in the city.

There was no response. Too exhausted for subtlety, Mira went straight for a threat. "The Council have reason to believe your people murdered a prisoner; the leader of the Cleaven, in fact. Now I could make that go away, or I could make it much worse. Which would you rather it be?"

Jiang-Li raised an eyebrow. "You finally chose a side."

Fatigue washed over Mira. For weeks her every decision had been scrutinised, like she was nothing more than a broken junk ship to be dismantled for parts. She had held it together. Just. Here, in her siren-song-woven privacy, she could not. "It's not about sides! Do you really think what we did – Kai and Nami and I – was wrong?"

"You ask if my son's life was worth this city. How do you think I will answer? He died for your Council to bicker about gills and for radicals to mutilate themselves. What a boon for the folk! What a worthy cause." Jiang-Li's words dug like barbed fishing hooks.

"Then why show me the pearl at all?" Mira had tried friendship, tried professionalism: every overture batted aside until only spite remained. She had an inkling of both the love and the hate Kai and Nami had for their mother.

"Everyone assumes that once you get to the top, the air is much clearer. The answers ripe as low-lying fruit. The truth is, it's a burden."

"One you don't think I can endure?" Mira was affronted.

"One I would not *want* you to endure! I know what you think. I'm cold. I have been so wrapped up in the Senate that I never loved Kai. Never gave him what Trishanjali shows you. I did not have the luxury of hoping my children would live full and mundane lives. I gave them a home, food, the education they needed to survive in a world where we dragons are, and always will be, instruments. Figureheads. Sacrifices."

Her words pushed against the siren song that bubbled the room, stretching it. The breadth of her outstretched emotions contracted as swiftly as it had come; Jiang-Li once more bound tight in her many layers. The dragon matriarch wished that Mira, a self-taught half-siren, could live a blissfully simple life. An easy life. But Mira had been all those things that Jiang-Li was envious of. The responsibility was less, but so was the control: caught between poverty and prejudice without the power to change either. No. Leadership was not the easy option. It was the *only* option if Tiankawi was to change.

The first drops of rain fell onto the window, trailing slow, singular paths down the glass. The droplets sometimes came together, beads that splashed on the window ledge below; but mostly they travelled alone.

Mira had seen so many impassioned declarations of late that she could sort the rice from the husks. Jiang-Li mourned Kai. That was clear. Emotions so raw they could not be false. The responsible, perfect son who had never defied her. His only act of rebellion was Mira. But the dragon matriarch did not talk about Nami in the same terms; she hardly talked about her daughter at all.

"I have a theory," Mira said slowly, working out her words as she spoke them. "Kai was the firstborn. Handsome, smart, so incredibly dutiful. Never questioned your methods. You did not have to worry about him. But Nami—"

"Nami gets her temper from her father," Jiang-Li cut her off.

"Your husband? Yes. I see the similarities. They both had this moral compass, this compassion without the patience to think through the consequences. Both just needed someone to guide them. Yet you didn't. Strange for someone who has calculated the cost and benefit of all things."

Jiang-Li's eyes narrowed. Body stiff as if bracing for impact. "What exactly are you accusing me of?"

Mira did not know the answer until she saw the dragon's response. Until the abacus beads slid across the frame and it all added up. "You wanted her to implode, didn't you? Sending your ill-equipped daughter to Tiankawi to fuck things up. Rile the local Drawbacks – whom your contacts had told you were tee-tering on the edge of violence. You expected her to use her pearl. Finish it. Finish the whole city perhaps. Except there was one thing you never counted on. That even though you didn't give a shit, Kai still loved her. Kai loved all of us." Mira's voice grew louder, surer as she continued. It was clear to her now how Jiang-Li had planned this. She had not come simply to mourn Kai, nor to renegotiate the terms of the peace deal.

Jiang-Li didn't want compromise – she wanted the city.

"Your parents were a love match. You and Kai were a love match. One that certainly would not have met with my approval."

"What exactly is your point?" Mira narrowed her eyes.

"Alon and I were no love match. We *had* to marry. Preordained from the day we were born, the last dragon in both lines. We had to make pearls!" The jewels glittered in Jiang-Li's hair, sharp and clear. "That was our duty. You cannot imagine how that feels. The whole vast ocean watching us. Not to celebrate a life, as other births were celebrated; but to celebrate a sacrifice to come. Three chances to put things right. If it were up to me, I would have kept going. A dozen, that was my plan. Spares to lose, spread our feel-ings, so that if the time came, it would hurt less.

"Alon couldn't do it. He left to get away from me, as much as he came to save Tiankawi. Nami is just like him. She wants to do it her way, screw the traditions, the wisdom that came before. Blame me then for capitalising on her nature. Her *emotions*. Yes, I used her. I used all of them to do right by Yonakuni. Just as you are now doing to protect Tiankawi."

"We are not the same," Mira said.

"Not yet, but already you've made decisions that fill you with guilt. Admit it. You wonder if you should have chosen the other path. Violence is still coming, whether you want it or not. When plumes of white smoke come from the north, Sobekki's signal, it means your way has not worked. The sand god will destroy us all."

A silence dilated between them. Mira shook with everything she felt but could not articulate. "That won't happen. I believe in Nami."

Jiang-Li did not even deign to respond.

"Where is it?" Mira asked, refusing to be distracted. They both knew what the conversation was really about, the only question of importance. The one she had entered the room to ask. The drastic option.

"You are not prepared," said Jiang-Li.

"No. Not prepared. But if I must. Your diplomatic party have all been arrested, Jiang-Li. It's me or no one."

"You aren't strong enough for the sacrifices that need to be made."

"You talk of strength like it is who can lift the most weight. The way I see it, it's about moving with the changing course of the river." Mira paced as she spoke, picking up the unused hairpins from the table, lining them up one by one like sentries in a row.

Jiang-Li was silent, lips firmly pursed. She had been given an opportunity to do it the easy way.

"Tell me," Mira said. Her voice reverberated through the room, making the furniture around them quiver, blasting like a gale in the dragon matriarch's face. Jiang-Li paled with the force of it, the lines in her neck straining as her lips remained closed.

"Where is the pearl?" Mira repeated. Her siren song rose, pouring from her lungs, through her vocal cords to engulf Jiang-Li like a shroud. The water dragon's eyes bulged, dark veins on her forehead popping, yet still she remained tight-lipped. A trickle of blood trailed down her left ear, another from her nostril. The sight of it made Mira sick to the stomach. The siren coercion everyone was afraid of, being used to full effect. Resist for too long and the song's compulsion would burst the blood vessels in Jiang-Li's brain.

Finally, pleadingly, "Tell me!"

Jiang-Li took one step forward. Then another. Feet scraping across the floor. They could hear the kumiho guards outside the room banging on the door, the scrape of bolts being pulled. Mira would not get another chance; she had blown it all on this.

One of the guards wrenched her arm behind her back, as if that would prevent her song. The other one, more canny, gagged her with a scarf. She was relieved to have her voice momentarily stopped. Jiang-Li's taunts rang in her ears. She was right. The more Mira used her siren power – the more she told herself it was an exceptional circumstance, a one-off – the more she came to rely on it. Addicted to the ease with which people complied. Everything became an exception; everything became a need.

Jiang-Li wiped the blood from her nose, looking down at it critically. She seemed to have come to a conclusion; to trust where she had not done before. "It's with the truth. In the last place they'd look."

Mira let herself be dragged out. The stolen hairpin was cold against her skin where she had slid it up her sleeve. It had been simple enough to swap it for a decoy. The deception should last long enough to enact the plan.

It had to.

Chapter Thirty-Nine

Nami grabbed Eun's hand, her dragon pupils dilated to see through the darkness of the dimly lit corridors. Water lapped at their feet, puddles at first, but becoming deeper as the passage sloped down, until it sloshed around their calves. Mossy seaweed slick against the walls gave off a shimmering green sheen. Intricately carved pillars lined the walls and vaulted stone ceilings swept overhead like they were in the ribcage of a behemoth. They passed under archways, the carved bodies of twin kelpies rearing upwards to form the point. Nami made the mistake of looking up, the hooves so close to her head that she winced away from the blow she was sure was to come. Something slipped past her thigh, brushing against her. She lashed out, grabbing at it, to find herself holding a massive flailing catfish. Its barbed whiskers flicked as it gaped at her, wiggling free of her hold and splashing back into the murky depths.

Mikayil and the others should be in place by now, their raid on Firth's camp timed to mask Nami and Eun's furtive entry into Manannán Keep. Nami tried not to linger on it too much. She had to trust them. The chinthe lieutenant was one of Mira's trusted allies; he would be able to keep the rest safe long enough for Firth to take the bait. There would always be a risk, of course, but no one could think of a better option given the time restraints.

Soon the water rose too high to wade any longer. They would

have to swim from here. Nami knew before she even asked that Eun would refuse to go back. Refuse the relative safety of being above the waterline. It felt like a homecoming of sorts. Another mission through another tower. This time she was the one petitioning for peace, for conversation rather than rage. So much had changed since she left Yonakuni.

"Hold on to me," she said as they approached a treacherous stretch of the passageway.

"Always," Eun responded so quickly that Nami could not help but chuckle under her breath.

"Titans below, you are shivering," Nami said with sudden realisation. The water here was cold, sending goosebumps across her flesh as she kicked her legs. Her dragon scale gave her some insulation, but Eun had no such protection. The archivist shrugged her shoulders, but the chittering sound of her teeth was a giveaway. She was a competent swimmer now, not quite at ease in the water but tolerating it all the same.

"Wait, I can help." Nami's eyes sought for Eun's but instead were irresistibly dragged to her quivering lips. Mouth open just a fraction. She wrenched her gaze away, waiting for the nod of permission. Her hands ran down the length of Eun's arms, over the curve of her waist, right to her feet, leaving a trail of fine water-weaved bubbles on her skin, building up a thermal layer around the archivist, a makeshift skinsuit. Gingerly, trying not to make a deal of it, she touched the wet robes that clung to Eun's chest and down her front, turning to focus on her back before the flush of her cheeks gave her away. Eun had stopped shaking. Instead her rib cage rose and fell in deep breaths. Nami's hands lingered on her shoulder blades, not wanting to break contact. Eun leaned back so that her body was pillowed against Nami's shoulder. A trust fall, had they been above the waterline.

Except they were below it now, in Firth's domain. His haven.

Nami turned away.

They finally reached the bottom of the keep. A ring of standing stones stood in the cavernous open space. Like knife blades, blunt edges pointed up towards the waterline. The granite rocks were double Nami's height, made even larger by uneven layers of algae, barnacles and hard coral, giving them a monstrous silhouette in the dim light from above. The stones were surrounded by a shallow ditch and a bank, ringing it like ripples in the water. Ominous and intimidating by design, in opposition to the sand god shrines in Tiankawi. Those had been filled with knick-knacks; shells and pretty water lilies just as likely to decorate the unassuming shelves as ornate statues and expensive cups of wine.

Nami swam tentatively forward towards the largest of the stones, sitting at the centre of the circle. She felt the thrum of it long before her hands even grazed the rough surface. The reverberations pushed her away in a steady but firm wave. Planting her feet on the ground, she countered with her waterweaving, her palm flat against the surface, feeling the prickles of the coral and barnacles scratching at her.

Wave upon wave of nausea struck her like a physical blast. Her head spun with it, incoherent at first as she stumbled to her knees. Her hand slid down the stone, not quite breaking contact. She tried to answer Eun's frantic concern, but could not battle the voiceless scream that filled every corner of her mind. It was as if all life, all water was simultaneously squeezed from her. Her eyes filled with tears, gills clamped shut, and she heard herself howl. She longed to beat her head against the rock, tear out chunks of her hair and shred her nails down her own skin. A void, endless and gaping, called to her; sang with the vicious mandibles of a bobbit worm, threatening to drag her down through the sediment and devour her whole.

The feelings fled as quickly as they had come, slipping like a low tide back to sea. Nami blinked, unsure of what had happened. Unsteady apart from where Eun held her, coaxing her back. The librarian had pulled her hand from the standing stone. Nami looked at her palm, surprised to find the skin unmarked. The anguish of it had felt like being burned alive and she had fully expected the scars to remain. How could all that emotion, all that pain simply be in her mind?

It came to her, like a shoal parting. Grief. That was how. The inarticulate rage with which she was intimately familiar, lashing out as it had done to the *Wayfarer*. The sand god's emotions. This might have once been a communication point for Iyoness, but right now, it was useless. All it did was magnify the pain.

In all the stories, titans were pairs, bonded for the whole of their lives. The titan manta ray had lived for centuries before it had become the foundations of the Iyoness haven. Centuries more it lay dormant, patient and placid as the waters above it. When love could span oceans and hundreds of years, who was to say how long sorrow would last.

"It's no use," she managed to whisper. "It's too far gone."

Eun signed with her hands, unable to use her voice underwater. *Try again. Not words.*

"I am not the champion you think I am."

Understanding. Compassion.

A slow clap sounded from behind them. "Your pity party is quite moving," said the familiar voice. Nami suspected he had been there a while, waiting for the right moment to make his entrance. In the darkness, he looked taller than expected. She recalled the spider crab carcass they had found in the ruins, wondering if perhaps it had been Firth's shell after all.

After a couple of weeks apart, she could see the cruel edges to him that she had always made excuses for. Labelling it as audacious when perhaps she had always known it was merely callous. She had perversely admired it even; sneered at the softness Kai and Mira offered.

Her sharp eyes moved away from Firth, seeing Sobekki loitering behind him, arms folded across his chest.

"You planned this from the moment you boarded the *Wayfarer*," she stated. Firth shrugged, not even denying it. "And you would have this sand god destroy everything. Everyone."

"Poetic justice, don't you think?" he said. He winked at Eun, unable to help himself.

"What exactly is the point? You destroy Tiankawi, then what? You rise up as some hero over the ruins?"

Firth looked at her for the longest moment and then he rolled his head back. An ungodly sound came from his mouth. A laugh. Not the good-natured chuckle she was accustomed to, but one unlike any she had heard. Like a carrion bird picking over bones. He bent double, clutching his middle with the stitch his merriment had induced. His auburn hair floating back up as he pulled himself upright. "Oh my dear, darling, spoilt little princess. They really did fuck you up in the gilded cage, didn't they? I don't want to rule. I just want everyone to pay."

A little boy who had seen nothing but violence in his home haven had come to Tiankawi to ask for help. His pleas were ignored, drowned out, along with those of hundreds of others. Instead they were thrown in cages with pakalots around their wrists. The titans alone knew what had happened to his brother, the story always evolving. Whatever it was had twisted and broken him out of sync. Not an ounce of empathy remained: none for humanity, nor for the folk who chose to live among them. This was the truth of him. Nami had only seen the smoke smouldering in him, but she had failed to see the flames.

If she could go back, ten or more years, perhaps there had been a time, a chance for him. Perhaps all the community projects Mira worked on, the ones Nami found so tedious and pointless, would have been worth it if they'd managed to bring one lost child out of the maelstrom. But it was too late now.

Firth clicked his fingers and familiar faces were shoved roughly from the shadows. Mikayil, Zidane, Jinsei. They had even found

Jalad, dragging him injuries and all. Her companions all had their hands bound behind their backs. Nami scanned their bodies for signs of harm, relief suffusing her when it looked like only Mikayil had sustained anything of note. A fresh bruise had spread across his left cheek, eye already starting to swell. She let a look of defeat slide across her features. They had known the risks.

"Rather pathetic distraction plan, even for you. Send a bunch of humans to raid our camp? Sobekki saw it coming a mile off, didn't even need the rest of us to pause from our meal before he had them rounded up."

"You will have to answer for your actions," Jalad said in an ill-advised moment of bravery. Wensum took great pleasure in backhanding him with one of her long arms.

"Don't worry. I will ensure you and your friends have front-seat tickets to the unfolding festivities." Firth looked wryly at the motley remains of Nami's group. "You know how easy you made it when you arrived in Tiankawi. So full of anger but no purpose. No real understanding of how things worked. I didn't even have to do very much to tip the scales, not really." He moved towards her, running a finger under her chin with the lightest of touches. Nami was frozen in place. It did not matter that she knew the truth; it would take more than one revelation to break the hold he had over her.

After a significant delay, she shoved his hand away. Firth's eyes danced as if it was all but a game. Moved in closer so that his whisper brushed her forehead. "Lynnette was having her doubts, but jealousy worked so well on her. Bedding you just made her more desperate for my attention. I have to thank you for that."

"Fuck you."

"Mm, right here? Right now? In front of your ... friend?" His gaze flickered behind her to Eun, rubbing salt in the open wound.

Nami kicked out, an impulsive shot between the legs, but he easily twisted to one side to avoid the blow. "It's a shame I couldn't just prise the pearl out of you. But the end result will be the same."

Nami glanced at the folk who had aligned with him: Sobekki, Wensum and Shizuku, watching from the shadows. "You have friends, family, communities back in the city! What empty promises has he made? Land? Titles? You think he will deliver that without stabbing you in the back also?"

"And you would have things remain the same? Pakalots and cages."

"No. I want change. But you have corrupted what that truly means. Change that comes at the cost of so many lives isn't the way."

"Still the naïve little princess. When will you learn that sometimes bloodshed is necessary."

"I agree. Bloodshed *is* necessary." Nami finally understood. Everyone kept talking about a conversation: Mira, Kai, Eun. She had misinterpreted listening as being passive. Letting Firth walk all over her. She had swung all the way from incendiary to compliant without considering there was something in between. It wasn't about being a pushover. It was about being an impenetrable, undeniable, unavoidable force.

Standing in his way.

Violence was back on the table, wielded with purpose: a clear endpoint. Her eyes flickered to Sobekki, the Yonakuni Protector of the Realm. She had hoped, had to hope, he would support her. For the sake of decorum, for the havens, for the lessons he had once tried to teach her when she was too young to listen. She slammed both hands on the central standing stone, trying to wade through the explosion of grief that swamped her brain. "I challenge you, here in this sacred space, in the heart of Iyoness, witnessed by the titan beneath us. A duel to end this feud."

Cordelia had laughed once upon a time when Kai challenged her to a duel. It was not the Tiankawian way. But they were not in the city any more. Tradition and ceremony had more weight in a space such as this, in the presence of a sand god who had lived for centuries and abided by sacred promises.

"I attest." Sobekki's voice rumbled low but clear, as everyone swivelled to look at him.

"I attest." They had not thought to gag Jalad, not thought his words could mean very much. They only needed one more. One more fathomfolk voice to legitimise the duel in the ancient ways.

I attest, Eun signed.

"You don't count," Firth snarled. He looked flustered. Even he had not expected this move. They waited for the sand god's response, but it remained silent. He looked relieved, escaping a fate he had not predicted. "There, you see."

Wensum gloated. Shizuku, on the other hand, looked torn. Their long arms knotted into fists, knuckles scraping the dirt.

"Garrett, Tephan, Captain Rannoch." Nami saw the changbi flinch as she listed each name. "The *Wayfarer* crew were your family. Firth would have had them drown: at the tsunami, at the shipwreck, at every point it did not benefit him."

Shizuku's gaze stayed fixed to their feet. Their face unreadable as the desperate hope Nami clung to began to wither in her chest. It had all been for naught.

"I attest," the first mate finally said, their voice cracking into the stunned silence. Waves of fury rolled from Firth, but it was too late. A quake rumbled beneath their feet, cracking the earth into fractured lines. One of the standing stones groaned and toppled forward. Nami yanked Eun out of the way as it thudded to the ground, dust dispersing into the water in thick clouds. The sand god was silent now, the litany of grief momentarily halted as all attention was turned to what was happening upon its back.

Chapter Forty

"A duel? Really? That's your master plan?" Firth threw his hands up as if Nami was a bothersome child whingeing to play a game. His criticism bounced off her, a waterproof layer since they had last met.

"Remain within the standing stones," Sobekki warned. It was like being back in the Academy, listening to her teacher drone on with his familiar explanation. Except this time she did not roll her eyes or whisper with friends. She listened to each and every word as if her life depended on it.

It did.

"This is a one-on-one duel. Waterweaving permitted."

Firth gave a mocking fist-palm salute as he moved towards the centre of the ring-shaped enclosure. Nami was about to follow when Eun tugged at her sleeve. "Be careful," she mouthed, her feather gills stretching at her neck. All Nami could do was nod, trusting that the gesture would be enough. The librarian slipped back between the stones as Firth watched them, sneer etched in every line.

"Begin!" Sobekki declared.

Firth dropped down, his angular face growing long and equine as he shifted into kelpie horse form. His auburn hair was lost in a mane of brackish seaweed, his coat grew green-tinged, like algae coated his fur, and his lower legs became a muscular fish tail. He turned, tail slamming from Nami's left with the force of a hurricane. She narrowly avoided it, darting out of the way. He came at her again, rearing up with his hooves, charging forward with his head. It took everything in her repertoire to keep moving, circling, dipping and twisting just out of reach, as his ruthless frontal assault continued.

He swung again and she ducked under, kicking with her foot into his vulnerable side. Darting this way and that, a nibbling little fish in the water, never still long enough for him to hit. The frustration was making him reckless, tolerating her weaker hits so that he could reach her. He barrelled forward and Nami was out of space, pinned against one of the standing stones. Each of Firth's hooves strong enough to break bones, to knock her out. He landed a blow on her head and another on her shoulder, the blunt force of it making her eyes spin. Something cracked inside her, pain shooting down her right shoulder and arm. Frantically she wriggled out of reach, swimming up and over him.

She kicked at his back to provoke him, another tail slap coming towards her head. This time she was ready. Evading the blow, she grabbed at the forked ends of his tail, using his own momentum to pull him down and freezing his lower body to the ground with a thick block of ice. He cracked the frozen shell almost immediately, but it took longer to shake off the weight, anchoring his movement and making him lurch lopsided. He launched at her again, and again she met the attack with a manacle of ice. Over and over. Dragging down his hooves, his tail, a saddle of it crushing across his back.

The kelpie was angry. He roared as he threw water at her, an intense blast tearing towards her and throwing her backwards. She slammed into another of the standing stones. Pain lanced down her spine and pulsed in the back of her head. Her vision unfocused, blurred at the edges. This was when she would usually shapeshift, using her dragon scale as armour, her larger size to balance things out, falling back on the old trick even when it no longer worked. She flicked her gaze up to her old martial instructor. Sobekki's face was impassive as always, but he met her eye and something seemed to swirl in those black pupils.

She ducked under Firth's rising tail slap just in time. The force cut into the standing stone behind her head. A deep crack bisected the grey stone, and the top half slid like a felled tree, toppling backwards into the water with a dull thud. Nami wove a rope dart into her hands, the rope a tight stream of water and the pendulum dart at the end sharpened ice. It kept her moving, forced her into light footwork, every movement precise so the weapon kept swinging. This was what she excelled at. Precision. Speed. Never keeping still. She tugged, the dart flying towards the gaps in Firth's defences. A mosquito hounding him. It cut across the neck, snapping at his fetlock and embedding deep into his withers.

Nami felt something inside her rising like water vapour. Buoying her upwards despite herself. The whiskers she kept concealed beneath her human form sensed his lumbering movements, the tension in his muscles before it was clear to the naked eye. The punches he landed barely hurt any more, like her dragon scale was there, protecting her soft skin, despite appearances. To be here, halfway between land and sea, halfway between humanity and folk: this was the fine balancing act Mira talked of, the one that had never made sense to Nami before. Finally she understood.

"You are bested, Firth. Destruction has its appeal. Who doesn't like to watch something burn?" She looked outside the stone circle, to the hazy shadows of the others still watching. She did not blame them for the choices they had made. She had made so many of her own miscalculations. "It is so much easier to hate, to protect yourself by expecting the least of other people. But at the end of the day, I'd rather be an idealist. A dreamer. I'd rather live in a world with people like Eun than people like you."

She spoke from the heart, not really thinking about how Firth would turn his gaze. Lick his bleeding wounds and charge towards the librarian with hooves rearing over her head like ice axes. Nami was too slow. Her legs kicked, but the scream ripped from her mouth could not propel her through the water any faster. She flicked out a handful of ice, needle-sharp daggers that thudded into the kelpie's muscular flank, but his downward motion barely paused. She would not get there fast enough. Would only be able to watch as his hooves stamped down on Eun's skull. Could only ...

Firth's hooves never fell. He was caught in a tableau, only the rolling whites of his eyes revealing that he was being held against his will. Beneath his feet, the water shimmered unnaturally, discoloured like a brine lake. Nami pulled Eun back. She pressed the other woman to her chest, holding her so tight that Eun cried out in muffled protest.

Only then did she see Sobekki's raised hands. The crocodile-headed fathomfolk had lowered his brow as he held Firth in place. Otherwise he had barely broken sweat. He had not intervened during the duel, in keeping with the ancient rules. But when Firth had broken the circle, when he had directed his attack towards a bystander, then Sobekki had responded. Nami had known better than to ask the Yonakunish guardian to take sides. Sobekki had one loyalty and that was to the haven. Neutral in all other things, and not known for his heart. She had been sure, and had convinced the others when they had hatched the plan, that calling for a ceremonial duel was how to get him on side. Making use of her knowledge, just as he had always told her to.

"This is not within the rules." Sobekki released his hold on Firth.

"Rules? What rules? The arbitrary rules designed to hold us back the minute we gain the upper hand? Telling the same lie that it is unfair when in fact there was never a chance of equality to begin with. Neither beneath nor above the waves." The kelpie turned his white-hot gaze back on Nami. Once she had mistaken that look for something else. Excitement. Even . . . love. She saw it now for what it truly was. Revulsion. "The duel is of little consequence. You lost before you even started."

He indicated her group of allies, bound and subdued. Shizuku and Sobekki, unlikely to lend a hand. Wensum looked like she was ready to cut the throats of anyone Firth asked her to. Nami's waterweaving was insufficient to change things. She was not as forceful as Firth. One voice made no difference.

Firth called to the water. It dragged from around Nami, rushing towards the kelpie's formidable waterweaving strength. He formed it, rough hooves pressing the flow, squeezing it down against all protestation. Water solidified to ice. A frozen weapon almost as tall as her – a greatsword – the blade wider than a handspan across.

A display of pure brawn. Firth's overwhelming power was one she could not hope to defeat. He raised it over his head, not with his limbs but with the might of his waterweaving. Up close, Nami could see the water jet edge that could slide effortlessly through bone; just dropping it on her would be enough.

The blade fell.

Nami pushed back. With her whole body, hands outstretched, she resisted Firth's waterweaving. Her feet slid backwards, inch by inch. Every muscle tensed, every part of her strained to the extent of her abilities. She could not hold him. She could do little but slow the pace of the blade's descent. One painful finger width at a time. In horror, she watched the edge slide into her injured shoulder. Blood burst from the open wound as the white-hot pain of it penetrated her concentration, bearing down as if to split her in two.

Alone she could not stop him. Could not stop the wheels he had set in motion, long before she had arrived in Tiankawi.

But she was not alone.

She pressed her hands against both sides of the huge blade. Palms flat against the ice-cold sheet, she lifted it off her in incremental movements. Firth's eyes widened in confusion at her sudden strength. His brows knitted as he pushed back down. Harder. The ice edge stalled in place, held between the equal forces pushing and pulling. The kelpie looked her up and down, head even swivelling to where Sobekki stood. The Yonakunish guardian for once was also caught off guard, his surprise like a heavy stone dropped into a well. He caught on fast, though, turning to the human captives, who still knelt. Thinking perhaps of the letter Mikayil had delivered to him.

Sobekki,

Once you tried to teach me about duty to my people. About playing to my strengths and not just trying to be a poor copy of my brother. I did not heed your words then, but I recall them now. The definition of "my people" has changed. I ask not for your help, but for your mediation. Yonakuni will thrive when Tiankawi thrives. You have my word. My friends will be captured. Loosen their bonds. Let me demonstrate a way forward.

For all of us.

Yours in disobedience,
Nami

Nami's power guided the greatsword's movements, but Eun's palm was pressed against her back, seconding her. Her other hand was outstretched, fingertips touching Mikayil's. They were linked together – Jalad, Jinsei, even Zidane – hand in hand. A team effort. They had never stopped practising waterweaving. Hiding in the ruins of Iyoness, Nami had extended her lessons to the others, filling their tired evenings. Moving little more than raindrops and puddles of water, but moving them all the same. Finding that linking together they could tap into undiscovered pools of power: for folk and humans alike.

The sword reversed its downward arc. Inching back upwards as if on an invisible winch. Nami felt the pressure of the oppositional forces twisting through every joint. "Now," she commanded.

The massive sword shattered into a hundred shards. Firth stomped his hooves and half the shards moved haphazardly towards her, but it was easier to deflect them now. Breaking it down, dividing the power into smaller pieces gave her the advantage. Firth flailed like trying to swat at a swarm of gnats. He had never had any finesse in waterweaving. Nami used her hands to direct the shards, grouping them like shoals of fish.

Firth tried to raise another weapon, an enormous volume of water coming into his control. Before he could finish, Nami flung a dozen of the ice shards at his head, roundhouse-kicking more towards his side, distracting him. The water slipped away from him. He changed tactics, barrelling towards her injured shoulder. He thought he could read her, control her. Truth was, she had also got under his skin. She had learned to listen. Watched him spar with the Drawbacks. Knew there were certain moves he instinctually employed when riled. She used the knowledge against him now, taunting him as she slid back. Ducking over and under, sending a slew of projectiles into his vulnerable flank. The water was filled with scales from his torn tail, his lower fins shredded like paper.

"Stop being a coward and face me!" he roared.

"You were the one who broke the duel rules." Part of Nami wished he had chosen the honourable route: the one that would have allowed her to manacle his wrists and take him back to Tiankawi to face justice before the Council and the people. But deep down, she had always known it would come to this.

"So you are judge and jury?" Firth's lip snarled upwards in an ugly sneer.

"No." Nami raised her arm to her left and then right. Indicating the others, whom Firth had failed to see, even after all they had done to support her waterweaving. "This is not my decision. It's ours."

Only then did he look wider. Only then did he see she had shared out control of the ice shards: to the humans, to Jalad. Zidane reached out a hand to Shizuku. The changbi examined his palm curiously for a moment and then placed their own webbed hand into his. Sobekki stood to one side, and Wensum, face a turmoil of emotions, recoiled from the invitation. The rest of them, Tiankawians – fathomfolk and human alike – had a choice in the matter. Together.

The shards floated in the water, pointed inwards towards Firth in a rough circle, some better controlled than others. His lips came together in a grim line and he shifted back down, shrinking to his handsome human form. Amber eyes twinkled as he raised them. "So you did it, princess. You learned to play the game. To win. But you will never—"

She would not remember who acted first. Was it her, denying him the opportunity to speak any more of the words that had intoxicated her for so long? Was it Eun, wanting to shield her from more pain; Jalad, angry at the folk who had betrayed his own; Zidane, bored and unable to wait any longer? She would never know for sure.

The ice shards snapped forward. A ring of blades cut deep into Firth's neck, across his chest and back. A coat of broken gemstones, glittering in the dim light. Blood trailed from the wounds like stinging tentacles, grasping in every direction for purchase. Surprise filled the kelpie's expression. Outmanoeuvred for the first and last time. He jerked, falling to his knees as his head slumped forward. The projectiles melted into seawater as the life seeped from his body.

Chapter Forty-One

Dan took one look at Cordelia, and pulled the shutters closed. She didn't even know what he said, what he did exactly, but the fugu workers collected their belongings and traipsed out without a backward glance, leaving only the two of them behind. The cavernous warehouse echoed without the habitual noise. The wide-open space of it disconcerting to someone accustomed to the hustle of cramped city walkways.

"That's coming from your wages," she snapped instinctively. Dan said nothing, filling the kettle with fresh water and heating it over one of the burners. The seawitch was picking at her elbow, lower limbs twitching. It was only then that she realised she had walked in without her tarbh uisge disguise. Just wandered in the front door without a shred of common sense. She hardly knew how she'd got from Samnang's cell to here. There could be a whole trail of devastation in her wake; she simply had no recollection.

"Went well, then?" Dan broke the silence finally.

"Yes." Cordelia's teeth worried at the inside of her cheek.

"Excellent. Well, now seems a reasonable time for an update." The kappa paused, taking her silence for assent. "The bad news is, I think you've blown your cover. The good news is, you've a visitor upstairs."

He said nothing more as she drained the cup of tea, sliding silently across the floor and up the internal spiral staircase to her office. She could see Gede's silhouette illuminated by her desk light through the frosted glass. He blinked as she came in, riffling through the accounts open on the desk. Normally those books would be locked away in the safe. This morning she had left them in plain view. She had not told Gede about the fugu manufacturing, not in full. Nor the swing to gill rot medication and dull weed after the deal she had struck with Mira. They had logos, registration certificates, licensing documentation, orders from a dozen apothecaries throughout Tiankawi. She was looking into warehouse storage and a second manufacturing facility. It was a legitimate business. Bigger and more organised than anything she had ever strived for before. This was her lure: words would not be enough, she knew that long before she set off down this path. Hard numbers might be. Sorry for murdering your father, would you like to be my business partner – laid out in columns and figures.

Gede closed the ledger. He looked older than his four and twenty years gave him reason to. Being on the Council had wrung him dry. Echoes of Samnang were traced in the line of his nose, the furrowed brow. His expression unreadable. "The business is a success."

"Yes, it deviated from the original plan, but I'm proud of it."

He wrinkled his nose. "So you *do* get proud of things."

"Don't be like that."

"Like what?"

"Like a petulant child."

"Child? You imprisoned my sister and murdered my father. I've taken it pretty well, all things considering."

"I didn't have a choice."

"That's a lie. There was always a choice. A choice to leave me out of every decision you made."

"You're too young—"

"No! That's what you've said in the past. Too young, too irresponsible. I stepped up. Everyone recognises that, apart from you. I'll never meet the standards you expect of me."

He was right. He had exceeded everything she had hoped for. Become the ally she needed. Yet she could never say the words he so desperately wanted to hear. The habitual jibes of scolding and criticism slipping from her mouth without thought. The worry that if she lavished praise on him, even the smallest sprinkling, he would become indolent with it. The abrasive feedback kept him sharp; it was for his own good.

He looked at her with round moon eyes and it made her deeply uncomfortable. She would try, for once, to give him what he wanted. "I'm sorry I killed your father," she said. It was like sliding her mouth against a grater.

"No you aren't. In all of this Cleaven business, he forgot that his own kids are freshwater. We're folk. Or maybe that's *why* he was so obsessed. A hypocrite trying to hide the truth by shouting about it the loudest." Gede didn't sound that upset that Samnang was dead. A small mercy. There was a false brightness to his voice that she recognised. He still wore the broken amulet around his neck, out of habit more than anything, she suspected. It would take more than this for him to adjust to his seawitch side.

"You've performed ... adequately," she said finally. The words were awkward as they tripped off her tongue, like a new taste that she hadn't decided on.

Gede raised his chin, bottom lip quivering just for a second before he nodded to accept her grudging praise. "A bargain: you will not force my hand again. Ever."

Cordelia was affronted. "I never forced your hand! Just some motherly persuasion."

"If you respect me, then prove it. You always said I should embrace my seawitch heritage. Well here I am, making a deal with you. Meet me as my equal."

They would never be one of those families like Mira and her mother, telling each other the secrets of the heart. They would never even be friends. That wasn't what being a parent was. It was about preparing your children for the dangers of a hostile world. Giving them the resilience, the knowledge and opportunities to thrive despite those who wished them harm. Qiuyue hated her. Gede certainly didn't like her. But she had done right by them.

"What would I get out of it?" She could not help but ask. Another might have made the symbolic bargain simply to appease their upset offspring, but she was not one of those fools.

"A deal from the Minister of Defence that the kumiho will not pursue any investigations into your ... new business."

She wanted to protest that it was all above board. She was legit now. Had filled out the endless documents that Mira had demanded of her. She also knew that the straight and narrow path wasn't always the most profitable, nor the most interesting. It was a peculiar request, but he had been through a lot. Watching his mother murder his father in cold blood was bound to be a life-changing moment. If he wanted reassurance, it was a small price to pay. Besides, he had not said she couldn't cajole or bribe him; simply that there would be no use of force. No *borrowing* his voice again.

She let him draw up the contract, checked the wording, guided his hand to sign on the line. His eyes widened as the ink sacs in his body sizzled with the terms of the deal. At least, she thought, she was here to see him sign his first bargain. That was a milestone.

"I've taken Qiuyue, by the way," he said. "She never wants to speak to you again."

"What?" Prickles ran down Cordelia's neck and her limbs flared in orange spikes before she could stop them. She did not comprehend his meaning. The statement flung at her with such disregard. Such disrespect. How dare he! Intervening in something that was none of his business. Qiuyue didn't need protecting from her, she just needed someone to guide her. Well, she would force him to ...

Realisation must have spread across her features. Gede was grinning from ear to ear. He had finally done it.

Outsmarted her.

Chapter Forty-Two

The chinthe were on the lookout. Even the smallest wisps on the horizon had to be reported to Mira. Every cloud that looked slightly suspicious. Jiang-Li had made it abundantly clear what it meant. All hope was lost; the sand god was coming to destroy Tiankawi. Everything they had built. All the sacrifices that had been made. Every time something good happened, it had been countered by something bad. Like the universe could not simply give, but had to take back. Kai's death balanced with the city's survival. All the meetings with the Fenghuang simply for him to be assassinated before the new policies were enacted. Every fear and doubt thrown back in her face over the course of the Council elections, the rise of the Cleaven and Fathomfolk First.

Cordelia had done one thing right. Her gill rot medication was working. Chi-Mae at the Ministry of Healing could not contain her excitement, pestering Mira incessantly for the source of the product. In the trials so far, both folk and humans had responded well to the new formula. It had not only paused the progression of the disease, the effects had been actively reversed in some participants. Minster Kelwin had already promised to scale it up within the year.

But what did it all matter when a force bigger than they could fight was moving towards their shores? Perhaps the prosperous

Jingsha humans had it right – they should be jumping ship while they had the chance. The titan would tear through all the careful reconstruction work and every skybridge that had been built.

Mira went down the stairs at the Tideborn Centre, into the exhibition room she had walked through with Jiang-Li. Eun's curated archives of newssheets and objects showed the sordid history of the Nurseries with utmost clarity. At the back was one of the Nursery cages that had been retrieved, exhibited as a reminder of what the Council hoped to bury. It had been furnished, if it could be called that, with a thin reed mattress. Belongings hooked to the sides: a few items of clothing, a mirror, shelves at the far end crammed full of possessions. Impulsively, Mira crawled into it, lying with her head pressed up against one end, her toes touching the other. Even with the door open, she could feel the criss-cross of the narrow pen around her, lacing her in. Could not straighten her arms overhead without brushing against metal. Boundaries. Walls. This was all they had had. Their only personal space in a camp of thousands fleeing civil war and violence.

She closed her eyes, but the hatched pattern was seared into the back of her mind. The smell of the mildewed bedding rose up towards her as she shuffled down the far end. Her head struck against the metal more than once, curls snagging on rusted joins. The enclosed space made her panic even now, even knowing it was just a museum exhibit. It was in the past, and yet it was too close for comfort. History could easily repeat itself once more.

Tucked behind a couple of other items, she found a sandalwood box far too opulent to be in this cage. Hidden in plain sight, as Jiang-Li had hinted. Mira hauled herself out of the cage as fast as she could, scraping the skin on her shin as she did so. It could have been her in one of these cages, had her mother not married a human. Had they not been given a land visa that allowed them the luxurious upgrade to the Seong slums instead.

She pulled out the hairpin from her inside pocket, the one she had pilfered from Jiang-Li's room. It glittered golden and inconsequential, a slip of a thing apart from the end where it abruptly protruded outwards like a hammerhead. The only giveaway of its true purpose. Kai and Nami had told her enough stories of their mother for her to read the signs. She wore her elaborate clothing as if it was armour, each earring and pendant carefully chosen to curate an image. Only the pearl hairpin stayed the same. From her arrival, the meetings with the Fenghuang, to her time in captivity: for someone who used waterweaving to alter her clothing, to proudly display her wealth and skill, it stood out in how unchanging it remained. How much she constantly fiddled with it, checking it was still there.

Such a small, fragile thing. It could break in Mira's hands, not even by choice. Bend out of shape if she simply pushed too hard. Yet it was, she was certain, the key. She placed it against the small lock, twisting it until she heard a click. The heavy lid groaned open, exhaling to present Jiang-Li's last dragon pearl. Brilliant white with a blue haze around it, it nestled on a silk cushion within. Larger than Kai's had been, firmer against her hand also. Although it looked smooth at first, the shell was porous, the imperfections catching against her fingers as she touched it. Minuscule bumps and blemishes making it not just an ornament, not just a peace stone. An egg.

Mira slammed the lid shut. It was too much. She had only touched Kai's pearl for a few seconds, the whole situation too fraught, too fast for her to remember much at all. This pearl was not Kai, she tried to remind herself. It was different. Amorphous as yet, without experience to shape it. But it could be.

It could be the sibling Kai and Nami had never met. It could be a wish to save a whole city. Or it could be a piece in this endless game, passed between hands and factions for as long as city and haven still fought. Who was she to make that decision?

She carried it over to the room that she had somehow claimed for herself. Fell into the hammock, the motion of it giving her something else to think about for a brief period. Above her, the long strips of stained wood on the panelled ceiling rose and fell. Sky and sea one and the same everywhere she looked.

"What have you got there?" her ama's voice said. Mira jumped, almost dropping the sandalwood box onto the floor. It slipped between her fingers, but she managed to catch it, shoving it to the far side of the hammock and hastily covering it with a blanket. Trish said nothing, concentrating on her slow descent down the stairs into the cabin. She moved slowly, the teapot in her hand swinging wildly, hot liquid slopping over the sides. Mira chided her gently, taking her burdens from her, but the older siren said nothing, simply removing two small cups from the folds of her sleeves. Her eyebrow quirking to say she was managing quite well, thank you, before Mira decided to worry her head off. It was only as Trish slid a small side table across the room that Mira noticed the other changes.

She had lain in the hammock oftentimes enough, the storeroom of the Tideborn Centre slowly becoming her bedroom without conscious intent. She had other places – Kai's apartment to sort out, and her mother's sampan always had space for her. More often than not, she had simply fallen asleep mid task, exhaustion superseding the effort of finding a bed to sleep on. The hammock had been Trish's suggestion. Clothes she had left strewn around the room were washed and folded in her absence, another indication of her mother's meddling. But now, looking around, she saw more. Her certificates hung on the wall; a carefully patched rug, moth-eaten but serviceable, was underfoot; a woven reed basket sat in one corner, filled with familiar well-worn clothes.

"Ama, what is this?"

"You practically live here; you might as well *live* here," Trish responded, her curtness offset by the warm tea she poured. The little details had added a layer of intimacy to the room, dampening the harshness of the wood and the hollow echoes that bounced through Mira's skull. It settled a noise in her brain that she was not even aware she had endured.

"You can't keep on at this pace for the rest of your days." Trish might as well have read her mind. "He sacrificed himself because he believed in you. In us. He wouldn't have wanted you to keep punishing yourself."

"Ama," Mira managed to say before all the words fled, washed away by the anguish she tried so hard to hold back. It had been months. People had been sympathetic at first, given her space, time, comfort. But life moved on.

She was expected to move on.

"Remember old Abdar?" Trish said.

"The makara uncle?"

"That's the one."

"Vaguely. I remember we used to share dinner with him."

Trish's mouth twitched. "We didn't share. He took pity on us. Once a week or so, when my wages couldn't stretch any further . . . I hated it, but we would slink up to his door and beg."

Mira's childhood memories altered with this new information. The shame painted on her mother's face juxtaposed with the way she made up for it now: constantly feeding people.

"Old Abdar helped anyone who needed it. The food from his plate, the robes from his back. He took us in after the house collapsed, gave up his bed so you had somewhere to sleep."

"I remember complaining that it smelled like him." Mira was subdued, not realising how oblivious she had been.

"Well, a few years later, he just disappeared. Went out for a walk and never came back. The whole of Seong searched for him, worried he had fallen or been arrested by the kumiho. Everyone. The street kids, the aunties, the harbour workers who barely took a day off in their lives, they all looked. Because he would have done it for them. Because he had never asked for anything in return."

"Did they find him?"

"Not until it was too late. He knew it was his time, took himself off somewhere quiet. Didn't want to make a fuss."

"But that's devastating. To be alone when so many people would've gladly been by his side. To fail to see that he was appreciated and loved after everything he had done for others."

"Devastating," Trish repeated. One word. She did not need to say more. The entire cabin crooning in key with her unvoiced siren song. The oaky notes of warmth and promise of comfort.

Mira drained her cup of tea before she spoke. Before she shared all that had happened with Jiang-Li, the Fenghuang, Samnang and Cordelia. Before she slid the box containing the last dragon pearl from beneath the covers of her hammock.

"Well," Trish said, mulling the word over in her mouth. "Another cup of tea?"

"It's not that simple."

"No, but even complicated solutions start somewhere. I'll get Ibhar and the others. You get Tam. Don't forget the flatbread."

The words didn't really make sense to Mira, the whirlwind of activity her ama had put into action.

"Flatbread, Mira," Trish said, as if explaining to a child. "If we are making a plan, people will want to be fed."

Chapter Forty-Three

The surviving members of the *Wayfarer* traipsed without complaint back up through the tower. Subdued. In dialogue with their own inner thoughts rather than each other. They emerged at sea level, where the azure sky looked painted on: too blue, too perfectly serene after what had just happened. The unexpected heat prickled on Nami's scalp and the back of her neck. Her whole body ached, shoulder pulsing with what was probably a fracture.

She sat down on the nearest rock, too exhausted to move, to speak, to do anything other than stare into the distance. This was the first death she had chosen. No one had forced her hand or manipulated her this time. She dipped her hand in a puddle of sea-water, rubbing at the palm, although no bloodstains were visible.

"Well, I for one think that at a time like this, it is important to sustain our metabolism. Consume to compensate for the energy depletions." Eun yelled like they were in a busy room, even though there was only silence. Only her, standing while the rest of them huddled in disparate groups. Everyone looked at her. Confused. Nami knew exactly what she meant. The nervous rambling was creeping back in, but Nami saw her. Knew her.

"We should eat," she translated. A task to unite them, something concrete and achievable. It was easier to focus them with an objective. It thawed out the artificial reticence between them.

A good-natured rivalry about who could catch the biggest fish sprang up. Shizuku debated whether the one huge pike they caught with their long arms was equivalent to the small net of herring Mikayil and Jinsei managed between them. Wensum, the only one who had abstained from the group decision over Firth, was subdued to one side. They had discussed if they should bind her limbs together. In the end, the line between sides was so blurred that none of them felt they could do so. The mundane chatter at least put them at ease, strengthening those tender new shoots of trust. It would take longer to form a solid walkway, but it was a start.

"You are smiling," Eun commented, jostling Nami so their arms rubbed against each other.

Nami touched her own face. Surprised. Eun was right. Despite everything, it was as if she was soaring overhead, spiralling in the eddies. But peace never lasted. Not while they sat atop a titan, an arrow still pointing towards Tiankawi. Not now that plumes of white smoke were puffing from the top of the keep.

"Shit," Nami said, jumping to her feet. Sobekki's signal. She had been too exhausted, too distracted to ponder the significance of his disappearance.

Manannán Keep had grown. As the sand god came closer to the surface, so did more of the former Iyoness haven. Four small islands had become one large one, with more derelict structures now visible in the shallows. The keep glared down like one of those ancient oak trees of storybooks. Austere, grey as the overcast sky that had loomed all around for weeks. Beyond first glances, however, especially when the rays of sunshine hit the curved walls, the granite glittered with a shimmer. Treasure embedded in deep veins for those patient enough to search for it.

The smoke lingered, not in voluminous clouds but in thin layer upon layer like sediment. The sky pushing down, collapsing over their heads. The warning Sobekki had given her before the *Wayfarer* had been destroyed: if they did not avert the danger, Yonakuni would act instead. Jiang-Li would take control of Tiankawi.

"Nami? What is it?" Eun asked.

Nami had never felt like a dragon before. The wisdom and leadership people assumed she had was simply a mantle, a threadbare family heirloom: too heavy and too big for her narrow shoulders. Even now she did not feel it. The generations of knowledge and authority failed to manifest with a decisive response.

But she felt *them*. Jinsei offering Jalad his arm, helping him to his feet as they watched the smoke continue to pour. The others tending the small fire and the fish they had started to grill. The community they had built on the ship, the divides and differences they had somehow overcome to reach this place. This equilibrium of understanding. It would always be teetering, on one side or other of the scales, always needing careful monitoring. But it was something they had built. A raw unpolished gem. Not Firth's, not even Mira's back in Tiankawi. Certainly not her mother's.

"It's a choice," she said, pointing towards the top of the keep. They had fought for the chance to make their own decisions, their own future. Not to replace one broken system with another. In that moment, she knew she could not allow the signal smoke to continue.

Sobekki was waiting for them by the huge brazier at the top of the keep. A massive heap of kelp stood behind him. He must have been collecting and drying the seaweed for days now, readying everything for this. He had enough to keep the signal going all day, long enough for the people of Tiankawi to see the message. Even without the smoke, only the most adamant optimist would see Iyoness raised above the waves, on a direct collision course with the city, and not fear the worst. The damage might already have been done.

Sobekki slammed down his tail before they could get any closer, the force strong enough to flick rubble and smouldering embers into the air. As they covered their faces, the heat and light dazzling them, he charged through the middle, straight towards Jalad, aiming punch after punch at the naga's chest until he lowered his guard and Sobekki hooked him with an ice-coated fist across the jaw. Jalad went flying backwards, skidding on the ground towards the edge of the keep. Nami acted on instinct, throwing up an ice wall to stop him from tumbling off the side.

Sobekki turned, taking on Shizuku and Wensum next. Fists and legs too fast, too strong for them to do more than defend against it. The onslaught was relentless and brutal. On the climb upwards they had talked about strength in numbers, hitting him from all sides. His fury crumbled their resolve. Frightening them, making them hesitate. Their teamwork disintegrating at the first hurdle.

Or at least that was what they wanted him to think.

"Now!" Nami yelled. Shizuku and Wensum crouched as she leaped from behind them, whipping the ice dart in her hand towards the chink in Sobekki's scales. He slammed it away, the water rope ricocheting before Nami yanked it back in. She had known he would do that. Sensitive to that old vulnerability. The rope looped round his back and she pulled it upwards, slashing the dart across his right eye. He yelled, hand raised to cover his face as blood spurted between his claws, and took a step back, not noticing that while he was distracted, the ground beneath them had been turned to a smooth sheet of ice. Surprise flickered across his face as he fell onto his back.

Nami stood over him, now brandishing a glaive made of water and ice. The length of the polearm reassured her, as did the curved moonblade under his chin. She knew better than to get any closer. She did not want to kill him; Sobekki was not her enemy. "There is still hope," she said.

"You did your best, better than I had expected. You took that smug kelpie down. But this isn't a practice fight, this is the real thing." His words were assured, despite lying on the ground with a blade to his throat. Too late Nami realised they no longer had the upper hand. Somewhere beside her she heard Mikayil groan and drop. Eun and Jinsei also crumpled, sounds of whimpered anguish following them. The ice underfoot had been transformed back to water. Chains of it pulling down on them, forcing them to their knees. Sobekki did not need to get close to use his water-weaving. Only Nami could resist the drag of the water under her.

"There's more than one way to win a fight," he said.

Nami was afraid, the worst of her fears realised. That she had led them down the wrong path. Making everything worse, just as they always said she would.

"Believe me when I say I'm sorry it has come to this." Sobekki drew his curved khopesh, but he did not sound sorry. He was right about one thing. Nami knew she was never going to win this fight. Not with all the weapons and waterweaving in the world.

"What will she wish for? With the potential of her last egg?" she demanded abruptly.

"I did not ask."

"You didn't?" she pushed, finding a space to wedge into. "You, who taught me never to blindly follow. To question. To seek knowledge and opinions outside of my own. You have put trust in a leader so out of touch that she left thousands of Iyonessians in cages rather than offer aid?"

"What?" Sobekki said, his voice wavering for the first time.

"Jinsei, tell him!"

The schoolteacher raised his head, straining against the water ropes. His voice was quiet, but magnetising all the same. He spoke of the Nurseries at full capacity. Cages only slightly bigger than a coffin, submerged and stacked on top of each other. Metal bars carpeted with algae and barnacles. Malnourished fathomfolk queuing up for thin rice soup, no more than children, despite the whiskers and dorsal fins. Children like Firth, who had grown up too fast, distorted by the rusted metal around them.

"Eun," Nami encouraged as Jinsei's words petered to an end. The archivist carried on. She talked of Nami's father, the Yonakuni envoy desperate for a way out. Signing an agreement that fathomfolk would sell their powers at the Onseon Engine, would wear pakalots around their wrists. How in striving to end the Nurseries, he instead condemned the folk to another form of injustice in its place.

Then Nami took up the story herself. Telling a different tale. The city state more verdant than they had ever seen. Baskets of red snappers, piles of water spinach and nets of mussels filling the long boats of the early-morning water market. People meandering across the skybridges at a pace that said they had nowhere to be in a hurry. Kappas chatting to humans; a rusalka and naga couple with their young babe in arms; a schoolteacher chaperoning a dozen small children, skin and scale, hide and fur mixing as they weaved through the other folk, feet and fins one and the same as they chattered. The Tiankawi Mira strived for. One Nami had grown to believe in too.

Sobekki said nothing, but nor did he add more seaweed to the brazier. It was easier to be bleak. Prepare for the worst. Hope was easy to shoot down, to mock as something for fools. If they didn't hope, then they would never be disappointed.

"Jiang-Li sent me to Tiankawi not to learn and grow wise. She sent me ignorant so that I would stumble around and set fire to the place. Make a mess she could sweep down and clean up. That's all I have ever been to her. A pawn."

"You are her daughter."

"And?" Nami saw that they were all pieces on the board. Jiang-Li would sacrifice her last dragon pearl on the flimsy evidence of a smoke signal. Perhaps Kai had meant something to her, but perhaps he had been the favourite merely because he had been more pliable. The good immigrant. "Tell me you believe in her every word, every action. That you have no doubts. That the Senate of Yonakuni will be fair and just to *all* of us, and you'll have no fight from me."

Sobekki's eyes flitted to Eun beside her, to Mikayil and Zidane. No. He knew as well as they did that Yonakuni would treat humans and freshwater folk with disdain. Mudskippers. Siltborn. The words curdled now against Nami's tongue, but once she had used them casually, never realising that prejudice ran both ways. A different way of carving it up, but divisions all the same.

"You cannot best me in a fight."

"I cannot. I've never been able to. But I'm trying a new strategy for size. Reason."

Sobekki had no words for her. No reproach. All he had to do was tail-slap her to the ground. Fling her off the side of the tower. Clamp his sharp teeth around her jugular. With his impenetrable hide and lightning reflexes, he was ready for that. She had used up all her tricks.

Instead, the Protector of Yonakuni stepped aside.

It was her turn.

Nami and Eun rushed forward, heat from the burning seaweed rising in thick waves from the brazier. Nami was halfway to pulling water from the sea to dampen the smouldering dregs when Eun stayed her hand. "The message is already out there, broadcast for the whole city to see. Putting the fire out will make no difference now. You've got to alter it."

"Alter it?"

"Change the narrative." Eun reached up with both hands, touching the sides of Nami's face. Wonder. Exhilaration. Pride. Unspoken but tangible as the spark between them. Reading the tired lines as if she was following a sentence on a page.

It lit a fire inside Nami. Glittering red embers that had always been there, hiding in the ash. She leaned in, longing suffusing her. Zidane cleared his throat, snapping them apart. Sobekki rolled his eyes, the others somewhere between bemused and embarrassed.

"Change." Nami grinned, running a hand through her hair as if it had been nothing at all. Her fingers laced about Eun's. A promise of things to come. Rather than distracting her, this time it made everything clear. Stilling all the clamouring noise to pinpoint a solution. Her gaze drifted to the smoke signal. Eun was right, there was no point in putting it out.

"Time for a new message."

Chapter Forty-Four

Mira took the steps two at a time, disregarding the other Council members labouring up the stairs to the Hall of Harmonious Eminence in their ceremonial robes, heavily embroidered sashes and painted silks. The weather had turned cooler, but it was still not an easy walk in full regalia. Once upon a time, Mira might have felt eyes on her, trying and failing to ignore the whispers about how last-season, how outer-district her attire was. No more. Every second pandering to them was a moment wasted. She reached the entrance before the rest of the party. The folds and pleats of her brocade outfit draped heavily on her left side, the loose shawl end pinned to her shoulder and cascading to the ground.

Her eyes moved towards the horizon, towards the white that might be clouds but might be something else. She would not know, trapped inside the hall as overpriced cocktails were sloshed on the floor and the ministers were officially sworn into office, trampling on each other as they vied for the position of new Fenghuang.

All the ambassadors were present. The ones from Dhinduk and Atlitya, and even Jiang-Li for Yonakuni, despite a paka-lot locked onto her wrist and a pair of kumiho city guards on either side. The Yonakunish party had funded civil unrest with the Fathomfolk First movement, might even have arranged for Samnang's assassination, but ultimately Tiankawi could not risk an outright war with the havens. Jiang-Li claimed ignorance; after all, she had been confined and guarded when Samnang had died. It was hard to make anything stick. They could not hold the sovereign ruler of another nation indefinitely.

Mira tapped her fingers impatiently through the quartet of musicians in the first chamber. The traditional sounds of the zither and bamboo flute did nothing to settle her nerves, nor did the overhead chatter of songbirds swinging in their gilded cages. The Minister of Healing shot a look in her direction, and only then did she realise her sigh was audible in the echoing acoustics of the space. She had to endure the official swearing-in ceremony, grit her teeth for the pageantry of it, before she had the floor. All the incumbent Council members had time allocated for an outgoing speech.

Her tolerance was low. The same droning voices were so much more aggravating this time. Like sand under her nails. Pointless self-congratulatory speeches as the Ministers of Healing, Agriculture and Ceremonies were duly re-elected. Gede came next, keeping his speech shorter, thank the titans. Just a couple more and—

She heard her own name without understanding. It wasn't time for her to speak yet. Gede beamed, Pyanis scowled, the rest looked on with blank expressions. Mira moved slowly through the crowd, wishing she had listened more closely, desperately hoping someone would fill her in.

"Minister?" said the junior official at the front. In his hands was the seal of office in a silk-padded box. Minister of Fathomfolk. She had forgotten entirely. It meant so little to her these days that she had not kept track. Pyanis repeated her name, impatiently this time, her voice growling like Cordelia's on a bad day. It shouldn't matter. In the grand scheme of things, it did *not* matter. Yet it was as if she were eight years old all over again. A scrawny, knock-kneed thing hoping for someone, anyone to call her name when picking teams. Staring down at the shoes she had long since outgrown but could not afford to replace, pretending not to care as tears smarted in her eyes. They had chosen her.

Behind her the double doors creaked open and Mira closed her eyes with a wry smile. An ensign in the chinthe came to her side, whispering the words she had expected in her heart of hearts when the sky had looked hazy this morning.

"Tell my mother. You know what to do," she ordered him swiftly.

The new Minister of Justice complained about respect for the traditions, glaring at her with arms folded into sleeves.

"A smoke signal has been sighted. My ensign has just confirmed it's from the crew of the *Wayfarer*."

"The ship is back?" Gede asked.

"Not exactly. They are on the ruins of Iyoness, on the back of a titan: the life-bonded partner of the sand god who died beneath our feet. It will be here before nightfall, and if it does not slow, the whole city will be destroyed." Her voice was calm despite everything she felt inside. Delivering the news like a monthly report rather than the end of everything.

The room erupted into chaos.

Jiang-Li's voice carried above the panic, a piercing counter-melody that cut through the uproar, the questions. "I warned you, Minister of Fathomfolk. I know you have my last pearl."

"Then what are we waiting for. Use it!" the Minister of Agriculture said, her eyes bulging.

"How exactly?" Mira had been asking herself that question since she had stolen the key. It had seemed like a good idea at the time, but now she had to come up with a solution. Watch it succeed or fail without throwing the blame on someone else.

"Destroy the titan," the minister replied.

"No," Minister Pyanis cut in. "A waste of resources! Of land! Subdue it." She leaned back on a wall and scratched at her inner elbow, a mannerism that echoed Cordelia. It would be just like the seawitch to insinuate herself into the Council.

"Iyoness is a fathomfolk haven. That land belongs to us, to Yonakuni," Jiang-Li said.

"Why should you speak for us? Atlitya would stake a claim also," the Atlityan ambassador snapped. He glared at the dragon matriarch, the smaller haven forever overshadowed by its more successful cousin. They were like aphids, swarming over the tender buds and leaves before they even had time to unfurl, not caring that their sap-sucking jaws were destroying the very resource they relied on.

"It's hurting," Mira said. They squabbled, not listening to her words until she pushed them all down with a single note of siren song rising with exasperation through her.

Listen.

Silence rang in her ears. The manufactured peace that she so wished could happen organically. She was disgusted that she had to use her siren song against them, and yet the instantaneous effect of it could not be denied. The power so easy to fall back on. Thrown off balance, she heard her own words tripping and falling face-first onto the marble tiles. "It's mourning the partner it lost. I ... the Tideborn Centre recruits and I have arranged for a memorial service. To respect that loss."

She waited for a response, belatedly realising from Gede's rapid blinking that they were still under her influence. Shit. She released them, seeing the fear flicker across the room. Jiang-Li was first to regain control over her vocal cords. "Let me get this straight. You will quell the wrath of a vengeful sand god by laying flowers atop a grave marker? The very grave we are standing upon?"

It sounded absurd when said aloud, but the others had nothing else to offer. No viable alternative other than to pull hers down.

Outside, noise built up. The chatter of many people, heavy steps and activity. One of the city guards opened a shuttered window to take a peek. A crossbow bolt whizzed through the gap and embedded itself in his chest. He flinched backwards at the impact, spinning on the spot before falling onto the ornate tiled floor. Dark blood oozed from under him.

More bolts followed, a scattershot into the shutters, splintering through the musicians' instruments and the fine furniture. More still found soft targets, deep in the thigh of a kumiho guard, one in the abdomen of a junior official.

"Cleaven!" Gede yelled as Council and onlookers alike screamed and retreated. As he ran to slam the window shut, a bolt tore across his cheek and shattered one of the larger birdcages near Mira's head. She dashed forward to help him, yelling to the dazed chinthe to bar the doors. The heavy double doors creaked under the combined effort, then finally slammed shut. Mira slid the huge iron bolt into place.

Sounds came from outside, curses and pounding fists, muffled but still clear enough to hear. Then a rhythmical *thud. Thud. Thud. Thud.* Mira met Tam's eyes across the hall, but no words were needed. They knew that sound. A battering ram. An organised riot, then. Or more. Samnang had known. Perhaps he had planned to be a martyr all along, to boil the blood of his radical supporters.

"What do they want?" the Minister of Healing asked.

"They are here for the pearl," Jiang-Li said.

"How do they even know it's here?" Mira demanded. The dragon matriarch shrugged. Mira wouldn't put it past her to fan the flames of rage in order to pick up the pieces afterwards.

Before she could ask, something exploded inside the room. She threw herself behind a chair, shielding her eyes as the bright sparks blinded her. Spots of light danced across her vision, ears ringing still as she looked. The Cleaven had hacked small holes in the window shutters. Big enough to drop something in. As she watched, she saw a spiky clay grenade roll through one of the gaps. Smoke spewed from it before it detonated. Terracotta shards flew across the room, a surprise parcel of twisted metal shrapnel hidden within. Mira ducked once more. Others had slower reflexes. Sulphur and iron filled the air. Kelwin, the Minister of Healing, had refused to cower, and now paid for it as one side of his face burned red raw with pieces of jagged metal embedded deep into his cheek and eye. He howled in pain.

"Back, back to the inner chamber," Mira shouted. She neither knew nor cared if she had put coercion into her voice, people limping to respond all the same. Too dazed to do anything but wait for the next round without her command. The huge double doors thudded again with the heaving of the battering ram, bulging and splintering with the concerted effort. The invaders would be through it soon. Hands tore strips of broken wood away, and the glazed anger of the mob beyond was visible.

"Free me," Jiang-Li demanded of the new Minister of Justice. The woman hesitated, looking around for advice and finding none. She nodded, grappling for the release on the dragon matriarch's pakalot-cuffed wrist. Jiang-Li was the most powerful waterweaver in the room. If anyone could hold them back, it was her.

A burly man had climbed through the wreckage of the door. His feather gills were mutilated, but that was not his only scar by far. Healed wounds criss-crossed his torso and he carried a machete in each hand with practised ease. Others poured in behind him, armed with crowbars and kitchen knives, glass bottles and three-pronged trident spears, clambering over each other in their haste. Mira wondered with a strange distance if they had climbed the stairs two at a time as well. If they had stopped to marvel at the roof tiles as she once had, the artisan skill in the murals they would surely now destroy.

She sang, throwing up a hundred kumiho guards before them, swords drawn. The mob hesitated for a moment, but when the illusory guards failed to attack, the man with two machetes swept straight through, the other Cleaven not far behind. Gede, Tam and the remaining guards met them, blades flashing. They had the skills to hold their own but had not been trained for the relentless fury before them. People so angry that mere wounds would not end the fight.

Something cracked, crisp and solid. Ice had frozen under the feet of the Cleaven, welding them to the floor. Jiang-Li raised her hands overhead, and for a moment, Mira allowed herself to hope. Then one of the humans pulled his foot free. Followed by another. The brittle ice layer was too thin, too weak to keep them. There was not enough water in the closed room. It would be different at sea level, but in here they were trapped.

"Back, back!" Mira repeated.

Gede, Tam and the stragglers retreated to the inner chamber with the others. They dragged the heavy furniture across and piled it against the ornate glass doors. There was no lock here. The designers never expecting the occupants would have to barricade themselves in.

Shit.

Mira took a precious moment to unpin her ornate brocade outfit, the long folds falling like shed skin in a circle around her. Beneath she wore loose-fitting trousers pulled in at the ankle, and a plain top. The pleats of material had concealed a large box in a satchel by her left hip, secured by a shoulder strap.

"There's a back exit," Minister Kelwin said, voice muffled by the scarf he pressed against his wounded face.

As Mira moved through the tight huddle of people towards the indicated door, someone grabbed at her bag. She swerved instinctively, glaring at the sharply manicured nails that had managed nonetheless to gain purchase on the strap. Jiang-Li scowled. "Give me my pearl."

"No."

"It's mine. My flesh and blood."

"Just as Kai and Nami are yours? You may have brought them into this world, but you don't get to make every decision for them."

"And you do? A convenient excuse to further your own ends," Jiang-Li shot back. She was not wrong. No one was without bias, without ulterior motive here. But that did not mean Mira would simply hand back the pearl to Jiang-Li and Yonakuni.

"There is time for this later; we need to go," she insisted. She tugged, but the dragon matriarch would not let go.

"The time is now!" With her free hand, Jiang-Li yanked loose her belt of jangling shells and threw it on the ground. The rumble of thunder and crackle of forked lightning flickered underfoot as though they stood upon a storm cloud. Out of each shattered shell, a pinprick light bounced, skittering across the floor, coming together in a mesmerising display. Hantu ayer.

Mira covered her eyes just in time as the tiny water spirits flashed together, dazzling white light bleaching the room and temporarily blinding those nearby. She twisted her bag out of Jiang-Li's grasp, stumbling and half crawling towards the rear door. The dragon matriarch roared, the hantu ayer water spirits under her control combining to form a giant humanoid shape edged in pulsing light. It reached for Mira, charging with singular purpose. Those between them were thrown back as if an invisible hand flicked debris out of the way. Mira dodged, skidding on the floor as she turned and aimed one throwing knife, then another towards the bright shape. The blades stopped dead in the air as if embedded in something dense. The hantu ayer form paused, its dazzling edge dimmed. Then it rippled and both daggers fell, clattering to the ground like leavings washed up by the tide.

Mira swore. The hantu ayer were at her throat now, pinning her limbs down. They broke from their humanoid form back into pinprick lights once more, pouring in through the gill slits in her neck. Crowding her, making her gag as her body tried to heave up the internal assault. Lacerating her throat from the inside out.

She dragged her reluctant body, feet scraping heavily on the floor, the last couple of metres towards the rear door. Jiang-Li folded her arms, watching. She had barely lifted a finger, leaving the hantu ayer to wreak havoc. Mira reached for the handle, fingers fumbling weakly for the brass ring.

Before she could get a grip on it, the door flew open. A hand axe slammed down towards her head, so fast it was simply a blur of grey. Too late to dodge, too late to do anything other than squeeze her eyes closed and wait for impact.

Her skull did not split open.

The axe was inches from her head. Quivering in the muscular arms of the Cleaven assailant but held frozen in place. The hantu ayer had poured from Mira's gills, forming an opaque fist that gripped the weapon in mid-air. It gave a twist, the attacker gasping in sharp pain as the axe went flying to the side. Behind her, Jiang-Li cursed and redirected the water spirits. She might want Mira dead, but the dragon matriarch could not risk her last pearl falling into Cleaven hands.

They clashed. The hantu ayer took out swathes of the Cleaven invaders with one slam, pushing them back down the narrow corridor they'd snuck up from. Mira retreated hastily towards the centre of the room. Both exits were now blocked.

"Do something!" demanded the Minister of Agriculture, hands on Mira's shoulders as he propelled her forward like a shield. Tam yelled. At the front of the room, the Cleaven had pushed through the flimsy stained-glass doors, wedging the survivors in a tight huddle between the two onslaughts. Jiang-Li rolled up her sleeves, flicking beads of sweat from her brow and freezing them, sending the projectiles into the front wave of attackers, shattering knee-caps and causing a temporary pile-up. Behind her, the hantu ayer were flickering, powers all but spent. Already some of the Cleaven slipped round the sides, the city guards doing their best to push them back.

Mira looked round the room for a weapon, for an alternative she could not yet see. On the raised dais a trolley held bamboo scrolls and lotus leaf papers. The ornately decorated tea set she had drunk from with Jiang-Li and the Fenghuang during the endless negotiations.

She swivelled. The server who had brought them tea and bamboo steamers of dumplings had not used the front or back entrance. They had appeared soundlessly at the Fenghuang's side with a lacquer tray. A discreet servants' entrance to the room. Her sharp eyes spotted it: there, the wall hanging was askew. Another way out.

"Tam, with me," she said. Her lieutenant moved immediately to stand at her side, scanning the room as she beckoned the others forward.

Jiang-Li backed up as she saw them moving towards the hidden doorway. "I'm not done with you!" she shot, not daring to turn her back on the Cleaven.

"Concentrate on not dying first."

The dragon matriarch moved her fingers like she was strumming a zither. From the vase of flowers on the dais, a stream of stagnant water threaded towards her. She sneered contemptuously, but nevertheless moulded it into a long double-edged water blade, edge emerald-green with scum. "Get on with it." When Mira did not respond, she added, exasperated, "If you are intent on living, then go!"

She swung hard at the nearest attacker. He moved in close as she left her side exposed. In a blur of unexpected speed, she feigned upwards and then cut down. The man barely had time to gasp as he keeled over. Jiang-Li flicked her sword, blood splattering the faces of those behind her as she brought the weapon back to the centre. Mira wrenched her eyes away, leaving the dragon behind.

Chapter Forty-Five

Behind the servants' entrance, a set of narrow spiral stairs led upwards. Gede went first, the others close behind. It opened out into a large kitchen area dominated by a central island. Clay pots lined the shelves on one wall: rice and pulses, fish sauce and salted black beans. Strings of dried fish and squid hung in bundles in the far corner, where a couple of servants hid in a nervous huddle.

"Is there another way out?" Mira asked without preamble.

The woman uncovered her tear-stained face to nod. "Across the servants' quarters and back down into the main corridor below us. On the other side of the courtyard are the Fenghuang's personal chambers. There's a hidden escape route in there."

They wasted no time, Mira heaving the woman up by the elbow to come with them, stumbling in the dim light. They descended another set of narrow stairs, Gede sliding the hidden door open just a little before indicating it was safe. Mira had not even known there was an inner square in the hall. Had never ventured past the first two formal rooms. The courtyard was an oasis of calm. A weeping willow grew in the centre, the long boughs bending over an ornamental koi pond below. Grey pebbles, uniform in size and shape, were placed in circular patterns like ripples.

Mira found herself calculating how much bigger the garden was than her first home. Or her second. The long, snaking line for a ladleful of freshwater from the communal store when it had not rained in months. Here the water trickled down a tiered water feature and tickled orange and white dappled goldfish.

The echoed sounds of fighting were not far off their position as they crossed the courtyard. The sound of running footsteps grew louder. Yells, a warning, and then a water dragon cut towards them. Kai? Mira's heart soared momentarily, foolishly hoping for something that could never be. No. It was Jiang-Li. The differences were clear now as she undulated towards them. She roared, and words were not needed for everyone to understand the meaning.

The dragon matriarch crashed into them, Mira holding onto her flank to steady her. Her hide was badly hurt, patches pink where scales had broken off. One of her eyelids drooped, the pupil oozing red. She lurched, unstable on her feet.

"Tam, help me," Mira said. The dragon was too heavy to carry in her true form. They could barely get her upper body off the ground, her long serpentine tail dragging along the floor. "Perhaps if we—" she began.

Tam shuddered strangely, dropping Jiang-Li's bulk. The words died on Mira's lips and they both looked down at the strange sight of a harpoon bolt piercing through his chest. He wrapped his hands around it as if in disbelief, blood spurting in short, sharp gasps. Then he was yanked backwards.

Mira screamed as she watched him being dragged back by the attached rope, body bouncing down the steps and scraping heavily on the pebbles in the courtyard. A weak struggle at first, and then nothing more than a rag doll. She tore after him, stopped only by Gede's grip around her waist. He yelled something, but she could not understand his words.

More harpoon bolts whizzed across the courtyard, slamming into Jiang-Li's prone body, embedding themselves in the pillars on either side. The angry mob of Cleaven moved, weapons drawn and feet thundering like a drum roll.

"Lead them," Gede said. His thumb was on Mira's chin, forcing her gaze away from Tam's prone body. He had been repeating the same words, over and over, but only now did they reach through the haze. Mira snapped back into herself.

"To me!" she demanded of the cowering councillors beside her. They surprised her, and themselves, by responding. Together they dragged the wounded dragon into the Fenghuang's chambers. The attackers had to pause to reload, giving them time. Gede brought up the rear, kumiho sword drawn, the blade trembling, clutched too tightly for too long. He hesitated at the doors, catching Mira's unvoiced question. Cursing under his breath, he ran back into the courtyard with a strangled battle cry.

Mira was too exhausted to be surprised. Numb more than anything. She did not know what he had seen as he searched her face, but he had found an answer all the same. Something that made him trust in the fractured plan they had discussed. Something that made him reckless.

Minister Pyanis stared back through the door. Her brows were pulled low, an unreadable expression on her pinched features. She leaned down towards Mira, ostensibly to check on the unconscious dragon at her side. Her voice was low, and it was unmistakably Cordelia's. "Don't fuck this up, saltlick."

Everyone else was too busy, too panicked to notice Pyanis straighten up and slip out into the courtyard. The doors slid closed behind her and all noise suddenly quelled. In the blur of the opaque, semi-shuttered windows, the shadow of tentacles striped the floor and walls around them. Growing bigger and longer with squelching, groaning sounds.

One of the Cleaven screamed. "Kraken!" Then all they could hear was the strike of metal and breaking of glass. Slick, moist sounds. Crunching and breaking. Tearing and then thuds. Silence.

The seawitch had finally taken responsibility. Or perhaps she had only gone to protect her son. It mattered not which was the truth of it.

Mira assessed the remaining survivors. Picked off, fallen behind. Fewer by far than the group that had first entered the ceremonial hall. Council members and junior officials, a couple of kumiho and chinthe. She pulled the sandalwood box from her satchel, opening the lid so that the hard gleam of the dragon pearl stopped all hushed conversation. She held it up to Jiang-Li's snout. The water dragon's whiskers moved reflexively towards the light source, her eyes rolling beneath closed lids.

Mira pulled the pearl away, watching as a frown settled on Jiang-Li's brow. She was aware enough. "I need you in human shape." The furrow deepened. "So we can get to safety."

The dragon did not respond, but her long body shrank before their eyes. Tail thinning and curling into two legs. Body curved into a foetal position. Naked, Jiang-Li was as vulnerable as the rest of them. Without the armour of dazzling ceremony that kept people at arm's length, she could be mistaken for just another folk labourer at the port; another worker at the Onseon Engine. One of the junior officials wrapped their coat around her shoulders and picked up the unconscious woman, now much lighter.

They moved through the extensive chambers: tea room, study, dressing room and bedchamber, searching for the hidden way out. The ashes in the hearth had been carefully raked into wave patterns and a cast-iron kettle hung over the unlit stack of logs. It was not a practical arrangement, burning wood when there were so few trees in the city. Nothing but a status symbol.

They felt at the panelled walls, looked underneath the seat cushions, pulled the room apart looking for the secret passage they had been told about. The kitchen worker shook her head, just as confused as the rest. "I've never seen it, I was just told ... It must be here!" Doubt lingered in her voice.

Mira felt the weight of the dragon pearl dragging her down

through the shoulder straps of her bag. She kicked at the rim of the hearth with all her frustration. It wobbled. She pushed hard at the frame. Her first impressions had been right: the fire was purely decorative. The whole thing slid open to reveal a ladder leading down.

The darkness was engulfing as they descended. Mira might have lost her nerve had it not been for the others following her, feet just above her head. Down they went, rung after rung after broken rung. She counted eighty-eight, one hundred and eighty-eight, two hundred and eighty-eight, then she lost count entirely but still she kept going. Just as her courage was about to fail her, she finally stepped down into a tunnel. The walls were warded with powerful waterweaving barriers, keeping the seawater from seeping in. As dim light pierced the edges of her vision, she finally allowed herself to consider what might happen next.

Mira shaded her eyes as she ascended the shallow stairs ahead of her, squinting into the afternoon sun. Paper and scrolls criss-crossed her eyeline like birds flying through the air. Beyond that, shelves and glass cylinders all in disarray.

The City Library.

Eun had laid the precious archives out to dry before she left, tasking Mira with watching over things in her absence. Of course, she thought guiltily, the whole thing had slipped her mind.

They ducked and moved around the labyrinth of lotus leaf paper and bamboo scrolls towards the door. A couple of dried leaves slipped to the ground and something keened in Mira's chest. A savage mob had broken in to murder the Council, the leader of Yonakuni and every other notable envoy and official in Tiankawi. They had managed to kill one of her oldest friends. How could the destruction of records possibly compare? Still, it made her think, not about the now; not about her own loss, endlessly echoing in her heart; but about what might happen tomorrow. How people might talk of this moment in Tiankawi's history. Would it be something they could look back on proudly, or would they bury it, embarrassed at another stain on the city state's history.

From the library steps, she could see the smoke signal billowing in the sky, clear as could be. White plumes puffing from one side of the open seas, and below them, an island mass that moved with alarming speed directly towards them.

"Use the dragon pearl!" cried a panicked junior official.

"Destroy the sand god before it destroys us," others chimed in.

"We've all lost so much," Mira said, wishing more than ever that Kai, even his ghost, stood at her side. The space remained empty. No Kai. No Tam or Mikayil, Trish or Nami. Not even Gede.

"It's too big, too dangerous. We are more important," the junior official responded.

"It was not so long ago that the Council said the same of fathomfolk. Look where that left us."

"You have to do something!"

All the voices, the push and pull of demands, and yet none of them were listening. Not really.

"I have," she said. "Just wait."

Chapter Forty-Six

Nami should not be so glad to see Tiankawi: the familiar obelisk towers of the Jingsha central district, the sprawling stilthouses and drifting boats around it. She should temper her soaring heart since the titan was about to ram straight into her new home, sending the whole place plunging to the ocean floor.

They had dashed across the Iyonessian ruins in twos and threes, looking for the ores that Eun had pointed out. Within the short time remaining, they had scavenged as best they could, regrouping atop the Keep. The message could not be snuffed out, but it could be altered.

Nami threw a handful of stone into the smoke. Waited. The white plumes continued to billow. Looked a little ruddy perhaps, but that might have been her imagination. Her heart beat a hundred times a minute, the weight of it a millstone about her neck.

Eun picked up a whole sackload, stumbling under the weight as she hefted it into Nami's arms. There was no hesitation on her determined face. No doubt. Together they upended the lot, the ore tumbling out. The smoke signal considered this newest offering, rolling it like an unfamiliar taste. Flames simmering a merry dance before licking out higher and stronger than before. Satiated, the signal fire belched.

The smoke poured from the keep, no longer white but vermilion red. A vibrant, pulsing colour. It pushed away the white, the signal that said they were doomed. Now it said something else.

Nami had not agreed a code with Mira. She could only hope they knew each other well enough: that the message would be clear. Crimson clouds puffed overhead and all they could do was wait.

The song reached them first. An echoing sound carried by the waves, a hundred voices or more in harmony. It grew louder, richer, filling the wind and sailing over to them as if through time as well as distance. It tugged their attention with its simple lyrics, its repetitive refrain pulling fleeting memories from Nami. A mourning song. A funeral song. She recalled it from childhood in Yonakuni, from more recent heated discussions with her mother and Mira over Kai's memorial.

Small bobbing skiffs and taraibune boats moved awkwardly towards them, the passengers robed in white and singing in unison. She sensed Trish within the chorus. Her siren song calm and familiar when everything was so uncertain. The ground shook beneath their feet. A tremor rippling from front to back as the titan manta ray spotted the wobbly lines of vessels coming out to meeting them.

"A memorial," Nami said. Mira had organised this as a sign of respect. An overture to making amends.

It could work.

It had to work.

Her hand still held Eun's. Fingers folded together like two halves of a shell. Now she beckoned to the others, pulling them closer together. Sobekki shuffled over with great reluctance, but Nami dragged him in anyhow. Shizuku offered their arm to a limping Zidane. Wensum stood awkwardly between Jalad and Jinsei. They huddled, folding arms and heads against each other. An end was coming. They had done their best, and whatever happened, they had finished on the same side.

⬤

Cordelia looked up, through the branches of the willow tree; at least the ones that were not bent and broken in pieces beneath her limbs. She lay still, her body weeping blue blood and black ink from multiple wounds. Trickles dripped between the pebbles like an oil leak. She could taste it in her own mouth, no longer bitter on her palate but something else. Verging on sweet.

"Ama," Gede said, voice hoarse. She heard him move, sit down heavily. Funny, his voice was so close. As if he leaned against her side. She could no longer turn her head in his direction. It wasn't that it hurt – the pain she could've tolerated. It was more that she couldn't feel anything at all. She recalled the Cleaven cutting her first limb, and then the second and the third. Beyond that was a blur. She'd rather not think about it too much. Thinking led to dread and panic, and that was no good for anyone.

"The kappa in the warehouse, Dan. Keep him on. Settle his debts, don't let the others poach him," she said. She had to force the words out now.

Gede rustled somewhere near her, his face blocking out her view momentarily. A concerned hand touched her cheek, her brow, but she could not feel it. Just a peculiar pressure. The side of his face was swollen, as though from a heavy blow, and a deep gash ran across his forehead, dripping blue blood down into his eye. He wiped it away impatiently, skin rippling in dots of colour as panic became visible on his features.

"You need to stitch that," she commented, trying to raise her arm to touch the wound. Her limbs refused to cooperate. She had not got round to showing him all her recipes. The formulas for her tonics and tinctures never written down. It was a shame they would die with her. He still had the dull weed business, the gill rot medication that was being lauded as the most significant health-care discovery in a generation. Those would run in her absence.

He would be okay. He just had to control his colourings now he had broken the charmed pendant around his neck.

Or perhaps . . . he didn't.

She refocused on the sky behind him. The clouds from the signal smoke had turned red. Red like the many sunsets she had watched from their family home, plotting everyone's path. Red like the dried jujube dates she scattered in her medicinal soups. Something revived in her chest, her hearts beating a little bit faster.

"Make sure Qiuyue wears a vest in winter. She feels the cold more like a human."

"Tell her yourself, Ama," Gede said. He was near tears. Silly boy, such a sensitive thing. Yet he made her proud. Vehemently holding her hand as if he could drag her back into the world of the living. "Promise me, Ama. Tell her yourself. Make me a deal."

But Cordelia could not hear him any more. Her mind drifted upwards like the smoke signal, lifting into the sky.

Mira covered her mouth as the smoke signal turned red. It terrified her, the bloom of crimson clouds in the near distance rolling closer.

"Red. It must mean bloodshed!" one of the Council members said.

"A sign to use the pearl. Destroy it, Mira, before it gets any closer!" another guessed.

Hands tried to grab the burden from her, as if she would relinquish it so easily. She curled herself around it, hugging the box as close as she should have hugged Kai at the end. It seemed to respond in kind. A warmth emanating so faintly that she thought perhaps she had imagined it. What did red mean? White was bad enough. Did red truly mean all hope was lost?

"Give me your burden, child. You are yet too immature to yield it," Jiang-Li said. Her voice rasped, lips pale with the blood loss, and she could barely prop herself on her elbows, but still her authority rang out. Mira had to do everything in her power to resist it. She was tired of chipping away at things. Paring away at the bruises on the surface to find there was nothing left of the fruit. Nothing untouched by the dark spots. She needed to try something different. Bite into it and hope the whole thing was still sweet.

"Give me the pearl," said Kelwin, the Minister of Healing. The kindly grandfather put out his hand. The clay pieces from the grenades were still embedded in the side of his face, caked with thickening blood.

Instead Mira's grip tightened. Who was to say his best was better than hers? They clamoured around her. Too many hands, too many voices for her to discern. Tugging at her sleeve, pulling at her precious parcel. Any more indecision and they would tear it from her hands. A mob by any other name. All wanting to serve their own.

"*STOP!*" she commanded. Everyone was caught in their tracks, frozen limbs reaching to yank at her hair, to retrieve weapons, scowls and anger half formed. She moved away from them all, leaving an empty space at the centre where she had stood. She could not hold the tableau for ever. She could not stop the pressures and demands. She knew that.

As she opened the box, the brightness of the pearl shone at her once more. She took it out, cradling the hardened shell in both hands.

It was just an idea.

Unformed as yet.

A million potential wishes.

One possible life.

She lifted it over her head. Her chin tilted defiantly at the Council, at the vermilion tide filling the sky. Her heart clenched in a tight, aching fist within her chest. It hurt to breathe. The colour of life. Of death. Love. Revolution. Change. What did it mean?

And then it changed.

Yellow. Sunshine yellow, as though the air bloomed with the first flower of spring.

It changed again.

Now green as the dripping vegetation on the vertical farms, as the lapels of her border guard coat. Green melted into bright orange: koi fish swimming in the ocean sky. Then blue as the clearest waters.

The smoke cycled through a myriad of colours.

A smile fluttered across Mira's lips. Nami was anything but conventional, but the message had been received. The rainbow after a storm, when water and light merged momentarily to create something beautiful.

She slammed the pearl down on the ground, as hard as she could. One word ringing as she spoke, not with siren song but something else. Hope.

"Live!"

The egg cracked. A crunch and a tear. Fracture lines splitting open. Light so bright it burned, burst from those seams. A turquoise shade at first, it grew more intense in a rush of sea foam until it was a piercing blue. The rays fanned out in all directions like a sunrise from a small sphere. Travelling upwards in columns, pillars that reached overhead to the smoky clouds. When they touched, the colour dissipated. Dissolving as though washed in water. Until the sea and the sky and the egg were an endless cycle: an ocean of cerulean.

A baby mewled. An uncertain hiccuping cry from the broken shards of the egg. Mira crouched down and picked up the newborn. Wiped the mucus from their face with the back of her sleeve. Watched those big round eyes blink open and the possibilities dazzle like stars in the night sky. The baby dragon wriggled in her arms, scrambling onto her chest and draping their head over her shoulder. Mira turned to the onlookers. Her song had long since ended, the final refrain carried away by the tide. They watched now because she had done something unexpected. Something new.

"What have you done?" Jiang-Li was the first to finally speak.

"This is no longer a bargaining chip. This is a child. *Your* child. If you want your wish, you'll have to convince them first."

"It's ... it's a babe. They can't even understand us, never mind speak! They won't be able to for years!" one of the junior officials said.

"Years to reform. To learn. To love. Isn't that what we all need?"

"This is all well and good, Minister. But what about the more immediate problem?" Minister Kelwin said without malice, gesturing to the looming sand god bearing down on them.

"If this is how the city falls, so be it. We have gills. We will survive. We always have." With that, she turned back to Jiang-Li, offering the hatchling to her. The dragon matriarch recoiled instinctively, just as the baby whimpered in distress. Mira stroked its tail. She had no plan beyond hatching the egg, beyond choosing a way that was not lined with fear or hate. The dragon nuzzled a long snout into the palm of her hand.

She had done what she could. It was up to Nami now.

Chapter Forty-Seven

Nami shaded her eyes with the back of her hand. The burst of blue light had come from nowhere. A response to the rainbow of colours they had put out. A conversation between Tiankawi and the titan beneath their feet. She blinked as the smoke signal disappeared altogether.

"The last dragon pearl has been hatched," Sobekki said, confirming what she intuitively knew. There would never be another Kai, but she had another sibling now.

She tugged at Eun's hand, not even stopping to explain herself. They ran down the winding stairs, the mourning song swirling around their ears and carried by the wind. A vertical wall of water had been waterweaved by those in the nearby boats, just as at Kai's memorial. Paying their respects to the titan whale shark that had died beneath Tiankawi's feet. Trish sat on the prow of the vessel in front, like a masthead siren of legend except her hair was grey and she wore a sensible shawl rather than a revealing dress. The curtain of water was wobbly; thicker in places, mere tap drips in others. Held up by inexperienced hands, but held up all the same.

No time to celebrate. Nami waded into the shallows, spotting a safe place to dive down to face the sand god once more. "I can't do it alone," she admitted.

Eun splashed after her, ungainly on the rough terrain but with a promise in the freckles of her cheeks. She wrapped her arms around Nami, brow against her cheek. It took Nami by surprise, not that she minded. She stroked the librarian's hair, breathing in her smell. Eun's lips reached the shell of her ear. A rush of words as if she pushed them all out in one breath, taking the chance while she had it.

"You have never been alone. Not since the day you wandered into the library and moved all the scrolls to the wrong places. Not since I watched you quell the flames in Webisu, fire and water all at once. Hoping that you would one day find a path to a change that uses words as much as fists. That smoulders long and steady and doesn't simply scald. Titans could not tear me from you."

Nami leaned down and cupped Eun's face in her hands, searching her grey-blue eyes. She had been so wrapped up in Firth, in their barbed relationship that drew blood with every twist, that she had not seen what was in front of her.

She did not have the words Eun had. Did not know how to express herself so eloquently. She could take it no longer, the feeling threatening to pour from her in one long ache. She kissed her. Eun's lips, hesitant, trembled against her own. Nami pulled away, afraid of breaking her, afraid she had overstepped some invisible line and misread everything.

"Is this … okay?" she asked. Eun's eyes remained closed, her long lashes dipped onto her pale skin. Her freckles a constellation across her nose and cheeks, one that Nami longed to trace and explore. Then she leaned forward with a hunger that was both an answer and a new question in one. Walkways they could navigate together.

When their lips met for a second time, Nami dropped her guard entirely. It felt like everything, this single kiss completing her when she had not even realised there was a piece missing. A circle rounded and whole. She had known what it would feel like long before her lips met Eun's. In the days and weeks before, she had always known.

It felt like home.

Eun pushed up further on her tiptoes, soft lips firm now against Nami's. Her hands twined around her neck, and when her mouth opened, Nami forgot to be afraid any more. Forgot to worry. The imperfections did not matter. Perhaps every kiss with Eun would feel this way. Every hour, every day, the sense of wonder. The surprise that of everyone, Eun had chosen her.

Nami pulled away, reluctantly this time. Eun emitted a bereft noise, lips wet and redder than before. Pupils dark with longing.

"I take it that's a yes," Nami said teasingly.

Eun blushed red, the colour spreading across her cheeks and even into her ears. "Yes," she confirmed.

Nami dived. The waters were warmer now, their journey bringing them back to the temperate climate near Tiankawi. The pectoral fins of the sand god rose and fell. Slower than before, like it was gliding through the water. Hand in hand, Nami and Eun swam under it, diving deep to avoid the unpredictable movements. The currents made it difficult to traverse and pushed them towards the titan manta ray's whiplike tail. Nami shuddered; she didn't want to be anywhere near that.

"A moment," she warned Eun as she transformed. Her silver scales rippled down the length of her serpentine dragon body and her whiskers unravelled from her cheeks. Her claws grew long and sharp, worrying her enough that she let go of Eun's hand for fear of cutting her. The foolish flicker of dismay when their contact was broken was countered only when the librarian rested her hands on the ridge of her spines.

In dragon form, Nami curved under the sand god's wing, corkscrewing in a moment of pure indulgence as Eun held on that bit tighter. The manta ray's eye was as big as the librarian. Silver-ringed with a storm cloud brewing at its heart. Nami knew the milkiness was the slow blindness of age, but all the same it felt like the titan had turned inwards.

"They mourn for you. For the partner who laid down their life to save Tiankawi." The sand god did not even acknowledge their presence. Nami tried again. "We would honour them any way you please. Build a statue, a shrine to their sacrifice. Name a building for them, a district."

Eun put pressure on her hide. Without words, her action told Nami that she was going down the wrong track. Nami felt the rising pressure, panic simmering at the surface. It should be Mira doing this. Mira, who had experienced both love and loss far beyond Nami's comprehension. Who continued to hope and to give despite the weight of it around her heart. Nami closed her eyes and spoke, but it was Mira she was talking to this time. "I wish we could undo it. I wish I could take back every stupid decision, every naïve choice that led to this. I wish I could have my brother back."

Her honesty cracked through her voice. The turmoil of all the emotions she had refused to give space to. She was supposed to be wise, to sacrifice when it was demanded of her. To live a life of virtue and integrity. Not to fuck up over and over again like a broken record.

Eun's hand touched Nami's dew claw, balancing her out. It was enough. Nami opened her eyes and took solace from her. "I want us to remember. All the wrongs. The sacrifices. The love that you shared across the oceans and centuries. We will remember, if you let us. If you want us to."

The eye turned. Slowly. Finally focusing on the two people swimming beside it. The voice when it came rumbled through their bones, conducted straight into their skulls. *The pearl?*

"It has hatched," Nami said. "A new start for us all. Fathomfolk and human."

The sand god did not respond. Still it moved. The stilthouses on the outskirts of the city were visible beneath the waterline now. Their spindle supports no more than toothpicks in the water.

"I am tired of anger for the sake of anger," Nami went on. "We cannot build a future on rage. We cannot build anything." Eun was looking at her again, eyes magnetised to her face. Her own face a promise. Buildings, walls might erode, might even collapse, but they could always be rebuilt. As long as the foundations were deep, the rest would come. As long as they learned from their mistakes rather than burying them in the sand. A future Nami had hoped for without being able to articulate, radiated from Eun's every pore, and she soaked herself in it.

The sand god ploughed into the outlying buildings of the northern districts. Pillars cracked and gave way under the sheer size of it. Buildings crashed into the water, lopsided as they plunged downwards. Nami could only hope the people had already fled. Debris littered the surface and she had to pull Eun further down, sheltering them both under the wing-like fin of the titan. It barely seemed to notice the devastation it left in its wake. The groans of the city as it cut a wedge into it, dismantling all the reconstruction work in one sweeping blow.

"Tell me," Nami shouted, not certain if her voice would even be heard above the destruction. "Tell me their name."

What?

"Their name. Your partner. The whale shark that lay beneath our city. What were they called? Perhaps ... we could name the hatchling for them."

The sand god made a sound, sonorous and low. A sound that could have been a name, carried on the waves. Or perhaps just a keen of pain. Either way, Nami knew that feeling. She swam closer, heedless of the danger, and laid her serpentine body across the gentle curve of the titan's white underbelly, hugging the grieving manta ray.

"I'm sorry," she said. Finally, after all the weeks and months of holding it in, she let herself cry. Bitter tears that would only ever be a drop in the ocean. She cried for the rivers and lakes that had been swallowed whole by the rising tide; for the havens clinging on and crumbling; for the city with a thousand voices pulled in so many directions it could only break; but most of all, for the people. People tired beyond belief but who somehow kept going, who saw the best in others when it had taken her so long. And for her brother, who always gave so much and asked for so little that he had given all of himself. Entirely.

How long they stayed like that, she did not know. Only that the rumble of movement around her subsided, the titan finally coming to a halt.

A dragonling should not carry the weight of the past. Of this name. Teach them. Love them. Ensure that this world is one they can thrive in.

The titan descended. Nami and Eun watched as the basalt columns slid downwards past them, as the honeycombed sandstone houses once more submerged into the water. Seaweed, dried in the wind, waved in loose fronds once more. Bleached coral bubbled as if taking a deep breath. Here, where the water was shallower than where Iyoness had been, structures on the sand god's back still rose above the waterline. But below, the titan manta ray rested its belly atop the ruins of the old Tiankawi. The long edge of one fin up against the Peak mountain, blanketing its northern side, embracing it like a tide against the breakers.

Epilogue

The dragonling curled around Trish's neck, their long tail tangling her braid, and yet she didn't mind. She didn't blame the little one. The noise of merrymaking and the heady spices rising from the bubbling pot at the centre of the table were an assault to the senses. Mira laughed as the dragon leaped across the short distance and licked her cheek with a long tongue. The bond that had grown between the two was a great comfort to Trish.

Jiang-Li had shrewdly named her new child Edo. The name meant estuary: where river met ocean. A bridge.

Named for the future rather than the past.

The dragon matriarch was too severely injured to tend to the dragonling at present. Nami had berated her to no avail; it was Sobekki's intervention that made her listen. Jiang-Li had returned to the renowned Yonakunish healers for respite, leaving Nami in charge of her new sibling. Jiang-Li had made it clear that this was not a permanent arrangement.

There would be a tussle ahead of them when the sands had settled. Negotiating where the dragonling would live, who would teach it, what they would get in return. But trade deals and territory negotiations were a matter for another day. All any of them could do for now was live.

Edo had taken to Mira, so much so that Nami had passed

over the responsibility with great relief. It was not easy, especially alongside all the demands of being Minister of Fathomfolk, but it was a distraction. Hour to hour, day to day: sleepless nights tending to the dragonling's endless mewling cries, their need for comfort or food. It took all of Mira's attention and it was exactly the distraction she needed. Watching Edo's clumsy steps, their brimming joy at the smallest thing – a new taste, a new smell – gave her back her smile, the laugh that her ama had not heard in a long time.

Trish put down her walking stick, easing herself slowly onto the chair as first Nami, then Eun jumped up to help her.

"You can help with *this*," Trish said, depositing a huge parcel of dulse cakes into the hands Nami had held out. The fabric-wrapped package bulged at the sides and the water dragon gave an experimental squeeze, bemused at what she heard.

"We said not to bring anything." Nami nodded towards the table, which was heaving with fishballs and prawns, a mountain of pak choi and napa cabbage, lotus root and water chestnut waiting to be cooked in the spicy broth simmering at the centre.

"Pah, you can never have enough food. Look at you, practically wasting away." Trish prodded Nami's ribs with a smack of her lips. Too skinny by far. Needed more meat on her. "As for you . . ." She turned her critical eye to the librarian awkwardly holding her other elbow, giving her the once-over. "When are you going to propose?"

"Ama," Mira warned from beneath an exuberant dragonling. Edo was trying desperately to reach for the pyramid of steamed buns, successfully pulling the bottom one out and making the rest tumble down. They squealed in delight.

"What? *This* one won't get round to it any time soon," Trish said, jabbing at Nami.

Eun wished the ground would open and swallow her whole when Mira's ama made the comment. Her words betrayed her entirely, upended onto the floor in an incoherent heap. "In a traditional courtship period, matters of matrimony are rarely discussed in the first few weeks. In fact, in Muyeres haven, the whole subject is considered taboo until a full six cycles of the moon have passed. I could send you some scrolls on the matter . . ."

She ducked her head so that her glasses obscured her eyes. Heat rose up her neck until Nami took her hand. Whispering conspiratorially, "She just wants an excuse for a new dress."

"I heard that," Trish said. She did not deny it, picking at the frayed embroidery on her scarf. "You offering to buy?"

"In time, once things have settled down," Nami reassured her with a wink. Eun's blush concentrated into two pink dots on her cheeks.

"They are already more than settled." Trish was content with that response, pointing with her walking stick for Mikayil to lend Tam's wife a hand with the twins across the table. The woman mouthed her thanks, wolfing down her bowl of soup dumplings while simultaneously nursing one baby against her chest. They had had their fair share of losses, it was true. Mourning that awful day of carnage and upheaval.

Then had come the waiting.

Weeks they waited, to see if the manta ray sand god would make the return journey north. Eun and Nami spent days submerged by the titan's side, asking the questions that everyone above the waterline wondered about. Until finally they had been able to return to the Council with an answer. It would stay. The people of Tiankawi could build upon its back as long as they remembered the sacrifices that had been made.

Eun had never been busier, furiously recording the momentous occasion. Standing proudly by Nami's side as she announced it to the rest of the city. It doubled the size of Tiankawi overnight.

Enough space to build half a dozen new districts. To take in more folk from the havens. To start from scratch and make sure it was right this time. Reason also to expand and alter the Council, to add new faces to the leadership list from the varied communities that made their homes in the city state.

They had argued for a long while about appointing a new Fenghuang. The symbolic position was much coveted. Mira had been at her wits' end, certain they were heading for another disaster, when Nami proposed the solution. Said it in such a matter-of-fact way that Eun could hardly believe the thought hadn't occurred to her first.

Give it to the titan. It was symbolic after all: the firebird that watched after the city; that arbitrated only in dire need. What difference did it make if the Fenghuang loomed above them in a palace of jade and alabaster, or below, silent but available, if they failed to hold to their own standards?

Between all the negotiating, Eun and Nami spent their days exploring, learning, sharing, inhaling every inch of each other. It should feel fragile to be this exposed. To reach out in the dark, uncertain if her tentative touch would be reciprocated. But it never felt this way. There was always light between them, bright enough for her to read the meaning in Nami's every action. The story they wove between them.

Finally, out of the shadow of the voices and opinions that had sought to mould her, Nami bloomed like a giant water lily. The spikes were still there, the deep channels of all the journeys she had travelled to get here, but hidden on the underside. She had unfurled to the sun, more expansive than Eun had dared hope. A safe harbour, and Eun the flower at her heart. They worked in harmony, Eun's knowledge informing Nami's action. It was a natural progression for them to run the Tideborn Centre together, freeing Mira for other tasks. Nami was reluctant to lead, but she could teach. Not through rote learning, books or scrolls;

she left that to Eun. She taught practical subjects: swimming, waterweaving, martial skills. People flocked from across the city to learn from the pair.

"Don't you know, Nami has grand plans. She and Eun are going to pester the Minister of Education until he agrees to reform," Mira said. Edo sat in her lap, cheeks fat with chunks of steamed bun. Mira lifted the squirming little dragon and kissed them with great relish. "Chew it, you greedy little fool."

"Petition! Eun simply thinks we could roll out a more inclusive teaching scheme across the districts. Cast our net wider," Nami said. Jinsei nodded enthusiastically from across the table.

"Build your empire," Trish agreed.

Nami raised her glass across the table at the kappa who sat quietly at Gede's side. "If anyone has an empire, it's Dan."

Everyone stared at Dan, curiosity written in their expressions. It was awkward enough that Nami had found him, reached out and rekindled their friendship. Now they would ask questions, and there was simply too much he could not say.

Into the silence, Gede leaned forward to grab the bottle of soju, missing it entirely and sending the liquid spilling across the table. People jumped to rescue dishes and mop up the mess, questions entirely forgotten. Gede wore a seemingly baffled expression, but his lip twitched at the corner as he drained the rest of his cup. He still bore wounds from the fight at the Fenghuang's residence, his right arm in a sling and deep cuts scarring his boyish looks. They aged him. Gave him a maturity he had never had before. One that became him, even if he was indifferent to the admiring glances of the junior officials who followed him round. He was far too busy with the city guard and unpicking the harm that had been done to his sister.

Cordelia had disappeared after the fight. Died, Gede had said, his throat bobbing up and down. Dan did not push him. Not when the seawitch's empire was his to inherit. It expanded rapidly, astutely managed by Dan's head for numbers and Gede supporting him from the sidelines. Promotional signs popped up in every district across the city. Advertisements in the newssheets and an army of converts hand-selling dull weed at every floating market. The gill rot medication was being rolled out in waves. Auntie Delia became a more affable character on billboards than the Cordelia anyone had met in real life. Dan was tempted to follow the trail back to find the head of the snake, but sometimes it was better to let sleeping titans lie. If Cordelia was alive, she would make it known, probably when the most profitable moment arose.

Besides – he glanced across the circular table at the motley group – this wasn't bad. Wasn't bad at all. It was not the life he had expected for himself, but then again, when did things ever go to plan? He missed his family. His bickering sisters and the cucumber pickles his mother made. He understood there was no going back: he was an escapee from jail, a drug dealer who had been part of a violent radical group. He did not want his family to find out. It was bittersweet to know they were safe and provided for, more stable than if he had stayed in Yonakuni in his poorly paid clerking role. He would never see the people they grew into, but they had the chance to grow into them all the same. Still, perhaps he would write to them. One day.

Trish pressed a dulse cake into her daughter's hand, ignoring her feeble protests about being too full. Mira rocked the now sleeping Edo in her arms, face blissful, although she would never admit it. The betrothal bangles glittered in the lamplight, but they no longer looked heavy on her wrists. Nami challenged Mikayil to an arm-wrestle, spitting in the palm of her hand with gleeful mischief as the chinthe lieutenant quirked his eyebrow and thudded his elbow on the table. Eun merely shook her head, pulling out a scroll from titan knows where and poring intensely over the words. Gede turned down the flame on the hotpot, quietly contemplative. Next to him, Jalad and Jinsei barely had time for anyone else, hands and lips wrapped up in each other. Poor Gede, stuck there next to them. Someone should really set him up. Nice boy like him, Trish could think of a few options.

Everyone else, people she had just met and others she had known for a lifetime, fitted in here. Belonged around the table, eating from the same pot. The soup had acquired flavours from everything they had thrown in: sweet and sour, savoury and spicy. A broth fit for their misfit family. Their misfit city. The work would never end. There would always be changes to make, but hope balanced it: for fathomfolk and tideborn alike.

Acknowledgements

The second book is notorious for being a difficult child, but I have been incredibly fortunate since my debut came out. My writing community has grown, both in width but also in depth. I am incredibly grateful to everyone who has offered support in any capacity: in developing my writing, my self-belief or simply filling my cup with enthusiasm and kindness.

Thanks as always to my agent Alex Cochran and the team at C&W for being in my corner. My UK editor Jenni Hill, who once again, forced me to confront all the plot holes and my lack of ship-faring jargon. Nazia Khatun, my publicist extraordinaire for lining up events with some dream authors, for the Asian drama recs and for the best cross-stitches I've ever seen. Maddy Hall for working a great deal of marketing magic behind the scenes. Brit Hvide, my US editor, thank you for bringing my drowned city to the US and believing in it. Kelly Chong, whose extraordinary cover art did most of the heavy lifting. Also thanks to (takes a deep breath): Ella Garrett, Joanna Kramer, Serena Savini, Jane Selley, Jessica Dryburgh, Jessica Purdue, Bryn McDonald, Ellen Wright, Angela Man, Nick Burnham, Natassja Haught, Rachel Hairston, Lauren Panepinto, Alexia Mazis, Dorcas Rogers, Tracy England, Louise Emslie-Smith and Camilla Smallwood. And I would be remiss without thanking Illumicrate for the stunning special edition and especially

Daphne Tonge for always championing underrepresented voice, including this one.

Thanks to my beta readers who reassured me that I did not in fact have to spend four years on a book for it to be any good, G. V. Anderson, Christy Healy and Bori Cser. You of swift reading speed and astute suggestions, I salute you!

To the authors further along the publishing journey who have taken the time to offer advice rather than bat away my random questions and worries, especially A. Y. Chao, Tasha Suri and Nick Binge. I hope I can be just as supportive to those coming up the ladder.

To the debut friends I met along the way as we stumbled through so many firsts in this process: Christy Healy, Sophie Clark, Frances White, Emma Sterner-Radley, Sarah Brooks, Esmie Jikiemi-Pearson, David Goodman, Mina Ikemoto Ghosh, Genoveva Dimova and so many more. I can't wait to keep celebrating all your successes.

To the Bubble Tea group for surprising me with the depths of your support and also the London food recommendations! The Manchester Write Club, especially Thomas D. Lee and Tamsyn McDonald, for giving me regular writing buddies, talking out sticking points in plot and drinking more library coffee than we really should. My cottagecore writing besties Jess and Gemma, thanks for crit partnering, tea, prosecco and face masks. My local board gaming and geekdom friends, thanks for getting me out the house now and then, even if we overestimate how much we like a hot tub.

To everyone else, from the extraordinary booksellers (Martha Lewis in particular), con and festival organisers, booktokkers, bookstagrammers, YouTubers, podcasters, reviewers and readers. Thank you for championing this messy book and bringing it into your heart.

Thanks finally to my family, who remain perplexed by the

whole endeavour but continue to buy multiple copies of my books. My mother who is quite possibly sending books to every Chinese auntie in Glasgow, alike in their inability to actually read it: thank you, that's probably for the best. My son who now wants to become a writer too, so he can just "stay at home with Mummy all day". And, saving the best for last, to Ken: my husband, my biggest cheerleader and best friend. Thanks for being in my tag team and for helping me appreciate every little win. Now let's buy another pointy weapon to celebrate.

extras

orbit

meet the author

Sandi Hodkinson

ELIZA CHAN is a Scottish-born Chinese-diaspora author who writes about East Asian mythology, British folklore, and reclaiming the dragon lady, but preferably all three at once. Eliza's work has been published in *The Dark, PodCastle, Fantasy Magazine*, and *The Best of British Fantasy 2019*, and her nonfiction has appeared on Reactor. She lives in the north of England with her partner and young child.

Find out more about Eliza Chan and other Orbit authors by registering for the free monthly newsletter at orbitbooks.net.

if you enjoyed
TIDEBORN

look out for

THE GODS BELOW
The Hollow Covenant: Book One

by

Andrea Stewart

In this sweeping epic fantasy comes a story of magic, betrayal, love, and loyalty, where two sisters will clash on opposite sides of a war against the gods.

A divine war shattered the world, leaving humanity in ruins. Desperate for hope, they struck a deal with the devious god Kluehnn: He would restore the world to its former glory, but at a price so steep it would keep the mortals indebted to him for eternity. And as each land was transformed, so too were its people changed into strange new forms—if they survived at all.

Hakara is not willing to pay such a price. Desperate to protect herself and her sister, Rasha, she flees her homeland for the safety of a neighboring kingdom. But when tragedy separates them, Hakara is forced to abandon her beloved sister to an unknown fate.

Alone and desperate for answers on the wrong side of the world, Hakara discovers she can channel magic from the mysterious gems they are forced to mine for Kluehnn. With that discovery comes another: Her sister is alive, and the rebels plotting to destroy the god pact can help rescue her.

But only if Hakara goes to war against a god.

1

HAKARA

561 years after the Shattering

Kashan – the Bay of Batabyan

The mortals broke the world. They took the living wood of the Numinars, feeding it to their machines to capture and use their magic. Once, the great branches reached into the sky, each tree an ecosystem for countless lives. By the time the Numinars were almost gone, the world was changed. The mortals tried, but they could not repair the damage they'd caused. As the skies filled with ash and the air grew hot, the mortal Tolemne made his way down into the depths of the world to ask a boon of the gods.

And the gods, ensconced in their hollow, in the inner sanctum of the earth, told Tolemne that the scorched land above was not their problem. The gods ignored his pleas.

All except one.

Maman lied when she told me there were ghosts in the ocean. Cold water pressed at my ears, the breath in my lungs warm and taut as a paper lantern. Shapes appeared in the murk below, towers rising out of the darkness. Strands of kelp swayed back and forth between broken stone and rotting wood with the ceaseless rhythm of breathing. There were no ghosts down here – just the pitted, pockmarked bones of a long-dead world. I forced myself to calm, to make my breath last longer.

A shark swam above, between me and the surface, its shadow passing over my face. I hovered next to a tower wall, not even letting a bubble free from my lips, my elbow hooked over the stone lip of a window. An abalone lay in my left hand, the snail curling into itself, the rocky shell of it rough against my palm. My blunt knife lay in my right. A shimmering school of small fish circled next to me, light catching their silver scales like so many scattered coins. I willed them to swim away. There was nothing interesting here. Nothing to see. Nothing to eat.

Somewhere beyond the shore, Rasha curled in our tent, silent and waiting.

The first time I went to the sea, my sister had begged me not to go. I'd held her face between my palms, wiped her tears away with my thumbs and then pressed her cheeks together until her mouth opened like a fish's. "Glug glug," I'd said. I'd laughed and then she'd laughed, and then I'd whisked myself to the tent flap before she could protest any further. "That's all that's down there. Things that are good to eat and to sell. I'll come back. I promise."

Always told her I'd come back, just in case she forgot.

I imagined Rasha in our tent, getting the fire going, sorting through our stash of dried and salted goods to throw together some semblance of a meal. The fishing hadn't been good lately and now I had a snail in hand, as big as my face. I could begin to make things right if I could make it home.

If I died here, Rasha would die too. She'd have no one to defend her, to care for her. I counted the passing seconds, my heartbeat thudding in my ears, hoping the shark would swim away. My

347

throat tightened, my chest aching. I was running out of time. I could hold my breath longer than most, but I had limits.

There was a stone ledge far beneath me – the remnants of a crumbled balcony. I had two things in hand – my abalone knife and the abalone. I *needed* that abalone and they were so hard to find these days. Each one would buy several days' worth of meals. But it wasn't worth my life. Nothing else for it. I dropped the snail and moved, slowly as I could manage, around the tower.

Its shell cracked against the ledge and the shark darted toward the sound.

I swam upward, the tautness of my chest threatening to shatter, to let the water come rushing in. The bright shimmer of the world above seemed at once close and too far. I kicked, hoping the shark was occupied with the abalone. My breath came out in short bursts when I broke the surface.

I swam for the closest rock, doing my best not to splash. Any moment, I imagined, the beast from below would shear off a leg with its bite. The water that had welcomed me only moments before now felt like a vast, unknowable thing. And then my hands were on the rock and I was hauling myself out of the water, my fingers scrabbling against slick algae and barnacles, doing my best not to shake. A close call, but not the first I'd ever had. Another diver was setting up on shore. "Shark in the ruins!" I called to him. "Best wait until it's cleared off."

He waved me away. "Sure. Children always think they see sharks when they're scared."

Did he think just because I was young that my eyes didn't work right? Went the other way around, didn't it? "Go on, then." I waved at the water. "Be a big brave adult and get yourself eaten."

He made a rude gesture at me before fastening his bag to his belt and dropping from the rocks into the water. Not the wisest decision, but he was probably just as desperate as the rest of us. I could smell the shoreline from my rock – sea life rotting under the heat of the sun, crisped seaweed, thick white bird droppings.

I wrapped my arms around my knees and watched him submerge

as I breathed into my belly, calming my too-fast heartbeat. Waves lapped against the shore behind me. Early-morning light shone piss-yellow through the haze, the air smelling faintly like a campfire. Not the most auspicious start to the day, but most mornings in Kashan weren't. My smallclothes clung to me, trickles of water tickling my skin. I'd head out again once I thought the shark had moved on. Or once it had taken a bite out of the other diver and had a nice meal. Either way, I'd slide into the water again, no matter the dangers.

I think Maman told me about ghosts in a misguided attempt to scare me. Like I was supposed to look at her, round-eyed, and avoid the ocean ever after instead of eagerly asking her if underwater ghosts ate sharks or people's souls. Had to admit I was a bit disappointed not to find spirits lurking around the ruined city when I'd finally hauled my hungry carcass to the shore and plunged my face beneath the water. Would have had a lot of questions to ask my ancestors.

Maman wasn't here to warn me away, and our Mimi had rid herself of that responsibility when she'd sighed out her last breath a year ago. We had no parents left. Besides, who was Maman to warn me against danger when she'd walked into the barrier between Kashan and Cressima? At least our Mimi had died through no fault of her own.

Sometimes I could hear Maman's voice in the back of my head as I swam down, down, so far that I started free-falling into the depths.

Don't go too far. Don't push yourself too hard. Stay safe.

And each time that voice in my head spoke up, I stayed down a little longer, until my chest burned, until I felt I would die if I didn't gasp in a breath. I couldn't listen to Maman's voice. Not with Rasha counting on me. Mimi had told me to take care of my sister. She'd not needed to say it, but I felt the weight of her last words like the press of a palm against my back.

This time of year, when the afternoon sun bore down on the water like a fire on a tea kettle, the abalone I fished for retreated deeper. They clung to the sides of the ruins, smaller ones hiding in crevices, their shells blending in with the surrounding rocks. Hints of metal and machinery lay deeper down, artifacts of the time before. All broken into unrecognizable pieces, or I'd have gone after them instead. There was always some sucker with money fascinated by our pre-Shattering civilization.

Rasha and I could eat fish, but abalone we could sell – the shells and their meat both – and children always needed things. It seemed I could get by on less and less the older I got, my fifteen-year-old frame gaunt and dry as a withered tree trunk. But Rasha was nine and I knew she needed toys, warm clothes, books, vegetables and fruits – all those little comforts she used to have when both Maman and Mimi had been alive. Every year got a little harder. More heat, more floods, more fires. Kluehnn's devoted followers prayed for restoration to take Kashan, to remake its people and its landscape, the way it had realm after realm. It was our turn, they said.

Couldn't say I relished the thought of being remade. I'd run if it ever came to that. I'd make for the border with Rasha and I wouldn't look back. Kluehnn's followers said that was a coward's choice. I was perfectly fine with being a coward if it meant I kept my bodily self unchanged and all in one piece.

I frowned as I glanced back at the shore, rocks fading into yellowed grasses and wilting trees. There should have been more divers out by now. I might have always been first, but others usually followed quickly, jostling for the best fishing spots.

It was deserted enough that I managed to find three more abalone once I got back into the water; only one other diver made her way into the ruins. My mind picked over all the possible reasons. A fire come too close? Rasha knew what to do in case of fire. A sickness passing through camp? It had happened before. I cut my diving short and walked back to our tent barefoot, the well-worn path soft beneath my feet, the scattered remains of dried seagrass forming a cushiony surface.

Ours was not the only tent pitched near Batabyan Bay. Together with the others we formed a loose settlement. This morning, though, three flattened areas of grass lay where tents had once been pitched. They'd been there when I'd left for the ocean.

Rasha had started a fire in the pit, the musty scent of burning dung drifting toward me. A covered cast-iron pot hung over it, the lid cracked to let out steam. She ran toward me, nearly bowling me over with a hug.

I squeezed her back until she wheezed. Maybe got a bit carried away, but she didn't complain. Her long black hair had some indefinable scent I only knew as home. Something of Maman and Mimi clung to the thick walls of our tent, permeating our clothes and our skin. I waved away the pungent smoke as I let her go, gesturing toward the empty campsites. "What happened over there?"

She shrugged. "They left just as I woke up. All three. Packed up their belongings and just hauled them out."

I smoothed the hair from her forehead. It was quick as instinct, the way I moved to soothe away her worries. Worrying was for me, not her. "Did they leave anything behind?"

She gave me a tentative smile before holding up a comb and a horsehair doll. I held my hand out for the comb. That one had been left by mistake. Tortoiseshell, carved with the face of Lithuas, one of the dead elder gods. Her hair flowed out to the tines of the comb, which had been left smooth. I should have been excited by the find; instead, uneasiness rose like a high tide. Most people would have scoured their campsite. Most people would have taken the time to find what they'd lost. The people here weren't rich, and the comb was a luxury, one that had passed hands from one generation to the next. No one carved the elder gods into combs anymore.

I lifted the abalone in my mesh sack. "I got something too."

Rasha's eyes sparkled, and her expression was a bulwark against anxiety. "Is it enough?"

I gave her a mock-startled look. "For what? What do you mean?"

She laughed before grabbing a pole to take the pot off the fire. "You know what."

"Pretty sure you called me stupid the other day, and stupid people have terrible memories."

"I was *joking*."

"Yes, being called stupid is a very funny joke."

"I said 'don't *be* stupid. You can't go to the mines.'"

I mussed her hair. "Please. Same difference. Besides, if the ocean stops giving us what we need, I might be able to find work at the sinkholes. I have to consider it."

She spooned out the porridge with the air of someone who'd come to the realization that this shitty gruel was her last meal. "No, you don't."

Ah, I'd ruined the mood in one fell swoop, hadn't I? Count on me to crush delicate hopes with the clumsiness of a toddler wandering into a seabird's nest. "We have enough, and I can dive deeper than most. Let's not think about it. Not when we have this, eh?" I brandished the comb. "I'll sell it at market with the abalone. And then yes, I'll see about the garden you want."

Wished she would answer me with a sly "So you *do* remember", but she'd never been as able as I was to recover a good mood. It was a big ask. We both knew it. I could buy the seeds and we had water, but the weather was unpredictable. Crops had to grow quickly to be harvested before heat or flooding ruined them. Only thing that would make them grow more quickly was god gems, and I wasn't going to risk the black market.

Magic wasn't for the likes of us.

Maybe a few herbs, though. Some small greens we could carry in pots. I could do that. I dug into the porridge she'd made, putting on a show of how incredible it tasted until she smiled again. I'd once gotten drunk on fermented mare's milk when a passing traveler had left a skin of it out after he'd gone to sleep. It felt like that, getting Rasha to smile, to laugh. But better. No pounding headache the morning after, only a soft satisfaction that for one more day, I'd mattered.

But both were fleeting feelings. When we made our way to the market, it was nearly empty. Two stalls remained.

I'd never been as attuned to the community as perhaps I should have been. Rasha and I were a unit, and I couldn't afford to let anyone too close in case I'd misjudged them. We were young, and though my sister didn't understand our vulnerability, I did. All it would take was two armed, halfway-skilled grown men or women, and our stash of food would be ransacked. Maybe they'd kill us both for good measure. The law didn't mean much when you lived on the fringes. We had one another and that was enough. Or I'd thought it was enough.

I took the abalone to one of the two remaining stalls, where a woman clasped her hands together, her face rapturous. Rasha clung to the end of my shirt. I could feel the tension in her fingers, in every errant tug. It unsettled me more than it should have.

"Hey, Grandma – where's everyone?" I plunked the abalone on her counter, though I had no idea if she wanted to buy it.

She didn't even seem to notice. "It's Kluehnn," she breathed, her eyes bright.

The back of my neck prickled. I *knew* right then what was happening, though I still searched for a gap, for some other explanation. Restoration had been coming to realms quicker and quicker these days, but it was too soon after Cressima. I wasn't ready. Rasha was too young, we were too small. "What, the one true god popped up out of the ground and gave everyone a holiday?"

She smiled and shook her head, wisps of white hair floating around her face like spiderwebs. "No. People have seen the black wall. It's moving over Kashan and it's on its way here. Everyone is setting their affairs in order. Restoration. It's our turn."

My heart pounded faster than it had with the shark overhead. I grabbed the abalone and Rasha's hand. I ran.

if you enjoyed
TIDEBORN
look out for

A LETTER TO THE LUMINOUS DEEP
The Sunken Archives: Book One

by

Sylvie Cathrall

A charming fantasy set in an underwater world with magical academia and a heartwarming pen pal romance, perfect for fans of Emily Wilde's Encyclopaedia of Faeries *and* The House in the Cerulean Sea.

E. is content with a solitary life in her extraordinary underwater home, until the discovery of a strange, beautiful creature outside her window prompts her to begin a correspondence with renowned scholar Henerey Clel. The letters they share are filled with passion, at first for their mutual interests and then, inevitably, for each other.

But when a mysterious seaquake destroys E.'s home, she and Henerey vanish.

A year later, E.'s sister Sophy and Henerey's brother, Vyerin, must piece together the letters, sketches, and field notes left behind and learn what their siblings' disappearances might mean for life as they know it.

CHAPTER 1

LETTER FROM E. CIDNOSIN TO HENEREY CLEL, YEAR 1002

Dear Scholar Clel,

Instead of reading further, I hope you will return this letter to its envelope or, better yet, crumple it into an abstract shape that might look quite at home on a coral reef.

I become exceedingly anxious around strangers, you see, and I dared only write this note after convincing myself that you would never read it. It is only now – when I can picture you disposing of these pages in some appropriately dramatic fashion – that I may continue my message without succumbing to Trepidation.

You do not know me at all, Scholar Clel, but after reading your most recent publication (as well as the four preceding it), I feel as though you have become a dear friend. I only wish a human companion ever brought me as much intellectual bliss as *Your Natural History Companion* does!

Surely you receive letters of this nature from eager readers all the time, though, so I will depart from flattery and approach the more pressing subject that inspired me to risk writing to you in the first place. As a Scholar of Classification, might you assist me from afar with an inquiry of relative import?

extras

A few tides ago, I encountered a species unlike any I have ever seen. Lacking a name for such creatures, I dubbed them "Elongated Fish". They cannot be Subtle Pipefish, as they do not possess needle-like "noses" and far surpass the approximate measurements you offered in your Appendix. (My Fish are also decidedly Unsubtle.) During my observation of the Fish, I noted the following additional traits: they are remarkably quick in the water, possibly crepuscular or nocturnal, and territorial to a fault.

Allow me to elaborate, if I may.

Yesterday, I sat by my window, watching glimmers of sunset from the surface dye the drop-off waters a stately purple. I do this sometimes when I feel most at odds with my Brain, you see, and find it quite effective. I was all alone – my sister Sophy recently departed on the Ridge expedition – though because you are also a Scholar, I assume you know about that expedition all too well – my apologies – and it was then that I witnessed a most unusual scene starring the Elongated Fish. Their colouring was a kind of magenta speckled with silver, but stretched almost transparent – like strands of hair about to break. Most bizarrely, their bulbous green eyes sat flat on the very tops of their heads rather than protruding in profile. From tip to tail, each measured longer than our house is tall.

O – my apologies again – I hoped to avoid boring you with biography, but I suppose the preceding paragraph might confuse you since you do not know where I live. You may have heard of the late, renowned Architect, Scholar Amiele Cidnosin – she who developed the first underwater dwelling, located a few hundred fathoms off-coast from your own Boundless Campus and colloquially called the "Deep House". Well, she was my mother, and I colloquially call it "home". While I am not a Scholar myself (and pray that you will forgive my boldness in writing to someone of your Academic prestige), perhaps you have encountered my esteemed sister Scholar Sophy Cidnosin (from the School of Observation at Boundless – o, I mentioned her just a few sentences ago, did I not?) or my (rather less) esteemed brother Apprentice Scholar Arvist Cidnosin. (Yes, our mother defied the typical Boundless custom and gave us what she deemed "Scholarly Virtue Names" – which we all promptly despised and altered. "Sophy" is short for Philosophy and "Arvist" (somehow) for Artistry. I dare not tell you *my* given name.)

Now you understand that I am uniquely privileged when it comes to observing marine life in its natural habitat.

I first noticed only one creature: a solitary ribbon lost in looping sojourns around the window. When she (?) first darted past my window I felt my heart vibrate. Her eyes rolled around in perfect circles as she executed repeated stalks – perhaps not quite grasping the presence of the glass that disqualified me as potential prey. (The sharks who frequent the waters just outside my chamber long since learned to ignore me.)

Some amount of time later – I found it hard to keep track of the hour – I marvelled at the moonbeams illuminating the Elongated Fish as she continued watching me. After ages of stillness, she flinched, folding and opening like a concertina. I assumed I startled her with my stirring until I spied an even larger creature pulsing its way around the house. As this second Elongated Fish sped closer, "my" Fish dashed towards the interloper, swirling into a furious helix. They wove around each other, tighter than thread. Tails choked necks and fins found wounds. I watched with rapt horror as they fell into the abyss below the drop-off together. Neither returned.

Now, considering your diverse experiences "in the field", as it were, I suspect you will not find this encounter especially impressive – and I confess that my Elongated Fish can hardly compete with the Exceptional Squid Skirmish my family witnessed at the Deep House in Year 991 – but the novelty of these unfamiliar creatures struck me. I adore how each "Epilogue" of your books invites readers to stop by your Laboratory Anchorage at Boundless Campus to share news of unusual sightings with you, but circumstances prevent me from coming in person. Still, I would be most grateful if you would consider assessing my account of these creatures from afar.

That is, of course, assuming you did not do as I asked by destroying this letter without even reading it.

Sincerely,

E. Cidnosin

P.S. Allow me to apologise for the rudimentary sketch of the Elongated Fish that I enclosed. Please attribute any unforgivable errors to my non-existent professional training.

LETTER FROM SOPHY CIDNORGHE
TO VYERIN CLEL, YEAR 1003

Dear Captain Clel,

Forgive this unexpected intrusion from your former "acquaintance-through-grief" – otherwise known as me, Sophy Cidnosin (well, Cidnorghe now, technically – as my wife and I are newly wed, we combined our family names in accordance with Boundless Campus custom).

If it helps, I also go by "E.'s sister".

When you and I met for the first (and final) time – just after Henerey and E.'s disappearance – I promised "to keep in touch" in that vague, non-committal way that one so often does. Well, I come at last, a year later, to make that promise less empty. I do not wish to resurrect painful memories for you; rather, I hope that the contents of this package will provide some comfort.

After I lost E., I tasked myself with putting my sister's belongings in order as a distraction. Even after the Deep House's destruction, E.'s safe-box – a funny, waterproof little thing designed by our mother – survived intact, tucked into a crack in the coral bed. When the salvagers presented me with the safe-box just days after the explosion, I wasted no time (nor spared any expense) in hiring a locksmith to open it. I expected to find the box stuffed with draw-ings, rare books, curious shells, and perhaps a family photograph or two. Imagine my surprise when I discovered that my excessively introverted sister kept a cache of countless letters, the bulk of them dating from the period just before her disappearance – and sent by your brother.

I am a researcher by profession, Captain Clel. When I face a problem, I investigate all evidence and form a hypothesis. But it seems that my logical self vanished when E. did.

I did not ignore the safe-box entirely during those early days. I was not so far gone. I sorted through the box's contents, arrang-ing the letters into neat stacks on my desk for safekeeping. (Oddly enough, it was at this point that I found that daybook of Henerey's I gave you when we met last year. Why, I wonder, would he store it in the safe-box and not take it with him?) Yet every time I thought about opening even a single letter, I felt half-sick.

My guilty conscience tormented me for tides as I resisted the urge to read E.'s personal documents. I considered destroying the papers that serve as her only physical remains – cramming them into a crucible in my wife's laboratory, donating them to my brother in the guise of "mixed-media art supplies", or sailing out to the vast trench in the sea that marks the site where our family home once stood and sending the letters to meet their maker. I suspect my sister may have preferred any of these more destructive options. She was quite a private soul. But, dear Captain Clel, I must confess that tragedy has equipped me with a new propensity for selfishness. I can ignore the lure of the letters no longer, even if that makes me a traitor to my own sister.

A few tides ago, then, I pledged to construct an archive of E.'s existence – which is to say that I have started looking through the letters at last. I realised, however, that my "records" have limita-tions. I may read only what E. received from others, not her own words (excluding those she sent to myself and our brother Arv-ist, of course, which I already possess). With the exception of this enclosed draft of her first letter to Henerey (which I intentionally placed before my letter in the package so as to pique your interest with mystery), I do not know anything about what she said to him.

My proposal, then: if you inherited your late brother's personal effects and do not object, would you consider sharing some items of interest with me? Though I imagine the process might be devastatingly difficult, I do hope that together we may make sense of their final days – and feel more connected to them. (I have also included an ambitiously high number of coins in this envelope to cover your potential postal expenses.)

In archival solidarity,

Sophy Cidnorghe

LETTER FROM VYERIN CLEL TO SOPHY CIDNORGHE, YEAR 1003

Dear Scholar Cidnorghe,

I neglected your envelope. As soon as I recognised your name I felt rather overcome. My husband, Reiv, read everything you sent aloud to me. When we finished, he suggested that "sharing with [you] some of [my] feelings about Henerey might prove cathartic", because he is from Intertidal Campus originally and believes that honest emotional expression is an essential act of self-maintenance.

He's right, no doubt.

Your project offers the kind of cleansing that appeals to me. I'm not one for words. That was Henerey's forte. But you are right to presume that I still possess every scrap of paper upon which he ever scribbled and every note he ever received from friend or colleague or stranger or enemy.

Unlike you, I have not touched his letters, nor felt any particular pull to do so. Unexpected deaths produce a museum's worth of detritus. In the early days, a courier seemed to arrive every other hour with another box of Henerey's things from his Anchorage room, his laboratory, his ship-quarters, or his carrel in the library.

I locked every box away without opening them. It seems we

respond to grief in different ways. I feared (and still fear) that even the sight of his fashionable shirts or messy handwriting would break me.

But perhaps I need to break. With the support of my husband, I will start looking for things that fit within the timeline you wish to explore. In the meantime, if there is anything else you would like to send me, go ahead. I was intrigued when E. referred to your role on the Ridge expedition. "Ridge expedition" is a phrase you don't hear thrown around much these days. Reiv and I used to read all the expedition missives together. Until they stopped, that is.

I have enclosed the cost of postage to reimburse you.

With gratitude,

Mr. Reiv & especially Mr. Vyerin Clel

P.S. Can't believe E. started this whole thing by sending him a letter out of the blue. He loved that, I'm sure. He also loved her – even surer.

LETTER FROM SOPHY CIDNORGHE TO VYERIN CLEL, YEAR 1003

Dear Vyerin,

Your reply made me feel so radiantly hopeful that I am writing back (as you well can see) just a day later – I trust you won't mind. Many thanks to Reiv for reading you the letters and helping us begin this exciting partnership!

I look forward to seeing anything from E. that you uncover. O, I almost forgot – I also have Henerey's first letter to E. for you, though she reread it so many times that it's nearly falling apart in places. I shall endeavour to make a fair copy for our purposes. Additionally, because you seemed to take particular note of the Ridge expedition and my (unforgettable and regrettable) involvement therein, I shall also make fair copies of some correspondence between E. and myself from around that time period. Perhaps that will be of interest to you. If not, feel free to discard the copies as you see fit.

Enclosed you will find a sum suitable to cover the cost of many letters to come. If you wish, we may also correspond via Automated Post missives so that we can speak with greater speed (when it comes to any shorter questions or clarifications). My A.P. callsign for electronic communication is 2.02.CIDNORGHE.

Does that suit you?

With excitement,

Sophy

AUTOMATED POST MISSIVE FROM VYERIN CLEL TO SOPHY CIDNORGHE, YEAR 1003

Dear Sophy,

Suits me very well. More to follow upon receipt of your package. Though I hate it on principle, I admit that Automated Post is far more efficient than waiting for letters to be delivered. (Still, I would wait any amount of time to get to know my brother a little better.)

Sincerely,

Vyerin

P.S. Reiv had to encourage me to write the above parenthetical. But that doesn't make it any less genuine.

Follow us:

f /orbitbooksUS

X /orbitbooks

▶ /orbitbooks

Join our mailing list
to receive alerts on our
latest releases and deals.

orbitbooks.net

Enter our monthly
giveaway for the chance
to win some epic prizes.

orbitloot.com